A. C. Koning is better known as Christina Koning, the award-winning author of nine previous novels, of which the most recent was Out of Shot, the fourth in a series of detective stories set in the 1930s. Koning has worked as a journalist, reviewing fiction for The Times, and has taught creative writing at the universities of Oxford, Cambridge, and London. From 2013 to 2015, she was Royal Literary Fund Fellow at Newnham College, Cambridge

End of Term by A. C. Koning is the fifth novel in the 'Blind Detective' series.

This edition published by Arbuthnot Books 2018
ISBN 978-0-9927467-7-3

Cover illustration and design by Marina Esmeraldo.

End of Term

A. C. Koning

ARBUTHNOT BOOKS

To the memory of all the brave and brilliant women who fought for equal rights in education and the suffrage—and the men who supported their endeavours.

'Better is wisdom than weapons of war.' (Girton College motto)

ACKNOWLEDGEMENTS

With thanks for their kind and generous help in the writing of this book to Professor Susan J. Smith, Mistress of Girton College, Cambridge, and to Hannah Westall and Jenny Blackhurst, respectively archivist and librarian of my *alma mater*—which bears only the slightest resemblance to St Gertrude's College. Thanks are also due to the distinguished astrophysicist Professor Paul Murdin, who read *End of Term* in manuscript and corrected some of the more egregious scientific anomalies. Thanks, too, to the Principal, staff and students of Newnham College, Cambridge, where I spent two happy years as Royal Literary Fund Fellow, and to Richard Reynolds at Heffers Bookshop, for suggesting a 'Cambridge book'.

CONTENTS

MATRICULATION

1

ONE, TWO, THREE, FOUR... The clock in Trinity Great Court struck twelve, its sonorous chimes echoing around that enormous space, which had seen so much coming and going of young men since its foundation nearly four hundred years before—some of them belonging to that doomed generation which had come of age in 1914. How many of those, thought Frederick Rowlands, had left these hallowed courts never to return? His commanding officer, Gerald Willoughby, had been one of them—although he had not in fact been a casualty of the War, Rowlands reminded himself. He recalled something Willoughby had said, which hadn't meant much to him at the time. They'd been under heavy fire at Polygon Wood, and were having to advance at the double. 'You might think this is bad, but it's not half as bad as the Great Court Run,' the young officer had laughed.

Smiling at the memory of his late friend, Rowlands paused for a moment, in the middle of the flagstone path that bordered the expanse of grass on which—he'd been informed a few minutes earlier—only Fellows of the College were permitted to walk. As he did so, a group of undergraduates loudly discussing Trinity's prowess on the river that morning barged past him. 'I say—look where you're going!' cried an indignant voice. 'Can't you see the gentleman's blind?' It was Maud Rickards, who had been walking a few paces behind, with Rowlands's wife, Edith. A chorus of sheepish apologies followed: 'Awfully sorry, sir!'

'Didn't see you, sir.'

'That's quite all right,' said Rowlands. 'Although they barely touched me,' he added to Miss Rickards, when the youths had taken themselves off. 'It makes no difference,' was the tart reply. 'They should make way for their elders and betters. If you ask me, there's far too much of this kind of boisterous behaviour going on—and from University men, too. It sets a bad example—not least to my girls.'

Rowlands wasn't about to disagree, although privately he felt some sympathy with the miscreants. What he wouldn't give to be out on the river, this afternoon, instead of trailing round some stuffy garden party! He knew Miss Rickards's intervention had been well-meant, but he'd disliked having his disability drawn attention to. He kept his thoughts to himself, however. In the space of the past couple of hours, since he and Edith had been met at Cambridge station by his wife's friend and fellow V.A.D., he had been discovering what a formidable woman she was. From her brisk instructions to the taxi-driver—'Now, don't go the long way round, will you? I live here and I'll *know*'—to the way she'd just ticked off the noisy rowers, it was evident that she was not to be trifled with. 'Maud's a dear, really,' Edith said, when they found themselves briefly alone. 'It's just her way. She was like that when we were at 1st London together. Always convinced she was right. She had some fine rows with Matron, I can tell you!'

Rowlands could well believe it. Now, as he felt his arm being firmly grasped by the determined Miss Rickards, he decided it was time to take a stand. 'I can manage quite well by myself, you know,' he said, gently disengaging his arm. 'I've had a lot of practice, haven't I, dear?'

'Oh yes,' said Edith, with the faintest note of irony in her voice. She'd seen some of the scrapes he'd got himself into, through his stubborn desire to be independent. 'It's just that there's a step here,' said Maud Rickards, sounding a little put-out. 'I didn't want you to fall flat on your face.'

'Thank you,' said Rowlands humbly. 'I wouldn't have enjoyed that.'

Emerging through the great gate onto Trinity Street, the three of them made their way towards King's, having already taken in Magdalene and St John's on their whistle-stop tour of the colleges. 'You might as well see something of the really beautiful ones,' Miss Rickards had said, with a laugh. 'I wouldn't want you to think they're all as hideous as our dear Gertie.'

'Cambridge *is* a remarkably pretty place,' said Edith, as they strolled along the narrow street, at the end of which, Rowlands knew, was one of the city's most spectacular views: that of King's College Chapel and the ornate Gothic gateway that led from King's Parade to the college's central court. He could picture this, even now, although he couldn't see it. As with much of his mental furniture, the image was linked with a memory—in this instance, with his first visit to Cambridge, the summer before the War, a year or so after he'd started the job at Methuen. He'd had a meeting with the bookshop manager at Heffers in Petty Cury, and had wandered around the market for a while, looking at the second-hand bookstalls, before doubling back along King's Parade and turning down Bene't Street, for a pint at the Eagle. Now *there* was a thought…

The two women were still admiring the view. Edith (whose brother had been at Worcester College, Oxford) said she thought it compared very favourably with that of the Radcliffe Camera. 'Wait until you've seen the Chapel's interior,' said her friend. 'It's said to be one of the finest examples of Late Perpendicular in Europe.' But they hadn't time for that now, regrettably, she went on. They'd have to hurry if they were to get a bite of lunch before they were due back at College. 'There's the new Dorothy Café, in Rose Crescent,' Miss Rickards suggested, with this end in view. 'They do a very good Welsh Rarebit…' Rowlands decided to leave them to it. 'I'm sure you both have a lot of things you want to talk about,' he said. 'I'll be in the Eagle, when you want me.' Because after all, he thought, entering the courtyard of the venerable hostelry—a former coaching inn—by way of its broad gateway, it really was Edith's show. She and her friend had a lot of catching up to do. He'd only be in the way.

With necessary caution, he made his way over the uneven cobbled yard and entered the bar on the far side of it, where he ordered himself a pint of Lacons' Best Bitter, and a Scotch egg to accompany it. There'd be tea and sandwiches later, he supposed—not that he was a great one for garden parties. Again, it was to please Edith that he'd agreed to come. She and Maud Rickards had met during the War, and had remained firm friends—although, perhaps inevitably, their paths had diverged, in the years since their V.A.D. days, owing to the demands of bringing up children, in Edith's case, and to those of working life, in Maud's. So it had been a pleasant surprise for Edith when she'd received the letter, two weeks before: 'It's from dear old Maud. You remember her, don't you? She and I shared digs in Camberwell, when I first started nursing. She's asked us to go up for the May Week Garden Party, at St Gertrude's…' This was the Cambridge women's college where Miss Rickards was employed as Bursar. 'There's a dinner that evening, too. Oh, do say you'll come, Fred! It'll be the most marvellous fun…'

Rowlands wasn't so sure about that—but he hoped at least that it wouldn't be too much of a bore. And it was true, as Edith had pointed out, that they hadn't been away together without the children for a very long time. He sipped his drink, savouring its agreeably bitter taste, and allowed his thoughts to drift, glad to be at a loose end for a while, and away from Miss Rickards's managing tendencies. It was pleasant sitting there in the relaxed atmosphere of a lunchtime pub, with its aromas of cigarette smoke and beer, and the sound of voices drifting in through the open window beside him. Although as a rule he tried not to listen to other people's conversations unless it was unavoidable, there was something quite beguiling about trying to guess—from the scraps of talk he could make out—what those around him were like.

That group outside in the courtyard couldn't be anything but undergraduates, with their loudly self-conscious talk of 'ploughing' in the end of term exams, and their boastfulness as to number of pints sunk and severity of hangovers afterwards. Those men in the room behind him must be racing men, to judge from the frequency with which they mentioned Favourites, Handicaps and Each-Way bets. Of course, they weren't far from Newmarket here. As for that couple on the other side of the window next to which Rowlands was sitting, they appeared to be having a lovers' tiff… 'I don't know how you've got the *nerve* to say that to me.' It was a young woman—a girl, really—who had spoken. Her voice was pitched so low that no one who wasn't sitting opposite—or beside her—could have heard it. 'I think that's about the most rotten thing I ever heard…'

It was immediately apparent to Rowlands that the speaker was unaware of being overheard—a fact that made him feel rather uncomfortable. He withdrew as far as he could from the window, but was reluctant to make any further sign that might give away his presence, such as shutting the window, or moving from his seat. 'If we're talking about "rotten,"' the young man to whom these remarks had been addressed now said, 'then I think the way you've been behaving's pretty rotten. I mean, stringing a chap along when all the time… No, don't go!' The girl must have made a move to do so. 'Not until you've heard me out.'

'I don't see why I should stay around to be insulted,' she replied. A moment later, came the sound of high heels stalking away. 'Oh I say! Dash it all, Diana—I didn't mean…' This was said in such a plaintive tone that Rowlands felt quite sorry for the lad. Never a good idea to cross a woman when she's in an unforgiving mood, he thought. As if on cue, he heard his name called. 'Fred! Oh, *there* you are! I've been looking for you everywhere…'

'Just coming.' He finished his beer. 'Where's your friend?'

'Hailing a cab,' said his wife. 'So there's nothing for you to do except pay the driver, and look pleasant.'

'I'll do my best,' he said, still pondering on the acrimonious little exchange he'd overheard.St Gertrude's College was of considerably younger vintage than the men's colleges around which the Rowlandses had been conducted by their hostess that morning. Built a little over sixty years before, in the Gothic style which had then been the fashion, it had the look of a different kind of institution altogether. 'People say it resembles a madhouse,' said Miss Rickards with a chuckle, as the taxi turned into the long drive that led to the entrance. 'It's the red brick, I suppose. Although nobody says it about Selwyn…' This was one of the newer men's colleges. 'Or Newnham, for that matter.'

'Perhaps it's being so far out,' said Edith, as, having driven under the arch of the gatehouse, the cab deposited the three of them in the courtyard behind it. 'It must be all of two miles.'

'Three,' replied her friend. 'Although it doesn't do the little beasts any harm to have the exercise. There is a bus,' she added, 'but most of them prefer to cycle to lectures. Our rowing team's extremely fit as a consequence. Now,' went on this forthright lady. 'Let's see where they've put you. I asked for a nice, quiet room in Tower Wing.' This, the college's most distinctive feature, Rowlands gathered, loomed over the gateway and was reached through one of a pair of oak doors on either side of the arch.

Their room was on the second floor. 'It has splendid views over the grounds,' said Miss Rickards, accompanying them to the door of the room. Rowlands forbore from pointing out that this wouldn't make much difference to him. 'I'm sure we'll be very comfortable,' he said; then, because he always liked to get a sense of the layout of places: 'I assume there's a floor above this?'

'Yes,' said Miss Rickards. 'There's Top Boots. It's College servants' rooms, and box rooms.'

'Can one get out onto the roof of the tower itself?' he asked. 'One can. But I shouldn't attempt it, if I were you. The stairs are very steep. We've had to warn the students on more than one occasion about holding midnight parties up there. Well, if you've got everything you need—there should be soap and towels—I'll leave you.' With this, the Bursar took herself off, suggesting that they should all meet an hour hence, in the lobby at the foot of the tower. The garden party was due to start at three. 'So you'll just have time to change your frock,' was her parting shot to Edith. 'Phew!' said Rowlands, when she had gone. 'That woman makes me tired.'

'Now Fred, that's not kind,' said his wife in a reproachful tone. 'She means well.'

'I know. It's just that she makes me feel like a rather unwieldy parcel that's lost its label. I'm not sure she knows what to do with me.'

'The fact is, she's not used to men. I think they make her feel awkward. She sort of over-compensates when they're around.'

'Well, I'm glad it's not just me,' he said.

Reaching the lobby at the bottom of the tower staircase a few minutes before three, they found that Miss Rickards had yet to arrive. 'She'll have things to organise, I expect,' said Edith. 'Goodness! *She* looks rather a dragon...' She was referring to the subject of one of the photographic portraits with which the walls of the lobby were hung: these, it transpired, were former *alumnae*, amongst them, the distinguished five who had formed the college's first student body, in its foundation year. 'Now *she's* rather lovely,' Edith went on, moving to another portrait. 'Rather fine eyes, you know—and such a lot of hair! How they managed with it like that, I can't imagine.'

'*You* had your hair long, when I first met you,' said Rowlands, with a twinge of regret for that lost glory. 'So I did,' was the reply. 'And very tiresome it was, too. Ah, here's Maud...' Because the heavy oak door which led out onto the passageway that ran beneath the tower was even now creaking open. But it wasn't Miss Rickards, after all, but a strange young woman who entered. 'The Bursar sends her apologies,' she said. 'She's tied up at present, but would be grateful if you would join her in the Fellows' Common Room for tea at half-past three. She suggests a walk in the gardens until then.'

'Thank you,' said Edith, since her husband appeared to have been struck dumb. 'I'm to take you there,' said the girl. 'Unless there's anything else you'd rather see? We have a rather good Egyptian collection in the College Museum, or there's an exhibition of watercolours by one of the Founders in the Old Library...'

'The gardens will do fine,' said Edith; then, as their guide led the way back through the doorway to the door on the other side of the arch, she hissed in Rowlands's ear: 'What's the matter, Fred? Cat got your tongue?

'I know that girl,' he said. 'I've just remembered where from. It was in the pub, earlier...'

'Tell me later,' said his wife, because they had by now caught up with their young guide. 'It's this way,' she said. High heels clicked on the tiled floor of the corridor, at the end of which, said Edith to her husband, was a spiral staircase: 'Rather an ornate one, with stained-glass windows going up it...' Years of acting as his 'eyes' meant she'd got into the habit of describing places for him. It seemed to surprise the girl. 'Oh, there's nothing up there worth seeing,' she said. 'Only supervisors' offices and students' rooms. If you follow me to the end of this corridor'—it ran at a right-angle to the first—'we can get out through the door at the end.'

'You've been most helpful,' said Rowlands, to make up for his earlier silence. 'Miss…?'

'Havelock,' said the girl. 'Diana Havelock.' She opened a door, and ushered them out onto a gravel path, with a flower border on one side and, it transpired from her brief description, a lawn and shrubberies on the other. 'It's all looking rather jolly just now,' said Miss Havelock. Edith agreed. 'Splendid delphiniums,' she said. 'I do so love that particular shade of blue.' They had by this time left the path and were crossing the lawn, towards where—to judge from the murmur of voices—a crowd of undergraduates and their guests was milling about. Cries of greeting were exchanged: '*Too* lovely to see you!'

'Topping day for it!'

'What is it that you're reading, Miss Havelock?' said Rowlands. 'Natural Sciences,' was the reply. 'Physics. I'm studying for my PhD, actually,' she added, with some *hauteur*. 'I see.' He hastened to correct his mistake. 'And what is your field, exactly?'

'Well…' Diana Havelock seemed about to reply to Rowland's question, but then something seemed to distract her—perhaps the sound of voices, coming towards them. A man saying, 'Agnes, my dear, I thought we'd been through all this?' and a woman's querulous reply: 'Yes, but you *said*…'

'I… ah… Will you excuse me?' said Miss Havelock abruptly. "There's someone I ought to…'

'Of course.' Before the words were out of his mouth, she had rushed off. 'How very odd!' said Edith. But before she could enlarge on this, they were hailed from a short distance away, and a moment later, Maud Rickards bore down on them. 'Glad you found your way. I asked Miss Havelock to go and find you…'

'She did,' said Edith. 'But…'

'Good, good. Now let me introduce you to some people. Ah, Professor Harding! And Mrs Harding, too… I hope the girls are looking after you?'

'Splendidly, thanks,' said the former. A youngish man, in spite of his title, thought Rowlands. Rather pleased with himself, too. His wife remained silent. 'Do let me introduce my friends, Mr and Mrs Rowlands,' Miss Rickards was saying. 'Mrs Rowlands and I were V.A.D.s together, during the War.'

'Ah, you ladies have the advantage of me, having seen war service,' said Harding. 'I wasn't in the War, I regret to say. Poor sight kept me out of it—the result, no doubt, of excessive reading,' he added with some complacency. Rowlands, who had lost his sight at the Third Battle of Ypres, had nothing to say to this, and after a minute or two more of inconsequential chat—'I hope you're enjoying Cambridge? We put on rather a good show at this time of year...'—Professor Harding left them, with a murmured excuse about needing to speak to the Mistress. His wife, who had scarcely opened her mouth throughout this exchange, except to agree that they'd been lucky with the weather, followed him. 'Now that,' said Edith *sotto voce*, 'is a very handsome man. I thought all professors were about a hundred, with sloping shoulders and white hair. Your Professor Harding can't be much more than forty.'

'Really, Edie!' said her friend in a tone of mock-reproof, and for a moment Rowlands caught a glimpse of a more girlish Miss Rickards. 'Your wife is quite incorrigible,' she added to Rowlands. 'Don't I know it?' he said. 'Although I must say, I'm a little surprised to find a male professor at a women's college. I'd assumed all your Fellows would be women...'

'Most of them are. Professor Harding is just a Visiting Fellow,' said the Bursar. 'But he's certainly been a great success with the undergraduates. He's a physicist...'

'Like Miss Havelock.'

'Yes. As a matter of fact, Professor Harding is supervising her PhD. She got the top marks in Physics in her Finals, and so the College awarded her a studentship to carry on her research.'

'Clever girl,' said Rowlands.

'Indeed. If rather...'

'Volatile? he suggested.

'Precisely. Ah, Miss Glossop! Have you had tea yet? It's set out in the F.C.R. for Fellows and their guests.'

Miss Glossop, who turned out to be a pleasant-sounding

female of about fifty, said that she had not yet had tea. 'I was looking for Honoria Fairclough,' she said. 'Wanted to ask her how she got on in the exam yesterday.'

'She's about somewhere,' was the reply. 'She and Avril Williamson are friends, aren't they? I'm sure *she'll* know.' With her customary briskness, Miss Rickards duly collared a passing undergraduate, whom Rowlands guessed must be the aforementioned Miss Williamson. 'Have you seen Miss Fairclough this afternoon?' she demanded. 'Miss Glossop wants her.'

'It was only that I wanted to know how she did in the Shakespeare paper,' said the English Fellow. 'But it can wait.'

'I *think* she's with Bobby Pearson's people,' said the girl doubtfully. 'I'll go and dig her out, if you like...'

'No matter,' said Miss Glossop. 'Although I *am* hoping she'll be one of my Firsts,' she added, as Avril Williamson, released from the obligation of tracking down her friend, scurried off. 'Miss Glossop is our Shakespeare specialist,' put in Miss Rickards. 'We're very lucky to have her.'

'Oh,' said Miss Glossop in a deprecating tone. 'I don't know about that...' But the Bursar was adamant. 'She got the best First in her year—and that's including the men. A pity,' added Maud Rickards, acidly, 'that she couldn't be awarded the same degree as the men.'

'Well, that's just the way it is, I'm afraid,' said the Shakespeare scholar mildly. 'I'm so sorry,' she went on, addressing the Rowlandses. 'I didn't catch your name. Is your daughter one of ours?'

'I'm afraid not. Our eldest is only fifteen,' said Rowlands, with a smile. 'Mr and Mrs Rowlands are old friends of mine,' said the Bursar. 'And they've *three* daughters, so they've every reason to take a good look round College...'

'Quite so,' said Miss Glossop. 'Ah, I think I see my young lady over there. Very nice to have met you, Mr and Mrs Rowlands. Do tell your daughter to think seriously about St Gertrude's when she comes to deciding on a university, won't you?'

Before Rowlands and his wife had a chance to discuss this interesting suggestion, they found themselves surrounded by a little knot of undergraduates, intent on reaching the tea-table, which had been set up on the far side of the lawn—or so Rowlands surmised from the general movement in that direction.

'...so I said to him, "You give me the pip, you really do..."'

'You didn't!'

'I most certainly did. I won't have chaps making mooncalf faces at me. And he isn't even a third year...'

'Girls, girls!' Miss Rickards's sharp tones cut through this gaily malicious chatter. 'Do look where you're going, Miss Thompson. Miss Harvey, your hat's on crooked. Please put it on properly. And try not to *shout*, Miss Ramsay.'

'Yes, Miss Rickards.'

'Awf'lly sorry, Miss Rickards.'

'Silly young things,' muttered the Bursar, as the now rather subdued young women continued on their way. 'If one could get their minds off the opposite sex for half a minute, they might be capable of doing something really useful with their lives. But instead all most of 'em can think about is getting engaged to some fatuous young man.'

'You don't consider marriage to be a "useful" occupation, then?' said Edith innocently, as they threaded their way between groups of staff and visitors, to reach the door that led to the Fellows' Common Room. 'I...' Miss Rickards realised that she'd been caught out. 'Of course marriage is useful. It's just that these girls have other opportunities, not available to most of their peers.'

'I'm sure they do,' said Edith. 'Although I can see why the pretty one with the fair hair—Miss Ramsay, isn't it?—might attract a bit of male attention...'

'Oh, she's a dreadful flirt,' groaned her friend. 'A pity, because she's got quite a good brain under that platinum blonde bob.' They had by now reached the Fellows' Common Room. 'Now this we're very proud of,' said the Bursar. 'It was only built two years ago, and it's given us a lot more room for entertaining—especially useful on occasions like this. The Old Library is charming, if you like that High Victorian style, but these rooms'—there were two, it emerged—'are so much more spacious and modern.' A subdued murmur of conversation, accompanied by a clinking of teacups, showed that others had already availed themselves of the F.C.R.'s superior amenities. 'Such a relief to be out of the sun,' said a voice next to Rowlands. 'I thought I'd *expire* if I had to stay out there another minute...'

'Good afternoon, Miss Crane. Miss Sissons,' said Miss Rickards. 'I hope you've got everything you need?' To their reply that this was so, she said that, in that case, she'd see about getting their own tea. 'I'll come with you,' said Edith. Rowlands, left standing rather awkwardly with the two Fellows, decided to introduce himself: 'How do you do? I'm Frederick Rowlands.'

'Alethea Crane,' said the one who'd complained of the heat. 'I suppose you must be one of the fathers?' It seemed to Rowlands that he was fated to be asked a version of this question all afternoon. He explained that he was accompanying his wife, who was a friend of the Bursar's. 'Not that we wouldn't be delighted if one of our girls were to be given the chance to come to St Gertrude's in the future,' he added, feeling that any standing he might have in that gathering was entirely dependent on his female relatives. 'Are any of your daughters good at biology?' This was the other Fellow—Miss Sissons. Rowlands smiled. 'I don't know. The eldest might be. She's top of her class in Mathematics.'

'Ah, if she's a mathematician, she'll be one of Professor Harding's select little coterie,' said Miss Crane, in a tone of voice that indicated she did not think much of the handsome don. 'Well, she's yet to sit her matriculation exams, so I don't think...' he began, when Edith and Maud Rickards returned, bearing cups of tea. 'Such a crush!' exclaimed the latter. 'There. Have you got that all right, Mr Rowlands?' She placed the full cup in Rowlands's hand with exaggerated care. 'Yes, thanks,' he said. Something about the exchange must have caused the Biology lecturer to look more closely at the man she'd been talking to. 'I say,' she said. 'I'm awfully sorry. I didn't realise...'

'Nothing to be sorry for,' said Rowlands, unable to suppress a feeling of irritation at the officious way Miss Rickards had once again drawn attention to his blindness. He hadn't crashed into anyone, or tripped over the furniture so far, and so he wished she hadn't felt the need to make such a fuss. 'Now, do have one of these cakes,' she was saying. 'Fred never eats cake,' said Edith, perhaps reading his scowl correctly. 'I've got you some sandwiches,' she added. 'Egg and cress. I didn't think you'd care for cucumber.'

'Yes, we really ought to have provided some heartier fare for the men,' said Miss Rickards. It was hard to tell from her tone of voice whether or not she was being sarcastic. Rowlands decided to ignore the remark. 'Miss Crane and Miss Sissons and I were just discussing the possibility of Margaret's applying to study mathematics,' he said to his wife. 'I gather Professor Harding's the man we should be talking to?'

'Yes they're all clamouring to attend his lectures,' said the Bursar. 'They can sit examinations with the men, too—they just can't expect to receive the same degree.' This was obviously a sore point, and one with which the other two academics were familiar to the point of weariness. 'If you'll excuse me,' said Miss Sissons. 'I see some of my parents over there... that is, the parents of my pupils. So nice to have met you, Mr Rowlands. I do hope your daughter comes to St Gertrude's.'

'I should circulate, too,' said Miss Rickards, hastily gulping down the last of her sandwich. 'Will you two be all right on your own? Miss Crane here knows everybody in College, so she'll be able to introduce you to anyone you want to meet. Only I see that Lady St Clare—she's one of our Trustees—needs looking after...'

'We'll be fine,' said Edith. 'It must be quite a responsibility,' she observed to their new acquaintance, as Miss Rickards bustled away. 'Organising an event like this, I mean.'

'Oh, the Bursar's marvellous,' agreed Miss Crane. 'She keeps the college ticking over with remarkable efficiency. We've over two hundred students, you know—to say nothing of teaching staff and Research Fellows. It's a lot to keep in check.'

'It must be,' said Rowlands, resolving to give Miss Rickards the benefit of the doubt in future. What seemed, at first sight, to be unnecessary fussing, was probably no more that a desire to ensure that everything was running smoothly, he told himself. An institution of this size would need a lot of organisation if it were to function effectively. His army training should have told him that.

2

'Well,' said Miss Crane. 'I don't know who else you'd be interested in meeting, but I can tell you who's here. There's the Mistress, of course...'

'Is she the tall, distinguished-looking woman in the grey silk frock?' asked Edith. 'That's her. She's talking to Dr Maltravers—our chaplain. He's Director of Music here, so I should think it's about the concert this afternoon. Some of the undergraduates will be singing madrigals, and some acting scenes from Shakespeare.'

'I look forward to that,' said Rowlands, meaning it—but Miss Crane laughed. 'Oh, the girls enjoy it, and it gives the parents a chance to applaud their little darlings' artistic prowess,' she said. It sounded as if she didn't care much for such endeavours—but then she was a scientist, he reminded himself. 'Come and meet Dr Bostock,' she was saying. 'She's our Modern and Mediaeval Languages Fellow—newly arrived from Oxford, so she doesn't know anyone, poor thing. It'll be a kindness to talk to her. People do tend to clump together at these events.'

The Rowlandses followed their guide across the room to a window embrasure, where the aforementioned Fellow was standing, nursing a cup of tea. This fact became apparent to Rowlands when, at Miss Crane's friendly greeting, the other gave a violent start, and was only saved from disaster by her colleague's intervention. 'Steady on! You nearly had that all down you...'

'You startled me,' said the young woman hotly. 'I'm sure I didn't mean to,' was the reply. 'Let me introduce Mr and Mrs Rowlands. They're guests of the Bursar's.'

'Oh.' If this was a sample of Dr Bostock's conversational style, it was hardly surprising she was all on her own, thought

Rowlands. He chose an inoffensive topic. 'Fine day for it,' he said. 'Yes.' This was hardly better. Dr Bostock was obviously one of those people with no small talk. 'We've just been admiring the gardens,' put in Edith. 'You're lucky to have such extensive grounds at St Gertrude's. It must be very nice for the students.'

'I expect so,' was the indifferent reply. Miss Crane being at that moment caught up in conversation with another member of the teaching staff—evidently a friend, for they were on first name terms—the Rowlandses found themselves rather landed with the reticent Dr Bostock. Rowlands tried again: 'I gather you teach Modern Languages? he said. 'May I ask which languages particularly?'

'French and Italian.'

'Ah. I read a little French,' he said. 'What have you read?' She sounded marginally more interested in this—'Although I don't think she was paying either of us much attention,' said Edith afterwards. 'She kept glancing out of the window all the while you were talking to her, as if she was looking out for someone. Rather rude, I thought.'

The conversation limped on for a few more minutes—Rowlands opining that it made all the difference to one's first impression of a work to have had a sympathetic teacher—or, in his case, a patient reader. 'Being blind, you know, I've had to rely on my wife to read aloud to me...'

'Unfortunately I don't read French,' said Edith.

'...so I'm lucky to have the use of some excellent Talking Books. I'm halfway through *Le Rouge et Le Noir* at present.'

'I'm doing Stendhal with my first years,' said Dr Bostock, with more warmth in her voice than before. 'They're making rather heavy weather of it.'

'Perhaps they need a Talking Book to bring it alive?' said Rowlands. 'Perhaps.' Something seemed to have distracted the Modern Languages Fellow, for she broke off suddenly. 'Do excuse me. There's someone I... I really must speak to...'

Then she was gone.

'Well!' said Edith. 'I must say...' But she was fortunately prevented from saying it by the return of Miss Rickards, very apologetic for having abandoned them. 'It's just that there's so much to see to at an event like this,' she said. 'With over a hundred guests, and then the dinner to organise tonight...'

'Surely you have help?' said Edith, as the three of them strolled out into the courtyard of the Fellows' Garden. Here, a sizeable contingent of Fellows and their guests had congregated, the better to enjoy the glorious weather. Several of the men— and no doubt some of the women, in such an emancipated gathering, Rowlands surmised—had lit pipes and cigarettes, and the smell of tobacco smoke mingled pleasantly with that of the roses on the garden wall. 'Oh, as to having help,' the Bursar was saying. 'It doesn't make much difference. It all comes back to me in the end.' She gave a martyred sigh. 'Which,' said Edith to her husband later, 'is Maud all over. She always did like to run the show.'

Feeling that he too might take advantage of the prevailing informality regarding smoking, Rowlands lit a cigarette, and paying only the most superficial attention to his wife's conversation with her friend, allowed himself to relax for a moment or two. It could be hard work, having to be on the *qui vive* the whole time—especially when, as now, almost everybody was a stranger to him. Being blind meant you had to concentrate extra hard if you were to follow what was being said—let alone get any sense of what your interlocutor was like. Over the years, since that day in 1917 when he'd been blinded by a burst of shrapnel, he'd developed ways of assessing not only something about a person's character but also something of their personal appearance, using the clues available to him.

Clues such as whether a person sounded old or young; whether they seemed cheerful or morose, subdued or outward-going. Physical clues—such as the vigour or otherwise of a person's handshake, and the height from which that handshake was offered—were something else to which he'd taught himself to pay attention. Dr Bostock's hand—a limp, cool hand, with no rings—had been unwillingly given, and hastily withdrawn. He'd had the impression of a small, slight woman with something on her mind. Painfully shy, he thought—for which one could only feel sympathy. But it had struck him that her stand-offishness was down to more than shyness. She'd seemed decidedly on edge, he thought.

The sun was warm on his upturned face, and the smell of the climbing rose on the wall behind—an Ena Harkness, if he wasn't mistaken—added to his sense of well-being. Really, you couldn't think of a more peaceful spot in which to pursue… well, whatever you felt inclined to pursue. Pleasant surroundings and three meals a day. These academics were living in clover, he thought. 'I most strongly disagree,' said a voice just beside him. 'If you follow that line of argument, there's no telling *where* it will end…' The speaker was a woman—not one of the Fellows (if that was what she was) to whom Rowlands had yet been introduced. 'I rather supposed you *would* think that,' said the man to whom she was speaking. Professor Harding. 'As a historian, you take a different view of these things…'

'I certainly do.' The speaker had a deep, rather attractive, voice. The voice of someone used to having her opinions deferred to, thought Rowlands. 'But my dear Miss Hall,' went on Harding 'Surely even you must agree that research without any *outcome* is… how shall I put it? Behind the times.'

'I don't see why…'

'No, let me finish. In a field such as mine, one becomes used to the idea that one's work has a practical application. After all, most of the advances we now take for granted in the modern world—electricity, radio waves—are the result of scientific enquiry. We scientists have a duty to pursue such enquiry to its limits, and to share our knowledge with mankind in general…'

'Very laudable,' said the woman drily. 'Do I take it that you believe the possession of such knowledge to be intrinsically *beneficial* to mankind—or womankind?' she added under her breath. 'Whether it's of benefit or not is beside the point,' said Harding. 'So you'd carry on regardless?' she persisted. 'Even if you knew your research might be harnessed to evil ends… such as those of the present regime in Germany, for instance?'

Harding sounded unperturbed by this. 'Science has always been at the service of those in power,' he said. 'It isn't up to the scientist to take issue with the way power manifests itself. But I see you don't approve of my philosophy, Miss Hall…' Harding sounded amused. 'Whether I approve or disapprove is hardly relevant,' said the History Fellow. 'But I do know quite a bit about the way power—and the patronage of the powerful—corrupts. I mean, take the Medici...'

'Oh, the Medici,' said Professor Harding, as if that were scarcely to the point. 'And then look at Francis I, and Leonardo da Vinci,' went on Miss Hall. 'Having to spend his time inventing war machines, when he could have been painting beautiful pictures...'

'Some of us,' said the mathematician slyly, 'prefer the war machines to the paintings. Well, must be pushing along. Let's carry this on at dinner, shall we?'

'Not if I can help it,' muttered the History Fellow under her breath. She took a step backwards as she said these words, not looking to see if there was anyone behind her, for her foot in its stout Oxford landed heavily on Rowlands's foot. 'Oh! I'm so sorry!' she exclaimed, although he had been too much of a gentleman to cry out. 'It's quite all right,' he said quickly. 'The name's Frederick Rowlands,' he added, thinking that he could hardly admit to knowing her name, since he'd only learnt it inadvertently. 'And before you ask, I don't have a daughter at St Gertrude's—yet.'

'Caroline Hall. I teach History.' She seized his offered hand and shook it vigorously. Definitely the Amazonian type, thought Rowlands. They seemed to flourish here—doubtless a result of all the bicycling and rowing... 'So you do have a daughter?' Miss Hall was saying. 'Three. Although only one of them seems like university material at present.' Dreamy Anne, though as fond of reading as her older sister, was more interested in fairy-tales than facts, while Joan, just turned seven, cared only for her collection of shells and beetles. 'Well, it gives them a splendid start,' said the historian. 'Not just the studying, but being with their peers. They form tremendous friendships, you know, which last them all their lives.'

At that moment someone came out of the French windows onto the terrace where he and his companion were standing. 'Ah, Miss Hall,' said a voice—a beautiful voice, thought Rowlands. Deep and resonant, with a peculiar timbre, that suggested… what? Fragility? No. Sensitivity, perhaps. 'I wonder if I might have a word?'

'Of course, Mistress.'

'It's about the running order for the series of lectures on New Directions in Philosophy next term…' She broke off. 'But I see I'm interrupting. Do forgive me.' Then to Rowlands: 'I don't believe we've been introduced. I'm Beryl Phillips.'

'Frederick Rowlands.' He held out his hand and felt, for a moment, her slim, cool fingers touch his. A tall woman, he thought, but—unlike the ebullient History don—a woman not much given to energetic bustle. This was a stately presence: dignified, commanding. 'Mr Rowlands has three daughters,' said Caroline Hall, in the manner of a conjurer pulling a rabbit out of hat. 'How fortunate,' replied the Mistress graciously. 'I hope you will bring your girls to St Gertrude's one day, Mr Rowlands.'

Rowlands bowed his head, in acknowledgment of this courtesy. Although how they'd be able to afford the fees for one daughter, let alone all three, was anybody's guess, he thought privately. 'We have scholarships, you know,' said the Mistress, as if she guessed this thought. 'Bursaries, too—although those are not *quite* so useful.'

'Thank you,' said Rowlands, with the feeling that a considerable favour had been conferred in those few moments—if only the favour of her attention. What a presence she had! 'With a few of her sort running the country, we wouldn't be in the mess we're in,' he thought. 'But I should leave you to your discussion…'

'Discussion? Oh, about the lecture… It was only,' said Beryl Phillips, in the same languidly offhand manner with which she had mentioned the scholarships, 'that I felt that as the organiser you ought to give the first lecture, Miss Hall. I'm happy to take the *second* week.'

'Just as you like,' said Miss Hall. 'The Mistress is an authority on Aristotle,' she added, to Rowlands. 'She's written such an interesting paper on the *Poetics*…'

'All I remember about that,' said Rowlands with a self-deprecating air, 'are his stipulations about drama having to evoke pity and terror…'

'Catharsis,' murmured Miss Phillips. 'The essential element in all tragic art…' She laughed. 'But you mustn't let me get carried away with my favourite topic. This is meant to be a festive occasion. We've all sorts of treats in store—the concert this afternoon, for one. I hope you're staying for that, Mr Rowlands?'

Rowlands said he was looking forward to it.

'Splendid. We've some talented musicians among us—some of whom will be doing double duty this evening, poor young things…'

'Oh?' said Rowlands politely.

'It's the College Dance tonight,' the other explained. 'The girls have been looking forward to it so much, haven't they, Miss Hall? And so our musicians will go from playing Bach and Chopin to dancing cheek to cheek—or whatever it is that they amuse themselves with these days.' Perhaps seeing his startled expression, the Mistress said drily: 'Oh, I'm quite *au fait* with all the latest tunes! As head of a women's college, one gets to hear rather a lot of them. The undergraduates are allowed gramophones in their rooms, as long as they don't disturb their neighbours at unsocial hours. At St Gertrude's,' she added, with what Rowlands guessed was a twinkle in her eye, 'we believe in a *complete* education for our girls. Not that we don't prize getting Firsts above an ability to dance the Rumba…'

'St Gertrude's does rather well for Firsts, I'm told.'

'Yes, we can hold our heads up,' was the reply. 'Of course, we impress on our students when they come here that they have to be even better than the men.'

'In my experience,' said Rowlands, 'women generally are, if you give them the chance.'

'Ladies and gentlemen,' proclaimed a voice from the steps behind them. 'I have been asked to summon you all to an Entertainment, which is about to start in Forest Court. The theme is 'Shakespeare's Women', and there will be music to follow.'

'Thank you, Angela,' said the Mistress. 'Miss Thompson is one of the stalwarts of our dramatic society,' she added, for Rowlands's benefit. 'They build the sets and make all the costumes themselves, you know.'

'Quite an endeavour, on top of all the other work,' he replied. 'Oh, it is. But Miss Glossop, our Director of Studies in English, believes that only thus will they gain a complete understanding of the workings of the theatre. It's been a pleasure talking to you, Mr Rowlands. But I see that my presence is required elsewhere.' Miss Phillips sounded as if this wasn't entirely to her liking. 'Ah, Lady St Clare,' Rowlands heard her say, as she was claimed by this distinguished visitor. 'How very good of you to come! Yes, we have been lucky with the weather...'

Rowlands was joined at that moment by his wife and her friend. 'I say—you were having a good long chat with the Mistress!' said Maud Rickards. 'Yes. Interesting woman.'

'Oh, she's marvellous! She was up in '97 when there was all the fuss about women's degrees, you know,' said Miss Rickards, taking his arm, as the three of them joined the general movement towards the exit. 'About whether women should be allowed them, that is. Can you believe they laid on special trains to bring M.A.s with voting privileges back to Cambridge to ensure the motion was defeated?'

Rowlands said he could well believe it.

'I wasn't at Cambridge myself at the time, but I gather there was almost a riot,' said the Bursar. 'The undergraduates hung an effigy of a woman riding a bicycle from the window above Macmillan's Bookshop in the market square, and another of a woman in cap and gown from a window in Caius—all of which they thought a great joke.' Miss Rickards wasn't laughing, however. 'If I didn't know better,' said Rowlands to his wife, when the Bursar, having escorted them to where the entertainment was to be held, had gone to supervise the seating arrangements, 'I'd say your friend had a bit of a down on men.'

'Can you blame her?' was the reply; then, in a softer tone: 'It isn't *all* men. She was engaged once, you know. He was killed at the Somme.'

'All right, all right. I'm sorry I said it. But you have to admit, that men are in rather a minority at an institution like this. It's hardly surprising that I'm feeling a bit got at...'

'Then you know how we women feel, most of the time,' said Edith, who always liked to have the last word.

At one end of Forest Court a small stage had been set up. Seating had been arranged in front of this; as he and Edith drew near, Rowlands could hear Miss Rickards's voice, directing operations: 'That's right, Thomas—a little more to the left with those chairs, if you please. We don't want to block the actors' route to the stage... Thank you, Mr Wainwright...' This was the Porter, with whom Rowlands had earlier exchanged a few words about their luggage. 'If you'd direct people *this* way...'

A few of the male undergraduates, and a couple of the younger fathers were roped in to help—Rowlands being prevented from joining them by his wife. 'They've plenty of willing hands,' she said. 'No need for you to exert yourself.' Although she knew perfectly well that he never shirked such duties as a rule. But he'd turn forty-five next month, which was no longer young, he supposed. Only he was damned if he'd let himself turn into an old man before his time... 'You're scowling, Fred,' said Edith in his ear. 'Do try not to scowl. You'll frighten the actors.'

Because now that the pandemonium of moving chairs and marshalling people to their seats had subsided, they could settle down to what was happening on stage: the quarrel scene from *A Midsummer's Night's Dream*, as it turned out. His irritation forgotten, Rowlands focused his attention on this—one of his favourite of Shakespeare's plays. It never failed to put the audience in a good mood. Around him, people were chuckling, as insults were exchanged between tall Helena and diminutive Hermia:

> How low am I, thou painted maypole? Speak!
> How low am I? I am not yet so low
> But that my nails can reach unto thine eyes...

'She's rather good, the little one,' said Edith, *sotto voce*. 'So I gather,' he whispered back. Even though he couldn't see the comic discrepancy in the two girls' stature, he could hear it, in the difference between their voices—one a shrill soprano, the other a thrilling contralto. 'And with those dark curls...'

'Ah.' He could picture it, now. 'The other one's fair, is she?'

'Yes. Rather statuesque.'

It was all he needed; memory supplied the rest. An open-air production in Regent's Park, before the War. Who was it he'd been with? Lizzie—no, Kitty—Carter. That was it. Pretty little thing she was, with those big brown eyes. Worked in a florist's shop. They hadn't really hit it off, though, and next thing he heard she was going steady with Joe Furnival. He was a nice chap, Joe—no side to him. He'd married Kitty the week before he'd been sent to France. Killed at Mons, poor fellow. Rowlands had lost touch with Kitty after that. Had she married again, he wondered? She'd be all of forty now. Funny how a few, half-remembered, lines from a long-ago production could bring back the past so vividly.

With something of an effort, he dragged his attention back to the here-and-now, and the next item on the programme—which was the casket scene from *The Merchant of Venice*. They were certainly choosing all the best-known bits, thought Rowlands—which made sense, of course. Always a good idea to meet one's audience halfway. And they—the actors—were making a decent job of it, too. Good to see it wasn't all swotting for exams. What was it the Mistress had said? *We believe in a* complete *education for our girls…* Well, this was certainly a demonstration of that admirable principle. He let himself relax, drinking in the scents and sounds of the garden in which they sat, along with the music of the words, and the dark fairytale they told:

O hell! What have we here?
A carrion Death, within whose empty eye
There is a written scroll…

The girl playing Portia had an attractive voice, he thought—warm and expressive, with just a hint of laughter. Even though it would have given her more chance to shine, he was glad they hadn't chosen the courtroom scene, in which Portia, disguised as the young advocate, turns the tables against Shylock. There was a cruelty to it he'd always found uncomfortable. The Princes of Morocco and Aragon having been given their comeuppance, and Bassanio having solved the riddle and won the lady, a brief hiatus ensued, as scenery was shifted and costumes changed for what was to be the third and final scene. This, according to the programme, was to have been the courtship scene from *Twelfth Night*—a play which would have presented a intriguing reversal of the girl-dressed-as-boy wooing a girl on behalf of the man she's in love with, thought Rowlands—given that all the actors were female. But just then came an announcement: 'Owing to the indisposition of Gwendolyn Hussey, who was to have played Viola,' said Miss Glossop, from the stage, 'there has been a change of programme...'

A change it proved to be. Instead of the light and shade of the comedy, here was unrelieved darkness:

> That which hath made them drunk hath made me bold:
> What hath quenched them hath given me fire.—Hark!
> Peace!

'It's her,' whispered Edith. 'The one who showed us around the gardens.'

'Diana Havelock,' said Rowlands, who had known the voice at once. 'Now she *is* good.' Because it was apparent as the scene progressed that hers was a different order of acting. The others had merely spoken their lines; she performed them.

> Give me the daggers. The sleeping and the dead
> Are but as pictures: 'tis the eye of childhood
> That fears a painted devil...

She sounded... what was the word? *Haunted*, thought Rowlands. As if, in that moment, she was seeing unimaginable terrors. He wondered how someone of her age—she couldn't be more than twenty-one, surely?—had come to know such things. When the scene was over, a momentary silence fell—broken at last by a smattering of applause. This grew, until it reached a crescendo. 'Bravo!' cried a voice from somewhere behind Rowlands. One of Miss Havelock's male admirers, evidently. 'I suppose she *was* rather good,' said Edith, not sounding entirely convinced. 'She's very striking of course, with that red hair, and those extraordinary eyes. Some of it's make-up, I imagine, but even so...'

'Yes,' said Rowlands. 'Even so.' It stuck him that there was something troubling about Diana Havelock—although he couldn't have put his finger on what it was. These very brilliant types often were a little unstable. *Volatile* was the word he'd used in describing the girl to Maud Rickards. But what he'd just witnessed onstage was indicative of more than mere unpredictability.

He was distracted from such thoughts by the beginning of the musical section of the programme—one to which he'd been looking forward. For while there was pleasure to be got from hearing Shakespeare's words spoken, he knew that one aspect of theatre —the visual—was forever closed to him. By contrast, *this* was unqualified enjoyment. As the St Gertrude's Madrigal Choir launched into a spirited rendition of 'Now is the Month of Maying', he surrendered to the moment and all it contained: the pure young voices, rising and falling, the scent of flowers on the warm, still air.

Beside and behind him the audience sat absolutely silent (aside from the occasional creaking of a chair, or involuntary whistling of breath), as the five voices wove their intricate patterns of sound. Scarcely had the last notes of this died away, than the choir moved effortlessly into the opening bars of 'Weep, O Mine Eyes'. This, though slower and more melancholy that the previous song, was entirely to Rowlands's liking, since his taste was always for the sombre. Gloomy stuff, Edith would have said, but he found it rather up-lifting.

Several more pieces followed: it was not a long programme, as guests would need time to bathe and change before pre-dinner drinks in the Library at six-thirty. From the faint rustlings and shiftings of weight on the chairs about him, Rowlands guessed that he was in a minority in wishing that the concert could go on longer. But, as the last song in the afternoon's entertainment reminded him, all good things come to an end. Had he known how soon that adage was to be proved to him, he might have savoured the moment still more.

The silver Swan, who living had no Note,
When Death approached, unlocked her silent throat;
Leaning her breast against the reedy shore,
Thus sung her first and last, and sung no more:
Farewell all joys; O Death, come close mine eyes;
More Geese than Swans now live; more Fools than Wise.

Dressing for dinner, Rowlands found himself in an unusually abstracted mood—so much so, that it drew the attention of his wife, as she stood helping him with his bow-tie. 'Whatever's the matter, Fred? That's twice I've asked you if you'd like me to fasten your cufflinks.'

'Sorry.' He pulled a face. 'I was miles away.' He held out his arms, so that she could thread the silver links through his cuffs. He was perfectly capable of managing this himself, but the small intimate service was one from which both derived satisfaction. 'It's always the same when you listen to music,' said Edith, with rare perspicacity. 'You go into a world of your own.'

'Well, it *was* rather beautiful. All that stuff about love and death. A reminder of one's own mortality, I suppose.'

'Mortality—fiddlesticks!' she said. 'You want your dinner, that's all. There!' She brushed a speck from the lapel of his dinner jacket. 'You look quite presentable. And my new frock is quite a success, if I say so myself. I wasn't sure about the colour—maroon can be a difficult shade to pull off—but I *think* it's all right, with my pearls to set it off...'

'I'm sure you look lovely,' he said, drawing her close for a moment. 'You *smell* lovely. What is it?'

'*Evening in Paris*.' He knew it was; he'd given it to her last Christmas. 'Don't, Fred! You'll mess my hair...' But she allowed herself to be kissed. 'Come on,' she said, disentangling herself. 'We'd better go down, or we won't get our sherry.'

3

Reaching the Old Library, they were met by a lively buzz of conversation, whose volume at times threatened to overwhelm the discreet strains of the string quartet that was playing in a corner. These, Rowlands guessed, must be the young musicians to whom the Mistress had referred, whose talents would later be employed in playing the latest dance numbers for the benefit of their peers. Because the room was filled with people, he was unable to form more than a cursory impression of its size; he guessed it must be large, to accommodate such crowd. That the walls would be lined with bookshelves he didn't need to guess, since the smell of old books and leather bindings, overlaid at that moment by cigarette smoke, confirmed this not-unreasonable assumption.

'See anyone we know?' he murmured to Edith, as the two of them entered. 'Yes. There's Miss Glossop.' And indeed their cheerful acquaintance of a few hours ago was standing a short distance away, accepting compliments on behalf of her students for the afternoon's performance: 'They were rather good weren't they? When one thinks that most of them finished their exams only yesterday...'

'Your Portia was most charming, I think,' said an attractively low voice with an accent Rowlands thought he recognised. He drew closer to the speakers—Edith's attention having been captured by her friend, at that moment. 'Miss Fairclough, you mean?' replied Miss Glossop. 'Not a bad little actress, is she?'

'I thought she was jolly good,' he said. 'Oh, good evening, Mr Rowlands! So glad you enjoyed it. Fräulein Kruger and I were just saying...'

'Perhaps you'd introduce me?'

'Oh! Of course. Ilse, this is Mr Rowlands. Fräulein Kruger is our German assistant,' she added to Rowlands, who held out his hand. '*Guten Abend*,' he said. 'You speak German?' was the reply. 'But that is wonderful!'

'I'm not what you'd call fluent,' he said. 'But I can get by, if I have to.'

'Ilse... Fräulein Kruger... has come back to us,' said Miss Glossop happily. 'She was an undergraduate here, weren't you, Ilse?'

'Yes. It is a great pleasure to be back in England,' said the German assistant. 'Especially since I am no longer welcome in my own country.'

'I see,' said Rowlands, who had had some experience of how things were in Germany not so very long before. 'I'm sorry to hear that. Where are you from, exactly?'

'Munich. I was teaching at the university there. At least...' She sighed. 'I was until last year. It was then that the authorities decided that they had no use for those like myself. We Jews are not true Germans, you understand. Others—and especially the young—must be protected from us...' Although she herself didn't sound very old, thought Rowlands. 'Well, *we're* very glad to have you,' said Miss Glossop warmly. 'Will you both excuse me? Only I must have a word with Dr Maltravers. We're putting on an extended version of 'Shakespeare's Women' for the undergraduates, you know. He's letting us use the Chapel.' She bustled off, and a moment later could be heard in earnest conversation with the Chaplain.

Rowlands turned once more to his new acquaintance. 'St Gertrude's seems like a fine institution,' he said. 'I've three daughters myself, and so I'm rather in favour of women having the same advantages as men.'

'Then you are exceptional,'was the crisp reply. 'There are not so many—yes, even here in Cambridge!—who think as you do.'

'I've rather gathered that.'

'We are of course very lucky at St Gertrude's to have such an excellent teaching staff—although we are not able at present to cover all the subjects...'

'Ah yes,' he said. 'Mathematics being one of the subjects not offered, I believe?'

'Mathematics, and Physics and Chemistry—we are v all the sciences, expect Biology,' said Fräulein Kruger own subject—Modern and Mediaeval Languages—we have supervisors for French, Italian and German, but not Spanish or Portuguese. And so the students—the women, you understand—must find supervisors in other colleges… those that will have them.'

'Why,' said Rowlands. 'Do you mean to say…'

'It is not every member of the University's teaching staff who will accept female students,' she said. 'Some are very much opposed to the idea that women should be educated at all.' Ilse Kruger gave an unamused little laugh. 'Certain Fellows of this university—I will not say their names—refuse to address the women students at all. It is as if we do not exist. "Gentlemen," they will say, when beginning a lecture—I know, because I have attended such a lecture myself—"Gentlemen…" Even though there might be twenty or thirty women sitting in front of them in the lecture hall. Or they will make a joke of us, and call us 'undergradu*ettes*'. You will think I am making a big fuss about nothing,' she said. 'Oh no,' said Rowlands. 'I don't think that at all.'

'*There* you are, my dear!' said a voice. It was a man's voice: elderly, Rowlands guessed, and what he would have called 'donnish'—all too appositely, in this case, no doubt. 'I was hoping I'd see you here. When are you coming to talk to my students about Goethe?'

'Good evening, Professor Giles.'

'But I'm interrupting…'

'Not at all,' said Rowlands. Introductions were performed, and then the older man said: 'I say, haven't we met before?'

'I don't think…' began Rowlands, but the other went on eagerly, 'Yes, yes. Never forget a face. I suppose you were in the War?'

Rowlands said that he was.

'Then it's likely you'll have come through my hands. Basic training. Aldershot.' Light dawned at last for Rowlands. 'Major Giles. Is it really you?' The memory of those mornings lining up for target practise in the bitter cold came back to him in a rush.

'The very same. Older and greyer, now, of course.'

'You taught me to shoot,' said Rowlands. A vision of a kindly, slightly ineffectual, figure in khakis rose up before his inner eye. Grey moustache and an eye-glass... *'All right, you men, fall in. Let's see what you can do at twenty paces...'*

The other man laughed. 'Didn't make a bad job of it, either, as I recall. Of course, *I* was too old to fight that time,' he added. 'Saw service in Africa, though, in '99.'

This interesting discussion was brought to an end by the sounding of the gong, and, after agreeing to meet up for a smoke after dinner, the two men separated—Professor Giles to join the procession of dons on its way to High Table, and Rowlands to wait for Edith. In all the excitement of meeting his former instructor, he'd quite forgotten Fräulein Kruger—all too easy, when one couldn't see if another person was still there. 'I must apologise for breaking off our conversation, Fräulein,' he said—uncertain whether or not he was addressing the empty air. 'But you know how it is when old comrades get together.'

'Yes, I know,' she said. So she had been there all along, he thought. 'It is the same in my country. Men like to talk of war.'

In the vast dining-hall, two rows of long tables ran parallel to the walls on which, Maud Rickards informed her guests, hung portraits of former Mistresses of the the College. 'All except the present one. She's still to sit for hers. Some Royal Academician's going to do it... I forget the name. Ah, here we are...' She steered Rowlands and his wife towards the table at the far end, which was on a dais, at right-angles to the rest. 'You're both on High Table—although seated apart. I hope that's all right? Oh, take care!' This was to Rowlands. 'There's a step.'

'Thank you.' He found his place without further assistance, giving way as he did so to Miss Havelock, who murmured her thanks as he stood back to let her pass along the narrow aisle that ran behind the table. It struck him that, as a PhD student, she must feel rather isolated, being one of such a small, select group (he supposed there must be others)—but he dismissed the thought. What, after all, did he know about it? With Miss Hall, the History Fellow, on his right-hand side, and Miss

Merriweather, a Geographer, on his left, he wouldn't be short of conversation, he thought. He was pleased to discover that the amiable Miss Glossop was sitting opposite, with Professor Harding to her left, and another man, to whom Rowlands hadn't yet been introduced, on her right.

A silence fell. '*Benedictus benedicat,*' said the Mistress, and, with a scraping of chairs and a clattering of heels on the bare wooden floor, the company sat down. At once an indescribable sound—midway between a shriek and a roar—arose from the body of the hall, as greetings were exchanged along the length of the tables, and plans were laid for the rest of the evening's festivities. 'One always forgets,' murmured Caroline Hall, as those at High Table waited for the first course—a salmon mousse—to be served, 'how much *noise* women make…'

Rowlands, to whom this remark had been addressed, smiled. 'It's no worse than a barracks mess-hall,' he replied. 'No, I suppose not,' said his neighbour. She must have taken a closer look at him then, for she said quietly, 'You're blind, aren't you? I thought so when we were introduced, but I wasn't sure. Only I had a brother who was with the East Surrey Regiment at Loos in 1915…'

'That was a bad show. He was gassed, was he?'

'Yes. Blinded by chlorine gas.' She emitted a sound that was not quite a laugh. 'It was our own side who released the stuff, Ted—my brother—said afterwards. But the wind changed, and it got blown back into the British trenches…' Miss Hall fell silent a moment. 'Ted's sight came back, after a few months, but his health didn't.'

'I'm sorry. It was rotten luck,' said Rowlands, who had heard this story before. There'd been a number of veterans of the Battle of Loos when he'd first arrived at St Dunstan's. They'd spoken of a yellow-green cloud descending over the flat fields, and burning all it touched. Some had taken off their gas-masks, which had fogged up with moisture, and so had no defence at all against the poisonous vapour.

Once more, Caroline Hall seemed to hesitate. 'Please don't think me presumptuous, but I wondered…'

'As regards eating and drinking, I can manage most things

without help,' said Rowlands, anticipating what she had been going to say. 'Only I'd appreciate it if you'd let me know if I've made a mess of myself. My wife would never forgive me if I spilt anything on my dinner-jacket.'

The History Fellow laughed. 'I'll let you know, don't worry. And it's pheasant tonight, by the way. They *are* doing us proud! Mrs Woolf was quite right about the usual standard of fare at women's colleges, I'm afraid.'

They talked of this and that for a few minutes more—what Rowlands and his wife thought of Cambridge, and if they had further plans for the weekend (Miss Hall recommended a visit to the Fitzwilliam Museum), but all the while, as plates were being cleared and replaced with other plates, and wine was poured, Rowlands was conscious of an undertone of sadness in Caroline Hall's manner. Perhaps his presence had stirred memories she'd rather have forgotten... It hadn't been lost on him that she'd spoken of her brother in the past tense.

As if at an agreed signal, he turned to his left-hand neighbour, as Miss Hall turned to the one on her right. Miss Merriweather—Enid—turned out to be young, jolly and talkative. As well as fulfilling her duties as a lecturer, she was an enthusiastic member of the College rowing team, he soon discovered; an interest in the sport was one Rowlands shared, and the next few minutes passed in an agreeable discussion of St Gertrude's creditable performance in the recent rowing contest against a crew from Lady Margaret Hall. It emerged in the course of this that Enid Merriweather was engaged to be married. 'He rows for St Jude's. That's how we met, actually.' The man in question was taking her to the dance tonight. 'It's mostly for the students, of course—but some of us younger members of staff are going.' Across the table, Miss Glossop let out a hoot of laughter. 'You make me feel about a hundred! I'll have you know, Enid, that some of us—whether young or not— can still put up a decent showing on the dance floor.'

'Now, Jane, you know I didn't mean *you*,' said the Geography lecturer, unabashed. This little exchange brought about a hiatus in the conversation Miss Glossop's two neighbours—Professor Harding and the other man—had been having over her head.

Rather rudely, in Rowlands's opinion. He hadn't picked up much of this, intent as he had been on the finer points of bumping and over-bumping, but the few phrases which had come his way had been enough to tell him that some abstruse scientific point was being discussed. Now, as plates were changed once more and a savoury distributed, Miss Glossop addressed her *vis à vis*: 'I hope you're enjoying yourself, Mr Rowlands? It must be rather a strange experience for you, being surrounded by all these women…'

'Not as strange as all that,' he said. 'Of course,' she smiled. 'You've got daughters, haven't you?'

'A mathematician amongst them, if I'm not mistaken,' put in Harding, in a self-satisfied tone. Then, to the man to whom he had been talking: 'Let's continue this later.'

'If you like,' said the other indifferently. 'Only I still maintain…'

'Shop! Shop!' cried Jane Glossop, perhaps tiring of being talked over. 'Mr Rowlands will think we're all dried-up academics, with nothing to say for ourselves beyond our respective subjects.'

'I don't think that at all,' said Rowlands. 'It's all been most interesting.' He addressed the man to Miss Glossop's left. 'I don't believe we've been introduced,' he said. 'The name's Rowlands.'

'Bristow,' was the curt reply. 'Professor Bristow is a physicist,' said Miss Hall. 'I'm afraid I can't tell you any more than that about his field of study, because it's much too complicated. Something to do with splitting atoms, isn't it?'

'Something like that,' Bristow agreed. He didn't ask Rowlands what it was he did for a living, but instead fell to demolishing his Devils-on-Horseback.

Feeling that he had encountered one of the drier academic types (Miss Glossop hadn't been far out in her characterisation, he thought) Rowlands turned again to Caroline Hall. Her subject, at least, wasn't too hard for the layman to understand, and her field of specialisation—the eighteenth century—was one that interested him. A discussion of the Age of Enlightenment and its brutal curtailment by the French Revolution took them through the pudding and cheese courses. Then the Mistress rose to lead her female staff and guests to the Senior Common

Room for coffee, and the men were left to their port.

Having done himself rather too well with regard to food and drink, and in need of a breath of air, Rowlands decided to leave the now-depleted High Table to its several conversations, and to enjoy his cigarette outside. Professor Giles—the only one there with whom he'd have liked a talk—was presently engaged with the Chaplain in what sounded like a rather deep discussion on Coleridge. He'd catch up with him later, thought Rowlands. As he left the Hall, by way of the main door into the corridor, he found himself engulfed in a cloud of tulle and taffeta, and the scent of warm, talcum-powdered skin, as a crowd of undergraduates—*en route*, he supposed, to the famous dance—surrounded him momentarily.

'Oops, sorry!'

'Awf'lly sorry...'

Did no one in Cambridge look where they were going? wondered Rowlands, remembering his earlier encounter with the Trinity rowing crew—but then it struck him that, to these young things, he was as invisible as... well, as they were to him. Excited voices drifted back along the corridor towards him, as he located the heavy oak door he thought must lead to the courtyard outside the cloisters, and beyond it, to the grounds.

'... like to see his face when he realises I've promised the first three dances to Ronnie...'

'... think the Greek God'll be there?'

'Not he! St Jude's men consider themselves *far* too grand for our poor little hop...'

'Says one who's got her eye on a Magdalene man...'

Smiling to himself at these girlish high spirits, Rowlands let the door fall to behind him. Ah yes. He knew where he was, now. Crossing the courtyard, where a fine old rose lent its perfume to the night air, he walked quickly through the archway. If he turned right, he thought, it would bring him to the spacious lawns where he'd walked with Edith a few hours before. He seemed to remember there was a rose garden... He set off across the lawn. It was good to be able to stride freely. One of the things he most resented about not being able to see was the way it forced one to walk at such a snail's pace. Surrounded by nothing but an expanse of grass, as he was at this moment, meant he could go as fast as he liked.

He wandered around for a few minutes, basking in the peace and quiet, which was broken only by the hooting of an owl, from the woodland beyond—and by the distant sounds of an orchestra tuning up. The strains of 'Lovely to Look At' floated out upon the night air. It must be the dance band for tonight's revels, he guessed, wondering how late the thing would go on. Not that it would make much difference to him and Edith. Tucked away as they were on the far side of the building, they were unlikely to be bothered by even the most raucous of parties. Reaching the borders of the rose garden, whose heady scents now enfolded him, he paused to light a cigarette. He'd just take one more turn around the grounds to clear his head, he thought, humming a snatch of the silly little tune under his breath.

Lovely to look at
Delightful to know
And Heaven to kiss...

Then, without warning, someone rushed out from beneath the arbour in front of which he had stopped, and ran full tilt into him. Rowlands had a fleeting impression of a warm young body in a satin dress—a scent of hair and skin. 'At last!' cried a voice. 'I'd almost give you up... Oh!'—evidently having realised her mistake—'What are *you* doing here?' No vengeful goddess could have sounded more indignant. Rowlands held up his cigarette—although in truth he didn't owe her any kind of explanation. 'Miss Havelock. I'm afraid you weren't looking where you were going.'

'I...' She mastered her temper with an effort, although she was still breathing hard. 'I thought you were someone else,' she said. She was trembling, he realised. 'It's so beastly dark out here. I say, I couldn't have a cigarette, could I?'

He offered the pack to her, and she took one, then held it to the flame of his lighter. 'Thanks.' She took a deep drag, and exhaled, seeming calmer now. Although something had happened to upset her a good deal, thought Rowlands. It didn't take much imagination to guess what that might be. She'd obviously been expecting someone, and that 'someone' hadn't turned up. This impression was confirmed when she said abruptly: 'What time is it, do you know?'

He checked his watch. 'Just on a quarter-to.'

'Damn,' the girl muttered under her breath. 'Well, that's that, I suppose.' She didn't offer any further explanation; nor did he expect one. For a few moments the two of them stood in silence, smoking their cigarettes. Then she said: 'Can I ask you something?'

'Ask away.'

'What I want to know is—how does one know one can trust *anybody*?' It was said in a tone of extraordinary bitterness. And it wasn't a question which really required an answer, he thought—flung out as it had been in the heat of the moment, to one for whose opinion the speaker cared not a jot. Realising this, he still took a moment to consider his reply. 'Well, one doesn't,' he said. 'One just has to follow one's instinct. And of course there are people one can trust,' he added, thinking that he needed to offer some firmer assurance. 'People who care about one. Who have one's welfare at heart...'

His answer seemed to disappoint her, for she gave a short, unamused laugh. 'It appears,' she said. 'That there aren't too many of those.'

'Don't you have a friend you can talk to?' he said, feeling somewhat out of his depth. If it was a disappointment in love to which her question had alluded, then he wasn't the ideal confidant... 'I don't have many friends here.' Again, that note of bitterness. 'And those I thought I had...' She broke off, as if she'd said more than she'd meant to. 'Oh, what does it *matter*?' she muttered, as if to herself. 'It's all a rotten mess. I wish I'd never got into it in the first place...' That did sound rather more serious that just a lovers' tiff. *A rotten mess*. Rowlands wondered anew who it was she'd been intending to meet in the rose garden. Whoever he was, he'd clearly let her down.

They had been walking slowly back in the direction of the college, and had by now reached the path which led around the side of the building. Diana Havelock dropped her half-smoked cigarette on the gravel, and ground it beneath her heel. 'Better go,' she said, in a bright voice quite at odds with her previous melancholic tone. 'I'll need to powder my nose before I'm fit to be seen. Thanks for the cigarette.'

Rowlands raised a hand in valediction. He had been going to wish her an enjoyable evening but then thought better of it. From what he had gathered, it didn't sound very likely she'd be enjoying herself much tonight, poor girl. He heard the soft crunch of her footsteps on the path, then the creak of the door opening, and closing behind her. A moment or two later, having finished his own cigarette, he followed the route she had taken back into the building, finding himself in the corridor that led in one direction to the main entrance, in the other (he hoped) to the Senior Common Room. As he stood there getting his bearings, it struck him how utterly silent it was, with not the slightest sound of departing footsteps, although it had been mere moments since his companion had left him. Well, it was a big place, he reasoned; doubtless there were any number of short-cuts he knew nothing about. But he was surprised, nonetheless, at how swiftly and completely Diana Havelock had vanished.In the S.C.R., he found his wife and Miss Rickards engaged in earnest conversation. '... so you see,' the Bursar was saying. 'It's all been rather difficult.' She broke off as Rowlands joined them. 'Don't let me interrupt,' he said. 'I was just after a cup of coffee.'

'I'll get it for you,' said Maud Rickards, even though he tried to assure her that he was quite capable of pouring one for himself. 'That sounded rather serious,' he said to Edith, when her friend had got to fulfil this promise. 'It is,' was the reply. 'Maud's quite upset. I'll tell you about it later.' They were interrupted at that moment by Professor Giles. 'I looked for you on my way out of Hall,' he said to Rowlands. 'We must have missed one another. Got waylaid by the Chaplain earlier. Awfully sound on many subjects, you know—but quite *wrong* about Coleridge. Insists the *Rime of the Ancient Mariner* is a Christian allegory, whereas of course...' He broke off. 'Forgive me. I really should come off my hobby-horse. I don't believe we've been introduced,' he said to Edith.

Rowlands remedied the omission.

'Oh, Professor Giles,' said Miss Rickards, returning with Rowlands's coffee. 'I've a message for you from Dr Maltravers. He says he's left the paper he was telling you about in your pigeon-hole...' Giles emitted a low groan. 'What did I tell you? The man's incorrigible. "Christian Mysticism in the Works of Samuel Taylor Coleridge". Written by himself, of course.'

'It all sounds fascinating,' said Edith diplomatically. 'Yes, it's reassuring to know that intellectual debates are carried out in such a good-humoured spirit,' said Rowlands. The English Fellow laughed. 'Oh, but I'm afraid the reverse is the case in many instances,' he said. 'You'd be appalled at the rancour some debates generate. I've known men practically come to blows over the use of the Subjunctive...'

'Then it's as well not all Fellows of this university are men,' said Miss Rickards tartly. The conversation continued in a desultory fashion for the next few minutes, taking in a variety of subjects—the now-familiar question of whether the Rowlandses were enjoying Cambridge, their plans for the rest of the weekend, and the programme for the next day (the Bursar was somewhat exercised by the problems of organising a College picnic)—before it became apparent that the party was starting to break up. Those who cared for a nightcap would find whisky decanters on the sideboard, said the Mistress, as she herself withdrew. 'Care to join me for a Scotch?' said Giles to Rowlands. The latter hesitated. If Edith hadn't been with him, he'd have liked the chance to compare war stories with his former Training Officer. 'Stay if you like,' said Edith.

'Well...'

'Tell you what,' said the older man, pouring himself what sounded like a generous measure of whisky. 'Why don't you see your wife back to her room, and you can join me afterwards?'

'Good idea,' said Rowlands.

'So what was all that about?' he asked his wife, as they crossed the courtyard which separated one side of the college from the other. 'What was all what about? Oh, Maud, you mean...' Edith yawned. 'I'm feeling terribly sleepy. It must have been all the wine. She was telling me—Maud, that is—about some queer goings-on in College these past few weeks. Poison-pen letters. Several of the dons have had them, apparently. I imagine it's the kind of thing that does happen at this kind of institution from time to time. It's got her quite rattled, though…'

'I'm not surprised,' said Rowlands. 'What does she want to do about it?'

'I'm not sure she wants to *do* anything,' was the reply. 'She was just getting it off her chest.' They climbed the stairs to the second floor of the Tower Wing. 'Well, I'm ready for my bed,' said Edith, as she unlocked the door. 'A cup of hot milk and a chapter or two of the new Agatha Christie is all I'm fit for.'

'Maybe I'll join you,' said her husband.

'No, you go and have your nightcap.' Edith yawned again. 'Take the key with you, though, because I've an idea I'll be asleep by the time you get back.'

CONGREGATION

4

Rowlands descended the stairs once more and let himself out into the grounds, glad of the chance to get another breath of fresh air before bed. He'd cut across the grass he thought, and get into the building through the door on the other side, instead of taking the long way round, past the Porters' Lodge. It was very quiet outside, with no sound of traffic: one would hardly have guessed it was a mere three miles away from the centre of Cambridge. It wasn't completely silent, however—from across the lawn, where a marquee had been erected, came the jaunty strains of a dance band:

Heaven, I'm in Heaven
And my heart beats so that I can hardly speak
And I seem to find the happiness I seek
When we're out together, dancing cheek to cheek…

Well, it wasn't quite 'Now Is the Month of Maying', thought Rowlands, but it wasn't far off. As he found the door he was looking for, he became aware that someone else was standing there, just inside the Gothic arch in which it was set. Someone who'd been imbibing rather heavily, to judge by the smell of whisky. 'Hallo!' he said. 'Who's there?'

''S'only me,' was the reply. Then followed an unintelligible word that might have been a name. A male voice, Rowlands was relieved to hear. Call him an old fogey, but he couldn't get used to the idea of girls getting tight. And this chap was certainly far gone—to judge from his slurred speech. 'I didn't catch that,' said Rowlands. 'What did you say your name was?'

'Wass it matter?' came the reply. ''Sall a washout.'

'I dare say.' Rowlands guessed this was a case of disappointed love. 'W'men!' muttered the young man, confirming this suspicion. 'Can't trussht 'em.' As he uttered this piece of sententiousness, he must have flung out an arm, for he lost his balance and staggered heavily against Rowlands. 'I say, steady on!' Rowlands gave the lad a shove, to set him back on his feet. 'What *you* need is a cup of strong black coffee, followed by a long walk back to town, to clear your head.'

But this suggestion met with resistance: 'Can't do that,' said the other thickly. 'Musshn't letta lady down. Sh'd be here...' He hiccoughed loudly. 'Shoon...' Since this was plainly not the case, Rowlands made another effort to persuade his young friend to call it a night, but with no more success than before. 'Gotta shtay... stay here,' he insisted, with the stubbornness of the very drunk. 'Said I'd meet her.'

Rowlands decided this was a lost cause. And there were probably worse places to sleep it off than in the grounds of St Gertrude's College, on a fine summer's night, he thought. 'You still haven't told me your name,' he said. 'If I see the young lady in question, I could mention that you're looking for her.'

''S ver' kind,' muttered the lad. 'Name's Sjwck...' From which Rowlands deduced that his name was Sedgwick. 'Lady... lady's name's Diana. Hvlck,' he added. Diana Havelock. It would be, thought Rowlands. He supposed this must be the unfortunate fellow he'd overheard having a row with the girl in the courtyard of the Eagle. 'Well, if I see her, I'll be sure to let her know,' he said again. Perhaps it was Sedgwick she'd been waiting for in the rose garden, too—in which case, Rowlands didn't fancy his chances of getting back in his girlfriend's good books. It wasn't his business, he was glad to say. Let these youthful swains sort out their own romantic tangles—he was for his nightcap, a jaw with old Giles, and then bed...

Leaving the unlucky Mr Sedgwick to his vigil, Rowlands pushed open the heavy oak door and went inside. Here, corridors went off to right and left, divided by a small lobby, from which a broad stone staircase rose. He discovered this by the simple expedient of walking into one of the marble pillars which stood on either side of it. 'Damn and blast,' he muttered, glad that it was only his pride that had been hurt. This place was built like a Gothic castle, with fittings to match. Fortunately, there was no one around to see him stumble; even so, he felt himself blushing at this momentary loss of equilibrium.

And so he was at the bottom of the steps when he heard the sound of rapid footsteps coming from the floor above, accompanied by the sound of breathless sobbing: 'Oh God. Oh God…'

'Is everything all right?' he called, already starting up the stairs. 'Oh, please! You must help…' It was a young woman's voice, sharpened by terror. 'I can't wake her…' Rowlands reached the top of the stairs at the same time as the girl did; he felt her stumble against him. 'I don't know what to do… Oh, you *must* help, you must!'

'It's all right,' he said. 'Just tell me what's happened. Is somebody ill?'

'Yes.' The girl made an effort to steady herself. 'It's… it's Diana. I… I'd gone to fetch her, you see, because she hadn't turned up at the dance, and she'd *said* she was coming… and she… Oh, it's *too* awful! I knocked on her door, and when there was no reply, I went in…' She drew a deep, shuddering breath. 'I thought she was asleep at first, but then…'

'You'd better take me to her room,' said Rowlands, to head off another storm of tears. But just then there came another interruption: 'I say, Wha's all the fuss?' came a voice from the foot of the stairs. It was the Sedgwick boy. 'Honoria? That you?' And Rowlands thought: Honoria Fairclough. Of course. The girl who'd played Portia. At the sound of her name, the girl only wept harder. 'Oh Julian,' she sobbed. 'It's Diana…'

'Wha's that about Diana?' demanded the youth. A moment later, he had stumbled up the stairs, and stood, breathing whisky fumes over the other two. Before she could launch into another round of explanations, Rowlands took charge. 'Come on,' he said. 'We're wasting time. Miss Fairclough, you'd better lead the way. *You*'—this was to Julian Sedgwick—'had better pipe down. You've made quite enough of a row already.'

Without further ado, the girl turned and set off along the right-hand corridor that led off the landing. This, Rowlands discovered, consisted of doors set at intervals along the right-hand side—students' rooms, evidently—and windows on the facing side. About halfway along a door stood ajar—presumably as it had been left by the girl, in her haste to fetch help. 'It's this one,' she said, confirming his supposition. 'All right' said Rowlands. 'You two wait here.' He grasped the doorknob and had pushed open the door, when there came a soft indignant yowl from about the level of his ankles, and a small furry shape shot past him, into the corridor. 'What on earth...?'

'It's the college cat,' said Honoria Fairclough, in a voice dull with misery. 'It likes to sleep on her bed...' At which she began to sob once more. 'Look,' said Rowlands. 'You've got to try and pull yourself together. Now. Do I understand you found Miss Havelock lying on her bed?'

'Th...that's right. Her bedroom's just across there—behind the curtain...' For the room was evidently part of a suite, consisting of a small sitting-room, with an arm-chair (against which Rowlands presently blundered), a desk and bookshelves. Beyond this was the curtain referred to, and behind *this*... 'Where ish she?' demanded Sedgwick, pushing past Rowlands. 'I wan' to see her...'

'Stay back,' warned the older man. But it was too late. 'Oh God! Diana!' cried the lad. 'Wha's wrong with her? Why's she jus' *lying* there? An' why's she that awful *colour*?' A curious gurgling sound rose from Sedgwick's throat, and he rushed back past Rowlands and out of the room. Doubtless to be sick, thought the other. Well, he had only himself to blame, silly boy...

Steeling himself, Rowlands took a step towards where he guessed the bed must be—the room was small—and almost tripped over something that was lying on the floor. A woman's high-heeled shoe. Another step brought his shins in contact with the edge of a wooden bedstead. He reached down and touched the thing that protruded from the end of the bed: a foot, wearing the fellow of the shoe he'd found. The foot was attached to a leg, clad in a silk stocking... Hastily, Rowlands withdrew his hand, and drew closer to the head of the bed.

Here, his questing fingers encountered something soft and silky—the famous red hair, he thought, with a pang of sadness. Gently, he laid his hand on Diana Havelock's head, which lolled on its slender stalk. There was no pulse in the throat, nor at the wrist of the hand that dangled off the edge of the bed. And yet her flesh was still warm. There might still be a chance, he thought. Kneeling down beside the bed, he threw aside the pillow, and tilting back the head of the unconscious girl so that her windpipe was unimpeded, pinched her lips apart, and blew a mouthful of air into her lungs. Was it his imagination or was there a response? He drew another breath, although something told him that his efforts were in vain.

'She's dead, isn't she?' Honoria Fairclough must have come into the room behind him. Intent on what he was doing, he didn't reply. Even though he knew in his heart of hearts that it was futile, Rowlands continued his attempts at resuscitation for a few more minutes. Suddenly, Miss Fairclough darted forward. 'What's *that*?' She picked something up off the floor, where it had rolled—and then dropped it again with an exclamation of disgust. 'How perfectly foul!'

'What is it?' he said, raising his head at last—although he had half-guessed. 'A hypodermic syringe. It was lying next to the bed...'

'Is it empty?'

'I... I don't know. I can take a look, if you like...'

'I should leave well alone,' said Rowlands grimly. This, then, was the reason for Miss Havelock's collapse—the reason why she would not be joining her friends at the end of term party, or ever again. He got to his feet. 'Come on,' he said. 'We'd better inform the College authorities what's happened.'

'Is she...?'

'I'm afraid so,' he replied, steering the other back across the little sitting-room, and out into the corridor. 'I don't think there's anything more we can do.' He took the key from the inside of the door, locked it, and pocketed the key. The least he could do was to make sure that no one else stumbled across this scene of horror, or, having done so, interfered with it. 'All right,' he said. 'You'd better show me the way to the Porter's Lodge...'

'Where's Julian?' said the girl. The answer to her question came a moment later, as the young man emerged from further along the corridor—presumably from one of the bathrooms, for there was the sound of a lavatory flushing. 'I... I felt a bit sick,' he mumbled. 'Don't worry about it,' said Rowlands. 'I imagine it wasn't a very pleasant thing to see. Come on,' he added, since the other seemed rooted to the spot. 'You'll be needed, too.'

'But...' protested the youth. 'What about Diana? We can't just... *leave* her there, like that...'

'The police will bring their Medical Officer,' said Rowlands. 'He'll make all the necessary arrangements.'

'The police?' This was Honoria Fairclough. 'Do they have to be involved?'

'I'm afraid it's unavoidable in such circumstances.'

'What do you mean?' said Sedgwick. All traces of the alcohol-fuddled youth of half an hour before had vanished. The shock, of course thought Rowlands. 'I mean when it's a suspicious death,' he said. 'Especially where drugs are involved...'

'Drugs?' The young man's voice had risen. 'You're talking rot...'

'Julian, *honestly*!'

'Diana'd never taken drugs in her life,' insisted the boy. 'She loathed all that sort of thing—you tell him, Honoria!'

They had by now reached the stairs at the far end of the corridor—the ornate spiral staircase which led, by way of the main corridor, to the Porters' Lodge. 'As I said, this is a matter for the police,' said Rowlands. 'It's out of our hands, now.'

At the bottom of the stairs, they met Professor Giles. 'There you are, Rowlands!' he said. 'Thought you said you were coming back to the S.C.R. for a drink?'

'I'm afraid a rather more pressing matter intervened. The fact is... there's been a death. It's Miss Havelock...'

'Good God! Do you mean she's had an accident?' said Giles.

'It's too soon to say—the police will have to look into it,' said Rowlands. At this, Miss Fairclough let out a sob. 'Steady on, old thing,' murmured Julian Sedgwick.

'The police? Are you sure?'

'I'm afraid so,' said Rowlands gravely. They had now reached the Porters' Lodge. 'Well,' said Giles. 'This is a shocking thing, and no mistake...' Then to the Porter: 'Wainwright, Mr Rowlands here has some rather distressing news...'

'Yes,' said Rowlands, addressing the Porter. 'We—that is, these young people and I—have just come from Miss Havelock's room. She's... she's had some kind of accident, it appears. A fatal one. You'd better call the police at once.'

'The police?' The Porter, a local man, seemed dumbfounded by this information. 'Why, what have *they* got to do with College, I'd like to know? Miss Havelock's room you say? I'll send the College Nurse to her at once...'

'It won't do any good,' said Rowlands bluntly. 'She's dead. And the police won't thank you for any further delay.'

The Mistress, as it happened, had not yet gone to bed, but had been writing letters in her sitting-room. When Rowlands, accompanied by Professor Giles, had broken the news of Diana Havelock's death, she had listened in silence. Only when Rowlands had finished speaking, did she permit herself a question—a restraint characteristic of the woman, thought Rowlands. 'I gather from what you've said that the police have already been called?'

'I thought it best,' said Rowlands. 'In cases such as this, the less delay there is before the authorities arrive, the better, in my experience.' She didn't comment on this—or indeed ask him what experience he'd had of such cases (although the answer might have surprised her). Instead she allowed another silence to pass. 'I suppose there's no doubt that it was drugs that killed her?' she said at last. 'We'll have to wait for the pathologist's report to know the precise cause of death,' replied Rowlands. 'But there was certainly some evidence in her room to suggest that Miss Havelock had been using drugs. The syringe...'

'Yes, yes,' said the Mistress, as if this unpleasant detail were too much to be borne. 'You must understand,' she said, 'that I'd like to spare her parents as much of this as possible.'

'Of course.'

'The College, too,' she added, with something of her old spirit. 'We can't have it said that this is the kind of thing that goes on at St Gertrude's... Drug-taking, I mean.'

'No, indeed,' put in Professor Giles. 'There are those who'd be only too glad to have some ammunition of this sort with which to attack the cause...'

'The cause?' said Rowlands.

'Of women's education. We're already under fire enough, as it is.'

'I suppose,' said the Mistress, interrupting this, 'I ought to see for myself what's happened before I telephone Diana's parents. Will you go with me, Mr Rowlands? You too, Professor Giles.'

'Mistress.'

'Then let's waste no more time.' And yet she hesitated once more. 'What about the Fairclough girl—Honoria? She was the one who found Diana, you say?'

'Nurse Blenkinsop thought she'd do best in her room. Girl's had a nasty shock,' said Professor Giles. 'Quite right. It's what I would have suggested myself,' said Miss Phillips. 'And Mr Sedgwick?'

'The Porter—Mr Wainwright—sat him down in the Porters' Lodge with a cup of hot, strong tea,' said Rowlands. 'I imagine the police will want to interview him in due course. Miss Fairclough, too,' he added. 'Although it may be that they'll be content with a statement from me, initially.'

'Yes, I'd prefer it if the students could be involved as little as possible,' said Beryl Phillips. 'So unsettling for them. If you're willing to talk to the police instead, Mr Rowlands, I'd be more than grateful…' Rowlands forbore to point out that it wouldn't be up to him to decide how the police should conduct their investigation. But maybe they, too, would put the concerns of the University before those of common procedure.

As he and Giles, with the Mistress slightly ahead, walked along the corridor that led to the main staircase, sounds of revelry drifted up from the lawns outside through windows left ajar on this warm summer's evening.

> It was just one of those things
> Just one of those crazy flings
> One of those bells that now and then rings
> Just one of those things…

'I'd better have a word with the Porter,' said Miss Phillips, as they reached the head of the stairs. 'He can go and tell the orchestra to stop playing.'

'Do you think that's wise?' said Giles, in a low voice. 'I mean... it'll only put the wind up the undergraduates. We don't want to start a lot of gossip. The fewer people who know about this the better, surely?'

'I see what you mean, but...'

'Might I suggest,' put in Rowlands, for whom this way of doing things was still something of a revelation, 'that the Mistress should send a message by way of Mr Wainwright to say that the music is too loud and the orchestra should limit itself to quieter numbers? Then nobody need be alarmed unnecessarily.'

'Excellent idea,' was the Mistress's reply. 'It's just that it seems so heartless, having it blaring out like that.'

In Room E14, they found the College Nurse in possession (Rowlands having previously given up the key). She confirmed what Rowlands had already discovered: the girl had been dead for over an hour, apparently after injecting herself with the contents of the syringe. 'I'd say from her colour, and the dilation of the pupils, that it was probably morphine,' said the nurse. 'But the post-mortem will tell us for certain.'

'Thank you, Nurse Blenkinsop.' Beryl Phillips was silent a moment, her gaze evidently focused on the dead girl, for she said softly, 'Poor child! What a terrible waste. She was one of our brightest students, you know, Mr Rowlands. She had a brilliant future ahead of her. To think it should have come to this...'

'Terrible waste,' echoed Professor Giles.

Rowlands murmured his agreement, but his thoughts were occupied by other matters: specifically, the changes which had taken place in the room since he had last set foot there. That the nurse had altered things was not in doubt; he cursed himself for not having insisted beforehand that nothing should be touched. As it was, she had evidently disturbed the body, in the process of examining it—as he himself had done, in attempting to resuscitate the dead girl. But there were other signs that evidence had been tampered with. As he entered the little bedroom, behind the Mistress and Professor Giles, his foot knocked against the discarded shoe he had found earlier—now lined up next to its fellow. 'Did you remove this?' he asked, holding it up. Nurse Blenkinsop agreed that she had. 'It didn't seem right to leave her lying there with only one shoe on, poor lamb,' she said. 'I thought I should tidy her up a bit.'

Rowlands suppressed a groan. No doubt the worthy Nurse Blenkinsop's idea of 'tidying up' had extended to the syringe. 'That nasty thing!' she said, when he referred to this. 'If you want to know, I popped it on the dressing-table, out of harm's way.' Which meant that any fingerprints on this or anything else would have been obliterated, thought Rowlands automatically. 'Does it really matter what's become of the thing?' said Giles. 'If I had my way, I'd throw it into the fire, and no questions asked...'

'I think the police might take a dim view of that,' said Rowlands. 'Oh, the police!' Professor Giles's tone showed exactly what he thought of that honest body of men. 'I must say, I wish we could have dealt with this affair without involving them...'

'Indeed. But unfortunately that won't be possible,' said the Mistress crisply. 'No.' Again, Rowlands was taken aback by the evident desire on the part of the other three to close ranks against the outside world. 'The police have already been called. Besides which...' He broke off. If Miss Phillips hadn't already worked out why the police had to be involved, he wasn't going to be the one to spell it out for her. But it wasn't in the nature of the academic mind to let a question go unanswered. 'Yes?' she said.

'It might turn out that this isn't an accident,' he said reluctantly. 'You mean suicide, don't you?' So she *had* worked it out. 'I'm afraid so.'

'That's preposterous,' said Giles. 'What reason did she have to kill herself? The girl had everything going for her. Why, she'd only just been awarded a research studentship...'

'I think,' said Beryl Phillips, 'we should continue this discussion elsewhere.'

'Quite right,' muttered Giles, with some chagrin. 'Hardly decent, with the poor lass lying there...'

'Although I think there was something troubling her,' said Rowlands, as—having given instructions to the nurse to lock up—the Mistress led the way back to the Porters' Lodge, to await the arrival of the police. As succinctly as he could, he described the encounter he'd had with Miss Havelock by the rose garden, and repeated her anguished question: *How does one know one can trust anybody*? 'What do you think she meant by that?' he said.

Beryl Phillips reflected a moment. 'It could mean anything.'

'These girls are always having love affairs,' said Giles. 'Probably some silly fellow let her down, that's all.'

'People have killed themselves for less,' said Rowlands. 'Yes.' This was the Mistress. 'I see what you mean. So you think she might have done it deliberately?'

'I couldn't say,' said Rowlands. 'One would have to talk to her friends, I suppose...' Although in the same instant he recalled something else Diana Havelock had said: *I don't have many friends here...*

'That, at least, can wait until the morning,' said Miss Phillips. 'The most urgent thing is to let her parents know. I think,' she went on, 'that I shall say it was a seizure of some kind. We don't know for certain that it was connected with... the other thing. Ah, here's Miss Rickards...' Because they had by now reached the entrance hall, where the Bursar was pacing around in some agitation. 'Oh Mistress—is it true?' she cried. 'About Diana...'

'I'm afraid so. Now, Maud, I'll need you to be my right hand in dealing with this dreadful business. As Mr Wainwright will have told you, the police have already been called...'

'Of course, Mistress. But what exactly happened? Did she have a fall?'

'We'll talk about it later,' said Miss Phillips, in a warning voice. 'I think this must be the police, now.' Because from outside, came the crunch of tyres on gravel, as two cars drew up. Car doors slammed, and a moment later, the heavy oak door opened and a man Rowlands guessed must be the police inspector came in, followed by two subordinates. Seeing the little party gathered there, he paused. 'Which one of you is Sidney Wainwright?'

The Porter declared himself.

'Inspector Brown. Cambridgeshire Constabulary,' said the newcomer. 'This is Sergeant Gotobed.' He didn't trouble to introduce the uniformed officer. 'Now then. I understand you reported a death. A Miss Diana Havelock…'

'She was one of my students,' said Miss Phillips.

'And who might you be, Ma'm?'

'Beryl Phillips. I'm the Mistress of St Gertrude's. These are two of my colleagues—Professor Giles, and Miss Rickards, our Bursar. And this is Mr Rowlands,' she added, without further explanation. 'This is a distressing business, Inspector.'

'Indeed, Ma'm.' The inspector's tone had changed in an instant from one of authority to one of deference. Rowlands suppressed a smile. He, too had been somewhat overawed by Miss Phillips. 'I feel sure,' went on the Mistress, in her clear, measured tones, 'that you will agree with me that the matter should be handled with the utmost discretion…'

5

It was a subdued group of Fellows and their guests who occupied the Senior Common Room. Most of those who had remained talking there after dinner had elected to stay on, until the police had finished their preliminary enquiries into the PhD student's death, in case—as Miss Glossop put it, 'any of us could be of any assistance'. As Miss Havelock's former Tutor, she felt morally bound, she said, to offer what insights she had into the dead girl's state of mind. 'Although I can't say I ever got to know her really well. If only,' she cried, 'she'd *said* something!'

'Now then, Jane, don't distress yourself.' This was the Chaplain, Dr Maltravers. 'We don't yet know that it was anything but an unfortunate accident...'

'I suppose not, but one feels as if one should have been able to *help*...'

'Do we know if she—if Diana—was engaged?' piped up Miss Hall, from her chair by the fire. She had been taking a last walk in the grounds before turning in, she said, and had returned to find College 'swarming with policemen'—as she put it. 'Sometimes,' she added in a studiedly neutral tone, 'a broken engagement can lead someone to... well, to do this sort of thing.'

This suggestion was received in silence, although nobody saw fit to contradict it. 'What do you think, Harding?' This was Professor Bristow, who had hitherto taken no part in the discussion. '*You* were her supervisor. Was the girl unstable, do you think?' The question, though innocent enough, seemed to have an edge of malice. Some professional rivalry there, Rowlands surmised. 'I... what on earth are you driving at?' spluttered Harding. 'I hardly knew her. I mean...' He corrected himself hastily. 'I was familiar with her work, of course. We worked together at the lab. But I didn't have much else to do with her...'

Professor Bristow blew his nose with a trumpeting sound. He appeared to be suffering from a heavy cold. 'Even so,' he said. 'You spent a good deal of time with the, ah, young woman. You must have formed an idea of her character. Rather an hysterical sort, wasn't she? Inclined to be overdramatic.'

'I don't know about that,' said Caroline Hall. 'She always struck me as rather clear-headed. Determined, too, in her own way.'

'The fact is, none of us knew her very well,' put in Miss Glossop. 'She was a reticent child.' The word seemed to have provoked a train of thought, for she added, in a low voice: 'Does anyone know whether her parents have been informed? This will be a dreadful blow for them. I believe she's an only child...'

'The Mistress was about to telephone when I left her,' said Professor Giles. There was a general murmur of satisfaction at this. 'If anyone's up to the task of breaking such news it's the Mistress,' said Caroline Hall. 'Although I don't envy her the job.'

'The question is—what do we do about the Dance?' This was Enid Merriweather, Rowlands's dinner companion—her liveliness now considerably diminished. 'Ought it to be called off?'

'The Mistress thought not,' said Professor Giles quickly. 'We agreed—she and I—that the less the undergraduates know about this, the better. Mr Rowlands very sensibly suggested that we should ask Wainwright to get them to lower the volume of the music, and so...'

'It's too late for that, I'm afraid,' said the Geography Fellow bluntly. 'There are all sorts of rumours flying around already. Harold and I heard some of the students discussing it, when we were walking back across Forest Court—didn't we, dear?'

'Something was said, certainly,' agreed Miss Merriweather's *fiancé* reluctantly. 'What exactly?' This was Miss Hall. 'I heard one of the St Jude's men shouting that... well, that there'd been a murder,' said Harold Armstrong. 'Told him not to talk such rot, but it means somebody must have let something out...'

'Wainwright,' said Miss Hall. 'The man's a terrible gossip.'

'Or it might have been one of the students who found her,' put in Miss Glossop. 'Honoria Fairclough, wasn't it, and the

Sedgwick boy?'

'I doubt it was either of them,' said Rowlands quietly. 'Both were much too shocked and distressed by what happened to go blabbing about it to their friends. And I gather Miss Fairclough's lying down in her room...'

'Well, regardless of who said anything, I think it's clear that the dance ought to be stopped.' Miss Hall again. 'We can't have the students spreading rumours of this sort. *Murder*, indeed!'

'No one's suggesting that this a case of murder, Miss,' came a voice from the door. It was Inspector Brown, followed by another man—his sergeant, Rowlands surmised. 'Although of course we can't rule anything out at this stage.'

'No indeed.' Caroline Hall sounded flustered. 'I was merely commenting on an absurd rumour that's going around College...'

'Ah, we don't take any notice of *those*, Miss,' said Brown. 'Now who's the gentleman who found the body?' Rowlands declared himself. 'Then I'll take a statement from you, sir, if you'll come with me.'

'Certainly,' said Rowlands, getting to his feet.

'I'd like to know,' said a voice that sounded as if the owner were having difficulty breathing, 'when the rest of us will be allowed to go home? I'm feeling far from well...'

'And you are, sir?'

'Francis Bristow. Professor of Physics and Fellow of St Jude's.'

'Make a note of that Sergeant, will you?' said the inspector. 'Yes, you don't sound very clever, if I might say so, Professor,' he added. 'Some nasty summer colds going about. You can go, sir, by all means. The rest of you ladies and gentlemen are free to go, too. Take their names and addresses, Gotobed.'

'Sir.'

'Come this way—Mr Rowlands, isn't it?' Inspector Brown stood aside to let his witness precede him out of the room. 'I won't keep you long,' he said, as they walked back along the corridor that led from the modern wing of the college, where the S.C.R. was located, to the older part of the building. 'All I need is to establish a few facts.'

'I'll tell you all I know,' said Rowlands.

'I'm obliged to you, sir. Ah, here we are. The Mistress—Miss Phillips—said I could use this room,' said the inspector, opening a door. Then, to the uniformed constable outside: 'All right, Smedley. Let's have you and your notebook, double quick. Mr Rowlands here will want to get home to his bed…'

'As a matter of fact I'm staying in college tonight,' said Rowlands, with a smile. 'My wife is, too—but I imagine she'll be sound asleep by now.'

'And a good thing, too. I think we'd all like to be in our beds,' said the inspector ruefully. 'Take a seat, sir, if you will. In front of the desk will do.' Then, as Rowlands took a step in what he hoped was the right direction, the other exclaimed: 'Good Lord! You should have said, sir. I didn't realise you were blind.'

'I try not to draw attention to it,' replied Rowlands drily. 'Do I take it that the chair isn't where I expected it to be?'

'Just a little to your left, sir… that's it. Mustard gas, was it, sir?'

'Shrapnel,' said Rowlands. 'The men who were gassed had it worse, I believe.'

'Bad enough, sir, I'm sure. I was with the Cambridgeshires at Thiepval Ridge,' he added. 'Made it home in one piece, though.'

'Lucky man,' said Rowlands. 'I am that, sir.' Inspector Brown cleared his throat. 'Now, about Miss Havelock… I understand you were in the vicinity when the young lady—Miss Fairclough—gave the alarm?'

'That's right. You've spoken to the Sedgwick lad, I suppose?'

'For what it was worth. Not what you'd call a reliable witness, is he?'

'He'd had rather a lot to drink,' said Rowlands. 'Although he seemed sober enough when I spoke to him last, poor fellow. Seeing something like that's enough to shock any man back into his senses, wouldn't you say?'

'Indeed, sir. So you heard Miss Fairclough give the alarm. Have you any idea what time that would have been, sir?'

'Around ten minutes to ten,' said Rowlands promptly. 'I heard the clock strike a quarter to while I was outside talking to young Sedgwick. We were talking for four or five minutes before I left him. I'd been inside the building no more than a minute when I heard Miss Fairclough call out.'

'Well, that's very clear, sir, I must say,' said the inspector. 'If all our witnesses paid as much attention to times and places, our job would be a lot easier—eh, Constable?'

The police constable's pencil ceased its scratching for a moment. 'Yes, sir.'

'All right. So you and Mr Sedgwick accompanied Miss Fairclough to Miss Havelock's room?'

'That's right.'

'Arriving when, approximately?'

'I'd say five to ten.'

'You're very clear about that,' said the police inspector. 'I made a point of checking my watch as I entered the room,' said Rowlands, holding out his wrist so that the other could see the instrument for himself. 'Interesting model,' said Inspector Brown, after looking at it for a moment. 'I suppose the raised dots are what enable you to tell the time?'

'Just so,' said Rowlands. 'One might almost think,' said the inspector slyly, 'that this wasn't the first time you'd been asked to give evidence in a case like this…'

'It isn't. But you were asking me about my movements earlier this evening…'

'Indeed. So you entered the room and found Miss Havelock lying there, apparently unconscious?'

'Yes,' said Rowlands. 'I… I attempted to revive her, but…'

'She was already dead.'

'Yes.'

'And did you notice anything else?' asked the inspector.

'I suppose you mean the syringe?'

'That's right, sir. It was you who found it, I gather…'

'Actually, it was Miss Fairclough who noticed it first. It was lying on the floor. She picked it up, so I imagine her fingerprints will be on it.'

'Not to worry, sir,' said the policeman. 'In a case like this, we don't bother much about fingerprints. I don't suppose we'll find any but Miss Fairclough's and the nurse's—and those of the dead girl, of course.'

Rowlands was silent a moment. 'I expect you're right,' he said.

'We've had a fair bit of experience of this kind of thing, sir,' said Brown, with a certain complacency. 'So you found the syringe—and then what?'

'I thought it best to notify the authorities. Since there was nothing more I could do for Miss Havelock.'

'You were quite sure she was dead by this time?'

'Oh yes. I believe she'd been dead about an hour. It couldn't have been more than that...'

'You seem very sure, Mr Rowlands.' There was an edge in the inspector's voice that had not been there before. 'Don't tell me you've had medical training?'

'I haven't—or not officially. I picked up a certain amount in the army—as one did in those days, of course. But that's not why I can be so precise as to the time of Miss Havelock's death. I saw her, you see—spoke to her, I mean—almost exactly an hour before I found her dead.'

The constable's pencil stopped its scratching. Perhaps he exchanged a startled glance with his superior; perhaps not. 'I see,' said Inspector Brown. 'So you're telling me you were the last to see the young lady before her... er... untimely demise?'

'Possibly,' said Rowlands. 'I don't know if she spoke to anyone else after she left me. But it's that I wanted to talk to you about, Inspector. The rather odd thing she said...' He gave a brief account of his meeting with Diana Havelock on the edge of the rose garden, and of the impression he'd received that she'd been waiting for someone—perhaps a man. 'I've no idea who it might have been,' he said. 'But she—Miss Havelock—seemed troubled and unhappy when she spoke to me. That remark about not being able to trust anybody... Well, it struck me as significant, that's all.'

'Perhaps because this man you mention had let her down, she decided to do away with herself?' said the inspector. 'Did she seem unbalanced in any way, when you spoke to her?'

'Not at all,' said Rowlands. 'In fact, she seemed perfectly lucid. Just—well, troubled, as I said.'

'Hmm,' said the other. 'Well, you've been very helpful, Mr Rowlands. 'Although I think I should tell you that we're not treating this as a case of suicide. After all, you were the one to find evidence of drug-taking in the young lady's room...'

'Yes,' said Rowlands. 'But I'm still not sure...'

'Death by Misadventure is the verdict I'm hoping we're going to get from the Coroner,' said Inspector Brown firmly. 'Kinder to her parents, you see...'

'Better for the College, too,' Rowlands couldn't restrain himself from saying. 'That too,' the other agreed. 'Very impressive lady, isn't she—that Miss Phillips? She wants this kept as quiet as possible, and I can't say as I blame her. Got daughters of my own,' he confided, as—their conference at an end—he rose to conduct Rowlands to the door. 'The thought of them messing about with drugs... it's enough to make your hair stand on end! If you ask me, they get a bit too much freedom, these girls. First it's "we want to be like the men—have the vote, get degrees, all that". Next thing you know it's cocktails and cigarettes and cocaine... to say nothing of this filthy stuff that's done for Miss Diana... Shocking waste,' he said, guiding Rowlands out into the corridor.

'It's certainly that,' said Rowlands.

On his way back to the Tower Wing, Rowlands passed a group of undergraduates, discussing something in low voices. It was immediately apparent to one with his propensity for picking up conversational clues, what it was they were talking about.

'...didn't know her well, of course. She was always a bit stand-offish.'

'...they're saying it was drugs.'

'...too awful. I don't know what Mummy will say.'

'I think it's a pretty poor show,' said one young man rather too loudly. 'Cutting the dance short like this. My exeat's till one, so I've over an hour to kill...'

'Why don't you get a punt out and go on the river?' said another male voice rudely. 'Do us all a favour and fall in.'

'Oh, very funny, Rowntree. Ha *ha*.'

'Well, I think you're all being perfectly horrid,' cried a young woman, with some feeling. 'Poor Diana's *dead*, in case you've forgotten, and all you can do is make stupid jokes. I call it pretty despicable.' Arrested by something familiar in the girl's voice, Rowlands came to a halt. 'Miss Thompson, isn't it?' he said. 'You were one of the people involved with putting on the plays this afternoon.'

'That's right,' she said. 'But…'

'I gather you knew Diana Havelock?'

'Not awfully well,' said Angela Thompson. 'We were in different years. She was a fourth year, so she'd already sat her Finals. I'm only a Second Year.'

'Even so,' said Rowlands. 'You knew her as well as anyone, I imagine.'

'Well…'

'Is it true,' put in another girl, 'that it was drugs that killed her?'

'I'm not in a position to say for certain,' said Rowlands. 'But it looks that way. Now, if you could tell me something about her…'

'I say, what *is* all this?' said the youth who'd complained about the dance being cut short. 'Are you some sort of policeman?'

'Shut up, St Clare,' said the other boy. 'Whoever saw a copper in evening dress? I apologise for my friend,' he said to Rowlands. It occurred to the latter that neither of the two young men was entirely sober. 'No, that's all right,' he said. 'I should have introduced myself. I'm a guest of the Bursar. Frederick Rowlands is the name. And I'm not a policeman—merely an interested party.'

'You were talking to Diana earlier,' said Angela Thompson. 'I remember now. It was at the garden party. You were with a lady in a lilac frock.'

'My wife,' said Rowlands. 'Miss Havelock was showing us the gardens. We only spoke to her for a few minutes. But I'd like to know a bit more about her. For instance,' he went on, 'someone else who knew her told me she'd never taken drugs. Disapproved of them, in fact…' There was a snort of disbelief from the St Clare boy. He must be Lady St Clare's son, thought Rowlands. Bumptious type. 'Would that be your impression, too, Miss Thompson?'

'I… I honestly couldn't say,' said the girl uneasily. 'As I said, I didn't know her very well. As for whether or not she took drugs… I've no idea. *I* certainly don't,' she added indignantly.

'Of course not,' said Rowlands. 'I wasn't suggesting anything of the sort. What about you, young man?' It was St Clare he now addressed. 'You seem to know something about it...'

'I?' was the astounded reply. 'I can't think *what* gave you that impression. I'm as pure as the driven snow, aren't I, Rowntree?' St Clare sniggered, as if he'd said something terribly funny. 'If dear little Diana's been meddling with the hard stuff, it's nothing to do with *me*...'

'Thanks,' said Rowlands. 'You've made that very clear. It's just that if any of you *do* know how Miss Havelock came by the drugs that were in her room, you ought to inform the police. Not to do so would be withholding evidence, you know...'

'Look, I'm off,' said St Clare, as if the topic under discussion made him uncomfortable. 'Coming, Rowntree? We can get a taxi from the Porters' Lodge, if you'll go halves.'

'All right,' said the other, somewhat reluctantly, it seemed to Rowlands. 'Be with you in a minute. Are you sure you'll be all right, Angela?'

'Perfectly all right, thanks, Miles. Brenda will keep me company, won't you?'

'If I must,' said her friend, a shade ungraciously. 'Besides,' went on Miss Thompson, 'I want to talk to Mr Rowlands about Diana. Although I don't know anything much—I wish I did! She was rather aloof, if you know what I mean, Mr Rowlands?'

Rowlands said that he did.

'Good night then, Angela,' said the youth. 'I'll see you tomorrow, shall I?'

'I expect so,' was the reply—no doubt an unsatisfactory one as far as Mr Rowntree was concerned, thought Rowlands, suppressing a smile. When the two young men had walked off, he addressed Miss Thompson and her friend. 'Is there somewhere we can talk?' He was getting tired of standing about in the corridor. 'We can try the J.C.R., I suppose. It's this way.' The girl took his arm. 'Come along, Brenda, if you're coming,' she said to the reluctant chaperone. 'With any luck, we should have it to ourselves.'

This proved not to be the case. 'Hullo!' said Miss Thompson. 'What are *you* doing here, Mainwaring?'

'Same as you, I imagine,' was the cool reply. 'Trying to find a spot that's not been overrun by idiots in dance frocks... Oh, I *do* beg your pardon! I didn't recognise you in your finery...'

'Very funny,' said Miss Thompson. 'I'm howling with laughter, as you can see. Now do push off, there's a good creature. This gentleman and I want to have a serious talk.'

'It comes to something,' grumbled the other, 'when one can't find a quiet place to oneself in the entire college. First it's that infernal caterwauling that passes for music that drives me from my room—and now this. Some of us have to work, you know...'

'Oh, ha *ha*!' said the girl Miss Thompson had addressed as Brenda. 'Just because you're a scientist, Mainwaring, doesn't mean you have it any harder than the rest of us...'

'I beg to differ. You Arts people don't know you're born.' But she got up, and gathered her books together. 'I was about to stop work anyway,' she said. 'There've been people shouting their heads off in the corridors all night. One can't hear oneself think.'

'Well, people are naturally upset,' said Angela Thompson. 'Upset about what?' When Miss Thompson told her, the girl went silent for a moment. 'That's beastly news,' she said at last, sounding genuinely shaken. 'I wish to heaven you hadn't told me.'

'You knew Miss Havelock, did you?' said Rowlands. 'Not well,' was the reply. 'I used to see her at the lab a bit. She... she was always decent to me...' Her voice seemed to catch in her throat. 'Do you know, I'd really rather not talk about it now, if you don't mind.' And with that she stalked off, letting the door slam shut behind her. 'I must apologise for the Mainwaring,' said Angela Thompson, after a moment. 'She doesn't usually fly off the handle like that...'

'She sounded quite distressed.'

'Oh, I shouldn't pay any attention to *that*, if I were you,' said Miss Thompson's friend. 'Mainwaring's always putting on airs. She's our resident swot. Takes herself *far* too seriously, if you ask me. Some say she's tipped for a First, but I'm not so sure. She works far too hard to be *really* clever.'

Having delivered herself of this crushing verdict, she flung herself down on one of the sofas with which the Junior Common Room was evidently supplied. Angela Thompson followed suit. Rowlands, rather more gingerly, seated himself on a sofa adjacent to this—whose springs, he discovered, had obviously suffered from the assaults of successive generations of St Gertrude's students. 'Well,' he said, without further preamble. 'What can *you* tell me about Miss Havelock?'

'As I said, I didn't know her well…' began Angela Thompson. 'We'd nod if we passed in the corridor—that sort of thing. It was only when I joined S.G.D.S. that I got to know her a bit better…'

'That's the dramatic society, is it?'

'Yes. She was one of the leading lights, of course. I just used to help out with scenery and costumes…'

'But you got to know her,' he persisted gently. 'I wonder if you could give me an idea of what she was like?'

There was a moment's silence, during which the girl considered her reply. But it was her friend who said: 'She thought a lot of herself.'

'*Brenda!*'

'Well, she did. Just because she'd got that College Studentship, when everyone knows that…'

'Shut up, Brenda!'

'Everyone knows what?' said Rowlands. But the girl, thinking perhaps she'd gone too far, was silent.

'What if she *did* think a lot of herself?' said Angela Thompson. 'She'd more reason than most. Getting that Double First, and then all the other things she was good at. Music and acting and all that…' Rowlands recalled the one sample he'd had of Miss Havelock's talent in this last respect. 'She was very good as Lady Macbeth.'

'Yes, but even then she was pushing herself forward,' said Miss Thompson's friend. 'Don't shake your head at me, Angela! You know it's true…'

'I think you'd better explain,' said Rowlands, tiring of this barbed innuendo. 'Oh, there's no mystery to it,' said the girl. 'Just the Havelock doing what she did best—getting herself noticed.' Well, she'd certainly achieved *that*, poor lass, thought Rowlands. But if the tastelessness of her remark had occurred to Miss Thompson's friend, it didn't prevent her from going on. 'When Gwen cried off because her cold was worse, it should have been the understudy who carried on,' she said. 'That's how we've always done things in the Drama Club. And *Twelfth Night*'s a comedy—much more suitable for a garden party! But then *she* said she wanted to do the daggers scene, and of course the Glossop's so in love with her that she let her do it...'

'Honestly, Brenda...'

It's like that, is it? thought Rowlands, making a guess as to the identity of the spurned understudy. 'Can I ask you something, Miss...?'

'Carstairs.'

'Miss Carstairs. Did Miss Havelock have many friends, do you think?'

The girl seemed taken aback. 'I... I couldn't say. She might have done—in other colleges, I suppose. People who did her subject, or worked with her at the lab, like Mainwaring. I'm not a scientist, so I don't know anyone of that sort...'

'Thank you,' said Rowlands. 'That's very clear. And you, Miss Thompson? You said you'd got to know her through the Drama Club?'

'Well... a little,' she admitted. 'But as I said, I wasn't particularly close to her. She was rather in a world of her own. I suppose scientists are a bit like that.' She thought for a moment. 'Honoria might be a better person to ask, because their rooms were on the same corridor...'

'Ah, yes. Miss Fairclough,' he said. 'It was she who went to find Miss Havelock when she didn't turn up at the dance, wasn't it?' He knew it was, but wanted to hear what she had to say. 'That's right. People were saying it was she—Honoria—who found her...'

'Yes.'

Angela Thompson shivered. 'How perfectly ghastly. Poor thing!' It wasn't clear whether it was Honoria Fairclough or the dead girl she pitied. 'Can you tell me a little more about what happened this evening?' said Rowlands gently. 'For instance—when was Miss Havelock's absence first noticed?'

'I don't know exactly. About nine or nine-thirty, at a guess. The band had played a few tunes, and then someone said had anyone seen Diana? She'd been in Hall earlier, and so we knew she was intending to come. She had a jolly nice frock on,' said Miss Thompson wistfully. 'Emerald green satin. Perfect with her red hair. She'd shoes to match, too…' Rowlands, remembering when he'd first become aware of the shoes, repressed a shudder. 'Go on.'

'That's all, really. Honoria said she'd go and see what had happened to her. When she didn't come back, we… Well, nobody noticed anything for a while. We were all dancing by then, you see…' Rowlands did see. 'When did you discover what had happened?'Angela Thompson thought about this. 'It must have been after eleven, because they'd put out supper and we—that is, Miles and I—were talking about having one last dance before getting something to eat…'

'And who told you the news about Miss Havelock's death?'

Again, she pondered for a moment. 'Can't say, I'm afraid. Suddenly, everyone seemed to be talking about something dreadful that had happened… No one quite knew what it was—until that idiot Roddy St Clare said there'd been a murder…'

'Thank you,' said Rowlands. 'You've both been most helpful. I'm sorry if I've kept you up late.'

'Oh, that's quite all right,' said Miss Thompson cheerfully. 'We never go to bed much before midnight, out of term—do we, Brenda?'

The other concurred with this.

'Then I'll walk with you as far as the Porters' Lodge, if I may,' said Rowlands, getting to his feet, as the girls did the same. 'I do have one more question,' he added, as if it had only just occurred to him. 'You said earlier, Miss Thompson, that you weren't part of Diana Havelock's set, but suggested—unless I'm mistaken—that there were others who might have been. I'm talking about drugs,' he added, in case this wasn't already clear. 'Can you tell me who might have given them to Miss Havelock?'

'I'm afraid not,' was the prompt reply. It was plain from Angela Thompson's manner that, even if a name had come to mind, she wouldn't have divulged it. 'As I said, I don't move in those circles.' She gave a little shudder. 'Gives me the pip, that sort of thing, if you want to know.'

'According to Mr Sedgwick, Diana didn't move in what you

call "those circles" either,' said Rowlands. 'In fact, he swears she'd never touched drugs of any kind.' They had now reached the bottom of the spiral staircase; to the left of this was the corridor leading to the Porters' Lodge, and the door leading to the Tower Wing. 'Oh, everyone knows Julian's in love with her,' said Miss Thompson with a touch of scorn. 'He won't hear a word against her.'

'Was he Miss Havelock's boyfriend?'

'He'd have liked to be,' was the reply. 'Poor Julian! He rather worshipped Diana. But I think he was just one of the men she kept dangling, if you know what I mean?'

'I think so,' said Rowlands, to whom this didn't come as a surprise. 'Well, if either of you think of anything else you can tell me, I'd be grateful. A note at the Porters' Lodge will find me—until first thing Monday morning.'

'I say—are you sure you're not a policeman?' said Brenda Carstairs, as Rowlands was about to take his leave of the two girls. He smiled. 'Quite sure. I'm just interested in getting at the truth, that's all.'

It was this—his unfortunate preoccupation with 'getting to the bottom of things', as Edith put it—which kept him awake for much of the rest of the night. Insomnia was a not-uncommon affliction for the blind, for whom the hours of darkness offered no respite from waking reality. This, combined with the wine Rowlands had drunk, and the over-stimulation of the brain brought about by the night's events, kept him wakeful until the small hours, so that when he eventually drifted off to sleep, the birds were already starting up their matitudinal racket in the trees that gave its name to Glade Court.

His mind kept returning to his last meeting with Diana Havelock. *How does one know one can trust anybody*? What exactly had she meant by that? Could she really have been referring to a broken love affair? And if not, then what *had* she been referring to? The words went round and round in his head. As for what he'd learned about the dead girl from her peers—that wasn't very conclusive, either. She was ambitious—that he knew already. She liked to 'push herself forward'—although that was a judgement made out of envy.

Of more interest was the other thing the Carstairs girl had said—about how she (Diana) had only got the College research studentship through some underhand means. He wondered what she'd been hinting. It might make sense to talk to her again, he thought. He fell asleep at last thinking about a green satin shoe…

What seem like only minutes later, he was woken by his wife's cheerful salutation. 'Wake up, sleepyhead! We don't want to be late for Chapel, do we?'

Rowlands groaned and turned over. 'I think I'll give Chapel a miss.'

'Got a bad head, have you?' Edith didn't sound very sympathetic. 'I knew having whisky on top of all that wine wasn't a good idea.'

'It wasn't the whisky.' Then he remembered exactly what it was. His sleepiness forgotten, he sat up. 'Edith. There's something I have to tell you.'

6

THE CHAPEL WAS FULL. Evidently the news of last night's terrible events had spread to the student body—those, at least, who had not yet returned home for the holidays—and the atmosphere was one of suppressed tension, conveyed by the nervous whispering that passed around the vaulted space like the sighing of wind in a cornfield. 'Oh dear,' murmured Edith. 'It looks as if we may have to sit separately…' But just then there came a hissing sound from near the front. It was the Bursar, prepared as ever for every eventuality—including the possibility that Chapel might be full to capacity on this most untoward of Sundays: 'I've saved you some seats…'

The Rowlandses had just sat down when a sudden silence announced the arrival of the Mistress, who took her seat to the right of the choir. A moment later, the strains of the organ heralded the procession up the aisle of the Chaplain and choir. As the choristers—all women, Rowlands supposed—seated themselves, Dr Maltravers took his stand in front of the altar. 'Dearly beloved brethren,' he began, and Rowlands listened once more to the familiar words, which had been a part of his life since early childhood, and which had sustained him in the darkest hours of his life—on the eve of battle, and in the military hospital, after they told him he would never regain his sight. '… the Scripture moveth us in sundry places to acknowledge and confess our manifold sins and wickedness…'

For form's sake, Edith had handed him a prayerbook and hymnal, knowing how much he disliked seeming different from the rest of the congregation, but he didn't need either, having long ago committed the words of both to memory. From around him, as the service went on, came muted rustling and creaking as people rose to their feet or, as custom dictated, sank to their knees. These homely sounds, overlaid by the sonorous tones of the Chaplain's voice, were punctuated, from time to time, by muffled sobs, and blowing of noses—indications that, for some, the beautiful words of Morning Service could not dispel the dark cloud that hung above them all.

'The Mistress read the Lesson very well, I thought,' Edith remarked—perhaps in an attempt to lighten the mood, as the three of them joined the general exodus from the Chapel, and made their way towards the Hall, and breakfast. 'Oh, yes. She always does,' said Miss Rickards—adding, with a brave attempt at a laugh, 'I've said to her that the theatre lost an ornament when she decided to go in for teaching.'

Rowlands murmured something expressive of agreement. The text of the lesson in question—the gospel for the Third Sunday after Trinity, about the man who invited friends to a feast, only to be fobbed off with various lame excuses—was a favourite, containing as it did verses which seemed particularly pertinent to one such as himself: *Go out quickly into the streets and lanes of the city, and bring in hither the poor, and the maimed, and the halt, and the blind...*

Had things been otherwise, he might have pointed this out; as it was, even such a mild joke would seem in poor taste, he thought—although the only allusion during the service to the previous night's events had been when 'our sister, Diana Mary' had been mentioned in the prayers, provoking another, quickly stifled, outburst of sobbing. Perhaps, thought Rowlands, she'd had some friends in College after all.

As they took their seats in the dining hall, where a subdued murmur of conversation mingled with the rattle of cups and plates, he decided to have another word with Honoria Fairclough—always supposing she'd recovered from her ordeal of the night before—in case she remembered anything that might be relevant... Although relevant to what? he asked himself, letting his thoughts drift away from the material reality of tea and toast to more nebulous speculations. The case, to all intents and purposes, was closed, wasn't it? Death by Misadventure would be the verdict—hadn't that chap Brown as good as said so? A sad illustration, to anyone who cared to see it, of the perils of taking drugs. Then why did he feel that there were still questions left unanswered?

'Fred, I've asked you three times if you'd like another cup of tea,' said Edith, with the exaggerated patience that came from long familiarity with her husband's ways. 'What? Oh, sorry. Yes, I'll have another cup...'

'And you've hardly touched your bacon and eggs.'

'No.' He picked up his knife and fork and made a half-hearted attempt at finishing his rapidly cooling breakfast. 'I don't seem to have much appetite.'

'Hardly surprising, under the circumstances,' said the Bursar. 'I don't think any of us feel much like eating today. When I think of that poor child...' There was the sound of a nose being blown sharply. 'Such a waste,' said Maud Rickards, in a choked voice. 'Dreadful,' agreed Edith, adding with uncharacteristic gentleness, 'You mustn't blame yourself.'

The three friends were seated at High Table, where the seating arrangements were much less formal than those of the night before, with Fellows sitting down wherever a space appeared, and leaving as soon as they'd finished eating, with no more ceremony that that displayed by the student body in the main part of the hall. Snatches of conversation floated towards Rowlands along the length of the table, as he did his best with a congealing rasher of fatty bacon, and an egg overcooked to rubberiness.

'Who would have thought it? She was such an exemplary student...'

'... so distressing for the parents.'

'... no idea she had anything on her mind, had you?'

He recognised the voices of Miss Hall, Miss Glossop, and Miss Merriweather—the latter explaining to a late arrival, Miss Kruger, the reason for the general upset. 'But I have heard nothing of this,' exclaimed the German Assistant. 'That poor girl! Was it suicide, do you think?'

'There's no suggestion that it was anything but an accident,' said Miss Hall quickly. 'Even so, it is a terrible thing,' said Ilse Kruger. 'A terrible thing.' She sounded close to tears, and after a few moments she pushed back her chair and went out, leaving her breakfast untouched. Then for a while there was silence in the Hall, except for the scraping of knives and forks against plates, and the chinking of teacups in saucers. Rowlands pushed aside the remains of his meal, heartily glad to have done with it. 'Well,' said Miss Rickards to her companions. 'If you've finished, perhaps we should adjourn to my rooms for coffee?' Both murmured their assent to this plan.

But as they were getting up to leave, the young woman who had been collecting their plates—one of the college servants, Rowlands surmised—addressed the Bursar in a low voice: 'Is it true, Miss—this awful story that's been going around? About Miss Diana, I mean…'

'I'm afraid so, Betty,' was the reply. The girl said nothing more for a moment, busying herself with stacking plates onto her tray; then she said: 'I'm very sorry to hear it, Miss. All of us kitchen staff feel the same. She was a lovely young lady.'

'Thank you, Betty.' Miss Rickards waited until the girl was out of earshot before adding, 'Something like this upsets the whole college. I shouldn't wonder if we have a few of the gyps handing in their notices—and I'd be the last one to blame them.'

The Bursar's sitting-room was to be found in the modern part of the college—'so much less draughty and inconvenient,' she said, ushering in her guests. 'Coal-fires are all very well, but such a lot of work for the maids. And I do like having my own gas-ring. It makes entertaining wonderfully easy.'

So saying, she bustled over to the far side of the room, where the said fixture was located, Rowlands guessed, and began taking cup and saucers from a cupboard. 'Edie, if you want to take your hat off, there's a mirror in my bedroom.' Edith went to carry out this suggestion, leaving her husband stranded in the middle of the room—which was, he discovered, by barking his shins on a chair or two, somewhat overfull of furniture. 'Do make yourself comfortable,' said Miss Rickards; then, as Rowlands prepared to sit down: 'I say—look out! You nearly sat on Webster!'

Before he could ask why this should be a cause of alarm—it was only a dictionary, after all (albeit an American one)… unless she was referring to the collected plays of the Jacobean dramatist—his hostess explained: 'The college cat. He likes to take his ease in here of a morning.'

'We've met, haven't we, Webster?' Rowlands reached down and, encountering no resistance, began to scratch the back of the animal's head. Soon, a loud purring ensued. 'Yes, he pretty much has the run of College, ' said Miss Rickards, setting down a tray on a low table. 'The students spoil him, of course—which is why he's so fat. I'm afraid he doesn't do much to earn his keep in the way of killing rats and mice, these days...'

'We can't all work hard for a living, can we, old man?' said Rowlands to the cat, which demonstrated its agreement with these sentiments by jumping up on Rowlands's lap, once he'd seated himself in one of the Bursar's comfortable armchairs, and settling itself down at once to sleep.

'Ah,' said the Bursar. 'There's the coffee.' Because, to judge from the gradual slowing-down of the bubbling sounds it had been making, the percolator had finished percolating. 'I got it on my last walking-tour of Italy,' said Miss Rickards, when Edith admired the elegant nickel-plated finish. 'I find the result—especially when using freshly-ground beans—is much more satisfactory than the beverage produced by the college kitchens.' The next few minutes were filled with the pouring out and handing around of the coffee.

A silence fell. It was not unlike the one which had earlier befallen High Table when Miss Kruger had mentioned suicide— a silence heavy with meaning.

Then Edith and Maud Rickards spoke at once:

'I think you ought to...'

'I wanted to ask you...'

Both stopped; then laughed. 'You first,' said Edith. 'It's your story, after all.'

'Very well.' Miss Rickards drew an audible breath, as if gathering her resources. 'Edith has told me,' she said to Rowlands, 'that you have had some experience of this kind of thing... and I thought that, given what's happened with this poor girl...'

'What exactly are we talking about?' he interrupted.

The Bursar shuddered. 'Letters,' she said. 'Vile letters. I've had one, and I know that others have, too...' She paused, as if weighing up the advisability of mentioning names. 'I suspect,' she went on, 'that Diana Havelock may have received such a letter.'

Rowlands took a sip of his coffee. It was, indeed, much better than the stuff they'd been served after dinner. 'Have you kept this letter?'

'I threw it in the fire.'

'A pity,' he said. 'If the police are to pursue the matter…'

'I'd prefer not to involve the police,' said Maud Rickards quickly. 'This has to be handled with the utmost discretion—don't you see?'

'Well,' said Rowlands. 'I'm not sure what I can suggest. Without any physical evidence, it'll be difficult to pin this down to a particular perpetrator…'

'There is some physical evidence.'

'Oh? I thought you said you'd burnt the thing?'

'Jane Glossop got one,' said the Bursar. 'As did Caroline Hall—although I gather she tore hers up, too. But I asked Jane to let me have the letter she was sent. In case there were any further repercussions.'

'Have you got it here?'

'Yes.' She got up and went over to the desk. There was the sound of a drawer being opened. 'Here you are.' She put it into Rowlands's hand. 'You're going to have to read it to me, you know,' he said with the ghost of a smile. 'Of course. Idiotic of me.' She went to take it back, but he held onto it. 'Just a minute. Let's see what we can learn from the envelope, before we get to the contents. I don't suppose we need bother about fingerprints,' he said, as if to himself. 'Whoever wrote this is bound to have worn gloves.' He weighed the envelope on his palm. 'It seems like a fairly poor quality.'

'Yes,' said Miss Rickards. 'It's just the cheap kind one can buy in any post-office.'

'And the address? Is it typed or handwritten?'

'Typed,' was the reply. 'I was pretty sure it would be,' said Rowlands. 'Most people have read enough murder mysteries to know that handwriting can't easily be disguised. Was it posted outside College, or did it come through the internal post?'

'Do you know, I didn't think to look,' said the Bursar. She took the envelope from him, and examined it. 'It's been franked,' she said. 'Posted the Friday before last—the 31st of May—in Cambridge. I must say,' she remarked to Edith. 'I see what you mean about your husband's detecting skills.'

'I haven't detected anything yet,' said Rowlands drily. 'May I have it back, please?' He took the envelope from her, sniffed it, and pulled a face. 'I wish I could tell you it smells of *Joy*—or *Evening in Paris*,' he added wickedly. 'Thus giving away the writer's sex. But I'm afraid it only smells of cheap paper—and cow gum.' He drew out the letter, a single sheet, and ran a fingertip across the surface. 'As does this,' he said. 'Now I *know* whoever sent these letters must be a reader of murder mysteries. It's quite a work of art, in its way.' Because instead of a typed note, the message had been constructed out of printed letters cut out and glued. 'You'd better read it,' said Rowlands; then, as Miss Rickards hesitated: 'Don't worry, I'm not easily shocked. I was in the army for three years, remember?'

The Bursar took the letter from him and cleared her throat. '*YOULL BE SORY FOR THIS YOU OLD COW MAKIN FAVOURITES OF TROLOPS LIKE HER*,' she read, with no more expression than if she had been reading out a crossword clue. 'I should mention that it's not punctuated and that three of the words—"sorry", "making" and, er, "trollops" are misspelt.'

'But not "favourites",' said Rowlands. 'That's interesting.'

'What is?' said Edith, who had been listening impatiently to this. 'It sounds like a lot of filth to me.'

'Yes, but carefully constructed filth. Can you remember,' he said to Maud Rickards, 'what was the substance of the note you received?' The Bursar thought for a moment. 'It said—as far as I can recall—that I was a silly, prating old fool, and that I'd rue the day I set eyes on "that red-haired hussy". I think that was the phrase used,' she added, suddenly sounding very tired. 'To tell you the truth, I could hardly bring myself to look at the thing. It seemed so full of spite…'

'And rage,' said Rowlands. 'Whoever sent these things is very angry with someone…'

'Red hair,' said Edith suddenly. 'That sounds like poor Diana

Havelock.'

'It does,' agreed her husband. 'Unless you can think of anyone else it might refer to, Bursar?'

'No...' said Miss Rickards hesitantly. 'So you think this was all directed at Diana?'

'It's hard to say, without seeing the letter Miss Hall received—and any others we don't yet know about,' said Rowlands. 'But on the evidence so far, it does seem a possibility.'

'That makes things even worse,' said Maud Rickards. 'If the letters were all intended to hurt Diana Havelock, then it looks horribly as if she were driven to do what she did because of it...'

'We don't know she received one of these letters, though, do we?' said Rowlands. 'We can find out,' was the Bursar's reply. 'Her room ought to be searched at once...'

'So you do think it might have been suicide?' said Edith to her husband, but he only shook his head. 'I don't think we should jump to conclusions. And there's another matter to consider—who supplied Miss Havelock with the drugs that killed her? It seems to me that everything else takes second place to that.'

'But surely...' began Miss Rickards, when the telephone rang. 'Bother!' she said, going over to her desk to answer it. 'Hello? Bursar's Office... Oh, hello, Mistress... Yes, he is, as a matter of fact... Shall I put him on? Oh. Very well, I'll tell him... There was one more thing, actually... Oh! She's rung off.' Miss Rickards sounded faintly put out. 'She—the Mistress—has asked if you could spare her a few minutes,' she said to Rowlands. 'I'll go with you, if I may.'

Edith having elected to wait for them in Miss Rickards' room, the Bursar and Rowlands accordingly made their way to Beryl Phillips's office, in the older part of the college. It was perhaps Rowlands's heightened sense of the atmosphere of dread and suspicion that hung over the place that made him more aware of the prevailing silence. As they walked along the seemingly endless corridors, their footsteps echoed hollowly. Instead of the lively chatter of young women which had filled the college and its grounds on the afternoon of the garden party, there was only a feeling of abandonment. 'The nymphs are departed,' said Rowlands, half to himself. 'What's that?' said his companion; then, without waiting for an answer (not that he would have had one to give her): 'I suppose I ought to tell her—the Mistress—about these wretched letters.'

Surprised that she had not already done so, he murmured his agreement. 'It's all so horrible,' exclaimed Miss Rickards. 'I feel that I should have acted sooner. Maybe this dreadful thing'—she meant the girl's death, Rowlands assumed—'might have been prevented.' There was nothing to say to this. Rowlands guessed that his wife's friend would torment herself with the thought for a long time to come. Certainly, she did not spare herself when relating what had happened to the Mistress. 'So you see,' she finished, as the latter heard her out without interruption, 'I blame myself. If it turns out that Diana received one of these letters...'

'There's no evidence to suggest that,' was the calm reply. 'All we know is that the poor child died in as yet undetermined circumstances. When—and if—we learn otherwise will be the time for such recriminations. Now, Bursar, if that is all you have to tell me, I wonder if further discussion could wait? I don't wish to trespass on any more of Mr Rowlands's valuable time than I can help.'

'But...'

'Another time, Maud—please.'

'What about the picnic?'

To this apparent *non sequitur* the Mistress must have raised an eyebrow or given some other sign of incomprehension, for the Bursar said: 'The end of term picnic for the undergraduates this afternoon. Shouldn't it be cancelled?'

The Mistress considered this a moment. 'I don't see why. The girls have been looking forward to it immensely.'

'Isn't it in rather poor taste to go ahead with it? I mean—with poor Diana...'

'I think it would be a worse error of judgement to cancel it,' said Beryl Phillips gravely. 'The last thing we want to do is to call attention to this distressing affair. Don't you agree, Mr Rowlands?' He wasn't sure he did, but then, he wasn't the one in charge of a women's college. 'I know it might appear somewhat callous, to carry on as if nothing had happened,' the Mistress went on. 'But I can assure you, it's the best thing for everyone concerned. I'm thinking of Diana's parents,' she added, when Rowlands looked doubtful. 'They're travelling up from the West Country today. They'll be staying in College, of course—you've made the arrangements, Bursar?'

The Bursar said that she had.

'Good.' said Miss Phillips. 'I think that'll be all, then.' When Miss Rickards had left them, she continued: 'You see, Mr Rowlands, the less fuss there is, the less they—Mr and Mrs Havelock—will have to endure from the Press.' Her contempt for this august body was all too evident from her tone. 'The least sniff of scandal, and *they'll* be coming around in droves... We need to guard against that as much as possible.'

'"We"?' thought Rowlands, aware that he was being conscripted into a plan not of his making. 'There'll be an inquest,' he said. 'I don't think you're going to be able to avoid that.'

'No, indeed,' she said drily. 'Naturally, there will have to be an inquest. It was about that I wanted to talk to you, as a matter of fact. You were the one who found the poor child's body...'

'Actually,' he said. 'It was Miss Fairclough who found her.'

'Yes, yes.' A faint note of impatience had crept into her voice. 'But you were the first, shall we say, responsible adult? Poor Honoria was naturally upset...' Again that word, he thought. Although there had been nothing 'natural' about Diana Havelock's death. 'What is it you want from me?' he said. If he had offended her by his bluntness, she gave no sign of it. 'I don't *want* anything,' she replied. 'Unless it's for this atrocious business never to have happened...'

She was silent a moment; then she sighed. 'All I ask is that when you are called to give evidence at the inquest—as assuredly you will be called—you say no more than you feel you must say about the unfortunate circumstances of Diana's death. There! I have said it. You will doubtless think me impertinent.'

Rowlands shook his head. 'I don't think that at all. You are trying to protect a young woman's reputation...' He broke off, conscious that he could have said more.

'And the reputation of this college, you were going to say, I think?' There was the hint of a smile in Beryl Phillips's voice.

'I confess that it is something which which I concern myself a great deal, Mr Rowlands.'

'I think I understand.'

'It has taken a considerable effort on the part of a good many people—men and women—to bring this college into being,' she said. 'Effort and time—and money, too. We could not exist without our benefactors. I was not one of the pioneers,' she went on. 'I am not quite old enough for that! But I was amongst those that came to St Gertrude's when it was still a relatively new institution. It had not been founded thirty years, when I was up. I remember the opposition there was then to the whole idea of women's education. I was there when those who should have known better hung effigies of women out of windows on the eve of the election, and lit a bonfire in the Market Square to celebrate the vote going against us. I was also present, in 1921—not so very long ago—when a crowd of male undergraduates stormed the gates of Newnham, our sister college, after the vote for women to receive degrees on the same footing as the men was once more overturned.'

Rowlands nodded. He had heard this story from Maud Rickards, but it lost nothing in the retelling.

'More than this,' said Miss Phillips, her tone pitched between sadness and scorn, 'I have seen for myself the vilification of women's efforts—the mockery and the belittling of even the brightest achievements, if those honours happen to have been achieved by female scholars. It is so easy for women's work to be dismissed, you see. And there are those—yes, even at this very university!—who do not think that women should be educated at all. So perhaps you will understand, Mr Rowlands, when I say that I will do almost anything to defend the reputation of this college—and to resist giving ammunition to those who wish us ill…'

NOTICES

7

Laundress Green was crowded with picnickers, on that fine Sunday afternoon. Descending from a taxi in Mill Lane, Rowlands and Edith, shepherded by Maud Rickards, joined the queue for those hiring punts and rowing-boats at the boatyard by the Old Mill Pond. Since it was almost three o'clock, the public houses on the waterfront—the Anchor and the Mill—had already closed their doors, but a few stragglers from the lunchtime drinking session still lingered in the street outside, breathing beery fumes and an air of contentment that Rowlands could not help but envy. A nice pint of Ruddles would have gone down a treat, he thought; as it was, he'd make do with yet more tea and sandwiches.

Miss Rickards was just then engaged in argument with the man hiring punts. 'I was told there would be a special rate for two punts,' she insisted, while the man—clearly out of temper from having to cope with the influx of loudly cheerful students and 'trippers' the fine weather had brought out—grew increasingly surly. 'Don't know nothing 'bout a special rate,' he said. Rowlands decided it was time to intervene. 'Come now,' he said. 'You'll be guaranteed a whole afternoon's hire for both punts. Throw in the price of a nice little rowing boat—suitable for three—and we'll call it quits…'

Grumbling that he'd never hear the last of it from the guv'nor, the man complied with this request, and the party—which consisted of six St Gertrude's girls and four young men—disposed itself between the two larger craft, with Rowlands and his two companions getting into the boat. Had he and Edith been on their own, Rowlands would have liked to try his hand at punting—something he'd only attempted once before, on that earlier visit to Cambridge, before the War. His passenger in the punt on that occasion had been a girl called Elsie; he couldn't remember how it was he came to meet her, or indeed, whether they ever met again—but it was a pleasant memory, full of sun and laughter, with the shadows of the willow trees along the bank casting shifting patterns on a pretty, smiling face…

'You seem in a good mood,' said Edith, as they settled into their respective places in the boat—the two women with the hamper of tea things between them; Rowlands getting to grips with the oars. It had been a while since he'd taken a skiff out on the river at Kingston; he really must try and get fit again, he thought. 'Well, what could be nicer?' he said. 'A picnic on the river—and not a cloud in the sky, I'll be willing to bet…'

'You're right,' said Edith, and for a moment she rested her hand on his. 'It's as blue as blue.'

'I knew it,' he said. Then, after listening a moment: 'There's a mill-race nearby—I can hear it rushing.'

'It's all that's left of the old flour mill,' said Maud Rickards. 'They demolished it some years ago. Improved the area a good deal, in my opinion…'

When the occupants of the two St Gertrude's punts had taken their places, with much giggling and shoving, and loud jocularity on the part of the boys as to which of them should take charge of the punting, the little fleet moved off, heading upriver towards Coe Fen and distant Grantchester. In the leading punt, piloted by Miles Rowntree, sat the object of his affections, Angela Thompson, next to a rather subdued Honoria Fairclough. Opposite her was Brenda Carstairs, beside a young man who'd introduced himself to Rowlands earlier as Peter Bradshaw. A humorous exchange between the two young men regarding the prowess of their respective colleges in the May Bumps, elicited the fact that he was a Magdalene man.

The occupants of the second punt included the lively Geography don, Enid Merriweather, whose *fiancé*, Harold Armstrong, was punting, two St Gertrude's students called Pamela and Judy (Rowlands never did catch their surnames) and a taciturn lad by the name of Loxley, who was reading Classics at St Cat's but—he later confessed—had hopes of publishing a novel.

As the punts moved out into mid-stream they joined a procession of others, mostly heading in the same direction. From all around came cheerful shouts of 'Mind out!' and 'Keep to your own side, why don't you?' as the flat-bottomed craft jostled for position on this shallow stretch of the river. Intent on manoeuvring his own vessel so that its passage through the water wasn't impeded by the punts, Rowlands paid little attention to this jovial banter. Edith was acting as cox, and so he had only to concentrate on the rowing, knowing he could trust her to keep him out of scrapes. His old dexterity with the oars had come back to him after the first few strokes, and he was able to relax and enjoy the sensation of being out on the river, with the slight breeze that you always got on the water ruffling his hair and cooling his labours.

From up ahead, girlish voices floated back to him: 'Oh, do look where you're going, Miles! You nearly ran us into the bank...'

'It's quite rural, this part of Cambridge, isn't it?' remarked Edith. 'Who'd have thought to see cows grazing so close to the city centre?'

'Oh, you'll see them on Parker's Piece,' said Miss Rickards airily. 'Midsummer Common, too. It's quite a feature. Now this bit we're coming to is called Sheep's Green... I say, watch out!' Because as they reached the bend in the river just before this stretch of meadow, the blaring sound of a gramophone heralded the arrival of a punt coming the other way. Before Rowlands had time to react, the larger vessel was upon them. 'Hard left—I mean port!' cried Edith, as the punter, seeing the danger too late, shouted something incoherent. With a supreme effort, Rowlands did as his wife had commanded, narrowly avoiding a collision, but bumping the edge of the bank with its overhanging fronds of willow. 'My hat!' gasped Miss Rickards. 'That was a near thing!'

Rowlands felt this was putting it mildly. 'You young idiot!' he shouted. 'You almost had us in the river!'

'Frightfully sorry,' drawled the youth who'd been punting. He sounded anything but sorry, thought Rowlands. 'Didn't spot you until a minute ago... I say, it's the detective chappie!' In the same instant, Rowlands recognised the voice as one belonging to the insufferable young man encountered in the corridor at St Gertrude's the previous night. 'It might be a good idea, Mr St Clare,' he said coldly, 'to pay a bit more attention in future.'

'It's Lord St Clare, as a matter of fact,' was the condescending reply. 'Not that you were to know. Well, if you've done with the lecture, we'll be on our way…' There was snickering from the other occupants of the punt. 'That's told the blighter, Roddy!' guffawed one. Hot with fury, Rowlands had little choice but to let it go at that, and—with the punt now moving out of his way—turn his attention to getting the boat away from the bank. But before the miscreants, still hooting with laughter, could make good their escape, Miss Rickards intervened: 'Just a minute. I'll want your names and colleges, please.'

At once the merriment subsided. 'Oh, *Lor'!*' said one. 'If we haven't gone and hit a Gertie boat…'

'I…' Suddenly Roddy St Clare didn't sound so cocksure. 'I didn't realise it was you, Bursar…'

'So it would seem,' was the crisp reply. 'Names and colleges—and be quick about it. I don't need to ask *yours*, Lord St Clare,' added Miss Rickards, with withering politeness. 'I'm sure the Dean of St Jude's is all too familiar with your face…'

I say,' murmured the offender. 'Is this really necessary? Mama will have a blue fit if I'm gated again…'

'You should have thought of that before you were impertinent to a guest of mine,' retorted the Bursar. 'No more prevarication, please. You've delayed us long enough.'

It was a crestfallen foursome—St Clare, and three friends styling themselves the Hon. Anthony Langland (Trinity), Piers Fox (Queens') and Christopher Bagott-Smyth (Peterhouse) who eventually went on their way, to the strains of *I'm Wearin' My Green Fedora*. 'I feel almost sorry for them,' said Edith, as their boat set off in the opposite direction. 'I don't think I've ever seen you quite so fierce, Maud.'

'That type doesn't deserve your pity,' said her friend. 'They think they own the river—to say nothing of the University. It won't do any of them a bit of harm to get a talking-to from the Dean of their respective colleges.'

The rest of the journey upriver passed without incident—Rowlands putting on a bit of speed in order to catch up with the St Gertrude's punts. The occupants of these, it emerged, had witnessed the whole episode, and were loud in their condemnation of St Clare and his cronies. 'What I don't understand,' said a voice Rowlands recognised as that of Brenda Carstairs, 'is what anyone sees in Roddy St Clare.'

'Go on!' This was Angela Thompson. 'You were saying only yesterday that he has a profile like Rupert Brooke's...'

'Well, so he has. It doesn't mean I *like* him. You're being awfully quiet, Miles,' went on Miss Carstairs, with the touch of spitefulness Rowlands remembered from his conversation with her the night before. 'I thought Roddy was a chum of yours? In fact, I'm surprised you aren't with him and the rest of his gang this very minute!'

Miles Rowntree said nothing for a moment—perhaps intent on navigating a tricky patch of river. 'St Clare's not so bad when you get him on his own,' he said at last. 'He's just a bit weak-minded, that's all. Hanging out with Tony Langland and his crowd hasn't done him any good, in my view.' A sensible young fellow, thought Rowlands, overhearing this conversation. He was glad, for Angela Thompson's sake.

Further upstream, the river grew wider and deeper, between broad, tree-lined meadows. Here were grazing cows enough to delight Edith, who had grown up in rural Dorsetshire, and still spoke fondly of her girlhood rambles across its lush green fields—a world away from the suburban streets where she had spent her married life. Reaching a suitable spot, the picnic party disembarked, and a small procession carrying hampers, cushions and rugs for sitting on made its way across the grass. 'I think here will do very nicely,' said Miss Rickards, when they had gone a little distance. 'Plenty of shade. I don't hold with all this sun-bathing the young go in for nowadays.'

Rowlands didn't agree—he loved the sun—but in the interests of harmony he set down the hamper at the place she had ordained. The young people, however, made for a spot a little further off, where the sun fell uninterrupted by the willow trees' shade. The next few minutes were occupied with spreading rugs and unpacking hampers—cries of delight greeting the appearance of the provisions put up by the St Gertrude's kitchens. 'Ham sandwiches—jolly good!' was Harold Armstrong's reaction to these substantial delicacies. 'I was afraid there'd be nothing but cucumber…'

'Never you fear!' said his *fiancée*. 'We women like our food too, you know. I say, pass us the mustard, will you?'

Soon, a contented munching—not unlike the sound of cows chewing a cud, thought Rowlands—prevailed over the sylvan scene, which his imagination peopled with girls in white linen skirts, sailor blouses, and wide-brimmed straw-hats, and with young men in striped blazers and white flannels. He knew these sartorial details belonged to an earlier time—the time when he was young—and that the reality was probably more prosaic. Young women nowadays were as inclined to wear shorts and trousers as their male peers; hats, too, were no longer *de rigeur*. He himself never wore a hat if he could help it—but that was for a particular reason. Hats shaded the eyes from light, and with his damaged vision, he needed all the light he could get.

'I hope,' said a voice, breaking into these reflections. 'They haven't forgotten the "deadlies"…' These, it transpired, were the chocolate cakes that were the speciality of the town's famous cake-shop, Fitzbillies, and without which no picnic could be complete. A quick search soon turned up the cakes, as well as strawberries and cream, and ginger beer or lemonade to wash the whole lot down. Disdaining these beverages, Miss Rickards had thought to bring along a Primus stove, on which she presently boiled a kettle for tea.

'I must say,' said another voice from somewhere near the ground. 'This beats revising for Finals…'

There was a murmur of agreement from the young man's peers. 'You never spend any time revising that *I'm* aware of, Peter,' said Angela Thompson, to general laughter. 'That's because I do all my revising in the middle of the night,' he replied in mock-offended tones. 'Well, I'm jolly glad to be done with the beastly things until next year,' said the young woman who'd been so concerned about the 'deadlies'. Pamela or Judy, thought Rowlands, who hadn't managed to distinguish one from the other. 'I've got another year of exams, so don't crow that yours are over and done...'

'Some of us wouldn't mind another year,' said the young man called Loxley. 'Anything rather than having to get a job...'

'What will you do?' This was Angela Thompson. 'No idea,' was the reply. 'The pater wants me to go into the family firm, but if Faber like my novel then it might not come to that...' Rowlands let his attention lapse. It was pleasant beside the river, with the smell of hawthorn blossom drifting across from the trees on the far bank, and no sound, beyond the desultory murmur of conversation, but the twitter of birdsong—was that a lark? he wondered sleepily—and the sighing of the breeze in the willow fronds. He stretched himself out on the grass, and closed his eyes...

'Anyone for a walk?' said Enid Merriweather, with her customary enthusiasm. 'Harold and I thought we'd have a look at the church.' This was Grantchester Church, Rowlands assumed. Having already had more than his fair share of exercise that afternoon, he was inclined to pass up the chance, interesting as it would have been to visit the church whose clock had inspired the famous lines. Brooke's poetry was out of fashion now, but during the War, and in the years just afterwards, it had seemed to encapsulate something—a particular kind of Englishness, perhaps—which had seemed worth fighting for. Then he heard Angela Thompson say: 'Come on, Honoria—a walk'll do you good. You can't sit here moping all afternoon...' He decided he'd join the expedition to the church, after all. This might be the only opportunity he'd get to talk to the girl.

Edith and Maud Rickards having elected to stay behind, the rest of the party set off, across another meadow—this one full of buttercups, to judge from the murmur of bees that arose from it. After a few minutes, Rowlands fell into step with Miss Thompson and her friend. 'Pleasant afternoon,' he said; then, to Miss Fairclough: 'I hope you're feeling a little better today?'

'Yes. I...' Her voice seemed to catch in her throat. 'You were very kind to me after...' Another pause. 'After what happened.'

Miss Thompson—sensible girl!—took her cue at this point, and fell behind to talk to Miles Rowntree. This was Rowlands's chance. 'I wondered,' he said, 'if anything else had occurred to you about yesterday evening?'

'I… I don't know. What do you mean?

'Did you notice anything untoward? I mean, when you first got to Miss Havelock's room…'

'I don't think so. Why are you asking? You don't think there was anything *suspicious* about Diana's death, do you?'

'I'm not sure,' he admitted. 'I suppose I'm just trying to get a picture. Perhaps, if it's not too painful for you, you could tell me as much as you can remember of the time between when you left the dance and when you arrived at Room E14…'

'All right. But I still don't see…' She drew a breath, as if collecting herself. 'I left the dance at around half-past nine, I suppose… I *told* that policeman all this,' she said; then went on: 'I got to E Corridor about three or four minutes later, and went into my room to get my shawl…'

'Yes, I'd gathered that your room was on the same corridor,' Rowlands interrupted. 'That's right. Diana was to have moved next term to a nicer set—because of getting the College Studentship, you know—but we've had rooms next to each other on E Corridor since the beginning of Michaelmas Term. Mine's E12A.'

'Go on,' he said. Ahead of them, Miss Merriweather could be heard talking about the geography of the Cambridge area. 'Before the Ice Age, the whole region was a swamp, with a ridge of gravel running through it. If you climb up Castle Hill—which is chalk, of course—you can see the river valley laid out in front of you…'

'Well, I got my shawl,' said Miss Fairclough, 'and then I went along to Diana's room, and knocked on the door…'

'Was there anyone else about? In the corridor, I mean…'

'No. Everybody was at the dance… although…' She broke off. 'That's funny! Now you mention it, there must have been somebody about, because I heard a door closing…'

'When was this?' Even though he knew it probably meant nothing, Rowlands felt a prickle of excitement. 'Just before I knocked,' said the girl. 'I'd forgotten it until now, because of what happened after…'

'Perfectly understandable. Have you any idea which room it was? Where you heard the door close, I mean?'

'I'm afraid not. I wasn't paying much attention. It might have been the one on the far side of Diana's… that's E15… or the one beyond that…'

'It doesn't matter,' he said. 'Then you knocked, and there was no reply…'

'No, there wasn't. So I knocked again, and called Diana's name…' Honoria Fairclough's voice faltered. 'When she… when there was no reply, I tried the door. It opened, and I went in… and found her.' They had by now reached the village, and their little group had bunched together, making anything but general conversation impossible. Rowlands judged, in any case, that the girl had had enough. 'Thank you,' he said, 'You've been very helpful.' He wasn't sure what to make of the information he had just received. It certainly bore thinking about, however.

Returning, perhaps half an hour later, from admiring the beauties of the fourteenth century church (whose clock, Rowlands was disappointed to learn, was not eternally frozen at ten-to-three), they passed other strollers, some of whom—to judge from the talk of 'scrumptious cakes' and 'spiffing scones'—were on their way to or returning from tea at the Orchard tearooms. Others were apparently enjoying more active pleasures: shouts and laughter came from one such group of youths, who—doubtless encouraged by the warm weather—had taken to the river. From all the yelling and splashing that was going on, Rowlands guessed that a swimming contest was in progress. On the bank sat an admiring audience of young women. 'Go on, Tom! You show 'em!' cried one, adding indulgently, 'Look at him, Mabel! Thinks he's God's Gift, he does…'

The voice was familiar—after a moment, Rowlands placed it as belonging to one of the maids from the College. He smiled and nodded as he went past. 'Good afternoon,' he said. The young woman who'd spoken—Betty something, wasn't it?—must have recognised him too, for she replied, ''Afternoon, sir. Lovely day for it.'

'It is indeed. Although I must say I'm not tempted to go in. Rather muddy, isn't it?'

Betty laughed. 'Oh, you can't keep my Tom out of the water! Loves it in all weathers. Champion swimmer, he is, too. Won all sorts of cups…'

'Good show,' said Rowlands. 'Well, I'll leave you to it, ladies.' As he walked off to rejoin his party, he heard the other girl ask, 'Who's that, then?' and Betty's reply: 'Gentleman as is staying at the college. Bursar's guest. *Lovely* manners.'

Reaching the place where the punts were moored, Rowlands found Miss Rickards in high dudgeon. 'Really!' she hissed. 'One would have thought Thomas Findlay and his friends might have found another part of the river in which to disport themselves! Edith and I have barely been able to hear ourselves think—have we?'

'Well…' said Edith.

'Quite apart from the racket they're making, those bathing costumes he and his chums are wearing are barely decent. He ought to consider the reputation of the college, in my opinion…'

'Why, does he work at St Gertrude's?' asked Rowlands, a little taken aback at this vituperative outburst. 'He certainly does,' was the reply. 'He's the groundsman. Does a good job of it, too,' she conceded, as their party began stowing the hampers and cushions away, in preparation for casting off. 'But he's a bit too full of himself, that one.'

The inquest was to be held on Wednesday; Rowlands would return to Cambridge on the morning of that day. He and Edith had taken a rather more subdued leave from their hostess than any of them could have anticipated on the Rowlandses' arrival in the university town three days before. Now it seemed as if a shadow hung over everything. Even the pleasure of seeing the girls and their grandmother again, and of hearing of all they'd been up to in those few days apart—a campfire party Margaret had attended with the Guides; Anne's coming top in French; Joan's learning to make cheese scones—was dimmed. It felt wrong, somehow, to be rejoicing in the presence of one's own children, when another family had been so cruelly bereft of their child.

Then there was the matter of work—of which there was

quite a bit to catch up with, after his extended weekend. For the past six years, as secretary of St Dunstan's, the institute for the war-blinded of which he was himself a member, Rowlands had been coping with the demands of running a large organisation—the administrative side, that is; Sir Ian Fraser, the head of the organisation (whom Rowlands still thought of by his wartime title of 'Major Fraser'), took care of all the public side. Just now he—the Major—was taken up with preparations for the Silver Jubilee, as well as with planning the celebrations for St Dunstan's twenty-first anniversary next year, not to mention plans for the new building at Ovingdean.

The more humdrum work fell to Rowlands—not that he minded a bit. Someone had to make sure that pensions and child-allowances were paid on time, and materials supplied for home-based workers. Making sure that typewriters (an essential piece of equipment for the blind) were kept in good order, and that telephones were installed as a priority in St Dunstan's houses, were other necessary jobs. All of this Rowlands saw as contributing to the general cause, which was making it possible for those, like himself, who had lost their sight in the service of their country to lead relatively independent lives. In this task he was ably assisted by his staff, which consisted at present of his secretary, Miss Betts, and Miss Harker, who took care of bill-payments and other financial matters.

With the thought of what the inquest later that week might reveal, and what his own contribution to this might be hanging over him, Rowlands was especially glad that he could trust Miss Betts to answer the routine letters, and to turn his occasionally rambling dictation into clear, concise, prose. Miss Harker was no less efficient when it came to dealing with the finances. Privately, he dreaded what would happen to the smooth running of the organisation if either of them took it into her head to get married—although so far neither had expressed such a wish. But good secretaries and bookkeepers were hard to find.

If there were times when he missed the excitement of the job he'd had before this one, when he'd worked as a receptionist in a busy firm of City solicitors—with the telephone ringing non-stop and clients dashing in and out of the office all day long—this wasn't one of them. With so much on his mind, his quiet office, with only the clacking of Miss Betts's typewriter to disturb the flow of his thoughts, seemed a haven—as did the peaceful surroundings of Regent's Park, where St John's Lodge, the St Dunstan's H.Q., was situated, and through which his walk from Baker Street tube took him each day.

Even so, it was hard not to be distracted by thoughts of what had happened a few days before, in the no less tranquil environs of St Gertrude's College, Cambridge. A young woman's life had been cut short, and the wrongness of this haunted Rowlands's waking hours. His unconscious mind, too, seemed unable to let the matter rest. It had been years since the bad dreams which had once plagued him almost nightly had troubled his sleep, and yet now they returned. Visions of a dead grey landscape, littered with corpses. Its broken stumps of trees and tangles of barbed wire a graphic expression of an unseen horror.

8

LIVERPOOL STREET STATION WAS a roaring maelstrom of sound: the grinding of engine wheels and the screeching of brakes; the blaring of announcements and the crying of news vendors; porters heaving luggage and guards ordering latecomers to 'Stand away, there!' combining in one extended cacophony, echoing and re-echoing from the great iron and glass canopy overhead. Rowlands, who relied to a very great extent on his hearing in order to find his way around, wondered if those in possession of all their five senses found this assault on their ears as disagreeable as he did. One got used to it of course—although somehow, in all his years of travelling into Central London, he never had. 'Pandemonium,' he murmured. A word coined by a blind poet, to designate the capital city of Hell. He wondered what Milton would have made of railway trains.

Having navigated his way successfully through the crowd to the platform where the Cambridge train had just come in, he bought a paper from a newsstand (his habit when travelling, to discourage unwanted conversation) and made his way along it, hoping to find an empty compartment. The newspaper might not do the trick—and he was in no mood for idle chatter. He found one that was unoccupied at last, and took his seat, having first pulled down the window, to allow some air to enter, then unfolded his *Times*. The main story, he knew from the man who had sold him the paper, was the continuing investigation into Saturday's train crash at Welwyn Garden City, in which fourteen people had died. That, and the crisis in Abyssinia, had dominated the news broadcasts on the wireless that morning, too.

The guard blew his whistle. From the platform came sounds

of scurrying footsteps, as people dashed to board the train at the last minute. To Rowlands's annoyance, the door of his compartment was flung open, and someone got on, sitting himself heavily in the seat opposite. At the same moment, a porter, about to slam the door that the newcomer had left open, was hailed by the latter in a peremptory fashion: 'Put my suitcase up in the rack for me, will you, my good man?'

'Train's about to leave, sir,' was the curt reply from the official, as he complied with this request. 'Surly fellow,' remarked Rowlands's fellow passenger, when the door had been slammed shut. 'He lost himself sixpence with that sour face of his.' The speaker sounded rather pleased at this outcome. It was then that Rowlands remembered where he'd heard the voice before. Reluctantly, he lowered his paper. 'Professor Bristow, isn't it?'

'It is. Have we met?'

'Briefly,' said Rowlands. 'At the St Gertrude's College dinner on Saturday.'

'Indeed?' There was a pause, as the other scrutinised his companion. 'Now you mention it, your face *is* familiar. Although, to tell you the truth, I had a lot on my mind on Saturday night…'

'I think we all did,' said Rowlands. 'Yes, I had my speech to plan,' went on Bristow, as if the other had not spoken. 'Fortunately, I was able to work on it all day Sunday.'

'Your cold got better then?' said Rowlands, recalling his last encounter with the physicist, in the Senior Common Room. The other seemed momentarily taken aback. 'What? Oh, that turned out to be nothing… Anyway, I worked on it, as I said, on Sunday and Monday, so that I was pretty much word-perfect when it came to deliver my paper yesterday evening. It was at the Royal Society,' he explained, although Rowlands hadn't asked. Professor Bristow chuckled—a harsh, dry sound, that bore little relation to full-throated laughter. 'I believe it went down very well,' he said. 'Yes, very well. Indeed, several of my colleagues expressed the view that it could lead on to greater things. Even…' He lowered his voice, as if speaking of mysteries beyond the ken of mere mortals. 'The Nobel.'

Rowlands composed his features into an expression of polite interest. 'Congratulations,' seemed excessive, given that the honour in question had not actually been awarded. 'What was your paper about?' he said, judging that this would give the man the opportunity he'd been angling for. But the professor of Physics seemed suddenly to be overcome by a fit of diffidence. 'Oh… It's a complicated subject,' he said vaguely. 'Quantum theory, you know. Wave mechanics. I don't suppose that means very much to you?'

Rowlands smiled. 'Not a great deal, no. But I'm always keen to learn something new.'

Bristow hesitated, then appeared to relent of his initial reticence. 'Well, if you really want to know, I'm working on the disintegration of nuclei by artificially accelerated protons,' he said. 'That is… we at the Cavendish are working on this.' Again, the dry little laugh. 'I can't claim *all* the credit…'

'It sounds fascinating,' said Rowlands, meaning it. 'But, as you say, a complicated subject for the layman.'

'Indeed.'

Perhaps it was the self-satisfaction with which this word was pronounced that prompted Rowlands's next question: 'Was that what Diana Havelock was working on, too? She was a physicist, wasn't she?'

'Eh?' was the startled reply. 'What's that? Oh, you mean the girl…' Professor Bristow considered a moment. 'I believe she *was* engaged in some kind of work at the laboratory, yes. Checking results and the like. In my field,' said the physics don with a laugh, 'there is, I fear, a great deal of routine work.'

'She was studying for her PhD, wasn't she?' observed Rowlands. 'Wouldn't that have involved her in more than routine work?'

'Possibly,' was the indifferent reply. 'Although I rather doubt it. These young women like to make themselves sound important. But I can assure you, Mr… er… that the work of any *real* importance is done by the senior members of the research team.' Such as himself, he didn't need to add. 'Of course,' said Rowlands humbly. 'I quite see that. But I'm interested, nonetheless, in what Miss Havelock was working on…'

'I really cannot see what possible interest…' began the other, when the guard appeared from the corridor. 'Tickets, please.'

'Oh, really!' exclaimed the elderly don irritably. 'I see no reason for this constant checking and re-checking of tickets. Surely the fact that I have already passed through the barrier at the station should be enough?'

'I'm afraid it's the rules, sir,' said the guard, to which Bristow's response was a contemptuous sniff. '"Rules",' he said. 'Rules, rules, rules. I'm afraid *that* is what is wrong with this country. Too many rules.'

'Surely,' said Rowlands. 'Society couldn't exist without them? And isn't science governed by rules—or laws, or whatever you call them?'

'Ah, but the laws of science are different, being based upon pure rationality, not craven superstition,' was the reply. After which, conversation lapsed. Professor Bristow took some papers from his briefcase and leafed though them, while Rowlands, his gaze ostensibly fixed on his newspaper, reflected on what had just passed—and in particular the physics don's remarks about Diana Havelock. That Bristow was a self-important old buffer was not in doubt; what was puzzling was why he'd made such a point of belittling her contribution to the research both were engaged upon. Suddenly, what Beryl Phillips had said about the undervaluing of women's achievements didn't seem so extreme.

The train passed through station after station: Broxbourne, Harlow, Bishop's Stortford... 'Would you close the window?' said the voice from the seat opposite. 'I find the dust intolerable.'

'Certainly.' Rowlands got up to do as he was asked, even though he had been enjoying the mild air, and the smell of the fields wafting in through the open window, as the train rattled along. With the window closed it was suddenly quiet. 'If you want to know what the girl was up to, why not ask Harding?' said Bristow suddenly. '*He* worked with her, after all.'

'Thank you. I'll do that.' Then Rowlands recalled the conversation in the Senior Common Room three days before, and Professor Harding's indignant reaction to the same remark from his colleague. Had there been something else implied, he wondered—the suggestion of an improper relationship between Harding and the girl—that had brought forth such a reaction?

There was probably nothing in it, but even so, it had to be considered...

Audley End, Whittlesford. As the train pulled into Cambridge Station, Professor Bristow, who had fallen silent after his last remark, again grew animated. 'If you'd oblige me by summoning a porter to help me with my suitcase, Mr... er... I'd be most grateful,' he said. But Rowlands was already getting to his feet. 'I can do better than that.' He swung the suitcase down from the rack and, having opened the door of the compartment, set it down on the platform. 'It's most kind of you to go to so much trouble, Mr... er...'

'Rowlands. It's no trouble at all.' He waited until the older man had alighted from the carriage, then picking up the suitcase, accompanied him to the ticket barrier. Outside the station building sat a line of taxicabs, with their engines running. 'Most kind, most kind,' murmured Bristow, as Rowlands saw him into one of these, then handed in the suitcase. 'St Jude's College,' said the don to the taxi-driver; then, as if the thought had just occurred to him, 'Can I give you a lift somewhere, Mr... er... Rowlands?'

Knowing it was a longish walk into town, Rowlands was about to accept the offer, when he was hailed by a familiar voice: '*There* you are, Frederick!' (He and Miss Rickards were now on first-name terms.) 'I've got a cab waiting. Oh, hello, Professor Bristow! I didn't see you there...'

'Dear lady,' was the reply. 'Delightful to see you, as ever. Well, if you're sure I can't give you a lift,' he said to Rowlands, 'I'll wish you good day.' With that the taxi took off, and with it the professor. 'Well, come along,' said Maud Rickards. 'We've time for a spot of lunch before things start.

'The inquest was held in a large, oak-panelled room in the Guildhall—a modern building, still only partly completed, in the Market Square. Around twenty or thirty people, by Rowlands's calculation, were assembled here—of whom just under half were onlookers, including members of the Press; the rest consisting of witnesses, police officers, and the Coroner's staff. First to be called were Inspector Brown and his sergeant.

Both gave a concise and workmanlike account of what they had found at the scene.

Rowlands, aware that Diana Havelock's parents were almost certainly present, was glad of the studied impersonality of the language both men used when describing the tragedy, and the respectful tone they employed when speaking of the deceased. People liked to make fun of the solemn formality of police procedure, but it was there for a reason, he thought. He wasn't looking forward to giving his own evidence—especially if, as seemed all too likely, he was questioned about the presence of drugs in Miss Havelock's room. With the Mistress's warning to say no more than was strictly necessary about the events of that sad evening, he was dreading the inevitable inquisition.

But, as it turned out, this eventuality never arose. Because the next to be called was the doctor who had examined the deceased. He gave his name—in response to the Coroner's question—as Ambrose Faulks. An elderly gentleman, Rowlands guessed from his voice—which, though precise in its pronunciation of medical terms, had a quavering note which intimated that its owner might be close to retirement. When asked for his opinion as to the cause of Miss Havelock's death, he paused for a moment, as if to ensure that he had the attention of the whole courtroom, then said: 'Heart failure.'

'Heart failure,' repeated the Coroner—perhaps for the benefit of his clerk, the tapping of whose typewriter was the loudest sound in the chamber. 'Had the deceased, to the best of your knowledge, Dr Faulks, a history of heart disease?'

Again, the old man took his time, shuffling through his notes. 'I believe she had scarlet fever as a child,' he replied at last. 'One of the consequences of which can be a weakening of the valves of the heart.'

'Thank you, doctor. That is admirably concise.' The Coroner cleared his throat. 'And was there anything else, in your opinion, which might have contributed towards the young lady's death from heart failure—apart from her childhood illness?'

Once more, Doctor Faulks seemed to be choosing his words carefully. 'There was a quantity of alkaloid of opium found in the body.'

'That is a medical term for the drug morphine, is it not?'

'It is.'

'And in your opinion, doctor, was the presence of this drug a contributory factor?'

'It's difficult to say,' said Doctor Faulks, with the guardedness so often employed by the medical practitioner. 'For a patient with a history of heart disease, it might well have proved a factor.'

'Thank you. I think we can draw our own conclusions from that. Have you anything you would like to add, before I call the next witness?'

The answer was in the negative. Was it Rowlands's imagination, or did a murmur of relief pass over the courtroom? He heard his own name called. Beside him, Miss Rickards made as if to get up, too—presumably so that she could guide him to the witness-box. He prevented her with a smile and a shake of the head. 'You are Frederick Charles Rowlands?' He said that he was. 'Mr Rowlands, will you tell the court as much as you can remember of the events of last Saturday night—the fifteenth of June?'

Once more, Rowlands recounted what had taken place: his walk in the grounds of the college, hearing the alarm given by one of the undergraduates—'That would have been Miss Fairclough, would it not?' interrupted the Coroner, with which Rowlands concurred—and then accompanying Miss Fairclough to Miss Havelock's room. As he described what he had found there, and his attempts to revive the dead girl, there was absolute silence in the courtroom. 'And so,' said the Coroner, when Rowlands had come to the end of this, 'realising that your efforts were in vain, you proceeded to notify the authorities?'

'Yes.'

'Thank you, Mr Rowlands. You may stand down.'

'Well done!' whispered Maud Rickards, as Rowlands resumed his seat beside her. He had to admit that the whole thing had indeed been 'well done'. For if he had not been asked any awkward questions, which might have cast doubt on the doctor's diagnosis, none of the witnesses who followed were afforded that opportunity, either. Honoria Fairclough, speaking in a voice so low it was an effort to hear her, said that she had called at Diana's room, and on receiving no reply, had gone in and found her friend, apparently unconscious. Unable to rouse her, she had called for help. 'You acted very sensibly,' the Coroner told her. The College Nurse, Miss Blenkinsop, stated that she had been called to Room E14 at around a quarter past ten, and had found Diana Havelock dead. She had done her best, she said, 'to make the poor lass comfortable' before the police had arrived.

The last witness to be called was Miss Glossop. As Miss Havelock's tutor, she was asked to give an account of the young woman's academic achievements, which she did in glowing terms. 'She was an ornament to St Gertrude's College,' she said, the calmness with which she spoke not concealing her emotion. 'We have lost a remarkable talent—both in the realm of science, which was Diana's chosen field, and of the arts…' Her own last conversation with Miss Havelock, on the afternoon preceding her death, had concerned the speech—an extract from *Macbeth*—the gifted young actress was to give as part of the college's end of term festivities. 'She said to me that she was very torn between the two worlds,' said the English don. 'Science offered great rewards, but one was necessarily obliged to share these successes with others, whereas the Arts—she was referring to the theatre, I believe—allowed the individual to shine.'

The Coroner thanked Miss Glossop for her testimony, which, he said was a judicious reminder of the loss to academe of so brilliant a scholar. It was his sad duty to pronounce a verdict on her untimely death, which from the evidence offered by Dr Faulks, he must conclude was from Natural Causes. Again—and this time Rowlands didn't imagine it—there came an audible sigh of relief from those assembled. 'Tell me who else is here,' he said to Miss Rickards, as the court rose. 'Well… The Mistress is here, of course—talking to Mr and Mrs Havelock, so we won't intrude. She'll be pleased with the Coroner's verdict…' Undoubtedly, thought Rowlands. 'And Professor Harding. Good of him to come. Of course, Diana was his star pupil… Ah, hello, Professor Giles! A sad day—but perhaps the best outcome under the circumstances…'

'Indeed,' said Giles. 'Good afternoon, Rowlands. You said your piece very well, I thought.'

'Thanks.'

'I don't suppose you'd care to come back to my rooms for a spot of tea? You, too, Bursar, if you'd like…'

'Thank you, Professor Giles, but I really must get back to College. End of term's always a busy time for me.' Maud Rickards turned to Rowlands. 'Goodbye, Frederick. Give my love to Edith, won't you?'

Professor Giles's rooms in St Jude's College, Old Court, had the smell of old books, pipe tobacco, and well-worn leather armchairs. Two of these had been placed in front of the fireplace, and on a low table in front of them—to judge by the enticing smell—was a plate of toasted muffins. 'Yes, I can't complain,' said the academic, when Rowlands remarked on the pleasantness of these arrangements. 'My bedder, Mrs Clark, looks after me very well… Ah, thank you, Emily.' That good lady, having just set down the tea-tray, made herself scarce. 'After Alice—my wife—died, I more or less moved into College. I've a little place out in the Fens, when I want to escape the world, but for the most part, the life of an academic bachelor suits me.'

Rowlands smiled, settling himself into one of the armchairs. 'A bit of a change from the Army, isn't it?'

'Not as much as you might imagine,' was the reply. 'One finds the same petty rivalries and clashes of temperament in university life as one does everywhere. At least in the army, one can take it out in physical activity. Here, it's all backbiting and skullduggery. *Much* more vicious…'

'You make it sound like a dangerous world,' said Rowlands, with a laugh. 'Oh, it is! When academic reputations are at stake, you know… I say, would you like a dash of whisky in your tea? I feel you've earned it.'

'Thank you.' Giles duly obliged, pouring a generous measure of Scotch into both cups. 'Well,' he said. 'Here's how.'

'Here's how.' Rowlands took a swig of his tea. Its warmth, augmented no doubt by the whisky, was comforting. Both men sat in silence for a few moments. 'A beastly business,' said the English don, at last. 'I'm glad it's over.'

'Yes.'

'The police obviously felt there wasn't enough evidence to investigate the matter of the drugs further—which in my view was the right decision… I say, will you have one of these muffins? They look rather good…'

'No, thanks.' Rowlands took another sip of his tea. 'Whatever that girl did or didn't get up to before her death… well, it doesn't concern us now,' Giles went on, taking a bite of his muffin. 'Terrible for her parents, of course, but at least they haven't had to deal with a worse verdict.'

With which Rowlands could only agree. 'I gather Professor Harding was at the inquest?' he said. Something was bothering him about the whole affair, but he couldn't for the life of him say what it was. 'Yes,' said the other. 'She was his student, you know. I believe he was the one who proposed her for the College Studentship, so that she could study for her doctorate. Much good it did her, poor child.'

'Mm.' Rowland set down his cup, his mood abstracted. If Harding had been the one who'd proposed Diana Havelock for the studentship, then why had he claimed he hardly knew her? Perhaps, he thought, it was no more than a necessary caution on the part of a married man, surrounded as he was by admiring young women… 'Do smoke if you like,' said Giles, already engaged in filling his pipe. 'Thanks, I will.' Rowlands extracted a cigarette from his pack of Churchman's and lit it, striking the match so that its flame was exactly level with the tip of the cigarette. A blind man's trick, and one he had perfected over the years.

He and his former training officer chatted for a while, recalling old times and long-dead comrades. Then Rowlands said he must go. It had been agreeable, after the strain of the inquest, to relax in that atmosphere of ancient peace, with only the striking of the college clock in the court outside, to disturb the quiet. With most of the undergraduates already gone down for the Long Vacation, Cambridge was assuming its soporific, small-town guise. So it would remain until the Autumn, when a new year would begin, and a fresh intake of students would arrive, to bring the place to life with their noise and frolics. Rowlands wouldn't have said so to Giles, but he'd be glad to see the last of it. The events of the past few days had coloured his view of the place—and not for the better.

The two men shook hands. 'It was good to see you,' said Giles. 'Don't leave it so long until the next time, will you?' Rowlands said that he would not. 'And give my best to young Fraser, when you see him...' This was Sir Ian Fraser, Head of St Dunstan's, and a blind war veteran with a long and distinguished career of public service. Yet to Austin Giles he would always be the young officer he had once instructed in the finer points of the Lewis gun. 'I'll do that, sir,' said Rowlands, falling as easily into old ways. Refusing the older man's offer of seeing him as far as the college gates, he descended the staircase that led from the professor's rooms to Old Court, and took the path to the right that led to the outer courtyard—its smooth flagstones between borders of cobblestones might have been designed for a blind man to follow, he thought.

As he did so, he became aware that someone was following *him*. Was he imagining things? He stopped, making a show of checking his watch, and the footsteps he'd heard behind him also came to a stop. Rowlands set off again, and at once the mysterious other did, too. Reaching the covered archway that led from Old Court to First Court, he turned to confront his pursuer. 'If there's something you'd like to say to me, then say it,' he said pleasantly. 'I'd like to know who you are first, though. I don't much like being crept up on.'

'I... I wasn't creeping,' said a voice Rowlands knew. 'At least... I didn't mean to. My staircase is just over there, and I saw you coming out of old Giles's rooms, so I thought...'

'Never mind all that, Mr Sedgwick. Tell me what it is you've got on your mind. In fact, you can tell me as we're going along. I've a train to catch, but I fancy a bit of a walk first.' Because suddenly Rowlands felt an urgent need to shake off the constraints of the day, after sitting for hours in that stuffy courtroom. Nor had his civilised but sedentary hour with Giles done much to relieve the feeling, oppressive to a man of his temperament, of having been cooped-up. The route to the station, he knew, was pretty much a straight line from Sidney Street to the Hill's Road. At this time of day, with most of the students gone, and the shops about to close, he'd be able to step out freely.

'All right.' Julian Sedgwick fell into step with him, as the two of them passed through the college's monumental gates and crossed over into All Saints' Passage. But it took the undergraduate another minute or two to come to the point. They had passed the junction with Jesus Lane, and the gate of Sidney Sussex, before he said: 'You were at the inquest...'—rather giving the lie to his story of having spotted the older man just a moment before, thought the latter. 'I was,' he said. 'I take it you were, too?'

'Yes. That is... I slipped in at the end, to hear the verdict.'

'Much the best one there could have been,' said Rowlands blandly, aware that he was parroting Professor Giles. 'I suppose so. For *her*,' said the young man, quickening his pace to keep up with Rowlands's long-legged stride. 'But...' He fell silent again. Sober, he was much more taciturn than his drunken antics on the night of the St Gertrude's dance would have led one to believe, thought Rowlands. 'What is it you're trying to say?' He slowed his pace, to give the boy time. 'It's just that... She wasn't happy,' Sedgwick said in a rush. 'There was something on her mind... I don't know what it was—she wouldn't tell me. But I can guess,' he added bitterly.

'Do you mean,' said Rowlands, 'that Miss Havelock had reason to do herself harm?'

'I don't know,' said the young man. 'I only know that something was troubling her... Or some*one*,' he added darkly. 'A man, do you mean?'

'Yes,' said Sedgwick in a low voice. 'I don't know who it was, but I'm sure she was seeing somebody... She'd become secretive.' He fell silent for a moment. 'There was one day last week when I rang her up. There was a new picture on at the cinema... *The Thirty-Nine Steps*,' he added, inconsequentially. 'I thought she might like to go, but she said she was busy... Then I'd heard that she'd been seen leaving St Jude's that same evening...'

'Was that the reason for your quarrel with Miss Havelock in

the Eagle last Saturday?'

'How do you know about that?'

'Just answer the question.'

'Yes, if you want to know,' said the young man miserably. 'I'd asked her—Diana—to meet me in the pub after she'd finished at the lab. She had to go there—to Free School Lane—to collect something... some papers she was working on. She was awfully late—I'd almost given her up, when she arrived. I... I'm afraid I rather jumped to conclusions...'

'You assumed she'd been with this man?'

'She didn't deny it. She told me not to meddle in things I didn't understand. I'm afraid I rather lost my temper...'

That must have been where I came in, thought Rowlands.

'She... she got angry and stormed off. We... we were supposed to meet at the dance that night but... but she never turned up. I thought she was trying to pay me out for the things I'd said earlier. I let myself get rather tight... Stupid, really.'

'We all do stupid things,' said Rowlands gently.

'I'll never forgive myself for letting her down,' said Julian Sedgwick. 'We were such good friends, at one time...' He made it sound as if he were looking back on a lifetime's experience, instead of an acquaintance that could have lasted no more than a few months, at most. But then Rowlands reminded himself how sharp the pangs of first love could be. 'When did you meet her?' he asked. 'Beginning of Michaelmas Term. She's... she *was*... a year older than me. I'd never met anyone like her,' said the young man forlornly. 'So... brilliant. And beautiful.'

'You were studying the same subject, I take it?'

'I'm a chemist. Diana was a physicist. But we used to meet at the lab.'

'The Cavendish, you mean?'

'That's right. I really thought she liked me,' said the youth. 'For a while I hoped...' He broke off. 'Oh, what's the use? It's all such a beastly mess...' They were passing the gates of one of the other colleges—Christ's, wasn't it? A group of dons emerging at that moment, in animated discussion of the merits or otherwise of the college port, made conversation momentarily awkward. 'You mustn't be too hard on yourself,' said Rowlands when they had got ahead of this jovial crowd. 'I don't think anything you said or did could have made a difference.' He meant to the fate that had overtaken Diana Havelock; but Sedgwick evidently gave his words another meaning. 'It would have made a difference to *me*,' he said, his voice low and bitter. 'I've got to live with the fact that I let her down, when she needed me...'

After this outburst, he said nothing more for a while, but tramped along beside Rowlands, as if he had little sense of where he was heading, and cared even less. 'It's all right, Mr Sedgwick—you don't have to accompany me all the way,' said Rowlands, after they had walked a little further. 'I'm quite capable of getting to the station by myself.'

'I'd like to go with you,' said the lad, with a gruffness that touched Rowlands's heart. 'I'm out of sorts. A walk'll do me good.'

'In that case, I'd be glad of your company.'

They passed Emmanuel College. Rowlands, whose memory for such things was a good one, recalled being struck by its imposing, neo-classical façade on his previous visit to the city. Such a beautiful place, he thought. But one could be unhappy just as easily in a place like this, as in any other, he supposed. He hesitated a moment before saying what he said next: 'Things will get better, you know. It may not seem so at present, but...'

'I just don't know if I can stick it,' muttered Julian Sedgwick.

'What—university, you mean?'

'University, chemistry, work—whatever you want to call it. It all seems so... well, *futile*.'

'I'm sure it's not that. But...' A thought struck Rowlands. 'Shouldn't you be going down, or going home—or whatever you call it? I thought term was over for the year?'

'It's the Long Vac,' said Sedgwick. 'I'm a second year—well, third year now. I'm supposed to be staying up to do some research... At least I *was*,' he added gloomily. 'Don't you have family you can go to?' said Rowlands. If anyone was in need of the consolations of home, it was this poor fellow, he thought. 'My people are in India,' was the reply. 'I've a great-uncle in London, but he isn't expecting to see me for a few weeks yet...'

At the station they parted, with more warmth on both sides

that might have been anticipated on meeting. 'You've been awfully decent, hearing me out like this,' said the young man, wringing Rowlands's hand. 'It's done me good to talk about her—about Diana, I mean.'

'I'm glad.'

'It isn't true, you know, about the drugs,' added Sedgwick, as Rowlands was about to walk away. 'Diana would never have touched the stuff. Someone must have planted it in her room…'

'Have you any idea who it might have been?' said Rowlands.

'No. But if I ever find out,' said the other quietly. 'I'll make him wish he'd never been born.'

9

The next few weeks were busy ones for Rowlands. He and his staff were fully occupied with making arrangements for St Dunstan's contribution to the Silver Jubilee celebrations which were at present exercising the nation. Every town and village had its street party or its garden fête in honour of Their Majesties King George V and Queen Mary's twenty-five-year reign; nor would St Dunstan's be outdone. Their celebration was to be held at the Royal Albert Hall. Lunch was to be provided for over five hundred St Dunstaners and their spouses, seated at tables arranged in huge circles around the tiers of the great arena. Coping with the increased paperwork this required—the sending-out of and responding to invitations—proved too much for even the industrious Miss Betts, and Rowlands was forced to engage a Temporary to assist her.

'I'm starting to wonder if we wouldn't have been better off limiting our share of the festivities to the odd Sale of Work,' joked the Major. 'All this is getting a bit out of hand, eh, Rowlands?' The latter smiled, knowing that in reality the Major was enjoying every minute of his latest 'campaign' in the service of the war-blinded. Only last year, Fraser had been instrumental in getting the Blind Voters' Bill passed. This allowed the blind person to be accompanied into the polling booth by a trusted friend or spouse, who would mark his voting slip for him, thus obviating the need for the voter to disclose his voting choices to outsiders.

Just now, as he and Rowlands shared a brief moment of respite from work in Fraser's rooms (the latter had wanted Rowlands's opinion on the speech he was to make at the Jubilee celebrations), the Major was enthusing about his current project—the provision of wireless sets, free of license, to blind servicemen and their families. 'It stands to reason, don't you see?' the Major was saying, pacing up and down the long, airy room which doubled as his sitting-room and study. 'The wireless is a vital resource for us. Its news bulletins are our newspapers, its talks our lectures… its plays are our… well, plays. And then there's the music…'

'Ah, yes, the music,' agreed Rowlands. 'We wouldn't want to be without *that*.'

'Nor should we be—and nor should we have to pay for it!' cried the Major, with the enthusiasm that reminded Rowlands that his distinguished colleague was still a young man at heart. 'Well, I think it would be a great thing if you could persuade the government to waive the license fee,' he said. 'Oh I will, Rowlands,' was the reply. 'You can be sure of that. Well, if you think the speech'll do,' he went on, reverting to the earlier topic of their conversation. 'I'll ask Doris to get some Braille copies typed. People won't care what *I* have to say, in any case. They'll all be waiting to hear from our honoured guest.' This was the Prince of Wales, newly-appointed as St Dunstan's Patron, following the death of Queen Alexandra. He was a popular figure, with an easy manner, and a talent for public speaking. He would bring a touch of glamour to the proceedings, Rowlands thought. Edith was already fretting about what she was going to wear… 'Would a full-length frock be absurdly over-dressed, do you think? It *is* a royal occasion…'

With all this, as well as his usual work, to engage him, Rowlands had little time to reflect on the troubling events in which he had been caught up at the end of the university term. When the excitement of the Silver Jubilee celebrations was over, there would be the Rowlandses' annual holiday to look forward to. For the past five years, this had involved a visit to Rowlands's sister and her husband—an old friend and former comrade of Rowlands's—who ran a hotel in Cornwall. Edith and the girls would go for a full three weeks, with Rowlands joining them for the last ten days of August. He could hardly wait. After the hectic few weeks he'd had, ten days by the sea, with nothing much to do, would be just the ticket.

The day of his departure arrived at last. Having telephoned

Edith to say which train he'd be catching, he locked up the house and set off. He was encumbered only with a light suitcase—most of his summer clothes had gone in the trunk with the rest of the family's luggage—and so was able to stride along at a good pace, in plenty of time to catch the ten past nine to Waterloo. After that, a short journey on the Underground would take him to Paddington Station, and a seat on the ten forty-five to Truro. Before leaving the house, he'd picked up the bundle of letters and postcards (most of which would be for Edith) which had been accumulating on the hall table. It crossed his mind to wait for the post, which usually arrived about this time, but he decided against it. Perhaps he'd catch the postman on the way...

As he walked along Grove Avenue in the sunshine, whistling softly under his breath, he wondered if he'd really needed to bring his mackintosh. But you never knew with Cornwall—the weather could change just like *that*... 'Mr Rowlands! Such a lovely morning!' His heart sank. ''Morning, Mrs Preedy.' His neighbour from two doors down was a pleasant, if talkative, woman of middle years. 'She's a dreadful gossip,' was Edith's opinion, less charitable than his own. He guessed the poor woman—a widow—was probably lonely. 'I said to myself when I saw you coming along,' said Marian Preedy, 'now *there's* a gentleman who looks as if he's off to enjoy himself...'

'Yes. The fact is, Mrs Preedy...'

'Oh, *do* call me Marian! We've known one another long enough, surely? It must be all of five years...'

'I believe it is. Now, if you'll excuse me...'

'Going anywhere nice?' It was the wistful note he heard, not the inquisitiveness, although that was there, too. 'Cornwall. My sister's place,' he added to make it seem less of an indulgence and more like familial duty. But Mrs Preedy wasn't fooled. 'How lovely!' she sighed. 'I used to holiday in Cornwall when I was a girl. St Ives, you know...'

'Very nice,' said Rowlands. 'And now...'

'I expect your wife and the dear girls are enjoying themselves already?' said Marian Preedy, with the sharpness that always took Rowlands by surprise. 'She has to know *everything*,' said Edith. 'Yes,' he said. 'I...'

'Oh, there's the postman!' interrupted this maddening woman. 'Just going up your front path. I'm expecting a parcel, so I must try and catch him. Give my regards to all in sunny Cornwall, won't you?' Rowlands—now in danger of missing the London train—had no choice but to rush off as quickly as he could, without intercepting the postman in his turn. Looking back on it afterwards, he wasn't sure how much difference it would have made had he done so—but that it *would* have made a difference, he was in no doubt.

It wasn't until some days later that Rowlands had cause to think about Diana Havelock again. The intervening time had been filled with the agreeable activities that seaside holidays offer: swimming, sailing (Jack Ashenhurst kept a small boat, for the use of his guests) and walking, being the more energetic of these. Nor were these pastimes usually solitary—although Rowlands liked to get out for an early morning swim before the rest of the household was up, and although he wouldn't have risked some of the cliff-top walks unaccompanied, it was always pleasant to stroll on the beach, with or without company. But with seven children, ranging in age from eight to fifteen, to keep amused, he found himself conscripted into their activities, too—organising swimming races, or keeping score for a game of beach cricket.

Since Jack and Dorothy, ably assisted by Jack's sister, Cecily, had the running of the hotel to think of, Rowlands was only too glad to shoulder some of the responsibility of looking after four lively boys, as well as his own three girls. Although the older ones were quite capable of looking after themselves, he thought ruefully, having just been told by his eldest daughter that she was off to play tennis with the Simkins twins, and that the three of them were later going to join her cousins in building a fire on the beach to cook sausages. 'She's growing up,' remarked Rowlands's sister, who had been a witness to this exchange. They were sitting on the hotel terrace, enjoying the last of the day's sunshine, while from below came the sound of waves crashing softly against the rocks at the cliff's foot. 'Yes,' he said, lighting a cigarette. Somehow it always tasted better in the open air. 'Getting pretty, too, with those long legs,' added Dorothy, when her niece was no longer in earshot. 'Although Anne'll be the beauty.'

'I think all my girls are beautiful,' said Rowlands, with a smile. 'The grown-up ones included.'

'That's nice,' said Dorothy. 'Although if you could see me now—getting fat and middle-aged—you might revise that view.'

'I very much doubt it.' It struck him as he spoke that she was the only one of his family whose face he had ever seen. She'd been a lovely creature at seventeen, with that mane of dark hair and those green eyes. He didn't imagine she'd have changed much at thirty-five. What *had* changed since her marriage to Jack Ashenhurst was Dorothy's attitude to life, thought her brother. Perhaps living with so mild-tempered a man had softened her combative nature. She was certainly less prone to flying off the handle than before; nor did she seems as fond of what Edith (never her sister-in-law's greatest fan) called her 'soapbox'.

Not that Dorothy's passion for social justice had been entirely quashed. She was still as likely to sound off about the iniquities of rural poverty in the West Country as she had been, in days gone by, to fulminate against the treatment of women factory workers, or to demand the right of universal suffrage, in the days before this was granted. Her attitude towards her brother, whom she had often taken to task for the alleged conservatism of his political views, was gentler, too. 'You're looking better,' she told him now, having studied him for a moment or two. 'Less strained. You looked awfully washed-out when you first arrived. I suppose you've been working too hard?'

'I don't know about that,' said Rowlands. Things have been pretty much the same as always.'

His sister gave a snort. 'Oh, you! You're as bad as Jack…'

'Did I hear my name?' said her husband, arriving at that moment, his halting step—the legacy of a bad fall two years before—heralding his arrival before he spoke. 'What is it I've done this time?'

'It isn't what you've done,' was the reply. 'It's that you'll never admit there's anything wrong, you men…'

'Well, there isn't,' said Ashenhurst. 'Or if there is, it's seldom worth making a fuss about, eh, Fred? Now, who wants a beer?' Both said that they would, and Ashenhurst went back into the hotel to fetch the drinks, returning, after a couple of minutes, with some bottles of a local brew. Accompanying him were Edith and Cecily, the latter carrying a tray with glasses and a jug of iced tea, for those who preferred this to beer. 'Dinner's at seven,' she said, seating herself with a grateful sigh in one of the rattan chairs with which the terrace was provided. 'Cold poached salmon—one of Mrs Jago's specialities. And aren't *I* glad not to be cooking tonight,' she added. 'It's too much in this weather. One hardly feels like eating at all.'

'I don't think Joanie and Vicky would agree with you about that,' said Dorothy, referring to her youngest niece and younger son, who were equally fond of their food. 'Where *are* the children?' said Edith, accepting a glass of iced tea from Mrs Nicholls. 'I don't think I've seen any of them all day...'

'Oh, they're somewhere about,' was her sister-in-law's reply. 'The older ones are having a bonfire party. I said the little ones should be back before dark—but that's hours away yet.'

'Is Anne with them—the older ones, I mean?' said Rowlands, aware of his middle daughter's tendency to wander off on her own. Usually she'd be found, after a lengthy search, curled up with a book somewhere. He knew that to be the case, and yet he was unable to suppress a mild feeling of anxiety where she was concerned, having once come very close to losing her forever. 'I saw her going down to the tennis courts with Margaret and the Simkins boys,' said Cecily, perhaps picking up something of Rowlands's mood. 'Which reminds me, I must ask John and Daphne whether they'll be joining us for dinner tonight. They did say something about going down to the Smuggler's Arms... And before I forget, *two* new lots of people will be arriving next week. The Favershams and the Bewlays. I thought we could put them both in the Old Wing...'

'Just as you think best,' said Ashenhurst.

'Perhaps I will have a beer after all,' said his sister, with a groan. 'I feel as though I need it. Why did we ever decide that having paying guests was a good idea, I wonder?' And yet

Rowlands was left in no doubt that Cecily Nicholls was quite contented with her life. A nice woman, he thought; what a pity she'd never remarried.

A companionable silence fell. From the tennis courts behind the hotel came the twang of tennis balls against racquets. Cries of 'Love-fifteen!' and 'Oh *beastly* hard luck!' pierced the warm summer's air. Rowlands drank his beer and shifted his chair a little more into the sun. It was pleasant to let his thoughts drift… to think of nothing… 'I was just saying to Fred how much better he looks,' said Dorothy. 'He was as white as a sheet when he got off that train.'

'Well, he's had a lot on his plate,' said Edith, a shade defensively. 'Organising the Silver Jubilee celebrations, for a start…'

'I *am* here,' put in Rowlands mildly. 'I think you two might do well to remember that.'

'Ah yes, the Jubilee celebrations,' said his sister, paying no attention to this remark. 'Yet another ridiculous waste of time and money, in honour of our glorious monarchy. I suppose *he* was there?' she added, knowing the answer full well. 'That idle playboy…'

'If you're referring to the Prince of Wales—yes, he was,' said Rowlands. 'Gave a decent speech, too.'

'Dottie would like us all to live in Russia,' said Ashenhurst affectionately. 'Where there are no kings or princes…'

'Yes, because they've killed them all,' said Edith with some acerbity. 'Let's not talk of killing on such a lovely evening,' said Ashenhurst. 'Who's for another beer?' But Edith, in her way as stubborn as her sister-in-law, wasn't to be diverted: 'You're right, Jack. Fred's had quite enough of that sort of thing to deal with lately, haven't you, dear?'

'That sounds exciting,' said Ashenhurst. 'What is this? Don't say you've been getting yourself mixed up in another of your murder mysteries, old man?'

'Nothing like that,' said Rowlands, heartily wishing that his wife hadn't felt the need to bring up the subject. 'I had to attend an inquest the other day, that's all…' As briefly as he could, he summarised the sad facts of Diana Havelock's death—keeping to himself what Julian Sedgwick had said about there being another man in the case. 'So you see,' he concluded, 'there's nothing mysterious about it. Just the pointless waste of a young life.'

'Poor girl,' said Cecily Nicholls softly. 'To lose everything, for one mistake...' She herself—married and widowed at twenty—knew all too well what losing everything meant, Rowlands thought. She got up and stood for a moment, looking out at the view, he supposed. When she spoke again, her tone was determinedly cheerful. 'I'll go and see about supper,' she said.

The last day of the holiday arrived, with the inexorability of all dread dates. School would begin in just over a week, but there was a great deal of preparation to be done before that, with uniforms needing to be let out as necessary, and projects set aside—Anne's promise to learn two new French verbs a day, Joan's cataloguing of her seashell collection—now hastily resumed. Margaret, with exams coming up later that year, should have been the most exercised by this looming deadline—but she, to her father's surprise, seemed to have lost interest in schoolwork. Revising had suddenly become 'an awful bore'. Overnight, it seemed, his studious daughter had become a fiend for tennis. When Rowlands expressed his bafflement, his wife had laughed. 'It isn't tennis which is the attraction, so much as her tennis partner,' she opined—meaning sixteen year-old Jonathan Simkins, Rowlands supposed. A nice enough lad, but surely... 'You've forgotten what it was like at their age,' said Edith, dropping a kiss on his cheek.

The weather having turned out glorious—as it never failed to be at the end of the holidays—a walk along the cliffs, with a picnic to follow, was proposed. The plan was to go from Coverack to Lizard Point, a distance of about ten miles, stopping for lunch and a swim, and then returning in time for an early supper. Dorothy, who had errands to run in Helston, and Mrs Nicholls, who was busy supervising the maids in getting the rooms ready for the new intake of guests, were not of the party, which otherwise consisted of the Rowlands family, Ashenhurst and his brood, and the Simkins boys—one of whom—Rowlands now knew—was Margaret's swain. He did his best, not altogether successfully, to banish this thought from his mind.

Having set out soon after breakfast, the little party was soon well on its way, tramping briskly across the sweet-smelling turf, between banks of gorse, with its heady, coconut scent. From far below, came the sound of the sea; from high above, the mournful crying of seagulls. It all felt like heaven to Rowlands, after so many weeks cooped-up in the city, and he drew deep breaths of the salt-tasting air. From up ahead, the voices of his children drifted back to him. Joan, to her cousin, Victor: 'No, that's a lapwing, not a magpie…' Anne, talking to Walter Metzner, who had come from his native Berlin two years before: 'I wish I were learning German. French is so beastly…' Margaret, to a Simkins twin (Rowlands supposed it must be Jonathan): 'Well, I'll have to ask Mummy, but I don't see why I shouldn't…' Shouldn't what? Rowlands wondered; then decided to let it go. He fell back a little, to where Ashenhurst was walking with Danny, his adopted son. 'I didn't say you couldn't take the boat out,' he was saying, 'I only don't want you to take her out alone.'

'But…'

'No "buts",' said Ashenhurst. 'The current's too strong around the point for you to go out on your own.'

'I've done it lots of times,' insisted the lad. He must be—what? Eleven or twelve? This was certainly a better place for him to grow up than Shoreditch, where he'd been born, thought Rowlands. He wondered fleetingly if the boy remembered anything of that time, or the dreadful events which had deprived him of his mother and grandmother; he very much hoped not. 'Even an experienced sailor has to respect the rules of the sea,' Ashenhurst was saying. 'Now stop pestering me, you little blighter, and let me talk to Mr Rowlands.'

When Danny had run on ahead, Rowlands said, 'He seems to be doing awfully well.' His friend laughed. 'Oh, Danny's a great chap. Getting to be a good sailor, too. Another summer, and I'll let him take over as boatman for the guests. But not yet.'

'We always want to run before we can walk,' said Rowlands.

'True,' laughed the other. 'Although in my case, the operative word is "limp"…'

'How is the leg?'

'Not so bad. I'll have to try a bit harder if I want to finish myself off,' said Ashenhurst wryly, alluding to the fall down icy cliff steps two winters before, when he had broken his leg—and been lucky not to break his neck.

'And Walter?' asked Rowlands, in a low voice. It had been around the time of Jack's accident that the young man (now fourteen) had come to live with the Ashenhursts. 'Walter misses his family,' was the reply. 'Not that he says so—but then he doesn't have to.'

'Have you heard from them lately—Frau Metzner and Clara?' These were Walter's mother and sister, whom Rowlands had last seen during the trip to Berlin which had ended with the German boy's coming to England. 'Not lately,' said Ashenhurst; then: 'We won't discuss it now, if you don't mind, old man.' Which Rowlands took to mean that if there *had* been any news, it had not been good. But then little news that was coming out of Germany was. 'How's young Billy?' he said, changing the subject—but not entirely. His nephew having been the reason he—Rowlands—had gone to Berlin in the first place. His friend laughed. 'Oh, Billy!' he said. 'He's just... Billy. I don't suppose I'll ever know what makes him tick.'

They reached Lizard Point in time for lunch—a plain but sustaining repast of bread and cheese, hard-boiled eggs, apples, and ginger beer—after which a game of beach cricket was organised, Edith having expressly forbidden bathing, until the requisite twenty minutes' digestion time had passed. She was persuaded to act as umpire, however, and so—released from this obligation (which both could perform only imperfectly), the two men wandered off along the white sand beach, pausing to light cigarettes, before strolling on their way.

Ashenhurst, who had spent much of his boyhood in Cornwall, recalled its beauties very precisely, so that listening to him describe the features of the landscape, Rowlands felt he was almost seeing it for himself. The broad, sweeping bay with its azure water. The rocky cliffs rising up from the beach. Lizard Point itself like a great sleeping dragon, its 'head' the most southerly point in the British Isles. As they walked, their talk was of old comrades from their army days; St Dunstan's and its recent financial troubles; and the worsening situation in Europe. Having been through one war, both dreaded the thought of another, and what it would mean for their children. 'But it won't come to that, surely?' said Ashenhurst. 'Hitler's all talk—like most demagogues…'

'I hope you're right.'

After they had been walking for a quarter of an hour or so, Ashenhurst said his leg was starting to hurt, and so they stopped to rest for a few minutes, seating themselves on a rocky outcrop at the foot of the cliffs. 'Used not to be such an old crock,' said Rowlands's friend ruefully. 'Time was, I'd have scrambled up those cliffs as easy as winking…'

'It's walking on sand that does it,' said Rowlands. 'Makes my legs ache too… Hello! Who have we here?' For at that moment, a dog ran up, barking. Rowlands, who was fond of dogs, held out his hand to be sniffed. The animal must have approved of what he found, for he stopped his racket, and allowed himself to be patted. 'Good boy,' said Rowlands.

'Chance! I say, Chance! Where have you got to, you rascal?' A man came panting up. 'I hope he's not bothering you?' he said. From his voice, Rowlands guessed him to be in his fifties; perhaps older. 'Not in the least,' he replied. 'He's been very friendly. What sort is he?'

'A flatcoat retriever. Two years old. He was the only liver-coloured pup in the litter, and so my daughter…' The speaker fell silent. 'Is that the colour that resembles autumn leaves?' enquired Rowlands, conscious of an awkwardness, but uncertain why it had arisen. 'It is.' The man seemed to make an effort to recover his composure. '*She* had auburn hair, you see, and so it was a good match…' Another odd little silence fell. 'Well,' said Rowlands, stroking the dog's sleek head. 'He's a fine fellow—aren't you, Chance? Hope you enjoy the rest of your walk,' he said to Chance's owner, as he and Ashenhurst began to walk away.

'Wait.' Surprised at the man's abrupt tone, Rowlands stopped in his tracks. 'I know you,' said the other. 'You spoke at the inquest. I believe,' he went on, his voice betraying the strain he was under, 'you're the one who found my daughter…'

Before Rowlands could reply, they were joined by someone else. A woman. '*There* you are, Reginald! And you've found Chance. I thought for a minute I'd lost you both...' The voice, which was warm and attractive, was not that of a young woman.

'Olivia...'

But she had already recognised Rowlands. 'You're the one who found Diana,' she said. Her voice was calm and expressionless, and for a moment, Rowlands caught an echo of her daughter's intonation. 'You were with her at the end, You tried to revive her. I must know,' she added softly. 'Was she... did she... suffer?'

'Olivia, dear—*please...*'

Rowlands drew a breath. 'Mrs Havelock, I'm so sorry. Please accept my condolences, both of you. I only knew your daughter for a very brief time, but I could tell that she was a remarkable young woman...'

'You spoke to Diana?' said Reginald Havelock.

'Only for a few minutes. She was kind enough to act as guide to St Gertrude's during the visit my wife and I were making to the College for the end of term festivities.'

'Of course. We wanted to go, but Diana said...' Havelock's voice failed him for a moment. 'She said it was too far to go, just for a garden party. How I wish,' he added, as if to himself, 'we'd insisted on going. Then none of this might have happened...'

'Don't,' said his wife. 'There's no sense in thinking that now.'

Another silence fell, broken only by the sound of the waves, endlessly rising and falling against the shore. 'Tell me,' began Olivia Havelock once more. 'Did she... did my daughter... seem peaceful, at the last?'

'Yes.' Rowlands caught at the word. 'Very peaceful.' Because the word *could* have sufficed to describe that absolute absence—the emptying-out of all that made a person a person—which was to be found in the dead. 'Thank you.' Mrs Havelock's voice was scarcely louder than an exhaled breath. 'Olivia, my dear,' said her husband gently. 'We really must go.' He didn't offer his hand to Rowlands. 'Thank you for what you did,' was all he said.

Walking back the way they had come, the two friends said

nothing for a while, both oppressed by the sadness of that chance encounter. Only when they drew near to the place where—to judge from the cheerful shouts of 'Oh, well played!' the game of cricket was still in progress—did Ashenhurst say: 'I felt so sorry for them both. But there seemed nothing one could say.'

'No,' said Rowlands. 'There's nothing to be said.'

TRIPOS

10

ARRIVING NEXT AFTERNOON AT Grove Avenue, they found Mrs Edwards, Edith's mother, already in possession—she having returned from visiting friends in Scotland the day before. The next few hours were spent in unpacking and, over supper, in comparing notes on respective holidays. Scotland was very pleasant at this time of year, said Helen Edwards: 'Although one never remembers to pack enough warm things. Rowena's place can be very draughty, even in summer...' The last-named was an old school friend of Edith's mother, who, with her husband, and—intermittently—children and grandchildren, inhabited a small castle in Perthshire. 'We were so hot in Cornwall we couldn't *sleep*,' said Joan. 'You should have come with us, Granny.'

'Perhaps I will, next year.'

After supper, when the girls had dispersed to their various activities—Joan to explore the garden, and hunt up her pet stag beetle, Anne to reacquaint herself with her books, and Margaret to write a letter (to whom she chose not to say)—the three adults sat over their coffee in the sitting-room. It seemed strange not to be able to hear the sound of the sea through the open windows, thought Rowlands. The blackbird's song made a pleasing substitute, however. He was glad it was Sunday tomorrow. One more day before he'd have to return to work, and all its muddles. He'd spend it in the garden, he decided. The lawn would need a good cut, and the kitchen garden would doubtless be a mass of weeds...

Edith was going through the pile of post which had accumulated during the previous ten days. 'Anything interesting?' Rowlands asked her. 'Mostly circulars. There's a new hairdresser's opening in the High Street. Special offer on Shampoo and

Set. Kingston Choral Society is performing scenes from *The Mikado* next month. We might go. The Wilmslows have sent us a postcard from Bognor Regis. *Weather fine. All well. Hope you are, too.* And there's a letter from Maud Rickards—quite a long one, by the feel of it...' She slit open the envelope with a paper-knife, and withdrew what was inside. 'It's two letters—one of them addressed to you. Shall I open it?'

'Yes, do,' he said. 'But don't you want to read Maud's, first?'

'All right. I'll give you the highlights. She's in Italy—Venice, this time. Or rather, she *was*. The letter's dated a month ago.' She began to skim through the pages of what was evidently a lengthy missive, reading out bits as the fancy took her: '"... most interesting visit to the Basilica San Marco... far too many tourists, however... enjoyable ride in a gondola along the Grand Canal... shockingly overcharged for it... splendid Titians at the Accademia... spoilt by an officious guard... reading *Stones of Venice*... things a good deal changed since Ruskin's day..."'

Suddenly Edith came to stop. 'Good God!' A strong oath, for her. 'Listen to this, Fred... "I've opened this to add a postscript before sending it at last (I never trust the Italian posts, as you know). I arrived back in Cambridge on Wednesday last to some rather shocking news. You will perhaps remember Thomas Findlay, our groundsman? It appears he was found dead—drowned in the river, near the Mill Pond—two weeks ago. Very sad for his family. I did not always see eye-to-eye with the man," added Miss Rickards, with scrupulous honesty, "but I am sorry that he is gone—and in such unaccountable circumstances. It is thought he must have hit his head, in falling into the river, because a strong swimmer, such as he was, would otherwise have been able to save himself." Well,' said Edith when she had come to the end of this. 'Maud sounds most upset.'

'Hardly surprising.'

'I suppose not—especially coming on top of that other distressing business...'

'What's that?' said Mrs Edwards. 'You know—I told you about it, Mother. That poor girl...'

'Won't you read me the other letter?' said Rowlands. 'Oh yes. There's a postscript about that, too. "The enclosed was waiting for me on my return from Venice—addressed to Frederick, as you'll see. I've no idea who sent it—the Porter could only tell me that 'a young gentleman' left it..." Curiouser and curiouser,' said Edith. She opened the envelope, and drew out the single sheet that was folded within. 'It's dated July 18th. St Jude's College.' She cleared her throat. '"Dear Mr Rowlands,"' she read.

'"You were decent to me, and so I thought you'd like to know what I've discovered, since we last spoke. It seems I was right all along—there was a man, and he's the one who did for Diana. You'll think I'm raving mad, I expect, but I can prove it, you see. I just need one more piece of evidence before I confront him. I won't write his name, in case this letter gets intercepted. I might be wrong, and it wouldn't do to tarnish a man's reputation without cause. I'll be in Cambridge, working at the Cavendish (for my sins) all summer, so if you want to hear my theory, I'll be happy to divulge it.

You said things would get better, but so far they've stayed just the same. She was everything to me. Now she's gone, there doesn't seem much point to anything.

Yours truly..."'

'Julian Sedgwick,' said Rowlands, before his wife could read out the name. 'Poor young devil! Does it give an address, apart from the College?'

'No. But Fred... You're surely not going to take this seriously? The boy sounds demented.'

'He's badly frightened, certainly. But not mad, I think. Damn! (Sorry, Helen.) This letter must have been sitting here for the past ten days...'

'It was written a month before that,' Edith pointed out. 'Even if you'd received it a few days earlier, what difference would it have made? You surely wouldn't have rushed off to Cambridge, instead of coming down to Cornwall?'

'I don't know,' said Rowlands. 'If I'd thought it was urgent enough, I might've. Anyway, all that's beside the point. I wonder if I should telephone now, or in the morning?'

'Don't be ridiculous,' said his wife. 'What are you going to say, in any case? That you've been away on holiday, and can't take any more time off to listen to his precious "theory"? Honestly,

Fred, I do wonder sometimes if all this detective stuff of yours hasn't gone to your head. You see mysteries in things that aren't mysterious at all...'

'Do I?' he said. 'Perhaps I do...'

'You surely don't believe this fantastic story about some man doing away with Diana Havelock? I suppose that *is* what he means?'

'It would seem so. I'll have to ask him.'

'Fred, you don't mean you're actually going to dash off to Cambridge on some wild-goose chase, just because a silly young man can't get over his girlfriend's death?'

'When you put it like that,' said Rowlands with a smile, 'It does sound rather absurd.'

'I think you should go,' said Helen Edwards, from the depths of the armchair where she had been quietly knitting. 'The poor boy obviously needs someone to talk to. A father figure. You mustn't let him down, Frederick.'

'*Mother*!' said Edith.

'Just what I was thinking myself,' said Rowlands.

Arriving in Cambridge the next day, which was a Sunday, Rowlands was struck by how completely the little market-town had assumed its late-summer guise. Instead of the clamour of young voices in the streets, and the constant danger (for a blind man) of bicycles whizzing past, a soporific silence lay over the place, broken only by the melodious clanging of bells, from the town's many churches—St Edward's, Little St Mary's, Great St Mary's, St Bene't's, St Andrew's, Holy Trinity—calling its denizens to morning service.

The college clock was just striking eleven as the taxi dropped Rowlands off in front of St Jude's main gate; he lost no time in making his enquiries of the porter. 'Mr Sedgwick? Don't think as I've seen him about this morning, sir. They sometimes sleep late of a Sunday, the young gentlemen... it being out of term,' the man added, in case the visitor should be unaware of this fact. 'Thanks,' replied Rowlands. 'I left a message for Mr Sedgwick last night, so he should be expecting me.'

'That's right, sir. It would have been the night porter, Mr Bailey, that took it.' He must have checked the row of pigeon-holes behind him, for he said: 'There's nothing there, now, sir. So he must have collected his messages all right—Mr Sedgwick.'

'Then could you direct me to his rooms? I seem to recall he's in Old Court somewhere...'

'Quite right, sir. He's in D17. Straight through the archway, past the dining hall, and you're in Old Court. Mr Sedgwick's staircase is third on your right. His room's on the first floor.' Rowlands nodded his thanks and then, grateful for the clearly marked flagstone path he remembered following on that earlier visit, set off across the main court. Although it was the first of September, the sun was still warm on his neck, and he was glad he'd worn his lighter jacket. If he succeeded in rousting Sedgwick out of his room, he'd suggest a walk by the river. It was too nice a day to sit around indoors...

Old Court was even quieter than the outer part of the college, where sounds—albeit faint—still penetrated from the street outside. Here, seventeenth-century brick walls enclosed what seemed a well of silence. If he hadn't just stepped out of a twentieth-century taxi-cab, Rowlands might have supposed himself back in a time when the fastest speed one could reach on land was that of a galloping horse, and when most people—in these cloisters, especially—took life at walking pace. How peaceful it must have been—must still be for some, he thought—to devote oneself to learning. Unhurried, untroubled by anything outside these ancient walls, the academic life must feel a kind of refuge. Although what was it old Giles had said? Something about its being 'all backbiting and skullduggery...' It occurred to him that his former training officer's rooms were just across the way. If he proved unlucky in tracking down Julian Sedgwick, he could always drop in for another chat with the old boy, he thought.

He found Sedgwick's staircase and climbed the creaking wooden steps to the first floor. There was only one door—its 'oak' was 'sported', meaning the room's occupant was in, but didn't want to be disturbed. Rowlands took this as a hopeful sign. Since the porter hadn't seen Sedgwick go out, then the likelihood was he'd be here, outer door closed, or not. He knocked, and waited. A few seconds passed. He tried again.

'Mr Sedgwick,' he called. 'Are you there? It's me—Frederick Rowlands.' Still no reply. Perhaps the porter was right and the young man was sleeping off a heavy night? Feeling increasingly foolish, Rowlands knocked again. 'Hello?' he called, louder this time. 'Anybody in?'

There came a shout from overhead. 'What's all the row?' Footsteps clattered on the stairs. 'Can't a fellow get some work done, without other fellows knocking down doors?'

'My apologies,' said Rowlands. 'But I'm trying to raise Mr Sedgwick. Only he doesn't appear to be in.'

'That's funny,' said the youth, who now appeared. 'I didn't hear him go out… I say, haven't we met before?'

'Twice,' said Rowlands drily. 'Although I rather think you had other things on your mind.' Angela Thompson being the main one, he didn't need to add. 'Of course. I remember now,' said the lad—Miles Rowntree—excitedly. 'You're the blind detective. Angela's told me all about you. Sorry if I yelled just now. I thought it was just some hearty playing tricks…'

'That's quite all right,' said Rowlands with a smile. 'So, as far as you know, Mr Sedgwick hasn't left his room this morning?'

'Well, he *might* have slipped out without my noticing,' said the other. 'Truth is, I've been swotting so hard that it's made me sleepy. I was just on the point of dropping off when I heard you knock. Law exams next term, you know. The pater says if I plough in my Part Twos, he'll cut off my allowance…'

'I can see you'd want to avoid that,' said Rowlands gravely. 'Well, if you see Mr Sedgwick in the next hour or so, perhaps you could tell him I've been looking for him, and that I'll be in the Eagle until lunchtime? I understood that he'd be in college today, but perhaps I was mistaken. Goodbye, Mr Rowntree. Sorry to have disturbed you.' He started to walk down the stairs. 'Hang on,' said Rowntree. 'Just give me a minute, will you?'

Once more, his footsteps thudded on the stairs. 'Up here,' he called. Rowlands accordingly followed. The door of Rowntree's room stood open. From inside came the sound of a sash being thrown up, and, a moment later, of someone—Rowntree—scrambling over the sill. 'I say, take care!' cried Rowlands, knowing they were two floors up. From the ledge outside the window, Rowntree's voice floated back. 'It's O.K.—I've done this lots of times. His window's open too, luckily…' By which he meant Sedgwick's window, Rowlands supposed. He waited, with bated breath, for the other to return. God forbid that a broken neck should be added to the tally of misfortune…

It seemed, however, that the youth had been successful in his mountaineering endeavours, for there was no sound of a fall—in fact no sound at all from the floor below. For what seemed a long moment, dead silence reigned. Rowlands was starting to wonder what was taking his young friend so long, when he heard footsteps coming thundering up the stairs. Seconds later, Miles Rowntree hurtled through the open door. 'My God!' he cried, in a voice of breathless horror. 'It's Sedgwick. I think he's dead.'

'How's the boy?' said Rowlands, when the inspector had closed the door of his office, and resumed his seat behind the desk. They were not to be disturbed, Brown had told the constable outside the door, for anything less than flood and fire. Seated at his own desk, a few feet away, Sergeant Gotobed threaded a fresh sheet of paper into his typewriter. 'Young Rowntree, you mean?' said Inspector Brown. 'He'll do right enough. A bit shaken—but then,' he remarked drily, 'he hasn't had much experience of such things. Finding a corpse,' he added, in case Rowlands should have missed his meaning. 'I suppose not,' was the reply.

'Whereas you and I, Mr Rowlands, have had a fair bit to do with dead bodies… and I *don't* mean because we've both been through the War,' said Brown. 'A more suspicious man than myself, sir, might think it an odd coincidence that you happened to be on the scene when the bodies of both these unfortunate young people—Miss Havelock and Mr Sedgwick—were discovered.'

If he'd thought to put Rowlands out of countenance, he didn't succeed. 'It isn't a coincidence,' said the latter. 'Well no, sir—that was just my fun. The only "coincidence",' said the inspector grimly, 'is the fact that both of 'em died from taking drugs…'

'It was murder,' said Rowlands. 'In both cases.'

There was a moment's astonished silence. The tapping of the typewriter ceased. 'I assume you've got some evidence to support that statement?' said Brown at last. 'Of course.' Rowlands took Julian Sedgwick's letter out of his pocket and handed it to the policeman. Another, brief, silence passed while the latter read it. 'It's dated middle of July,' was the inspector's first comment. Rowlands explained about Miss Rickards's having been abroad, and about his own absence on holiday. 'So he—Sedgwick—didn't know you'd received his letter,' said Brown. 'Yet he was expecting you to visit him this morning, you think?'

'I telephoned the Porters' Lodge at St Jude's yesterday evening,' replied Rowlands. 'The porter said Mr Sedgwick wasn't answering his door, but that he'd leave a message in his pigeonhole to say I'd call on him next day—today, that is.'

'I see. And did Mr Sedgwick collect his message, do you know?'

'I assume so. It wasn't there when the porter looked just now.'

'And what time would you say this was, sir—that you telephoned, I mean?'

'Let me think,' said Rowlands. 'It was after dinner—so about eight p.m.'

'So Mr Sedgwick must have picked up your message sometime after that. I'll have a word with Mr Bailey—that's the night porter—to see if he remembers exactly when the lad did this. It'll help us to establish the time of death, if nothing else,' said Inspector Brown. The cautiousness with which he pronounced this last phrase put Rowlands on the alert. 'You do see that this has to be a deliberate killing, don't you?' he said. 'The boy obviously knew something about Diana Havelock's death—something that would incriminate whoever was responsible. It's all in his letter...'

Brown was silent a moment. 'That's certainly *one* way of reading it,' he said at last. 'But there's another construction one could put on what he says—and one that accounts for the poor young man's death. He was sweet on this girl, wasn't he? Supposing he found out she *was* seeing another man? He'd have been mad with jealousy—and what could be more likely than that he'd try and put the responsibility for her death onto his rival? He writes you this hot-headed letter—and then thinks better of it, when he knows he's going to have to account for his cock-and-bull story. He can't face up to it, and so...'

'You think he killed himself,' said Rowlands. 'Out of remorse for telling lies about someone else—and because he knew I was coming to see him...'

'That's about the size of it, sir,' said the other with some complacency. 'I mean, he as good as says he can't bear to go on living any longer...'

'I don't believe a word of it,' said Rowlands. 'For a start, he doesn't name the man—so if he'd had second thoughts, as you suggest, he had only to say he'd made a mistake. You saw what he said about not wanting to traduce the suspect's reputation...'

'"Suspect" now, is it?'

'I believe so. I think if you were to find the man Julian Sedgwick was talking about in that letter, you'd find his murderer—and Diana Havelock's, too.'

'That's a serious allegation, Mr Rowlands.'

'I meant it to be. Good heavens, man,' cried Rowlands, doing his best to control his temper. 'How many more of these young people have to die before the police will treat these crimes for what they are? Not accident. Not suicide. But cold-blooded murder.'

There was a brief—perhaps sceptical—pause. 'Well now,' said the inspector. 'That's putting your cards on the table, and no mistake.' He gave a dry little cough. 'We—the police—don't usually fling around phrases like "cold-blooded murder" unless we've some good hard evidence to prove it. And this letter of yours...'

'It isn't just the letter,' said Rowlands. 'There's the conversation I had with Miss Havelock on the night she died. Something was troubling her—I'm sure of it...'

'Yes, but...'

'There's also the fact that she was waiting for someone—a man, presumably—in the college rose garden, just before I met her. I'm convinced it was that—the fact he hadn't turned up—which had upset her.' Rowlands considered mentioning the poison-pen letters, but then decided against it. He'd have a word with Maud Rickards first. 'At the very least,' he said, 'you might look into who it was she was expecting to meet. Even if it all turns out to have been perfectly innocent, it might help to determine Miss Havelock's state of mind on the night she died.'

Inspector Brown sighed. 'This is all speculation, Mr Rowlands. You can't make a case for murder out of that.'

'Can I ask you something?' said Rowlands. 'When the Medical Officer came to examine her body, were there any signs that Miss Havelock had been coerced into taking the drug that killed her? Any marks on her body—bruises, say?'

'What makes you ask that?' said Brown sharply.

'Because when I found her—before Nurse Blenkinsop so obligingly "tidied her up", she was missing a shoe,' said Rowlands. 'That suggested to me that she'd fallen—or been pushed—back onto the bed, and that, in such a position, she would have been helpless if a determined person wanted to plunge a needle into her arm.'

'That doesn't prove anything,' said the inspector—but, for the first time, he sounded uncertain. 'She might have kicked off the shoe as she lay down...'

'*Both* shoes, perhaps,' said Rowlands. 'But *one*? It seems most unlikely. If she'd been intending to take the drug for recreational purposes, she'd have made herself comfortable, surely? Not kicked off one shoe and hobbled lop-sidedly over to the bed. If it was suicide... well, I imagine your experience of that is wider than mine, inspector, but I suspect that most people who set out to kill themselves do so with some forethought and deliberation. I think she was pushed—and probably held down—as the drug was administered. If you'll look again at the post-mortem report...'

'What do you know about that?' snapped the inspector.

'Nothing you haven't just told me,' said the other.

Neither spoke for a moment. The typewriter, too, fell silent. From the corridor outside came shouting. 'No, no, no...'

'Stow that racket,' said a stern young voice—a police constable, presumably.

'As it happens,' said Inspector Brown slowly, 'it appears that there *was* some bruising on the girl's upper arm. The M.O. said she might've walked into a door. I wasn't informed about the shoes,' he added resentfully. 'By the time my men and I got there, it had all been made ship-shape. That nurse...'

'She was only doing what she thought was right,' said Rowlands. 'If anyone's to blame it's me. I should have mentioned the shoes before. But it didn't seem particularly significant at the time.'

'No. Well, it casts a different light on things now,' said the policeman. 'Given that...' He seemed afflicted by a recurring cough. 'Given that there was bruising on her upper arm, you were going to say?' said Rowlands. When the other didn't see fit to reply, he went on: 'When will the post-mortem results for Julian Sedgwick be ready?'

'The M.O. said three o'clock. I must say,' said Brown. 'You seem to know rather a lot about this kind of thing, Mr Rowlands.'

'It isn't the first such case with which I've been involved,' Rowlands admitted. 'But the reason for my question was this: how was the drug administered this time? Because when I found him, after Mr Rowntree raised the alarm, Sedgwick was sitting in an armchair, in front of a window which had been open for some time. He was quite cold, and *rigor mortis* had passed off, so my guess is that he'd died some hours before. My point is this. I find it hard to believe that a fit young man such as he was would have allowed himself to be overpowered, or would have tamely sat there, while his murderer stuck a hypodermic needle into his arm. He was in shirtsleeves, it's true, so this would have been easier than had he been wearing a jacket. And yet, even so...'

'What are you suggesting?' said the inspector. This time, there was no hint of scepticism in his voice. 'I wonder if perhaps some other method of rendering him unconscious was tried first? was the reply. 'Chloroform, perhaps. I couldn't detect any traces when I examined him, but the pathologist may have better luck...'

'All this is pure supposition,' said Brown, after a pause. 'Even with your evidence about the shoes, it's far more likely that this is just another case of a young person with too much time on his hands indulging in harmful substances. There's obviously a lot of this stuff going around. My men are doing their best to track down the supplier. *He's* your murderer, Mr Rowlands!'

'Without a doubt,' said the other. 'Whoever's been peddling this stuff is as implicated in the deaths of these two poor children as the man who plunged the needle into their arms. But there's still the matter of intent to kill. I think Diana Havelock was murdered—for what reason, I don't yet know. Julian Sedgwick found out who'd killed her, and why. That's why *he* had to die.'

'You seem very certain.'

'Oh, I am. In my situation, inspector, one gets a feeling for this kind of thing. Call it a blind man's instinct. I've known something was wrong ever since I set foot in St Gertrude's College for that blasted garden party. I can only blame myself for not having acted on that suspicion sooner.'

11

Having signed a receipt for Sedgwick's letter, and given an assurance that he would not leave the country until after the inquest, Rowlands left the police station, and wandered disconsolately along St Andrew's Street towards the town centre. It was now past one o'clock, and he realised that he'd had nothing to eat since breakfast—the strain of the past two hours having taken away all thoughts of such refreshment. Deciding to remedy this omission with a visit to the Eagle, he was about to cross Downing Street on his way to that hostelry, when a car shooting out of the turning nearly ran him down. A violent hooting of a klaxon ensued. 'Look where you're going, can't you?' yelled the driver, with what seemed to Rowlands some injustice. He'd only just stepped out into the road. If the chap hadn't been going too fast, he'd have seen him earlier. 'Road-hog!' he shouted back, with some relief to his feelings.

To his surprise, this satisfying insult was received, not with a furious riposte, but with a burst of loud laughter. A moment later the driver of the car—indifferent to the stream of traffic that was building up behind—jumped out onto the pavement and clapped Rowlands on the back. 'My dear old Spy,' cried this surprising individual. 'I nearly did for you just then. Can you ever forgive me?'

'Hello, Loveless. I think,' said Rowlands, 'you'd better move your car. From the sound of it, people are getting rather irate…'

'Let them,' said the other, but he climbed back in, without bothering to open the door of the car—evidently an open-topped roadster. 'Well, don't just stand there,' he said to Rowlands. 'Hop in. Then you can help me find a good place to leave this crate.'

'You'll be lucky, said Rowlands, but he did as he was told,

his mood considerably lightened by the appearance of his old friend. Even though the circumstances under which he and Percy Loveless had met had not been conductive to friendship, Rowlands had found it hard not to warm to the man, whose sometimes provocative behaviour concealed a more sensitive spirit.

When the vehicle—'a Brough Superior. Nifty little thing, isn't she?'—had been parked half-on and half-off the pavement outside St Bene't's church, and the two men sat face to face over their pints in the Eagle's back bar, Loveless said: 'So what are you doing in Cambridge, old Spy? Not still chasing corpses, I hope?'

'I might ask the same of you,' said the 'spy', without answering the second question. Loveless laughed. 'Me? I'm earning my bread-and-butter, old man. Painting pictures—one in particular, that is.' He took an appreciative draught of his beer. 'That's a nice pint. You don't seem to get the same depth of flavour in London beers... Yes, I'm here on a commission,' he went on. 'Doing the portrait of a certain Miss Beryl Phillips...'

'The Mistress of St Gertrude's,' said Rowlands. 'That's the one,' was the reply. 'Why, do you know the dame? I suppose she's a fearsome old trout...'

'Not at all. She's a remarkable woman. Highly intelligent. You'd do well to watch your step with Miss Phillips.'

'Hmph,' said the artist. 'You make her sound rather formidable. Well, I shall see for myself, I expect. And how's your delightful missus?'

'Topping, thanks.'

'Not with you today?'

'No.' Rowlands hesitated. 'The fact is, I'm here on a police matter.'

'I knew it!' crowed Loveless. 'You never could stay away from the criminal classes, you dear old Spy. Speaking of which, how's my portrait looking?' This work, whose title—*Portrait of a Spy*—was the origin of the artist's teasing nickname for his friend, had been exhibited at the Royal Academy's Summer Show in 1929, and now hung in the Rowlandses' sitting-room. 'It hasn't changed, as far as I know—unlike the subject,' said the latter ruefully.

'What nonsense! You're looking as disgustingly fit and youthful as ever,' said Loveless. 'A little greyer about the temples, perhaps. A few more lines about the eyes...'

'Thanks,' laughed Rowlands.

'She hasn't asked to reclaim it then?' The question wiped the smile from Rowlands's lips. 'No,' he said. The woman to whom Loveless was referring had bought the painting, before presenting it to Rowlands's wife. Which of the two had a greater claim to it, was still a moot point. 'You haven't run into her lately, I take it?' asked Loveless slyly. 'Not lately, no.'

'She's living in Ireland now, you know.' Loveless signalled to the barman. 'Two more of these, if you'd be so kind... Yes. Married some fellow who owns half of County Wicklow. Spends all his time hunting or fishing—or whatever it is these types enjoy doing...' Rowlands said nothing, but finished his beer. 'I saw her at a ball in Dublin Castle, at the end of last year,' his tormenter went on. 'She was as beautiful as ever—more beautiful, if anything...'

'You forget,' said Rowlands quietly. 'I've never actually seen her.'

'Ah, Celia's the kind of woman whose fascination doesn't depend on looks alone,' said Loveless, as their beers arrived. 'She's the classic *female fatale*. Maddeningly elusive. An enigma...'

'I think' said Rowlands, holding up his fresh pint. 'You'd better not have any more of these. I don't know whether I'd describe Miss Phillips as a "femme fatale" or not, but I'm quite sure she won't be very amused if the man who's to paint her portrait turns up drunk.'

'All right, all right,' said Loveless. 'I can take a hint. If that subject's out of bounds—and I *don't* mean Miss Phillips—why don't you tell me about your latest murder mystery?'

A—necessarily edited—account of the events which had brought Rowlands to Cambridge occupied the time between collecting the car (just then attracting the attention of a patrolling police constable) and arriving at St Gertrude's. They had reached the long straight stretch of the Huntingdon Road before Rowlands paused for breath. 'My word,' was Loveless's comment. 'You *have* got yourself into a ticklish situation, haven't you, old Spy?'

Rowlands admitted that this was the case.

'I mean to say, you're going to make it very awkward for these ladies'—it was thus he referred to the staff and governing body of St Gertrude's—'seeing as how they've swept the whole affair under the carpet...'

'It wasn't like that,' said Rowlands. 'They were concerned for the College's reputation, that's all.'

'Now you're giving the "carpet" a jolly good shake,' went on his irrepressible friend. 'And all sorts of nasty things have fallen out. Dead bodies, for a start... Good God!' he exclaimed suddenly. 'You might have prepared me...'

'For what?' But, since they were now turning off the main road into the long drive that led to the college, it wasn't hard to guess. 'That... that monstrosity,' babbled Loveless. 'That Victorian vulgarity. That acreage of blood-red brick...'

'I do wish, said Rowlands mildly, 'that you'd keep your hands on the wheel.' For the car was now swerving wildly from side to side, as Loveless accompanied his excoriation of all things Victorian with suitably 'continental' gestures. 'In any case,' he went on, as the car lurched to a halt at last. 'You know perfectly well I couldn't have prepared you for any such thing—given that I've only the vaguest idea what the place looks like.'

'For which you should give thanks,' was the reply. 'I suppose,' added Loveless, 'I can leave the car here?' He opened the door and got out. 'Well, come on! Aren't you going to show me where I've got to go?'

In the Porters' Lodge, they found Wainwright berating one of the assistant porters for some misdemeanour. '...don't care whether it was or it wasn't a quiet time, you'd no call to leave the desk unattended... Ah, Mr Rowlands, sir!' he cried, on seeing the latter appear. 'What can I do for you?' Rowlands explained that he was here to see Miss Rickards. 'Just an unofficial visit,' he said. 'It's Mr Loveless you've been expecting, I imagine...'

'Are you the artist gentleman, sir? The Mistress said as you was to go straight up. She's in her room, now. *You*,' he added to his junior, 'can show Mr Loveless the way. Any bags to bring in, sir?'

'Just the one,' said Loveless. 'But there are my painting materials, too...'

'Right you are, sir. I'll get one of the lads to bring them to your room,' said Wainwright. 'You're in Forest Court. Room B6. I'll let the Mistress know you're here.' While he was telephoning, Loveless took the opportunity to cast his eyes around the lofty spaces of the entrance hall. What he saw appeared to fill him with gloom. 'Just as I feared,' he muttered. 'The place is a monument to the High Victorian style. Soaring Gothic arches. Shiny marble pillars. Endless vistas of corridor...'

'I believe the grounds are very pretty,' said Rowlands. 'If you're thinking about a setting for your painting...'

'No, no,' was the reply. 'I must have the authentic backdrop—blood-red gables and all. The architect was Waterhouse, you know. I believe this is considered a fine example of his work,' said the artist with a shudder. 'All right, sir.' Wainwright had now finished his call. 'The Mistress will be pleased to see you. George here will take you up... And mind you come straight back,' he added to the lad. 'No passing the time of day with the maid-servants—is that clear? Now, Mr Rowlands, I'll just see if the Bursar's in, shall I?'

But before he could pick up the phone, there came the sound of rapid footsteps along the corridor which led from the hall to the older wing of the college, and a voice said, 'Frederick? What are you doing here?'

'Good afternoon, Bursar.' Rowlands turned with a smile to greet her. 'I met Mr Loveless in the town, and he offered me a lift to St Gertrude's, as he was coming up here himself. It seemed too good an opportunity to miss.'

'Of course,' she said, distracted by the appearance of the artist from what might otherwise have been the obvious question—what was Rowlands doing in Cambridge in the first place? She addressed the newcomer: 'I'm Maud Rickards. We spoke on the telephone.'

'Delighted,' said Loveless. 'You know, I pictured someone older...'

'I'm quite old enough,' she said drily. The mental picture

which came to Rowlands in that instant of the diminutive Miss Rickards, towered over by Loveless, who was well over six foot, made him smile. 'Welcome to St Gertrude's, Mr Loveless. Has the Mistress been informed of your arrival? She has? Good. In which case, I'd better not keep you. I expect we shall meet again at dinner...'

'I very much hope so. Until tonight, then.' Loveless managed to make it sound like an assignation. 'Goodbye Rowlands. Give my regards to Mrs Rowlands, won't you?' Rowlands said that he would. The two men shook hands, and Loveless, accompanied by the assistant porter, swept off along the corridor. 'Well,' said Miss Rickards, when the echo of their footsteps had died away. 'So *that's* the great Percy Loveless. I must say, he was rather less alarming than I'd feared. I was expecting someone more bohemian in appearance, but he seemed quite respectable...'

'It's summer. He's left his cloak and fedora at home,' said Rowlands. 'And he *does* know how to behave himself. You needn't worry about him *vis-à-vis* the Mistress.'

'Oh, I'm not worried about the Mistress,' said Miss Rickards. 'Now then. I'm going to order some tea to be sent up for our guest, and some for ourselves—and then you're going to tell me why you're here.'

When Rowlands had finished speaking, his companion said nothing for a moment, but set down the teacup she was holding, as if it were suddenly too heavy. 'So you think she was murdered?' she said at last. 'And that poor boy too?'

'The evidence certainly points that way,' said Rowlands. They had been sitting on either side of the fireplace in the Bursar's sitting-room; now she got up, and began pacing up and down, as if staying still had become intolerable. 'It's all so horrible. But are you *sure*, Frederick?'

'It's for the police to be sure,' he said. 'But if it turns out that Julian Sedgwick was killed in the way I suspect, then it makes Diana Havelock's death seem a lot more suspicious.'

Miss Rickards stopped her restless moving about. 'I suppose I'll have to tell the Mistress,' she said. 'God knows how she'll take it... a *murder* in College...'

'Not just this college,' he reminded her. 'And I should let the police inform her. It's just possible I'm wrong,' he added, not believing it for a minute. 'But if she—Diana—was murdered, who could have done it?' cried the Bursar, as if the question had just occurred to her. 'I hope the police will find that out,' said Rowlands. 'You know what it means, don't you?' she persisted. 'It means that somebody who was here that night—some man—was responsible.'

'Yes,' he said. 'It does seem likely.'

'One of the undergraduates, do you think?'

'It's possible. Or a member of staff...'

'I can't believe it,' said Miss Rickards, sitting down again. 'I mean when one thinks who was there... Professor Giles, the Chaplain, Professor Harding... it all seems too absurd. The idea that any of *them* could have done such a thing...' Her voice tailed off. 'It must have been someone from outside College,' she went on. 'A tramp... or an escaped lunatic...' Rowlands forbore from pointing out that a tramp or escaped lunatic would have been far less likely to get past the porter and pass unnoticed through the college than a member of the University. 'I'm sure the police will consider every eventuality,' he said. It would of course mean that all those she'd mentioned—and others she hadn't, including himself—would have to be interviewed as to their movements that night. He didn't say this, however.

'What I don't understand...' Before Miss Rickards could continue, there came a knock at the door. 'Now, who can that be?' she said; then, raising her voice: 'Come in!' It was one of the college servants. 'Oh, miss,' she said. 'I didn't mean to intrude...'

'That's quite all right. What is it, Mabel?'

The young woman hesitated. 'It's Betty, miss. She's come over queer again. Crying and carrying on... Mrs Doggett sent me to ask was it all right to send her home?'

'Quite all right,' said Miss Rickards. 'She lives off Mill Road, doesn't she?'

'Yes, miss. Ainsworth Street. Number twenty-three.'

'She'd better go in a taxi. Tell Mr Wainwright I said so.'

'Thank you, miss.'

'We can't have poor Betty crying her eyes out on the bus, can we?'

'No, miss.'

When the girl had gone, Maud Rickards let out a sigh. 'As if this dreadful business with poor Diana isn't bad enough, I'm having problems with the staff,' she said. 'Thomas Findlay's death has unsettled them all. Two of the girls have left already. Oh, they didn't *say* it was because of that, but I know the signs. Now it looks as if Betty will be next. She hasn't been the same since it happened, poor thing. She was engaged to him, of course…'

Rowlands recalled the lively scene by the river at Grantchester, the day after the end of term ball. 'Yes, I think I gathered that much,' he said. 'Why don't you tell me what happened?'

The Bursar reached for her cup and took a sip. 'Cold,' she said, putting it down again. 'Well, it was all rather strange…'

'In what way?'

'To begin with, there was the fact that Findlay'd given in his notice. It was right at the end of term. It wasn't as though he'd been at St Gertrude's very long—only a couple of years. Our people usually stay with us for life, you know… the men, that is. The girls stay until they get married.'

'Did he say why he was leaving?' asked Rowlands.

'Only in the vaguest terms. He'd got plans to start his own business, he said. I must confess, I didn't pay much attention. I was too angry with him for letting the college down, like that… and at *such* an inconvenient time, too! It sounds selfish,' said Miss Rickards, 'but I was just about to go away on holiday, you know. Having to advertise for a groundsman to take his place was the last thing I felt like doing…'

'When was this exactly?' interrupted Rowlands. 'You said it was the end of term, I know, but…'

'It must have been the day of the inquest,' said Maud Rickards. 'That was a Wednesday, wasn't it? I remember I had a *mountain* of things to do before the weekend, when I was leaving for Italy…'

'Did anything else strike you as strange?' he said, trying to keep her to the point. 'Did I say strange? I meant perverse. I mean, here he was, giving up a perfectly good job for no good reason. I know we don't pay top rates here, but we're on a par with the rest of the university… I said to him, "Is it the money, Thomas? Because if so, it may be that we can come to some arrangement." He practically laughed in my face.'

'Perhaps,' said Rowlands. 'He'd come into some money of his own?'

'Perhaps.' Once more, Maud Rickards sighed. 'If so, he didn't have long to enjoy it, poor fellow.'

'You said in your letter that Findlay's body was found in the river—whereabouts, exactly?'

'It was at the Weir, by the Mill Pond. You remember—where we hired the punts from that impudent fellow…'

'Yes. Do they have any idea how it happened? I mean, he was a strong swimmer, wasn't he?'

Maud Rickards did not reply at once. Then she said: 'You seem awfully interested in all this, Frederick. You can't possibly think it has anything to do with this other dreadful business?'

'I'm always interested when someone dies in untoward circumstances,' he said. 'Had he been drinking, do you know?'

'I haven't the least idea,' she started to say, when the telephone rang. 'Bursar's office. Bursar speaking… Oh, hello, Edie…' Rowland's heart gave a thump. 'Yes, he is, as a matter of fact… Would you like to speak to him? It's Edith,' Miss Rickards added unnecessarily, as she handed Rowlands the phone. 'What is it?' he said at once. 'Is anything wrong?'

'I could ask you the same question,' his wife said. 'No, there's nothing wrong—at least, not at home. The police telephoned, however…'

'Oh?'

'An Inspector Brown. I think he must have been the one you spoke to before, over that business with the Havelock girl…'

'He was. I saw him this morning. Go on.'

'He said to tell you that the inquest is on Tuesday, and that you'll be called. What *is* this, Fred? Has there been another death?'

'I'm afraid so. It's the Sedgwick lad.' He heard her gasp. 'Did Inspector Brown say anything else?'

'Only that they—the police—will be asking for an

adjournment…' That means it's murder, thought Rowlands grimly. 'Thanks,' he said. 'I think, as that's the case, I'd better stay in Cambridge until after the inquest. It isn't ideal timing…' Murder never is, he thought. '…but I'll try and get home as soon as possible.'

'But Fred… what happened?' she said. 'I can't really discuss it now, Edie. I'll write to you tonight. Give the girls a kiss from me, won't you?'

'All right.' There was resignation in Edith Rowlands's voice. She knew her husband only too well. 'Be careful won't you?' she said—having seen the results of some of Rowlands's less cautious activities in the past. 'I will. You look after yourself, too,' he said. He replaced the receiver in its cradle. There was silence for a moment. 'You'll be wanting somewhere to stay,' said the ever-practical Maud Rickards. 'I can put up at one of the pubs in town,' Rowlands replied. 'Don't be silly, Frederick. You'll stay here, of course. Apart from anything else,' added Miss Rickards, with the first glimmer of humour she had shown, 'you can help entertain Mr Loveless.'

Dinner turned out to be an unexpectedly pleasant affair. There still being a month to go before the start of Full-Term, those present were few in number—several members of the teaching staff having yet to return from their holidays. Amongst them was Rowlands's lively young friend, Enid Merriweather, who was, he gathered, currently engaged on a tour of archaeological sites in Greece, accompanied by her *fiancé*, the robust Mr Armstrong. Miss Sissons and Miss Crane were spending the summer together in Austria. 'Eating a great deal and tramping a great deal more,' read the postcard they had sent to the Senior Common Room.

'Lucky for some,' was Miss Glossop's cheerful comment. 'I hope *you've* had a pleasant summer?' enquired Rowlands, who was sitting beside her. 'Splendid, thanks. My mother lives in Hampshire—the New Forest, you know—so I usually spend the first few weeks with her. She's not in the best of health, so I try and visit as often as I can. The rest of the time it's been work, work, work,' she added, as if this were the most delightful thing in the world. 'My book on Keats is coming out in the Autumn, so I've had the proofs for that to correct. And aren't there a lot a howlers I've missed!' Rowlands wondered if he wasn't a little bit in love with Jane Glossop. She was so perfectly his idea of what a female academic should be.

Miss Kruger was on Rowland's other side; Loveless was seated opposite, between the Mistress and Miss Hall. The artist hadn't seemed surprised to see Rowlands, when the party had assembled for a pre-prandial glass of sherry, in the Old Library. 'Still around, old Spy?' he'd said, at what had seemed to Rowlands an unnecessary volume. 'I wish,' said his friend, feeling that the joke had gone far enough, 'you wouldn't call me that.'

'I suppose under the circumstances it isn't very tactful,' replied the other. 'But then I'm not renowned for my tact,' he added unrepentantly. 'How did the painting go?' said Rowlands, hoping to steer the incorrigible Mr Loveless onto the subject dearest to his heart: his work. 'Oh, I won't make a start on that for a day or two yet. I need to make a few more charcoal studies first. Lay the groundwork. But *what* a subject!' he cried. "Divinely tall, and most divinely fair..." Do you know, I think this will be one of my best pieces...'

'You hit it off with Miss Phillips, I take it?'

'I believe I did. She tolerated my absurdities, at any rate. But what can you expect, if you're Pallas Athena, and a mere mortal comes to call?' From which Rowlands gathered that his friend was rather smitten by Beryl Phillips. If Miss Phillips herself felt any surprise at seeing Rowlands again, she concealed it well, greeting him with her usual cordiality, and expressing no curiosity as to what had brought him to St Gertrude's. Since their number was small, the conversation at dinner flowed with an easy informality which seemed almost that of a gathering of old friends. Which, Rowlands supposed, most of them were, having lived and worked together under one roof for a good many years.

The truth of this was pointed up by the passing mention of an absentee. 'Isn't Dr Bostock in College this evening?' the Mistress wanted to know. 'She's asked to have a tray in her room,' was the Bursar's reply. 'Poor thing!' This was Miss Glossop. 'She suffers very badly from headaches, I understand.' A murmur of polite concern went around the table; then the conversation moved on to other, more interesting, topics. A substantial donation to the college library fund. 'To buy books?' asked Rowlands. 'Well, not exactly,' Miss Glossop admitted. 'The fact is, that our lovely new building—completed last year, you know—is rather draughty. We can't have our girls freezing to death while they work...'

He agreed that this would be unfortunate.

Then there was the money left over from the fund for modernising the swimming pool, which had badly needed it, after thirty-five years of regular use by undergraduates and staff. 'The question is: how to spend it? said the Bursar. '*Some* of us think it would be best spent on improving the college heating system... or indeed the sanitation,' she muttered under her breath. 'A summer-house would be nice,' said Miss Glossop wistfully. 'Perfect for reading-parties.'

Miss Hall expressed her concern about an invitation that had been issued by the college's political society to the secretary of the British Union of Fascists. 'I really don't know if we should be giving a platform to this kind of thing,' she said. 'Although I suppose one must consider freedom of speech.'

'Couldn't some of your students get up an anti-fascist caucus to heckle the blighter?' said Loveless. 'I'm sure they will already have thought of that,' said the History don. 'But I'm afraid that all too often such protests get out of hand...'

Rowlands, who had been present—with Loveless, as it happened—at just such a political gathering, was inclined to agree with her. There was an ugliness abroad in these times which could flare up at the slightest provocation. 'I think,' said the Mistress, with her customary air of calm authority, 'we can trust our girls to keep their heads. We'll leave you gentlemen to your port, I think.' With that, she rose and swept out, followed by the female teaching staff, and leaving Rowlands and Loveless at table with the College Chaplain.

12

Dr Maltravers did the honours with the port, and refused a cigarette. 'I've given up,' he said apologetically. 'Doctor's orders. Used to enjoy a smoke in my army days.'

'Which regiment was that, sir?' asked Rowlands, lighting his own Churchman's. 'I was attached to the Devonshires. We saw action at La Bassée and Givenchy Ridge. Of course I was a non-combatant,' added the Chaplain. 'I was never of the persuasion—unlike some of my more, ah, *militant* colleagues—that our God is a God of War. But you yourself were a soldier, were you not?'

'Royal Field Artillery. 56th London Division.'

'I suppose it was during the War that you lost your sight?'

'It was. We were at Passchendaele. The gun I was operating was hit. There was a lot of flying shrapnel.' Rowlands took a sip of port. 'I was luckier than the man next to me. He was killed instantly.' For an instant, an image of that staring white face, freckled with blood, flickered across his consciousness. Wilson. Wasn't that his name? Yes. Joe Wilson. The last face he'd ever seen, as it turned out. Mercifully, the Padre (as Rowlands now thought of him) didn't try and offer any bromides about God moving in mysterious ways, but turned instead to the other member of their party. 'And you, Mr Loveless? Were you also a combatant—or were you…' He hesitated a moment. 'In a reserved occupation?'

'Not I,' said the artist trenchantly. 'I've never been a pacifist—not like your precious Bloomsbury lot. No, I volunteered for the Artists' Rifles. Got a commission soon after I was sent to France.' He exhaled a mouthful of aromatic smoke. 'Can't say the experience did much for my drawing, although I did learn to handle a Lewis gun...'

'But how foolish of me!' cried Dr Maltravers. 'You're the artist who painted *A Burial Party*, are you not? A very fine work, in my estimation. It portrays the reality of war most affectingly...'

'Thanks,' said Loveless, adding, with uncharacteristic modesty, 'I don't think it's the worst of my big pieces. But then with a subject like that, one would have to be a complete fool not to make something of it.' As the conversation moved to a discussion of public art, and whether it could ever produce anything first-rate, it occurred to Rowlands that he would never get a better opportunity to question Maltravers about the events of last June. He accordingly waited for a lull in the conversation, then said: 'You were at dinner on the night of the end of term dance, weren't you, sir?'

'I was,' replied the clergyman. 'Why do you ask?'

'I was hoping you might be able to give me a rather more complete picture of that evening than I was able to form for myself,' said Rowlands. The chaplain said nothing for a moment. 'You are referring to what happened *after* the dance, are you not?' he said at last. 'The death of our poor Diana...'

'I'm interested in anything—however apparently insignificant—which might cast a light on her death,' was the reply. 'Surely,' said the other, 'the police have already gone into these sad events very thoroughly? I myself,' went on the padre, with some small attempt at humour, 'was grilled—is that the term?—for upwards of half an hour. Alas, I could tell the good inspector nothing of any consequence. I was at High Table for the first part of the evening, then in the Senior Common Room. I saw and heard very little of what went on—unlike you yourself, Mr Rowlands.'

'It's just that period— from when we were all at dinner and the time when... when Miss Havelock's body was found, that I'd like to know more about,' said Rowlands. 'Who was there, where people were sitting, and what was said...'

'I'm still at a loss to understand *why*,' said Dr Maltravers. 'If the police were satisfied...'

'It may be that the police will see fit to re-open the investigation,' said Rowlands. 'I see,' said the other thoughtfully.

'And you're helping the police with these enquiries, I take it?' Rowlands neither confirmed nor denied this assertion. 'Very well,' said the chaplain, apparently drawing his own conclusions from this. 'I'll tell you what I can.' He thought for a moment. 'I was seated at High Table next to the Mistress, as I recall, with... yes... your good lady on my right hand side. She was most interested in the College's plans to institute a scholarship for music students. One of your daughters is musical, I believe?'

'Yes,' smiled Rowlands. 'The middle one. And next to my wife?' He would ask Edith for her own impressions, he thought, but it wouldn't hurt to get a bigger picture. 'I believe that was Dr Bostock,' said the chaplain. 'A rather reserved young lady.' Dr Maltravers hesitated a moment, as if he could have said more. 'Now, who was on *her* other side? Miss Kruger, I think. Have you met our Miss Kruger? A very intelligent young woman. She was obliged to leave Germany in rather a hurry, I gather. Fortunately, St Gertrude's believes in looking after its own...'

'And across the table?' prompted Rowlands. Loveless, he noticed, had said not a word since the start of this interrogation (if that was what it was) but merely smoked his cigar, and from time to time replenished his glass. 'This is better than Pelmanism—or that game with objects on a tray,' said the chaplain, with some enthusiasm. 'Across the table... Ah, I can tell you *that* precisely. Directly opposite me sat our unfortunate young lady. Diana Havelock,' he added, in case this had not been immediately obvious. 'Very striking she looked, too—in a vivid green frock. Miss Crane was next to her, I believe, and Miss Sissons next to *her*. Those two are inseparable,' he laughed. 'On Miss Sissons's left was... let me think... Ah yes. Miss Merriweather's Intended. Armstrong's the name, I believe. He's a very fine oarsman. Got his "blue" last year...'

'Who was on Miss Havelock's right?' persisted Rowlands. 'That was Professor Harding, our Director of Studies in Mathematics.

'I see,' said Rowlands, trying not to show that this was of any particular interest to him. 'But of course, Professor Harding was her supervisor, wasn't he?'

'I believe so,' was the reply. Dr Maltravers considered a moment. 'You know, that's rather odd...'

Rowlands held his breath.

'Given that he *was* her supervisor,' said the chaplain, 'One would have thought that he and she would have had a good deal to talk about… being scientists, you know. Yet they didn't exchange a word, as I recall.'

'That *is* rather odd,' said Rowlands. 'Perhaps,' he suggested, 'Professor Harding was engrossed in talking to his other neighbour—Miss Glossop—or rather, the person who was sitting on Miss Glossop's other side. Professor Bristow, I mean.'

'Yes, I'm sure you must be right. But it makes me wish I had taken the trouble to talk to Diana myself. Poor child, she looked rather lost, I thought…'

A silence followed. 'Thank you,' said Rowlands at last. 'That gives me a very clear picture of *your* end of the table. I think I can remember mine. Now, here's another poser for you, sir. Can you remember at what point—and if possible, in what order—people started to leave? I mean when dinner was over…'

'Well, the Mistress was the first to leave, of course, taking the ladies with her, so that we men could have our port and cigars…'

'Didn't some of the undergraduates leave before that?'

'So they did! I was forgetting that. Yes, the girls were given permission to go early, because of the dance…'

'Did that include Miss Havelock?'

'I suppose it must have. Do you know, I don't recall…'

'Around half-past eight, wasn't it?'

'That sounds about right.'

'Which brings us to the second part of the evening,' said Rowlands. 'The Mistress and female members of staff having already left to go to the Senior Common Room, we were down to just the men. Yourself, Professor Harding, Professor Bristow—who moved to sit next to him after Miss Glossop left—and Professor Giles, who was also at my end of the table. Was there anyone else—apart from myself, of course? Mr Armstrong, perhaps?'

'No, he'd left. Gone to escort young Enid Merriweather to the dance,' said the chaplain. 'Jolly young couple…'

'We all shifted places a little, didn't we?' said Rowlands. I believe I heard you talking to Professor Giles…'

'That's right. I was telling him about my paper on Coleridge. You know it's quite extraordinary…'

'Can you remember anything else about that part of the evening?' interrupted Rowlands. 'Between, say, half-past eight and a quarter to nine? Did anyone get up to leave before then?'

'Well, you did,' was the reply. 'So I did,' said Rowlands with a smile. 'I'd decided I needed some air. So you see, I wasn't in Hall when the rest of the party broke up. Can you remember who got up to leave after that?'

Dr Maltravers paused a moment, perhaps to collect his thoughts. 'I don't recall exactly,' he admitted. 'To tell you the truth, I was so caught up in what I was saying that I can't be sure of anything else…'

'Professor Harding was still talking to Professor Bristow, was he?'

'He might well have been… Yes… I believe he was…' At last, we're getting somewhere, thought Rowlands. But his hopes of establishing a clear picture of events were dashed a moment later. 'I know they were both still there when I went to fetch my paper on Coleridge to give to Professor Giles,' Dr Maltravers went on. 'He takes a very *narrow* line on certain subjects, you know… *The Rime of the Ancient Mariner* is so much *more* than just a literary curiosity…'

'So you left the dining hall before the others?' Rowlands interrupted. 'Yes, that's right,' was the reply. 'I collected the paper from my study and went to put it in Giles's pigeonhole. I had my sermon to look over for the next day, and so I decided not to join the ladies in the Senior Common Room, after all. It wasn't until the Mistress sent for me, to tell me the dreadful news about poor Diana, that I rejoined my colleagues.'

'Thank you, Padre,' said Rowlands. 'You've been a great help.'

Soon after this, Dr Maltravers hurried off to Evening Prayers, leaving Rowlands and Loveless to make their more leisurely way to the S.C.R., and the chance of a cup of coffee or a brandy before turning in. 'So that's how it's done, eh?' said Loveless, as the two friends emerged into the long corridor which ran past the dining hall—at the appearance of whose red brick Gothic arches the artist had exclaimed in mock-horror. 'I've always wanted to know.'

'What *are* you talking about?'

'Your interrogation of old Whatsisname. Maltravers. I must say you softened him up quite nicely. Getting him to talk about his army days. Very professional.'

'I'm glad you think so,' said Rowlands drily.

'Have you decided who did it, yet?'

'Who did what?'

'Oh, come on, old man! You forget I'm familiar with your "methods". You've got a hunch that somebody did for her—our lady in the green frock. From the way you were grilling the old padre, my guess is you've narrowed it down to two or three suspects...'

'You read too many murder mysteries,' said Rowlands with a laugh. 'I'm interested in what happened that evening, yes—but only so that I can eliminate certain possibilities...'

'Such as?'

'Diana Havelock was killed sometime after a quarter to nine, when I spoke to her outside the rose garden, and before ten to ten, when her body was found. During that time, which was a little over an hour, someone—probably a man—went to her room, knocked her off her feet onto the bed, and stuck a syringe full of morphine into her arm. I need to find out which of those present that evening had the opportunity to do so. I'd hoped that Dr Maltravers might have helped me whittle down the list of potential suspects...'

'And has he?'

'No. That confounded Coleridge paper of his meant he was absent at exactly the wrong time.'

'You don't think he...'

'I don't. He's a clergyman, damn it!'

'That doesn't necessarily rule him out...'

'As I said, you read too many detective stories.'

'Founded in 1511 by Lady Margaret Beaufort, who also founded Christ's College, St Jude's College is the second largest college in Cambridge. The gatehouse is crenelated and adorned with the arms of the foundress. Above them, you will observe a tabernacle containing a statue of St Jude the Apostle. St Jude is renowned as the patron saint of lost causes, and it is traditional for a garland of flowers to be placed on the head of his statue on the night before final examinations—thus, it is supposed, improving the chances of undergraduates who fear they may do badly…'

Murmuring apologetically, Rowlands edged his way through the crowd of tourists listening to the guide on the pavement outside St Jude's. He was pleased to have managed this without treading on any toes. In general, he managed to get about pretty well, by following a simple set of rules. Where possible, when walking along a street, he'd keep within arm's length of a wall or fence; these acted not only as a useful support, but as a sounding-board, enabling him to judge distances of approaching vehicles—and people. It didn't prevent occasional collisions, but for the most part he found others got out of the way if one walked with sufficient purpose. From the earliest days of his blindness, he'd hated the thought of looking helpless.

So it was with a confidence borne of familiarity with the route that he went in, crossed First Court, and, passing under the archway, entered Old Court. Here, by contrast with yesterday's heavy quiet, he found a commotion. '…never heard anything so ridiculous in my life,' a disdainful young voice was saying. 'I'm a member of this college, I'll have you know, and I want to get to my rooms…'

'Now then, sir,' said another voice—also that of a young man, Rowlands guessed—'I've got my orders. No one—member of the college or not—is allowed up them stairs…'

'But I don't need to go upstairs, you dunderhead! My rooms are on the ground floor…'

'Be that as it may… *sir*,' said the police constable (for so Rowlands judged him to be). 'You're not getting past this door.'

'What seems to be the trouble, Lord St Clare?' said Rowlands. The young man whirled round. 'Oh,' he said. 'It's you again.' He didn't sound very pleased at this, perhaps remembering their previous encounter. 'I'm trying to persuade this booby to let me into my rooms. I've a ton of work to get on with, and he's being thoroughly obstructive.'

'Perhaps,' said Rowlands quietly, 'if you could see your way to being a bit less offensive to a man who's only trying to do his job, we'd all get on a lot better.' There was a stifled explosion—which might have been a laugh—from the man in question. 'Well, of all the…' spluttered St Clare. 'I take it,' said Rowlands, ignoring this, 'that you didn't spend last night in your rooms?'

'What of it?' said the youth rudely. 'It's out of term. Some of us have better things to do than spend our summers hanging about in College. St Tropez is *much* more to my liking…'

'But you weren't in St Tropez last night, were you?'

'No, I wasn't, worse luck!' said St Clare. 'Not that it's any of your business, but I spent Saturday to Monday at the Mater's…'

'She'll vouch for you, I imagine?'

'Of course she'll vouch for me! I say, what *is* all this? Has something happened?'

An answer to this question arrived just then in the person of Inspector Brown, accompanied by his sergeant, and another man. 'Oh Lord!' muttered Roddy St Clare. 'It's the Master…'

'All right, Bullman?' said the inspector to his subordinate. 'Sir,' replied Constable Bullman. 'And you're here, are you, Mr Rowlands?' Brown went on, his tone non-committal. 'Mr Rowlands was the one that found the body,' he said, by way of explaining Rowlands's presence to the head of the college. 'I see,' said the latter austerely. 'How do you do, Mr Rowlands? I'm Hugh Bradbrook, Master of St Jude's. Distressing business, this.'

'Very,' said Rowlands.

Roddy St Clare could keep silent no longer. 'What's all this about a body?' he said. Instead of answering him, the inspector directed his fire at Constable Bullman. 'I thought I said you was to keep members of the public away?'

'Young gentleman said as he wanted to get into his room,' was the wooden reply. 'Wouldn't take no for an answer… until *this* gentleman told him where to get off, sir,' added the constable, in a distinctly warmer tone. 'That'll do, Bullman. The fact is, Mr… er…'

'It's Lord St Clare,' snapped the youth.

'Indeed. The fact is, your lordship, these rooms on this

staircase are out of bounds. We can't have people tramping in and out, while the police are trying to do their duty...'

'But...'

'I should cut along, Lord St Clare, if I were you,' said the Master, in tones of sublime indifference. 'Spend an hour or two in the University Library—*I* should! Do you the world of good. As soon as the Inspector has finished with your rooms, you'll be free to come and go, as before. Am I right, Inspector?'

'Quite right, sir.'

'I suppose *nothing* I say will be of any use...'

'Not in the least, sir.' The five of them stood in silence for a moment, as the boy stormed off, muttering under his breath. 'A rather quick-tempered young man,' observed Dr Bradbook. 'His father was the same. Now then, Inspector. What is it you have to tell me, regarding this unfortunate incident? You say you have reason to suspect that foul play was involved?'

'Yes, sir. If you'll come this way, sir...' The two policeman, followed by the Master and Rowlands, climbed the stairs to the first floor. The inspector opened the door of Sedgwick's room and they all trooped in. 'The fact is...' Inspector Brown's stiffly official tone could not disguise his embarrassment. 'We had a tip-off, that... I mean to say, the post-mortem has *established* that the lad... Mr Sedgwick, that is... was rendered unconscious before he was killed.'

'Good Lord!' said the Master. 'How appalling. You found evidence of this, you say?'

'Indeed, sir. Threads of a cotton material... possibly a handkerchief... were found in the young man's nostrils. It seems likely...' The inspector cleared his throat. '...that chloroform was used.'

'And then this drug—the one that killed him—was administered, you think?'

'Yes, sir.'

The Master was silent a moment. 'Why in the *world*...' he began; then broke off. 'Such a bright young man,' he continued eventually. 'Doing great things in the chemistry field, I understand. You're certain,' he added, as if the inspector might not have considered this possibility, 'that it couldn't have been suicide? Sometimes pressure of work, you know…'

'I think the chloroform rules that out,' was the reply. 'I see,' sighed Dr Bradbook. 'But there was something else you wanted to show me, was there not?'

'That's right, sir. If you'll observe these scratches on the windowsill here—next to where Mr Sedgwick's body was found—you'll see that they're quite fresh…'

'By Jove, so they are! Do you think that's how the… the…'

'How the killer gained entry, sir? I do.'

'But…' protested Rowlands.

The inspector cut across him. 'The door was locked at the time the body of Mr Sedgwick was discovered. You said so yourself, Mr Rowlands. So the window's the only way in. The young man on the floor above—Mr Rowntree, isn't it?—gave a very good demonstration of how they get in and out of these rooms when the door's locked.'

'You don't seriously think young Rowntree had anything to do with this?' demanded Rowlands. 'Why, he's the one who found Julian Sedgwick's body…'

'Not necessarily a reason to rule him out,' said Brown. 'But we're looking at every possibility. Anyone could've shinned up that drainpipe and got themselves onto the ledge below the window there…'

'Yes, it looks the only likely way in, if the door was locked,' murmured the Master. 'I'm grateful to you for telling me all this, Inspector. Although *what* I shall say to poor young Sedgwick's parents, Heaven only knows… They're in India, you know. Colonial Service. I must write at once, I suppose. I'll leave you to carry on, Inspector.' The other men said nothing more until after he had gone. 'Miles Rowntree was utterly shocked by what he found yesterday morning,' said Rowlands. 'I've seen cases of shock, and I know the symptoms. His teeth were chattering so hard he could barely speak, and his hands were like ice. I thought he was going to faint. You can't fake such reactions.'

'I haven't said a word about Mr Rowntree,' said the inspector mildly. 'Other than to mention that he was the one who showed us the window trick… which,' he added, 'we'd have found out without him, given the scratches on this windowsill and the one above.'

'You haven't ruled him out, though?'

'I haven't ruled anyone out. Although as it happens,' said Inspector Brown gloomily, 'it won't be up to me to rule in or rule out suspects for very much longer. Given as how the Super wants to bring in Scotland Yard...'

'Ah.'

'Yes, said the detective, not without a hint of bitterness. 'Seeing as it's now a murder case, he—Superintendent Horrocks—thinks we local men might be in need of some expert advice.'

'I think you're quite expert enough to handle this case by yourselves,' said Rowlands quietly. 'Thank you, sir. But like I said, the higher-ups don't agree. So Chief Inspector Douglas of the C.I.D. has been assigned to the case... Did you say something, sir?'

Because Rowlands had been unable to suppress an exclamation when he heard the name. 'Only that Alasdair Douglas is a good man,' he replied.

'Know him, do you, sir?'

'I do. And I don't think,' said Rowlands, 'that you'll have any trouble with the Chief Inspector. He believes in giving people a free hand.'

Crossing Old Court once more, it occurred to Rowlands that he ought to look up Austin Giles, if only to bring him up to date with developments. It might also be useful, he thought, to get Professor Giles's version of the end of term dinner: perhaps *he* had remained in the dining hall long enough to see in what order the other male guests had left? Once Rowlands knew *that*... but there the thought tailed off. The trouble was, there were so many variables. Just because Diana Havelock had been waiting for someone in the rose garden after dinner, didn't mean that this unknown person—presumably a man—had been among the dinner guests. He might have arrived later; the college had been swarming with visitors—most of them undergraduates from other colleges. And there *might* have been no connection at all between the man Diana Havelock had been waiting for in the rose garden and whoever had killed her... although

Rowlands didn't think this was very likely. He wondered if anything more had been heard of the poison-pen writer. He must ask Maud about it tonight.

There was no answer when he knocked on Professor Giles's door, however. It struck him that he'd no idea if the English don was even in Cambridge. Many of them were still away on their holidays, apparently. He wished he'd thought to bring paper and pen, so as to be able to leave a note—then remembered that he could do so at the Porters' Lodge. It would give him an opportunity to check at what time the message he'd left for poor Julian Sedgwick had been picked up. No doubt the police would already have done this—but there was no harm in making sure. But the porter (the man he'd spoken to before) seemed to have no idea about this. 'You'll have to ask Mr Bailey,' he said—this being the night porter. 'Thanks,' said Rowlands, although he hadn't been much help. 'Oh, one other thing... Is there a spare set of keys kept in the Porters' Lodge?'

'Do you mean keys to all the rooms, sir?'

'Yes.'

'There's only one set of spares—whoever's on duty keeps that with him, in case he has to let any young gentleman who's mislaid his keys into his room. They do that all the time,' he confided. 'I see,'' said Rowlands. So that put paid to *that* theory, he thought. ''Course, when the day porter—that's me, sir—goes off duty, he hangs 'em on the hook here, for when the night porter takes over.'

'And what time's that?'

'Eight o'clock, or thereabouts.' Around the time I telephoned the college with my message for Sedgwick, thought Rowlands. Now, I wonder... While he was still considering the implications of this, someone else came in. 'Any letters for me, Flitton?' he asked; then, catching sight of Rowlands: 'Hello! I... I was hoping I might see you. There's something I must talk to you about...'

'Mr Rowntree. Of course. Shall we find ourselves a pub?' said Rowlands, cutting short what seemed likely to turn into a confession. 'All right,' muttered the lad, and the two of them made their way out of the college gates and across Bridge Street to the

Mitre—which, with its twin establishment, the Baron of Beef, was a mere two minutes' walk away. Even before they were seated, with their pints in front of them, the young man burst out: 'Is it true, what they're saying about Sedgwick?'

'Is *what* true, Mr Rowntree?'

'That… that his death wasn't an accident.'

Rowlands took a sip of his beer. 'Do you mean was it suicide?' he said cautiously, not sure how much the police had disclosed about the circumstances of Julian Sedgwick's death. 'No,' replied Rowntree. 'I mean—was it murder?' The dreadful word hung like a foul smell in the atmosphere of the quiet pub. 'Where did you get that idea?' said Rowlands. 'Oh… I don't know, Someone said something which made me think… It *is* true, then?'

There seemed little point in fencing. 'Yes, it's true.'

'I knew it!' cried Rowntree. 'All those questions that policeman was asking me… They're going to say I did it! Just because I was the one who found him… It isn't my fault if I knew how to get into his room…'

'Calm down,' said Rowlands. 'No one's saying anything of the sort. Here.' He pushed Rowntree's untouched pint towards him. 'Have some of this. You sound as if you need it.'

Rowntree did as he was told; then started up again: 'You weren't there when that policeman interviewed me. He kept asking if I'd heard anyone moving about downstairs—in Sedgwick's room—the night before I found him,' he said, in a trembling voice. 'And he kept on and on about how I'd got into the room. But *all* of us climb in and out like that, when we can't get in any other way. You ask any man in College…'

'I'm sure the police will do just that,' said Rowlands. 'Don't distress yourself, Mr Rowntree.' For the young man, evidently overcome by the strain of the past few hours, seemed close to breaking down. Giving him time to pull himself together, the older man went on: 'If you *were* to remember anything about what happened, I'm sure it would be of immense help to the police. Inspector Brown is a very competent officer, you know. He's not in the business of making unfounded accusations.'

'I expect you're right. It's just that it's all so beastly. Sedgwick was a decent chap.' The young man took a swig of his beer. 'I'd like to know who did that to him.'

'I say, what'll you have, old man?' Some people had come in. Loud voices filled the pub. 'Make it a pint of the usual. And none of your swill from the bottom of the barrel, eh, landlord?'

'Oh hell,' muttered Rowntree. With which judgement Rowlands was inclined to concur. Because the voices were familiar as those of Roddy St Clare and his friends. Any hope that his own presence might have been overlooked was dashed the next moment. 'Well, if it isn't the Blind Detective! And young Miles Rowntree, no less. I must say, I'm *surprised* at you, Rowntree, consorting with such types...'

'Shut up, St Clare.'

'Charming—I *don't* think! I suppose it was your *friend* here who got me chucked out of my rooms...'

'Come along, Roddy,' put in another voice, which Rowlands recognised as belonging to one of the punting party from a few weeks ago. 'As it happens, I had nothing to do with it,' he said quietly. 'But for what it's worth, Lord St Clare, I'd suggest you co-operate with the police as much as possible. They're bound to find the stuff when they search your room, you know, so it'll look better if you come clean.'

'What are you talking about?' St Clare almost shrieked. ('He went as white as a sheet,' said Rowntree afterwards.) 'I don't know what you mean by "stuff"...'

'Drugs, if you prefer,' said Rowlands. 'Cocaine, in your case, I'd imagine.'

'How... how dare you!' protested St Clare feebly; then, furiously, to Rowntree: 'Was it *you* who sneaked on me?'

'Mr Rowntree and I had more important things to talk about,' said Rowlands. 'And I should be careful of calling a man a sneak. You might find yourself on the receiving end of a good thrashing. No, the advice I've given you is based on my own observations. I know you're part of a set that thinks drug-taking is smart, and that the police are foolish—but I can assure you, it's quite the other way around.'

There was a moment's shocked silence, then the youth said, in a strangled voice, 'This beer's disgusting. I'm not paying for such muck. Come on, Tony, we'll take our custom elsewhere.' With that St Clare and his friends swept out. Another silence fell—this time of relief. 'I'll pay for the beers they left,' said Rowlands to the landlord. 'No need, sir. It was a pleasure to hear that lad taken down a peg or two,' was the reply. 'It was glorious!' burst out Miles Rowntree. 'Simply glorious. Roddy St Clare's a frightful blister. He's the sort that gives Cambridge men a bad name.'

SCARLET DAYS

13

AINSWORTH STREET WAS ONE of the streets of brick terraces close to the railway station—houses built fifty years before for railway workers and their families, Rowlands supposed. To reach it, he'd crossed the great green space of Parker's Piece, where he could stride without fear of colliding with slower moving pedestrians (although he'd needed to keep a sharp ear out for bikes). Number twenty-three was halfway along; he'd stopped a milkman on his way back to the dairy with a float full of empties, to check he was on the right track. Reaching the house, he knocked and waited. After a brief interval, the door opened and a woman put her head out. 'We don't want nothing,' she said. Before she could shut the door again, Rowlands put his foot in the gap. 'I'm not selling anything,' he said. 'I wanted to speak to Betty, Mrs…'

'Dimock,' was the truculent reply. 'And who might *you* be—asking for my Betty, as cool as you please?'

'Let's say I'm a friend…' he began; but just then a voice he recognised as that of Miss Dimock herself called from the back of the house: 'Who is it, Mum?'

'Says he's a friend.'

'Tell him to go away,' was the girl's response, delivered in tones of flat misery. 'You heard her,' said Betty's mother. 'She doesn't want to talk to you—or anyone.'

'It's about Thomas Findlay,' said Rowlands. There came the sound of footsteps. 'What's that about my Tom?' said Miss Dimock, coming to the door; then: 'Why, it's the gentleman from College! You needn't have kept him standing there, Mum… Won't you come in?' she said to Rowlands. The room into which he stepped—straight off the street, for there was no hallway—was over-full of furniture, he soon discovered. Armchairs, a sideboard (into which he blundered), a dining table and chairs, took up most of the available space. 'I'm sorry to trouble you at such a difficult time,' he said. 'But I've a few questions I'd like to ask you.'

'Questions?' said the girl. 'What sort of questions?'

'May I sit down?' asked Rowlands, since this had not been suggested. 'Oh. Yes. Why don't you? Mum, make us a pot of tea, will you? And bring the best cups...' At Miss Dimock's behest, Rowlands sat down in one of the old-fashioned wingback chairs that stood on either side of the hearth, waiting until her mother had removed herself to the kitchen, before broaching the topic that was uppermost in his mind. 'First of all, let me say how sorry I was to hear the news of Mr Findlay's death,' he said gently. 'I understand you and he were engaged to be married?'

'That's right,' said Betty Dimock. 'Next Easter we was to have put up the bans. Now...' She could not go on. 'I'm sorry if this upsets you,' said Rowlands. 'No, it's O.K.,' she said, blowing her nose sharply. 'Matter of fact it does me good to talk about it.' She gave a shaky little laugh. 'Just think,' she went on. 'We'd have been married by now, if he'd had his way, the great baby...' Another sniff. 'That's all he was, see? No harm in him, really.'

'I thought you said the wedding was to have been after Easter?' said Rowlands. 'Oh, it *was*. Only Tom says why did we need to wait all that time, when we had the money to do the thing at once?'

'And did he?' said Rowlands. 'Have the money, I mean...'

'He *said* he did,' replied the girl. But she sounded uncertain. 'Had he been given a pay-rise, perhaps?' prompted Rowlands, careful not to let her see his interest in the matter. Betty Dimock laughed. 'What! The College handing him a rise, when he'd only been there two years come Michaelmas? I don't *think* so.'

'Could it have been a legacy, then?'

She considered the possibility. 'He didn't *say* nothing about a legacy. Leastways, not to me... Although...' She broke off, as her mother appeared with the tea-tray. 'Put it down there, Mum. I'll pour out. How do you like it?' she asked their guest. Inwardly cursing the interruption, Rowlands replied that he'd have it as it came, thanks. 'This money,' he persisted. 'Have you any idea where he got it?'

Suddenly she was on her guard. 'Why are you so interested?' she demanded. 'Has he... had he... done something wrong?'

'I don't know,' Rowlands admitted. 'That's what I'm trying to find out. But I can promise you, Miss Dimock, that whether your *fiancé* did or didn't get himself involved in something he shouldn't have isn't going to make the least difference to him now...'

She thought about this. 'All right,' she said. 'What do you want to know?'

'Three things,' said Rowlands. He took a sip of the powerfully strong brew. 'Firstly: when was it, to the best of your recollection, that Tom—Mr Findlay—first mentioned the fact that he was expecting to receive this money?'

Betty Dimock was silent once more. 'It was end of term,' she said at last. 'We'd been to the pictures—his treat—and he suddenly come out with it. "I hope you've got your bags packed for the honeymoon," he says to me. "Because we won't have to wait until next summer to tie the knot, or my name's not Tom Findlay..."' This time, she couldn't repress a sob. 'Sorry,' she murmured, after an interval. 'I'll be all right now.'

'Were you aware that Mr Findlay had given up his job at the College?' asked Rowlands, hoping he wasn't about to add to her burden of misery. But she seemed unperturbed by this. 'He *said* he was going to do it,' she replied. '"Think of it, Betty," he said to me. "No more slaving away for sixpences here and there, when we've got our own concern..."'

'He meant setting up a business of his own, did he?'

''S'pose so,' she said indifferently. 'But then he always did like to talk big, did my Tom...' Rowlands sensed that she was nearing the end of her patience where his questions were concerned. 'One last thing,' he said. 'Was the Anchor pub at the Mill Pond a regular haunt of Mr Findlay's?'

She seemed startled by this. 'No,' she said. 'Why should it have been? Tom lives... lived... in Chesterton. Other side of the river. His local was the Green Dragon. He wouldn't have traipsed halfway across Cambridge just to go for a pint. I couldn't believe it when they told me where he'd been found.

"The Mill Pond?" I said to that policeman—the one who brought the news. "What business had he at the Mill Pond, on a fine August evening?" He *said* he was playing cards that night with Wilf and Ernie,' she added bitterly. 'But *they* said he'd never set foot in the Green Dragon all night.'

A short while later, Rowlands made his way back along Mill Road—a busy thoroughfare lined with small shops and cheap restaurants—thinking all the while about what he'd learnt. He was now in no doubt that there had been something suspicious about Tom Findlay's death. It wasn't just the timing of it—so soon after the girl's murder (for he was convinced that it *was* murder)—but the odd circumstances. The fact of Findlay's having given in his notice, without warning, at the end of term. His boasting about having come into money. Above all, the fact that he, a strong swimmer, should have failed to save himself when—as it appeared—he'd fallen in the river, close to a pub he wasn't in the habit of frequenting...

'It all adds up,' murmured Rowlands to himself. And what it added up to was murder. Another in what he was sure must be a chain of related killings, rather than the random accidents each had seemed to be. '*Look out*!' A hand shot out, and grasped him just above the elbow. 'You nearly walked right into the path of that bicycle...'

'Major... I mean... Professor Giles. You're right. I wasn't paying attention,' said Rowlands. He'd been about to cross Bridge Street, by the Round Church, to catch the Girton bus. 'It's a bad spot, that,' said Giles. 'Motorcars and bicycles coming at one from all directions. Still, no harm done, I trust? It's good to see you, Rowlands.'

'You, too,' he replied. Then he remembered what had brought him to Cambridge, and what he had found there. 'I called at your rooms earlier, as a matter of fact...'

'Yes, I've...er... just got back,' said the older man quickly. 'Spent a few days at my little cottage. Very quiet, but it suits me down to the ground.' They had by now crossed the road. Giles consulted his watch. 'Four o'clock. A little early for a snifter, but...'

'So you haven't yet been into College?'

'As I said, I've only just got back. Out of term, you know, I come and go as I please.'

'Then you won't have heard…' Rowlands broke off. 'Perhaps,' he said, 'we should go to your rooms. This isn't something to be talked about in the street.'

'That sounds rather alarming,' said Professor Giles. 'Yes,' said Rowlands. 'I'm afraid I've got some rather bad news.'

A little over an hour later, Rowlands arrived back at St Gertrude's College. He'd just have time to bathe and change, he thought, before setting out again. Over his arm was the dress suit he'd hired from Ede and Ravenscroft in the town, after accepting Professor Giles's invitation to dine at St Jude's that evening. 'Of course you must come, my dear fellow! And do extend the invitation to Mr Loveless,' the English don had added, when Rowlands had explained about his friend's presence at St Gertrude's. 'We keep a modest table at St Jude's—but quite acceptable, I think you'll find.'

Loveless was only too happy to accept. 'I could do with a break from all these women,' he said. 'To say nothing of the provisions. Luncheon was mutton stew and boiled cabbage—with nothing but water to drink. And such high-minded conversation, you wouldn't believe…'

'Do you good, I should think,' was Rowlands's reply. He himself felt more than a little guilty for abandoning Miss Rickards—who had after all been kind enough to invite him to stay at the College. But when he explained why it was that he and Loveless were to forgo the pleasure of her company at dinner, she only laughed. 'No need to apologise, Frederick. In your shoes, I'd do the same—like a shot! St Jude's has one of the best cellars in Cambridge, I believe. And they don't stint themselves when it comes to the food, either…'

If there had been a pleasant informality about dining in Hall at St Gertrude's, owing both to the smallness of the numbers, and (Rowlands suspected) because most of those present were women, with less regard for such flummery, the St Jude's version of the daily ritual was an altogether grander affair. The surroundings—a sixteenth century hall with a magnificent hammer-beam ceiling decorated with armorial devices— lent an aura of dignity and splendour to the proceedings. 'Now *this* is more like it!' exclaimed Loveless, as the two of them followed their host, Dr Giles, and the other Fellows of the College, into the great room. 'Like something out of a Holbein—all black and crimson and gold...'

'Describe it in more detail, will you?' said Rowlands, whose senses had been stirred by the mingled scents of candle-wax and polished wood, as well as by the enticing aroma of cooking drifting from the kitchens across the passage. Loveless obligingly did so, revelling in the finer points of linenfold panelling, heraldic stained-glass and antique silver candelabra. 'Some marvellous paintings, too. I believe that one *is* a Holbein... But then they all look as if they've stepped out of a painting, these old boys, in their long black scholars' gowns...'

He was silenced—as they all were—by the sounding of a gong, followed by that of a bell, heralding the saying of Grace. This—again, in sharp contrast to the brisk two-word blessing employed by the women's college—was a long affair in Latin, of which Rowlands understood no more than one word in three. It was followed by the scraping of chairs, as everyone sat down. Rowlands found himself seated next to the Master; Dr Giles was on his left, and Loveless on Dr Bradbrook's other side. 'Mr Loveless is an artist,' he heard Giles explain to the Master. 'He painted that remarkable portrait of Miss Sitwell, you may recall...'

'Ah, yes,' murmured Dr Bradbrook. 'Miss Sitwell, to be sure...'

'And a holy terror she turned out to be,' said Loveless. 'Constantly complaining. The studio was too hot or too cold, or she found the pose uncomfortable...' Rowlands, who had had experience of Loveless's studio—and of the rigorous demands he made as a portraitist—was inclined to sympathise with the poetess. 'And this is Mr Rowlands...'

'The Master and I have already met,' said Rowlands with a smile. 'Yes, yes, of course. You were the gentleman who... Most upsetting business,' said the other; then, in an undertone: 'I assume there's been no further word from the police?'

Rowlands replied in the negative. Further conversation was

interrupted by the arrival of the soup course—a vichyssoise. From his first taste of this, it was apparent that Maud Rickards's prediction concerning the standard of cuisine at St Jude's was to be amply fulfilled. Nor did the glass of Chablis which accompanied it disappoint. The Master's question had evidently caught the attention of one of the Fellows sitting opposite. 'What's that about the police?' he said. 'Don't say someone's been pilfering from the college cellars again?' This jovial sally was met with silence. 'I'm afraid it's a good deal worse than that, Dr Wilmshurst,' said the Master. 'We've had a death. One of the undergraduates. A scientist. Julian Sedgwick.'

'Good Lord! You don't say?' said the man who'd spoken. 'What was it—a motor accident? These young chaps are always racing around like lunatics...'

'It wasn't a motor accident—or indeed, an accident of any kind, regrettably.' The Master took a spoonful of his soup. 'It happened in College,' he said. 'The young man was found to have died from an overdose of morphine. The police have formed the opinion that it was a deliberate act.'

'Do you mean it was suicide?'

'The police have reason to believe that it was murder.' Once more, Rowlands observed the peculiar effect of the word on the atmosphere of a room. It was as if a chill had descended on the company, which no amount fine wine and rich food could dispel. 'Murder? But surely...' broke in a voice he knew, from across the table. It belonged to Professor Harding. 'Isn't that jumping to conclusions? I mean, saying it wasn't an *accident* isn't the same as proving it was a deliberate killing...'

'No, indeed,' said another voice. Professor Bristow. 'One must have *proof*. Something we men of science insist on, eh, Harding?' he added with a dry chuckle. The soup plates were cleared away and a dish of grilled soles in a cream sauce served. More wine was poured (a Sancerre, this time). Rowlands sipped his gingerly. With the conversation having taken the turn it had, he wanted to keep his wits about him. 'I believe the police have all the proof they need,' he said. 'Rowlands here was the man who found poor young Sedgwick's body,' put in Professor Giles.

'You seem to make rather habit of finding bodies.' This was Harding, again. His jovial tone veiled an undertone of aggression. Rowlands smiled. 'It isn't something I've particularly enjoyed, I can assure you.'

'What's that about finding bodies?' said a voice from further along the table. 'Don't say there's been more than one?'

'Dr Harding was referring to the incident at St Gertrude's last term, I imagine,' said Bristow, tucking into his fish. 'You mean the girl who died?' said the man who'd asked about bodies. 'But that *was* an accident, surely?'

'I understand that the police aren't satisfied with that verdict, either,' said Rowlands. A brief silence followed this statement, during which the only sound to be heard was the scraping of knives and forks against plates. At length, someone along the table made a remark about the proposed land speed trials, due to be held the next day in Utah. 'They're saying Campbell's aiming to break his own record of 276 miles per hour…'

'One really rather wonders what the point of it is,' said another voice.

'Why, to prove that he can do it, I imagine.'

Plates were cleared, and the next course brought to the table. 'Ah,' said Professor Bristow. 'What have we here? The roast beef of Old England, I declare!'

'Do you know,' said the Master. 'I think the beef we get at St Jude's is as good as any I've had—even at Rules, you know…'

And there the earlier topic of conversation might have petered out, if it hadn't been for Loveless. 'But we were speaking of murder,' he said, taking a swig of the excellent Burgundy which had just been poured. 'Do you know, I've often thought that *I* might make a good murderer? Who would suspect an artist? Yet one's opportunities are legion. How many men, after all, find themselves alone in a room with a beautiful woman as often as I do, and—having placed her in a chair, or posed her on a *chaise longue*—can get close enough to do the deed, without exciting the victim's suspicions?'

There was laughter at this. 'Disposing of the corpse might present you with rather more of a problem,' said someone. 'True,' said the artist cheerfully. 'Yes, the actual killing would be the easy part. Concealing it would be an altogether trickier matter.'

'I've always felt that pushing somebody over a cliff was the only really foolproof method,' put in an elderly Fellow. 'Murder and disposal of the body in one…'

'You won't find many cliffs in Cambridgeshire,' objected the first. 'No, but you could always lead your intended victim to the top of Great St Mary's,' said the other. The Master cleared his throat, evidently having decided that things had gone far enough. 'A rather macabre conversation, if I might say so,' he said. 'My apologies,' said Loveless. 'The joke was in poor taste. But as an outsider, I find it hard to believe that anything bad could ever happen in such a beautiful place. Why, sitting here in this splendid room, one might think oneself back four hundred years, in the time of Good Queen Bess…'

'Who, incidentally, rode her horse into this very hall, during a state visit,' said the Master, his good humour now restored. 'Which is not to say that bad things didn't happen in *her* day, too. Burnings and beheadings and the like. Fortunately, such things are no longer our concern…'

The talk moved on to other things. A trip to Florence, undertaken with some of his students by Dr Osgood, a Classics don. The walking tour of the Lake District from which Dr Harding and his wife had recently returned. 'I hope you took better care this time,' said the Master. 'We can't afford to lose one of most eminent scholars through some unfortunate accident. Dr Harding is a climber,' he explained to Rowlands. 'He does not consider a holiday well-spent unless he has tackled one of the major peaks. Last year, it was nearly the death of him.'

'A minor accident, nothing more,' said Harding airily. 'Even the most experienced climbers have accidents, you know, Master.'

'Yes indeed, accidents will happen,' murmured Professor Bristow. 'What's this they've given us for pudding? Can it be syllabub?' It was indeed syllabub—and sweet enough to have pleased the sugar-loving Queen herself. A savoury of devilled kidneys followed, after which the company—with the exception of the Master, who said he had some letters to write—repaired to an upstairs room for port, madeira and fine old Stilton.

'I don't know about resorting to murder,' remarked Loveless sleepily, 'but I can quite see how one might eat and drink oneself to death in such surroundings...'

'But seriously,' said the man who'd speculated about pushing his victim off the tower of the University church. 'Since we're on the subject—hasn't everyone, at one time or another, thought about doing somebody in? I know *I* have.'

'How do you know that some of us haven't?' This was Harding. It struck Rowlands that he was somewhat the worse for drink. 'What—thought about murder or committed it?'

'Committed it, of course. It stands to reason,' said the physicist, 'that there must be scores of people walking around who've got away with it...'

'You don't have a high opinion of the police, then?' asked Rowlands, keeping his tone light. 'Oh, the police do what they can, I've no doubt,' said Harding. 'But I maintain that—faced with what I call a really *intelligent* murder, the police could do nothing...'

There came a dry chuckle from across the table. 'And who is she—your intended victim?' said Professor Bristow. 'For I presume it *is* a "she" with whom you would like to do away?' There was more laughter at this. 'He's got you there, Harding!' said the man who'd introduced the topic. 'One of your conquests, is she?'

'I was advancing a hypothesis,' replied Harding coldly. 'But since some of you seem inclined to make a joke of it, we'll leave it at that. Pass the Madeira, Osgood, if you've finished with it...'

The conversation turned to College matters: the appointment of one Fellow or another to this Board or that. The altering of some regulation relating to the History Tripos. Most of it was impenetrable to Rowlands, and—to judge from an unsuccessful attempt to stifle a yawn—to Loveless, too. 'Can't think what's got into me,' the latter said, apologising for this lapse. 'It's not even midnight. Of course I was up rather early this morning. Miss Phillips is a stern taskmistress...'

'Yes, Rowlands tells me you're painting her portrait,' said Dr Giles. 'I should think she must make rather a fine subject.'

'Oh, magnificent,' was the reply. 'Such *presence*, you know.

And those eyes! She must have been a great beauty, in her youth…'

'She was,' said Giles quietly. 'Not that she would thank me for saying so.'

'No indeed! Her mind is on higher things.' Loveless accepted the port from his neighbour and replenished his glass. 'I don't mind admitting that she quite terrifies me,' he said. 'When she fixes me with that penetrating gaze, I seem to feel myself a small boy again, being ticked off for some misdemeanour.'

'I had an aunt like that,' said one of the younger Fellows reminiscently. 'Used to make me learn strings of Latin verbs before breakfast.' A collective shudder seemed to pass around the room at this evocation of female authority. Then Harding said, 'Time I was off. Agnes worries if I'm out too late.' After this, it wasn't long before the rest of the party broke up—only a couple of the elderly dons whose names Rowlands had failed to catch, seemed inclined to make a night of it. He and Loveless were accompanied to the gate by Dr Giles. 'Good night, Rowlands. I expect we'll meet at the inquest tomorrow… It was a pleasure to meet you, Mr Loveless. Please give my regards to the Mistress, won't you?'

'He seems a nice old boy.' remarked the artist, as he and Rowlands strolled back through the quiet streets to where he had left the car. 'An old Army man, you say?'

'Yes. He taught me how to strip down and load a rifle.'

'And yet he looks such a peaceable type! But then it's hard to imagine any of them getting up to anything more bellicose than quibbling over some point of Anglo-Saxon grammar in the columns of *The Times.*'

'What did you think of Harding?' said Rowlands, when they were driving back along the Huntingdon Road—mercifully deserted at this time of night (Loveless was an erratic driver).

'It's funny you should ask me that,' said his friend. 'If you want my opinion, I thought he seemed a bit full of himself.'

'In what way?'

'Well, you know… laying down the law like that… about murder, of all things!' Loveless chuckled. 'I hope you noticed the skilful way I introduced the subject?'

'I did. And I'll thank you not to do it again... I say, take care!' Because at that moment the car swerved violently. 'It's all right,' said Loveless. 'It was only a cat. I'm pretty sure I missed it. What were we talking about?'

'You were giving me your opinion of Professor Harding.'

'So I was. Yes, a rather conceited type. Those good-looking men so often are. Women fall for them, and it makes them think they're irresistible. He didn't like it one bit when that other fellow went for him...'

'Professor Bristow, you mean?'

'I can't remember all their names. Dried-up looking sort. Made some crack about our boy's fondness for the ladies. *He* wasn't amused, I can tell you!'

'He didn't sound very pleased, it's true,' said Rowlands. 'But then he might have felt it was a bit near the bone, given that one of the murder victims was his student...' Loveless let out a whistle. 'No wonder he looked daggers at the other chap. 'I'd venture to guess that the victim was a woman...'

'It was. Her name was Diana Havelock. A brilliant young physicist.'

'Our lady in the green frock, unless I'm much mistaken?'

'That's right.'

'And you think our handsome friend was involved with the girl?' said Loveless. 'I don't know,' was the reply. 'But I'm going to find out.'

14

No more was said on the subject until after they had arrived back at the College, where—having roused the Porter to let them in, and collected the keys to their rooms—they made their way along what seemed an all-the-more endless network of corridors to reach them. 'This place gives me the horrors,' said Loveless. 'I don't know how these women stand it, frankly.'

'They're used to it, I imagine,' said Rowlands. 'Some of them seem quite fond of the place.'

'Can't imagine why. I mean, one can understand getting sentimental about the beauties of St Jude's, or Trinity. But a Victorian red-brick warren like this…'

'I think the architecture is beside the point. Mrs Woolf said it was having "a room of one's own". Time and space to devote to study. The *right* to study…'

'I hadn't realised you were such a feminist, old man.'

'I surprise myself, too,' was the reply. They reached the door of Loveless's room. 'Care for a nightcap?' he said. 'I've a bottle of whisky to hand…'

With the thought of tomorrow's inquest in mind, Rowlands declined the offer. 'Pity,' yawned his friend. 'I was looking forward to quizzing you some more about your murder mystery. I take it tonight's gathering gave you another bunch of suspects to consider?'

'I wouldn't go that far. But it certainly gave me some food for thought.' Loveless laughed. 'You're a close one, old man! We'll meet at breakfast, no doubt.' The two men said goodnight, and then Rowlands, wishing he'd had rather less to drink than was the case, continued on his way towards his room. Was it his imagination, or had the place grow larger since that morning?

It was certainly quieter. Instead of the homely sounds of maids clanking mops and pails, as they did out the rooms, and of girlish footsteps hurrying along corridors, there was utter silence. From somewhere outside in the grounds, an owl hooted.

He reached in intersection between one corridor and another. It was this way, surely—wasn't it? With a growing sense of being caught up in some vivid dream of escape, he set off in the direction he thought was the right one—only to find himself, a few moments later, back at the place from which he'd set out. Yes, here was the heavy oak door that led out into the grounds; here the marble pillar, and the staircase… He tried another corridor, with much the same result. Ridiculous, to have got himself lost. He was deliberating whether it might not, after all, be best to go back to the beginning—even if it meant having to ask for help at the Porters' Lodge—when the sound of a voice, quite close by, almost made him jump out of his skin. 'Mr Rowlands.'

'Oh!' For a moment, he stood foolishly gaping. 'Good evening, Mistress.' But she, evidently unperturbed by his appearance at that late hour, was already opening a door. 'Perhaps,' she said, 'if you can spare a moment, we could talk?'

It was her study in which they found themselves; he recalled its odour of leather-bound books and furniture polish. There was another smell, too—he realised that she must have been smoking. 'Would you care for a drink?' she said. 'I have some sherry…'

'No, thank you.'

'A cigarette, then?' This he accepted, taking one from the sandalwood box she offered him—a Turkish brand. She lit it for him, then lit one for herself. 'Do sit down,' she said, after a moment. It struck Rowlands that she seemed curiously distracted. This was not the calm, impassive woman of their previous encounters. Something had evidently unsettled her. It was not hard to guess what that might be. 'The police were here earlier,' she said. 'They wish to re-open the investigation into Diana Havelock's death. Not that I am telling you anything you don't already know,' added Miss Phillips. 'I gather,' she went on, 'that it was you who found the Sedgwick boy?'

'Yes.'

Beryl Phillips was silent a long moment. 'You must think me a very foolish, obstinate woman,' she said at last. Rowlands shook his head. 'I don't think anything of the sort. You couldn't have known…'

'*You* did.'

Again, he refused the suggestion. 'I didn't *know* for certain. It was just a feeling… no more… that something wasn't right.'

'Well, your "feeling" or instinct—call it what you will—has been proved correct,' she said. 'That inspector… Inspector Brown… said that Diana was probably overpowered by… by her murderer… and that a dose of morphine strong enough to kill her was then injected.' She paused, as if considering this appalling fact, before continuing: 'He told me that a similar method was used to kill Julian Sedgwick.'

'That would seem to be the case,' said Rowlands.

The Mistress gave a long, shuddering sigh. 'What I don't understand,' she said, 'is *why*? Do you have any idea, Mr Rowlands, what reason anybody could have had to take the lives of these two young people?'

Rowlands hesitated. But then it occurred to him that she would hear sooner or later about the letter Julian Sedgwick had written, and what it alleged. 'I can only speculate as to why Miss Havelock was killed, but I believe from something Mr Sedgwick told me that she may have been involved with someone… with a man, I mean.'

'I see. And you think this man was the one who…' She broke off. 'It seems likely,' he said. 'I think whoever it was must have been afraid that his involvement with Miss Havelock would be discovered, and hoped to silence her—making her death look like an accident.' Miss Phillips considered the implications of this. 'Then the man… whoever he is… must have reasons for wanting to conceal the affair… such as the fact that he is already married.'

'I think that's a reasonable supposition.'

'It's all so horrible,' she said. 'To think that… that a St Gertrude's girl…'Again, she seemed to check herself. 'I expect you think it absurd, to care about such things… the reputation of the College, I mean… when two young people have lost their lives…'

'I don't think it's absurd at all.'

'The fact that the… the *perpetrator* might be a member of the University… perhaps even a member of the teaching staff… makes it all the more…' She let the sentence die away. 'I suppose there's no possibility,' she went on at last, 'that this… this *individual* could have come from outside?'

'It's possible,' he replied. 'But not very likely, I'm afraid.'

'Then let me ask one thing,' said the Mistress, her voice now perfectly steady. 'Find this man, will you, before he destroys another young life? Find him, Mr Rowlands—and bring him to justice.'

At ten o'clock on Tuesday morning, the courtroom at the Guildhall was less crowded than on the previous occasion Rowlands had set foot there; he reminded himself that it was now out of term. Nor was any member of Julian Sedgwick's family present—even the uncle in London the boy had referred to at their last meeting had evidently not thought it necessary to put in an appearance. Once more, Rowlands listened to the police evidence, followed by that of the Medical Officer, before being called to give his own—an experience which necessarily brought back unpleasant memories. Of entering Sedgwick's room—his heart already heavy with dread—to find the boy's lifeless body, slumped, cold and still, in its chair. Of feeling in vain for a pulse, and of trying to calm young Rowntree, who'd kept shouting, 'Can't you *do* something?' Yes, these were things he was going to find it hard to forget.

As the inspector had intimated, an adjournment was requested and granted—the suspicious circumstances of Sedgwick's death having made this inevitable. Now it was up to the police to gather the evidence which would lead to a prosecution for murder. For the time being, at least, Rowlands's part in this sad history was over. But as he got up, in order to make his way towards the exit, he heard a voice he knew—a voice with a strong Scots burr—say, 'You'll no' be leaving yet, Mr Rowlands? I'd hoped we could have a wee chat.'

'Chief Inspector.' Rowlands held out his hand and felt it firmly grasped. 'I wondered if I might run into you.'

'Aye, I thought I'd better come down for the inquest. Inspector Brown here has been putting me in the picture as regards the case,' he added, as they were joined by that officer. 'Oh, I don't think…' began the latter, clearly somewhat abashed at being given the credit for this by the man from Scotland Yard, but his superior went on: 'Och, this is your patch, man. Consider me a mere observer. It seems to me,' he added, as the three men moved towards the exit, 'that you've made considerable progress already. That piece of evidence concerning the fibres of cotton fabric in the laddie's nostrils, now…'

'Yes, well…' began the inspector, sounding decidedly uncomfortable. 'The fact is…' But his superior officer affected not to hear him. 'If you've nothing better to do, Mr Rowlands,' he said, 'you might stroll back to the police station with us—if that's all right with you, Inspector?' Brown mumbled his assent. 'Mr Rowlands and I are old friends,' explained the Chief Inspector. 'Old comrades-in-arms, you might say—eh, Rowlands? I've known him come up with some very ingenious solutions to the stickiest of crimes…'

'I don't know about that,' said Rowlands meekly. 'But I'd be interested to hear how the investigation is developing. There's something I ought to mention which may or may not have a bearing on it…' At the police station, he outlined as briefly as possible what he had learned from his visit to Betty Dimock. The two senior police officers heard him out in silence. Then Chief Inspector Douglas uttered a grim little laugh. 'Well,' he said. 'As if this case wasn't complicated enough, you've gone and found us another corpse, it would seem! What do you say, Inspector?' For the latter had evidently shown by some look or gesture that he had his own thoughts about this. 'The man's death—Thomas Findlay's, I mean—was an accident,' Brown said stubbornly. 'He drowned, while under the influence of drink. It's all in the file.'

'It was certainly made to *look* like an accident,' said Rowlands. 'As were the other two deaths.'

'You're saying he was killed, this groundsman fellow of yours, because he was blackmailing our murderer?' said the Chief

Inspector. 'I'm suggesting it might be worth looking into, is all,' replied Rowlands. 'I think Inspector Brown might have his work cut out looking into the two deaths we *know* to be murders, without taking on any more. Am I right, Inspector?'

'You are that, sir,' said Brown. 'Speaking of which,' went on the Chief Inspector, as Rowlands—thinking himself dismissed—got up to leave, 'who do you fancy for the starring role? If I might put it like that. Come, Mr Rowlands,' he went on, when Rowlands did not reply at once. 'Don't pretend you haven't given this some thought.'

'I'm sure Inspector Brown already has a list of suspects.' The Inspector gave a deprecatory rumble. 'That's as may be,' said Douglas. 'Saving your presence, Inspector. But it's *your* list I want to hear.'

'All right.' Rowlands sat down again. 'It seems to me that if we're agreed that whoever killed Diana Havelock also killed Julian Sedgwick, then our suspects must belong to one particular group—those who have remained in Cambridge, or returned to Cambridge, after the end of term. Which rules out most of the undergraduates, except the handful of third and fourth years staying on for all or part of the Long Vacation...' He paused a moment, considering how best to put what he had to say. 'Of these people, there are some who fall into both this category and another—that is, those who were guests at the St Gertrude's end of term dinner. As I've said, one can exclude most of the undergraduates, apart from the few I've mentioned. Which leaves certain members of the University teaching staff...'

'Their names, Mr Rowlands?'

'I think the Inspector will already have their names.'

'Even so.' While Rowlands was talking, the Chief Inspector had been filling his pipe; now he lit it, and having got it to draw to his satisfaction, began puffing away contentedly. 'I'd like to hear it from you.'

'Very well. If one excludes Dr Maltravers, the Chaplain at St Gertrude's...'

'On what grounds?'

'He's the Chaplain.'

'Hm,' said the Chief Inspector.

Inspector Brown gave a cough. 'As it turns out, he *does* have an alibi. He was seen by one of the ladies—a Miss Glossop—going into his room at around the time the girl was killed. He was still there—writing his sermon—when the news of the girl's death broke.'

'So we can wash *him* out,' said Douglas. 'Go on with what you were saying, Mr Rowlands.'

'All right. Well, that leaves three people. Dr Harding, who was present at the St Gertrude's dinner, and returned to Cambridge from holiday a few days ago—I'm not sure exactly when—Dr Bristow, also present at the dinner, also in Cambridge during the crucial period, and Dr Giles... But I'm sure *he* can't have been involved,' said Rowlands. 'Why not?' demanded the Chief Inspector. 'He was at this dinner, you say?'

'Yes, but...'

'And he's still in Cambridge?'

'He was away when Sedgwick was killed. He has a cottage in the Fens, I believe...'

'Nothing easier than for him to get back earlier than he says he did, do the deed, then pop back to his cottage, appearing next day as innocent as you please,' put in Inspector Brown. 'We'll be checking his story, o' course.'

'I don't think Professor Giles is our man,' said Rowlands. 'I know him quite well, as a matter of fact. He's a very decent sort.'

'So are a number of murderers of my acquaintance,' said Douglas, meditatively puffing on his pipe. 'You can't rule out a man on those grounds—even if he *is* a friend of yours, Mr Rowlands.'

'The man we're looking for is a younger man,' said Rowlands. 'Someone attractive to women...'

'I suppose it's Professor Harding you're thinking of?' said Brown. 'We've already talked to him. He was away in the Lake District when young Sedgwick was killed. His wife supports his alibi.'

'As you said yourself, alibis can be faked,' said Rowlands. 'So that just leaves... what's his name? Professor Bristow,' said the Chief Inspector. 'What's *his* story?'

'He was at the dinner all right,' said Brown. 'But we can rule him out for the Sedgwick murder because he was lecturing in London on the Saturday evening. *Very* keen to tell me about that, he was. Thinks he might be in line for some big prize—he's a scientist, you know. Funny old party.'

'We'll have to check his story, of course,' said Douglas. 'But it looks as if we can forget about Professor Bristow.'

'Quite apart from all that, he's too old,' said Rowlands. 'Julian Sedgwick was convinced Miss Havelock was romantically involved with another man. I find it hard to see the crusty Professor Bristow in the role of lady-killer…'

'You never can tell,' said Brown owlishly. After this a silence fell. Then all three started speaking at once:

'One thing…'

'It seems to me…'

'Are we certain…'

'You first, Inspector,' said the senior officer courteously. 'You don't mind, do you, Mr Rowlands?'

'Not a bit.'

'Well, sir, it's like this,' said Inspector Brown, clearing his throat in a nervous manner. 'We're assuming on account of this letter the boy sent that the perpetrator is a man. But—with respect—we've only Mr Rowlands's say-so to go on… about what young Sedgwick said to him I mean, and so…'

'Good point,' said the Chief Inspector, in what struck Rowlands (who knew him rather well) as a drily amused tone. 'What do you say to *that*, Mr Rowlands? Ought we to have ruled out one of the St Gertrude's ladies as our murderer? After all, Diana Havelock was killed on College premises…'

'Yes,' said Rowlands. 'But I still think…'

'Come, man! It isn't like you to base your suspicions on such flimsy evidence,' said Douglas, still in the same faintly humorous tone. 'The word of a young man who was—let's face it—besotted with the young lady in question. Naturally he'd be inclined to all sorts of jealous imaginings.'

'It isn't just what Sedgwick said.' As soon as he'd blurted it out, Rowlands regretted it. 'Oh?' came the reply. 'I hope you haven't been withholding evidence from the police, Mr Rowlands?'

'No,' said Rowlands, now feeling distinctly uncomfortable.

Briefly, he summarised the affair of the poison-pen letters.

'You say there were threats against anyone who seemed to favour her?' said Inspector Brown. 'I should have been told about this before, Mr Rowlands, I really should...'

'It didn't seem important at the time,' said Rowlands. 'After all, the police were treating Miss Havelock's death as an accident until very recently.'

'Fair enough,' conceded the police officer grudgingly. 'Still, I should like to see those letters. If anyone—man or woman—has been making threats, it needs looking into.'

'And it might offer us another lead,' put in the Chief Inspector, who had been listening to this exchange with what Rowlands guessed was some enjoyment. 'Do you think it's possible that our letter-writer and our murderer might be one and the same?'

'It's possible, o' course,' said Brown, a shade warily. 'Although in my experience, sir, these poison-pen types tend to work off their venom on paper, if you get me? It's not impossible that one of 'em could have taken things a stage further...'

'Always a first time for everything, you might say.' The Chief Inspector occupied himself with knocking out the ashes from his pipe. 'Well, it opens up a number of fresh possibilities. Perhaps we should take a run up to this ladies' college of yours, and see if we can get a line on these letters. You say the Bursar's the one who informed you of the affair, Mr Rowlands?'

'Yes,' admitted Rowlands, with an inward groan. He could imagine only too well what Maud Rickards would say when she found out that her confidence had been betrayed. 'Don't look so grim, Mr Rowlands,' said the other. 'I'll make sure to tell the lady—Miss Rickards, is it?—that you gave us the information under duress.' He *is* enjoying himself, thought Rowlands. 'No need,' he said. 'Miss Rickards and I are old friends. I'm sure she understands that the police have to do their job.'

'An admirable supposition,' was the reply. 'Would that all members of the public were as understanding—eh, Inspector?' The Chief Inspector got to his feet, with a certain effort. Always a heavy man, he had grown more so in recent years. 'Best be on our way, I think. Aside from these letters, I want to take a look at the girl's room. Not that there'll be much to see, after nearly three months. Any traces of our killer will have been obliterated long ago.'

Outside the police station, Rowlands took his leave of his old friend, Chief Inspector Douglas. 'I expect I'll see you around,' said the latter, as they shook hands. 'When this case comes to trial, if not before.'

'Indeed,' said Rowlands. If Brown had not been standing there, he might have added: 'Let me know how things develop.' But he knew that as far as the good Inspector was concerned, he had already outstayed his welcome. The car drew up and the two police officers, accompanied by the sergeant, got in. 'Give my regards to Mrs Rowlands, won't you?' said Douglas. 'I take it you'll be going back to London, now?'

'That's right. Goodbye, Chief Inspector. Inspector Brown.' Rowlands raised his hand as the police car drove away. Yes, he'd be heading home soon, now that the inquest was over—but first, he'd have a walk to clear his head. Two hours in a stuffy courtroom, follow by another hour being grilled by the police, had given him the beginnings of a headache. A walk, followed by a pint of ale and a sandwich in one of those riverside pubs, would be just the ticket, he thought.

St Andrew's Street was busy with lunchtime traffic—buses roared up and down, and crowds of pedestrians jostled one another at the crossing-points. Rowlands was glad to turn down quieter Downing Street, which led, he knew, past the Science Department of the University towards Mill Lane and the river. Something was nagging at the back of his mind, but he couldn't think for a moment what it was. Something to do with the river. Those pubs... yes, that was it... As he reached the junction with Free School Lane, the furious ringing of a bicycle bell made him jump back. These bicycles! Cambridge could certainly be a dangerous place... 'Look where you're going, can't you?' shouted a voice. Young. Female. 'I almost ran you over...'

'I'm sorry,' he said. 'I didn't see you.'

'No, that's perfectly obvious... Oh, it's you,' said the girl. In the same moment, Rowlands realised who it was. 'Miss Mainwaring, isn't it?'

'Yes.' She'd brought her bike to a standstill. 'I'm awfully sorry

I shouted at you. But I didn't see you until too late. I was just on my way to the lab,' she explained. 'I suppose I must have been thinking of other things...'

'No harm done,' said Rowlands. 'I say,' he went on, as she seemed about to cycle off, 'I couldn't ask you a tremendous favour, could I? Only I've always wanted to see what a working laboratory's like. I don't suppose you could let me take a look around?'

'Well... I don't know,' said Gillian Mainwaring. 'I *suppose* it'd be all right...'

'Splendid,' he said.

The Cavendish Laboratory took up almost the whole of one side of Free School Lane, it transpired. 'We're coming to the main building now,' said Miss Mainwaring, who was wheeling her bike. 'I'll just chain this up, and then... I suppose it *is* all right,' she muttered dubiously. Just inside the main gates she found a space in the bicycle rack for her machine. 'What is it you'd like to see?' she asked, when she'd done this. He smiled. 'I do appreciate this most awfully,' he said. 'And I promise I won't take up too much of your time. One thing, though—could you make sure to *describe* everything as minutely as possible? Only as I can't actually see, I'd like to be able to picture things...'

'Oh.' She seemed taken aback for a moment. Perhaps she hadn't realised he was blind, he thought. When she spoke again, it was in a less recalcitrant tone. 'I'll try,' she said. 'Do you want me to describe the buildings first?'

'If you don't mind.'

'All right. Well, the one we're about to go inside is the main building, as I said. It's not very interesting to look at—just a big Victorian building, built of pale yellowish stone. Three stories. Rows of tall windows—those are the labs. I've never really looked at it before.'

'That gives me an idea. Thank you.'

'The really interesting building is the "Crocodile",'she said; then gave an embarrassed laugh. 'That's not its real name—it's the Mond Laboratory—but it's got a crocodile carved on the outside, so that's what we call it...'

'Perfectly logical,' said Rowlands. 'It's a yellow brick building,' his companion went on. 'The entrance bit is in the shape of a drum. It's just through the archway, here—look! Oh, I'm sorry,'she added. 'I forgot for a moment that you can't…'

'Your description makes me feel as if I can,' he said. 'A drum, you say? That sounds very modern.'

'Oh, it is! It was only completed two years ago—just before I came up. It was designed by Professor Kapitza,' she added, in a reverential tone. 'That's why it's got a crocodile on it. It's his nickname for Professor Rutherford, you see…'

'And that's a laboratory, you say?'

'Yes. But only for people working on certain programmes. Magnetic fields and the like. I'm only a third year and so…'

'Was Miss Havelock working on that kind of thing, do you know?'

'Diana? I'm not sure. She might have been,' was the reply. 'We didn't have much to do with one another on a day to day basis…' He nodded politely at this, wondering why, if that was the case, she'd been so upset when she heard the news of Miss Havelock's death. But then she said: 'I… I really admired her, you know? It sounds silly, but… she was a sort of heroine of mine.'

15

THEY ENTERED THE MAIN building via a short flight of steps and a set of heavy wooden doors. Miss Mainwaring, her earlier reluctance forgotten, it seemed, was eager to point out salient features. 'To our left is the battery room. It supplies power for the whole building—especially for demonstrations in the lecture room. And that's the magnetism room. It has to be extra-stable, and so it's got a concrete floor. The labs and lecture rooms are up here…'

Still talking, she led him up a broad staircase to the first floor. She opened a door. A powerful smell of chemicals was emitted. 'This is the Large Laboratory. It should be empty just now, with the first and second years away.' Rowlands followed her into a large, echoing space. 'Nobody's here,' whispered his guide with evident relief. 'Only Mr Stanley. He's one of the demonstrators… 'Is it all right if I bring my… my uncle to look round?' she called to this factotum, who was busy with some task at the far end of the long room. Stanley must have made some reply, inaudible to Rowlands, for Miss Mainwaring continued with her description of the laboratory.

To this Rowlands listened with only half an ear, distracted by a growing realisation. This, then, was the world in which Diana Havelock and her unfortunate admirer, Julian Sedgwick, had spent the greater part of their time at Cambridge. It struck him then that the clue to what had happened to them lay here, within these walls—and not in their respective colleges. Because if anything linked these two young people and the man he suspected of murdering them both, it was the Cavendish Laboratory.

'…about sixty feet long, and thirty wide, with four tall windows looking out onto the street, and twelve benches, each fitted with a Bunsen burner,' said Miss Mainwaring. 'There are microscopes on all the benches, of course, and racks for test-tubes and bottles of chemicals... although the really noxious stuff is kept in the Poison Cupboard. I say, are you really interested in all this?'

'Rather,' said Rowlands. 'Only I think, if you don't mind, that I'd like to see where Miss Havelock worked. She was a physicist, not a chemist, wasn't she?'

'Yes. She worked over in the Mond Lab, most of the time, I think. With Professor Harding. I... I'm afraid I don't know much more about it. Atomic Physics isn't my field, as I've said.'

'It's not important,' said Rowlands—although he had a feeling that it was. 'I'm just interested, that's all. There can't be many women working in this area... Science, I mean.'

'No, Diana was the only one in her year. There are two in mine—Rosalind Fielding and me. And Miss Cartwright, of course—but she's one of the lecturers.'

'I can see why you have to work so hard,' he said. 'It must matter very much that the men shouldn't be the only ones to take the prizes...'

'Oh, as to *that*,' said Gillian Mainwaring with a touch of scorn, 'I don't think we've anything to worry about. Diana got the top marks in her year, you know. That's why College offered her the research studentship...' She broke off suddenly. 'Why *are* you so interested in what Diana was up to?' she demanded. 'It seems to me you've done nothing but ask questions about her since we got here...'

Rowlands hesitated; then made a decision. 'I'm trying to find out what happened to her,' he said. 'This seemed a good place to start. It appears that her death wasn't an accident, after all. Nor was it suicide.'

'You mean it was *murder*?'

'I'm afraid so.'

Gillian Mainwaring thought for a moment. 'Well, if you think it would help, I can show you where some of the physicists work—I think Diana spent some of her time in these labs, when she wasn't in the Crocodile building. We'll have to go up to the next floor.'

'I'd appreciate that very much.'

They climbed the stairs. 'In here,' said Miss Mainwaring, 'is the Electrical Room. It's full of apparatus…'

'Don't worry, I won't touch anything.' The room smelt dry and airless, with a faintly acidic odour that made Rowlands think of battery acid. 'Can you describe it a bit?' he asked. 'All right. The large object is an electro-dynamometer. There are also three mirror galvanometers, a glass-plate electric machine, and a Holtz electric machine… I can't let you touch them, I'm afraid…'

'I don't want to,' said Rowlands. 'Hearing about them is quite enough.' Miss Mainwaring was still brooding on what he'd told her. 'But who would *want* to murder Diana?'

'That's what I'm trying to find out,' he said. 'Do they have any idea who did it?'

'The police are following some leads.'

'And you're helping them—is that it?'

'Something like that.'

'Gosh! I've never met a detective before,' said Miss Mainwaring, as they emerged from the Electrical Room. 'What's across the corridor?' said Rowlands, still keen to get a more complete picture of the place. 'That's the Radium Room. It's kept locked, when not in use, though…'

'Jolly good thing,' said Rowlands. 'I say, I *am* having an interesting time!' They began walking back towards the stairs. As they reached the head of these, there came the sound of voices. At this, Gillian Mainwaring froze. 'Quick,' she muttered. 'In here.' She seized Rowlands's arm and pulled him towards another set of doors. These she pushed open, and the two of them tumbled inside. He didn't need to be told to keep quiet.

Footsteps sounded outside. 'I think you'll find that my results are accurate,' said a voice, disconcertingly close at hand. It was Professor Harding. He and whoever he was talking to must be standing on the other side of the door, thought Rowlands, praying that neither man would take it into his head to enter the room in which he and Miss Mainwaring had taken refuge. To be caught trespassing—for he supposed that was what he was doing—would be embarrassing, to say the least. But Fate was on his side, it seemed. Harding's colleague, whoever he was, mumbled a reply which Rowlands couldn't catch, and then the two men moved off. 'Oh please—do let's wait until they're gone,' whispered Miss Mainwaring. 'I'll get into awful trouble if anyone finds out I've been showing you the research labs. All this part of the building's out of bounds to anyone but fourth years…'

'Then I'd better clear off as soon as possible,' said Rowlands. 'We can't have you getting into hot water on my account. And I've taken up too much of your time, as it is.'

'I don't mind,' she said, as—the coast being clear—they emerged from their hiding-place and descended the stairs towards the exit. 'I was only going to check some results in the lab. Pretty routine stuff. Helping you with your sleuthing has been much more fun… If it *was* of any help,' she added. 'Oh, it was. I'm very grateful,' said Rowlands, as they shook hands. 'It's given me a much clearer picture of things than I had before.' Which was true, as far as it went, he thought—although he'd have given anything to see inside the 'Crocodile'. That, he was sure, was where the truth about Diana Havelock's death was to be found. But he'd already prevailed on Miss Mainwaring's good nature enough. And so, reluctantly, he took his leave.

As he went out of the main gate, a group of tweed-jacketed young men barged their way past him, talking loudly of papers they'd published or were about to publish. Marvelling at the obliviousness of the younger generation where their elders were concerned, Rowlands made his way along Botolph Lane—a quiet little alley running parallel to the main road. In the drowsy warmth of the September afternoon, sounds were magnified, and he fancied he heard a footfall behind him. But when he stopped to listen, there was nothing. Reaching the junction, he crossed Trumpington Street to Mill Lane and the river.

A bare three months before, he and Edith had stood, with Maud Rickards and her party of St Gertrude's girls, in the queue for Scudamore's boatyard. The contrast between that busy, summer scene and the one he found now could not have been greater. It being a weekday, the riverside was almost deserted, even though there was still warmth enough in the sunshine to make the prospect of a punt up the river not unattractive. The pub, however, was doing good business for a Tuesday lunchtime, to judge from the buzz of conversation—interrupted briefly at the appearance of the newcomer—he could hear as he came in. He said as much, as he stood waiting for his beer to be poured. 'Ah, we do all right,' agreed the landlord. 'Busier in the summer, o' course.' He pushed the pint of Ruddles across the bar towards his customer. 'That'll be one-and-nine.'

'Thanks. I expect it gets even busier when the undergraduates are back,' said Rowlands, with a smile. 'It does that, sir,' was the reply. 'Queens' College is just across the way. We get a lot of their young gentlemen in here.'

'Larking about, I shouldn't wonder.' Rowlands took an appreciative sip of his pint. 'One-and-nine, you said? Sorry, I've only got a ten-shilling note.' He was handing over the money, when the door opened behind him and someone else came in. 'Be right with you, sir,' said the landlord, counting out Rowlands's change. 'Yes, we do get some high-spirited ones,' he chuckled. ''Specially with the river so close. Chucking each other in all the time, they are…'

'Playing the goat,' said Rowlands. 'Only to be expected of the young. Although wasn't there a rather nasty incident a few weeks back? Fellow drowned, didn't he?'

'That's right, sir.' Suddenly the landlord didn't seem quite so friendly. 'Local lad, he was. Not one of my regulars, though… he was from over Chesterton way. Yes, sir—what can I get you?' he said to the man who'd just come in. 'Usual, is it?' So this, at least, *was* a 'regular', thought Rowlands, moving a little way along the bar to allow the other to get to it. He—the newcomer—must have nodded in response to this enquiry, or made some other wordless sign of assent, for the only sounds that followed were the clinking of coins on the counter, and a hoarse murmur that might have been thanks, as the glass was set down.

'Bit of a shock, when something like that happens,' Rowlands went on. 'It was, sir.' From his manner, it was plain that the landlord had no wish to prolong the conversation. But then a voice piped up from the end of the bar. An elderly man, guessed

Rowlands. 'Some o' these young fellers can't hold their drink, if you want my opinion...'

'You think so, do you?'

'I do. Seen 'im staggering about, that young chap. Drunk as a lord, 'e was. Never 'ad more'n a pint far as I could see...'

'Now then, Josiah. No call to speak ill of the dead,' said the landlord. 'Who's speaking ill of 'im? Only saying what I saw,' replied the old man shrilly. 'Seen 'im plain as day. He was perfickly sober when 'e come in. Staggering all over the place when 'e went out, not half an hour later. Didn't have *time* to drink more'n a couple of pints. Only *seed* 'im drink the one...'

'Tha's right, Josiah, you tell 'em,' put in another voice, with a humorous intonation. Somebody else chuckled. The old man was evidently a 'character', whose pronouncements were taken in that spirit by those who knew him. 'As you say,' said Rowlands, conscious that it would be impolitic to ask further questions, with the landlord standing there. 'Some men can't hold their drink. Sad, in this particular fellow's case—but all too true.' There was a general murmur of agreement at this piece of sagacity, and then a silence fell. It was familiar to Rowlands as the kind that preceded a call for Last Orders. Good drinking time, that shouldn't be wasted on idle chat. It seemed to him in any case that he'd got as much as he was going to get out of the landlord of the Mill and its clientele.

Then, as time was called, something else struck him. It was as the landlord, having made his familiar announcement, came out from behind the bar, and went through to the back of the pub, to call time in that quarter, too. 'I hadn't realised there was another room,' said Rowlands to the man next to him, who merely grunted. But this had put an idea in Rowland's head. 'Was that where he was sitting, that night—the man who drowned?'

'Might've been,' was the landlord's reply, as he returned from his errand. 'Why d'you want to know?'

'Just curious.' Conscious of the man's disapproval, Rowlands finished his drink, and got up to leave. 'Good day to you.' As the door fell-to behind him, he heard the landlord say, 'There's a sight too much *curiosity* about, if you ask me...' Not when it's a case of murder, thought Rowlands grimly—because he was now pretty sure that that was what Thomas Findlay's death had been.

All the circumstantial evidence pointed to this: Betty Dimock's account of her *fiancé's* change of heart regarding the timing of their wedding; his decision to quit his job at the College; and the hints he'd dropped that he'd come into money, were given a more sinister colouring by what Rowlands had just learned. That Findlay had arrived at the pub apparently sober; that after just one pint of beer he'd been 'staggering' drunk. That the Mill had a back room, where the young man had taken his drink—doubtless to wait for whoever it was he'd come to meet. Here, screened from general view, it would have been easy for the other man to 'dope' Findlay's drink, with the fatal results that ensued when a man incapacitated by alcohol fell—or was pushed—into the river.

The sun had gone in by the time Rowlands left the pub, and—still turning these disturbing facts over in his mind—crossed Granta Place to where the Old Mill had once stood. Now all that was left to mark the spot was the weir, which fell with the roaring sound he'd noticed on his previous visit, and emerged thought a culvert on the far side of the bridge that separated the upper and lower reaches of the Cam (here called the Granta) from each other. A chill little breeze had sprung up, as he crossed the bridge. Here he paused a moment, resting his hands on the low wall which enclosed the mouth of the culvert, in order to gauge its height from the ground. It wasn't very high at all—no more than two-and-a-half or three feet. He calculated how easy it would be to tip a man the worse for drink over the edge of the wall and into the roaring maelstrom beneath. Yes, he thought, it could very easily be done. With this sombre thought, he walked a short way along the upper reaches of the river. He reached a second bridge—this one made of iron—which crossed the mill-race at the point where it discharged itself into the Mill Pond below.

Here, the sound of rushing water grew louder, masking all other sounds, so that it wasn't until his assailant was almost upon him that Rowlands realised that the uneasy feeling he'd had earlier—the feeling that he was being followed—wasn't just morbid imagination. Something—a sixth sense—made him turn, but before he could cry out, a savage blow to the head made him stagger; a hard shove in the back did the rest. The last thing he recalled was of vainly trying to save himself as he fell down, down, towards the tumbling waters. Then the waters closed over his head, and he knew nothing more.

Rowlands came to in a strange room. It had a hospital smell. He knew a bit about such places, having spent enough time in one—it was 1st London General—when he was recuperating from his wounds in the summer of 1917. But this was different—for a start, it was quiet, with none of the sounds of men groaning, or crying out in the grip of nightmares, he remembered from that wartime sojourn. And it wasn't his eyes which hurt this time, but his head, which ached liked fury. He went to feel for the source of the pain and found that even that slight movement sent a red-hot bolt of agony through his skull. Although stoical by nature, he was unable to suppress a groan.

'He's awake,' said a voice, and there came a rustle of starched clothing, as someone—a nurse, presumably—drew near to his bed. A cool hand was laid upon his forehead. Cool fingers took his pulse. 'I'll tell Sister,' said another voice, younger than the first. A door opened and closed. 'Where...?' he started to say, but the nurse who'd taken his pulse made a shushing sound. 'Now, you just lie nice and quiet,' she said. 'But...' Again, the shushing sound. 'Sister'll be in to see you soon. She'll tell you all you need to know.'

It was easier to surrender: to lie back on the cool, crisp pillows and drift once more into unconsciousness. But there were questions he needed to have answered. 'What happened?' he said to the Sister (positively crackling with starch, this one), when at last she appeared. 'You've had a nasty knock on the head,' she told him. 'Not the first one, either, by the look of it.' Which was true enough; he'd been in the wars more than once, these past few years. 'I fell in the water,' he said. 'Someone pushed me...'

'Don't worry about that now,' said the Sister firmly. 'The best thing you can do, Mr Rowlands, is to get some rest. Nurse'll give you something to help you sleep.'

Some time later—was it hours, or days?—he woke to find his wife sitting beside his bed. 'Oh Fred, what *have* you been up to this time?' she said when she saw he was awake. 'I've been so worried.'

'I'm sorry,' he started to say, but she put a finger on his lips. 'You're not to talk. The doctor said you're very lucky to be alive. If that man hadn't pulled you out of the water in time, you'd have drowned.' A confused memory of struggling in icy cold depths surfaced. 'How long have I been here?' he said. 'Two days. Now that's enough, Fred—or you'll have the Sister after me...'

When he woke again, Edith was gone—had she really been there, or had he dreamt it?—and Sister McAllister stood at the foot of his bed. 'You've visitors,' she said with a disapproving sniff. 'I've put them off for as long as I was able but they won't be denied any longer.' The smell of Old Virginia tobacco which clung to Chief Inspector Douglas's clothes preceded him into the room. Inspector Brown was with him. 'Five minutes,' said the Sister, in a tone which brooked no opposition. 'Formidable woman, that,' said the Chief Inspector admiringly. 'Well, Mr Rowlands, I didn't expect to see you here.' Rowlands pushed himself up into a sitting position. The ache in his head had receded somewhat, but he still felt woolly-headed. 'Tom Findlay was murdered,' he said. 'You must see that now, Chief Inspector? The method was exactly the same as the one that was tried with me...'

'Yes, yes,' was the soothing reply. 'Dinnae fash yersel, Mr Rowlands. You've had a crack on the head and...'

'Have you caught him—the man who pushed me in?' interrupted Rowlands. 'We're pursuing several lines of enquiry.' This was Inspector Brown. 'The landlord at the Mill thought it might have been a student "rag"...'

'It wasn't a rag—it was attempted murder,' said Rowlands impatiently. 'I spoke to the landlord. Naturally, he doesn't fancy the idea that one of his customers was a murderer...'

'No. Well, you can see his point,' said Douglas. 'Do I take it you were in the pub, before the… ah… attack?'

'That's right. No law against a man buying himself a drink, is there?'

'None,' said the Chief Inspector. 'Only I understood that you were heading back to London after the inquest…'

'I was.' Rowlands hesitated. 'I decided to pay a visit to the Cavendish Laboratory first, that's all.'

'The Cavendish?' said Inspector Brown sharply. 'Why would you need to go there?'

'It happens to be where two of our murder victims worked,' said Rowlands. 'I thought I'd like to see for myself what the place was like.'

'Hmph,' said Douglas. 'Seems to me you're still working on this theory of yours about Professor Harding—who also works at the Cavendish, I believe?'

'Yes, well…'

'The fact is,' went on Douglas. 'We might have to revise our thinking about that…'

'I know he's got an alibi for the Sedgwick killing,' said Rowlands. 'But even so…'

'Things have moved on since then,' said the senior policeman. 'You've been lying here in your hospital bed for two days and so you haven't heard. We've had a confession.'

'*What!*'

'Aye, I thought that'd surprise you.'

'You mean that Harding…'

'It isn't Professor Harding who's confessed,' said Douglas. 'It's someone we hadn't even considered. A woman. Miss Evadne Bostock.'

'That's preposterous,' said Rowlands. 'That woman could no more kill somebody than she could fly.'

'As it happens, I'm inclined to agree with you,' was the reply. 'But we can't afford to ignore even the most outlandish claim, unfortunately. In the meantime, we're continuing to look into the movements of our *other* suspects—amongst them, the gentleman you're so keen on. So I'd appreciate it, Mr Rowlands,' said the Chief Inspector, with an attempt at severity, 'if you'd cease your, ah, activities, as far as this case is concerned. Otherwise you're likely to alert our perpetrator—if you haven't already done so—making our job all the more difficult, eh, Inspector?'

'That's right,' said Brown. 'Not that I wasn't grateful for your help in the matter of the Sedgwick lad,' he added handsomely. 'That tip about the fibres in the nostrils—that put us on the right track, as you might say. But now, as the Chief Inspector says, you'd best leave things to us. You've already had a narrow escape...'

'I know all that,' said Rowlands. 'But I really don't see...'

'Time's up,' said Sister McAllister, appearing with the silent alacrity of her kind. 'All right,' said Inspector Brown; then to Rowlands: 'I'll be needing a statement from you, Mr Rowlands. If we've any hope of catching the man who attacked you, we'll need a full description...'

'That's one thing I can't provide,' said Rowlands ruefully. 'Unless you count a prickling feeling in the back of the neck...'

'Ah, we all have *those*,' said Brown. 'Trouble is, they don't stand up in a Court of Law.'

At Visiting Time that evening, Edith was accompanied by Maud Rickards. It was she who had telephoned the police station and the hospital, after Edith had rung, frantic with worry, to find out where her husband had got to. 'So I suppose I'm in your debt,' said Rowlands, when this had been explained to him by his wife. 'Which makes me feel all the worse,' he added, with a sheepish grin. 'I suppose you mean the business with the letters?' said Miss Rickards. 'Yes, I *wasn't* very pleased when that Inspector fellow asked me about them... and then there was all the nonsense that followed, with Evadne Bostock confessing to murder. If you ask me, the woman's mad.'

'What do you think made her do it?' said Rowlands. 'Confess, I mean. She's no more capable of murder than you or I...'

'Why, my dear good man, it was those letters, you see. She must have been overcome with guilt...'

'She *was* the poison-pen, then? I guessed as much.'

'Of course she was! As I've said, the silly woman was eaten up with guilt, and so the next thing we knew she'd confessed to murdering Diana Havelock.'

'Impossible,' said Rowlands. 'I know that,' said Miss Rickards. 'And you know that. But the poor woman's demented.'

'How does she say she did it?'

'Oh, the police haven't let on about that! But I rather think,' said the Bursar, 'that it was "murder" in the metaphorical sense. She wrote those letters—which *were* rather filthy, it's true—and thus drove poor Diana to despair… Hence "murder".'

'So she believes Miss Havelock committed suicide?'

'I imagine so. With an hysterical type like Evadne Bostock, anything's possible. By now, she's probably convinced herself that she went for the girl with a carving knife…'

'What will happen to her?' asked Rowlands.

'The Bostock? I've no idea. One thing's certain,' said Miss Rickards. 'She can't stay at St Gertrude's, after this. I imagine,' she added, with just the faintest shade of malice, 'they'll send her back to Oxford.'

'Fred, you're looking tired,' said Edith, who had listened in silence to this exchange. 'Time we were going. I'll be in tomorrow. I've left you a change of clothes,' she added. 'And some clean pyjamas.'

'I'm not staying here another day,' he said. 'Hospitals give me the horrors. You can pick me up in a taxi first thing tomorrow. We'll journey back together.'

'Fred, are you sure that's wise? The doctor said you've had concussion. And your lungs are still congested. What if it turns into pneumonia? You oughtn't to take the risk…'

'I'm perfectly fine,' he retorted peevishly—although he knew she had a point. Being exposed to mustard gas in '15 hadn't done his chest any good. Nor had the ducking he'd received two days ago improved matters. 'I've an idea,' said Miss Rickards, with characteristic decisiveness. 'Why don't you come back to St Gertrude's, Frederick? We can put you up for a day or two, until you're fit to travel. I'm a qualified nurse, as Edith knows. I'll keep an eye on you.'

'Well…' said Rowlands.

'Good. That's settled. I'll come and fetch you myself in the morning. Come along, Edie dear. You ought to have an early night, if you're to catch the nine-thirty train.'

LONG VACATION

16

AND SO ROWLANDS FOUND himself once more installed at St Gertrude's. His semi-invalid status meant he wasn't obliged to get up for meals, but had trays in his room—an arrangement which suited him very nicely, since it excused him from having to make polite conversation with the St Gertrude's Fellows, most of whom, he knew from Maud Rickards, were preoccupied with one topic above all others: that of the poison-pen letters. Who'd had one, who hadn't had one, and what on earth College was coming to, were themes on which the learned ladies had yet to exhaust themselves, apparently.

He had several visitors, however. The first of these was Percy Loveless, bearing a bottle of whisky. 'Thought you might need a little pepping-up,' he said, handing it over. 'Thanks,' said Rowlands. 'Only don't let that dragoness see,' added the artist. 'She gave me a *very* fishy look when I asked if you were fit to see people. Said you needed absolute quiet and bed-rest…'

'Amongst her other admirable qualities, Miss Rickards is a conscientious nurse. As you see, I don't always obey her orders.'

'Yes, I wondered why you were up and dressed,' said Loveless, settling himself down in one of the armchairs with which the St Gertrude's guest room was provided. 'I was expecting to find you at death's door, after being bashed on the head and shoved in the Mill Pond…'

'You make it sound like something out of the Keystone Cops,' said Rowlands. 'Oh, I'm sure it was most unpleasant,' replied his friend. 'But if you will go poking sticks into wasps' nests, my dear old spy, you must expect to get stung.'

'I dare say you're right. Do you want some of this?' Rowlands brandished the bottle. 'There are some glasses in the sideboard, I believe.'

'What—whisky at ten o'clock in the morning? said Loveless in a tone of mock-horror. 'Your dragoness would have my guts for garters. In any case, I can't stop. Must get back to my easel, you know…'

'It's going well, then—the painting?'

'Famously, thanks. If Pallas Athena hadn't had some letters to write'—it was thus he had taken to referring to the Mistress—'I'd be hard at it right this minute.'

'Well, thanks for the Scotch,' said Rowlands. 'Although if you're not going to drink it, you might put it away in the cupboard. I'd rather my nurse didn't see it.'

'Right you are. I say, Rowlands,' said Loveless, when he had accomplished this. 'I'm awfully glad you're not drowned. Conversation over the port's been a bit dull since you left, with old Maltravers the only other man in College.'

After he'd gone, Rowlands sat for a while, thinking about all he'd learnt in the past few days. He was now all the more convinced that Diana Havelock's murderer—the man who had also murdered two others, and had tried to do away with Rowlands himself—was connected in some way with the Cavendish Laboratory. It was so conveniently close to the river, where Thomas Findlay had died and where Rowlands's fatal 'accident' had been staged. Then there was the fact that two of the victims had worked there—that, above all, was a clue. It had to be Harding, he thought. And yet Harding had been in the Lake District when Julian Sedgwick was killed…

Round and round went his thoughts, so that his head (still sore from the blow it had received) began to ache. If only there was a way of breaking Harding's alibi… He was still puzzling over this when Maud Rickards came in, to see if he wanted anything. 'You're looking very white,' she said. 'Are you sure you should be out of bed?'

'I'm fine. But there was something I wanted to ask you. Did you ever find one of those letters—the ones Dr Bostock wrote—when you searched Diana Havelock's room?'

The Bursar hesitated. 'Would you like a cup of coffee?' she said. 'I was just going to make one for myself… No, I didn't find any letters in her room. At least…' She broke off. 'How do you take your coffee? I'm not sure there's any milk...'

'Black's fine. You were about to say something,' he said. 'Hmm?' She seemed distracted, clattering cups and saucers about. 'You said you hadn't found any letters. Then you seemed to remember that you had...'

'All right. I *did* find a letter, but not the poison-pen kind. It was just a note, really.'

'What did it say?'

'It said, as far as I can recall,' said Miss Rickards: '"Meet me in the Rose Garden, at 8.30pm." That's all.'

'Was it signed?'

'No.'

'I don't suppose,' said Rowlands, 'that you recognised the hand?'

'I didn't. Frederick, what *is* this?' Because he had got to his feet, unable to remain seated, when the proof of what he had suspected for so long was within his grasp. 'I hope you've kept the note?' he said. 'I... I believe I did,' was the reply. 'I bundled it up with a lot of other stuff that was in Diana's desk. Notebooks and essays and scientific diagrams. It'll all have to go to her parents, of course...'

'Where is it now?'

'It's where I left it—in a drawer of the desk in my office. Frederick, I *insist* you tell me what this is all about.'

'It's quite simple,' he said. 'That note is probably the best concrete proof we've had so far of the identity of Diana Havelock's murderer.'

In the Bursar's office, Rowlands was barely able to contain his impatience as the Miss Rickards unlocked a drawer. 'Here we are. A great pile of stuff. I've no idea exactly what's here.' She began unloading the contents of the drawer onto her desk. 'Essays. Examination papers. Notebooks. A journal. I think I put your precious note inside that...'

'Where did you find it—the note?'

'It was in her dressing-gown pocket,' said the Bursar. 'You know, I'm not sure we should be going through her private things...'

'We don't have any choice,' he said, conscious that he was

being rather hard with her. 'I suppose not,' she muttered, flipping through some pages. 'Ah, here we are! I knew I'd put it somewhere...'

'Perhaps,' said Rowlands, 'you could put it away safely, until the police can examine it? It's probably too much to hope that there'll be any fingerprints on it apart from yours and Miss Havelock's, but we mustn't rule out the possibility.'

'Do the police really need to see this?'

'It's evidence, Maud. Proof that someone—whoever he is—made an assignation with the girl on the night of her death...'

'We don't *know* it refers to that night...'

'No, but there's a strong possibility. You said you found it in the pocket of her dressing-gown? Isn't it likely that she put it there soon after she received it—rather than carrying the thing around for days? But even without that probability, there's the fact that she *was* intending to meet someone that night in the rose garden. I came upon her while she was waiting. And so that note is a really important clue...'

'I'll put it in an envelope,' said Maud Rickards. 'Now Frederick, I really think you ought to rest. You shouldn't be out of bed, you know.'

'Never mind that,' said Rowlands. 'You mentioned there was a journal amongst these papers. I think we ought to take a look at that, too.'

'But surely...' began Miss Rickards. Just then a frantic mewing came from outside the window. 'It's Webster,' she said. 'He *will* climb up. We won't get any peace unless I let him in.' She accordingly did so, and the cat jumped over the sill, making at once for Rowlands, who put out a hand to stroke the animal. 'I know it's not very pleasant to have to pry into all this stuff,' he said. 'But there might be something—however small—that will help us to find who killed Diana, and silenced Julian Sedgwick.'

'All right.' She began leafing through the book. 'I suppose you want me to read it aloud?' she said. 'If you would.' He smiled. 'I'm rather restricted to Braille, these days.'

'Where do you want me to begin? The journal goes back to the start of the Michaelmas Term... that's October last year. It seems to be mainly lists of lectures she attended. College functions… Tea parties… That sort of thing.' She turned a few more pages. 'Perhaps you could just glance through all of that, and see if anything catches your eye,' he said, sitting down on one of the room's worn but comfortable chairs. Webster immediately jumped up onto Rowlands's lap, where he settled himself down and began to purr loudly.

'Very well.' She turned some more pages. 'There's a good deal about her work. Notes on 'spinning electrons'—whatever those are—and 'tunnelling through a potential barrier'… Can't say it makes much sense to me…'

'She was working on quantum theory, I believe,' said Rowlands. 'With Dr Harding.'

'Yes, he's mentioned quite a bit.'

'Can you give me an example?' he said, careful not to let his interest show. 'Hmm… hmm… Here we are,' said Miss Rickards. 'It's from Lent Term. March 5th… "Saw Dr Harding after my Practical…" She'd have been doing her mid-term examinations… "He seemed pleased with my results. If I can keep this up, H. thinks I might stand a good chance of getting the studentship…" Nothing suspicious in that,' said Miss Rickards. 'No indeed,' said Rowlands. 'Perhaps you could read on a little?'

'Here's an entry from two weeks later,' said the Bursar, after a moment. '"March 13th. H. convinced my research on anti-electrons will get me the studentship. Wants me to work with him on his own project. What larks! Late nights in the lab with the handsome Professor…" It doesn't prove anything,' she said, a shade defensively. 'Lots of girls get these silly crushes…'

'I'm sure they do. Read on a little, will you?'

'If you insist.' She sounded increasingly reluctant. 'This is from April 15th—beginning of the Easter Term: "Another 'all-nighter' in the lab with H. Work coming on really well. H. says I'm the best student he's ever had. None of the men he's taught have half my feel for the subject, he says…" You mustn't think,' put in Miss Rickards, 'that there's anything improper implied by an "all-nighter". They quite often work late, the research students, when they've a big project in hand. Why, I myself used to sit up till five in the morning sometimes, to get an essay done…'

'You're saying that what Miss Havelock felt for her tutor…'

'Supervisor,' said Miss Rickards mechanically. '...that what she felt for her supervisor was a purely intellectual passion.'

'Is that so hard to understand?' said the other hotly. 'Must every relationship between a man and woman be about Sex?'

'I wouldn't dream of suggesting it,' he said. 'But we've only got as far as the Easter Term. Is there any mention of Professor Harding after that?'

'I don't see why you're so convinced that Robert Harding is mixed up in all this,' she said, turning another page. Then she fell silent, as she read what was written there. 'All right,' she said in a low voice. 'It may be that it went too far...' Without further preamble, she began to read, her voice subdued. '"Another all-night session at the 'Crocodile'. Such a sense of my own potential! I've never felt like this before. H. says I'm the only woman he's ever met who could truly understand him. He and I are a perfect match, he says. There's no limit to what we can achieve together..." You were right,' said Miss Rickards. 'There *was* something between them.'

'It might only have been an affair of the mind,' said Rowlands gently; although he did not believe this. Harding's remark about Diana Havelock's being the only woman who could understand him smacked uncomfortably of the seasoned philanderer. 'Is there any more in that vein?' he asked. Miss Rickards turned over some more pages. 'It's almost all to do with work,' she said, unable to keep the relief from her voice. 'There are a couple of references to meeting friends... "A.T. asked me to tea..."

'Could that be Angela Thompson?'

'It could. Then there's this: "J.S. proving tiresome about H. Told me I risked 'compromising' myself—as if I were some character in a Victorian melodrama!"'

'I assume 'J.S.' is Julian Sedgwick,' said Rowlands. 'She *did* give him short shrift, poor lad! Does she mention Harding again?'

'Only cryptically,' said the Bursar. '"Attended H.'s lecture on atomic theory"—that was 7th May—"Interesting divergence from Dirac's view..." There doesn't seem to be anything of a more personal nature. Perhaps,' she added hopefully, 'it really *was* just a schoolgirl crush.' Rowlands gave a non-committal murmur. The fact that Diana Havelock's references to her supervisor had diminished didn't necessarily indicate that her feelings for him had done so. 'Anything else?' he said. 'Well, there's this: "May 22nd. H. has told me—unofficially, he says—that I've got the College Studentship. O frabjous day!" Nothing untoward about that.'

'Nothing at all.'

'Then there are a couple of other mentions: "Saw H. in lab"—that was on the 25th, a Saturday—"H. looked in to give me the good news..."—that'll be about getting the studentship. Then there's nothing until the end of the month. The 31st.'

'What does it say?'

'It's about her work, mainly. "Working on my research proposal at the Cavendish today. H. suggested following up my work on the polarisation of atomic nuclei by focusing on Dirac's theory of arbitrary perturbations. Was halfway through this, when I had another idea. Something no one else has thought of, I'm convinced..." *No one* is underlined,' said Miss Rickards. '"Wave mechanics is the future, I'm sure of it..." It breaks off there.'

'What—completely?'

'No. There's a gap of a few days. She didn't write every day. There's a brief entry on 5th June: "Working in lab all day. I'm so excited about this change of direction. Making progress!" 7th June: "As Heisenberg has shown in his Uncertainty Principle, certain pairs of physical properties, such as for example position and speed, cannot be simultaneously measured, nor defined in operational terms, to arbitrary precision. The more precisely one property is measured, the less precisely the other. I think I have found a way of taking this further, using Dirac's relativistic wave equation..." Then there's nothing until 12th June: "Saw H. this morning. He says it's no go. I begged him to reconsider, but he wouldn't see sense."'

'It sounds,' said Rowlands, 'as if he was ending it.'

'It does, doesn't it? Perhaps,' said the Bursar, not sounding entirely convinced, 'he'd come to his senses...' Or that he'd decided to put a stop to an affair that was threatening to compromise his reputation at the University, thought Rowlands. 'Anything else?' he said. 'Nothing more about Professor Harding, that I can see. Unless...' She turned a page. 'You know, Frederick, I *do* feel rather bad about reading the poor child's private journal,' she said. 'Some of it's rather extreme.'

'Read it,' he said. Maud Rickards cleared her throat nervously. 'This is the last entry, written on the 14th…' The day before she was killed, he thought. '"I can't believe he could let me down like this, after all the things he said. It's such a betrayal…" That's underlined. "And he calls himself a scientist! To let this happen, without a word in my defence, is unforgivable. When I said I'd take it to the University authorities, he said I'd only make things worse for myself. Who would believe me—a mere woman?"'

'It sounds as if she was threatening to expose him, said Rowlands. 'Is there any more?'

'Just this: "I'm not going to let this rest. There's too much at stake—my work's too important—for me to let this go. If H. won't stand up for me, then there are others who will. That man can't be allowed to get away with this…" It breaks off there,' said Miss Rickards. 'It's just blank pages after that.'

Rowlands thought again of Diana Havelock's words to him by the rose garden that night. 'Can one trust *anybody*?' It seemed as if the answer to that question was one she'd already worked out for herself, poor young thing. 'Well,' he said, when Miss Rickards had closed the book. 'It seems from what you've read that she was intending to take things further. That remark about going to the University authorities…'

'Yes. You don't think…?' She broke off. 'But it's too absurd,' she said. 'Robert Harding might be a rather vain and self-satisfied man, but I can't see him as a murderer.'

'Perhaps not,' said Rowlands. 'Even so, I think you'd better let me have that note and the journal. The police ought to see them.'

'But Frederick—surely you don't intend to go to the police station *today*? You're not well enough to go out, in my opinion…'

'I'm feeling a great deal better,' he said. 'Is there anything else in that heap of papers which might be of interest, do you think?'

'Really, Frederick…'

'Please,' he said. 'I'm relying on you.'

Maud Rickards sighed. 'Edith *said* you could be pig-headed.

All right. What is it that I'm supposed to be looking for?'

'I don't know exactly. Something that adds to what we know already. It's possible there may be nothing at all. Then again, there might be a vital clue to the whole affair.' Still holding the journal, into which he had slipped the letter in its fresh envelope, he waited while Miss Rickards sifted through the pile of documents. 'It seems to be mainly scientific papers. Notes on her research project. It doesn't mean very much to me, as a non-scientist.'

'I don't suppose there can be many—even in Cambridge—who'd find it easy to understand the kind of things Miss Havelock was working on,' said Rowlands. 'You can say that again! Here's one of her papers: *On Some Applications of the Theory of Arbitrary Perturbations in Quantum Mechanics*. Here's another: *The Disintegration of Nuclei by Artificially Accelerated Protons*. They sound like something from one of Mr Wells's wilder fantasies.'

As the Bursar opened the drawer in order to begin restoring the papers she'd taken out to their place of safe-keeping, Rowlands got to his feet, dislodging the cat, who registered a polite protest. 'Sorry old chap,' murmured Rowlands. 'You'll have to find somewhere else to sleep. Well, I'm off. See you later, Maud.'

She accompanied Rowlands to the door. 'I still don't think…' she began; but he cut across her. 'My dear girl, you worry too much. I promise I won't get into any more scrapes, if that makes you feel any better.'

'Not much,' she said, opening the door. 'But I don't suppose you'll be told…'

'No,' he admitted cheerfully. 'Edith says I'm incorrigible. Hallo! Do you want to go out, too, old fellow?' This was to Webster, who had taken the opportunity of making a dash for it, almost tripping Rowlands up in so doing. This put him in mind of another occasion—the first time he'd entered Diana Havelock's room, on the night of her murder. The cat had rushed out in just the same way, from the room it which it had been shut up. Almost certainly by her murderer, thought Rowlands. 'Don't I wish you could talk,' he murmured, as the cat stalked off along the corridor. 'You'd be able to tell us who was in her room that night, and who killed her—wouldn't you, Webster old lad?'

At the Porters' Lodge, Rowlands made an enquiry, and received an answer which gave him pause for thought. So Harding *didn't* live in College—being of course a married man. Might it not have been possible for him to have returned to Cambridge a day earlier than he'd said, in time to kill Julian Sedgwick? Rowlands felt a surge of excitement. If one could only break the man's alibi… He was sure it had been Harding's voice he'd heard outside the research lab at the Cavendish, and Harding who'd followed him to the Mill, and tried to kill him. Yes, it all made sense he thought. 'Could you call me a taxi?' he asked the Porter (not Wainwright, this time, but the younger man). 'Very good, sir.'

Then someone came along the corridor, and a familiar voice said: 'Going somewhere?' It was Loveless. 'I thought you were confined to barracks?'

'I've taken French leave,' he said. 'Pity. I was just going to see if you were planning to lunch in Hall. Last time we met, you seemed well on the way to recovery, so I thought…'

'Cab's on its way, sir,' interjected the Porter. 'I've got a better idea,' said Loveless. 'Why don't you cancel the taxi, and I'll run us both down to the Eagle for a pint?'

'That sounds like a fine idea,' said Rowlands. 'Perhaps you'd run me to the Police Station first?'

'More sleuthing, is it?' said Loveless. 'That's what I like to hear!'

But when they reached the St Andrew's Street Police Station—Loveless having parked the Brough quite illegally on the pavement outside it—neither Chief Inspector Douglas nor his subordinate officer were to be found. 'If it's important, sir, you're welcome to leave a message,' said the police sergeant behind the desk. 'I'll make sure as the Inspector gets it.' As there seemed more to be said than could easily be conveyed by a note, Rowlands decided against this. 'I don't suppose the Chief Inspector said where he and Inspector Brown were going?' he asked the man on duty, whose response was no more illuminating than before: 'I couldn't tell you, even if I knew, sir.'

'Well, that's that.' Rowlands recognised a dead-end when he came to it. 'Looks as if it'll have to be the pub after all,' said Loveless cheerfully. 'I for one am ready for a pint. Working in the smell of oil paint gives one a thirst, you know.' Rowlands, however, had another idea. 'I wonder,' he said to the sergeant, 'if you could direct me to Park Parade?'

'Nothing easier, sir,' said the policeman. 'You go straight down St Andrew's Street into Sidney Street and then along Bridge Street and turn right into Thompson's Lane. Keep going straight and you'll reach Park Parade. You can't go no further,' he added. 'Because of Jesus Green. It faces onto it, see?'

'I think so,' said Rowlands. 'Got that?' he said to Loveless, who seemed less than pleased at this development. 'I say, old man—what about our pint?'

The sergeant gave a dry cough. 'If I might make a suggestion, sir? There's a nice little pub on Magdalene Street—just opposite the College, and only a stone's throw from Park Parade. Landlord's a friend of mine. Keeps his beer very well. I'm sure you gentlemen won't be disappointed in the Pickerel.'

'Thanks,' said Rowlands. 'Come on, Loveless. What I want to do shouldn't take long.' The artist seems satisfied with this, making no further comment until they were in the car, and driving at a rather greater speed than Rowlands would have liked along the route suggested by the sergeant. 'I think,' said Loveless at last, slowing only fractionally to avoid a cyclist ('these people do take their lives in their hands, don't they?') 'that I'm owed some kind of explanation. Do I take it this is another of your detecting forays?'

Rowlands explained what he had in mind.

'So you intend to beard the handsome Professor Harding in his den? Isn't it rather risky? I know you've got "form" in these matters,' said his friend, 'but surely if your suspicions are correct, then the man's a murderer. More than that, he's already tried to murder *you*.'

'I can't help that,' said Rowlands, as the car took a sharp turn to the right. 'Besides,' he added, with a smile. 'You're with me, aren't you? He's hardly going to tackle us both at once.'

'Good God, these miserable little lanes,' muttered Loveless.

'One can't get up any sort of speed... I can't say I really fancy confronting this individual,' he went on, in answer to Rowlands's remark. 'I'm a painter, not a professional bodyguard.'

'You went through the War, didn't you?' said Rowlands. 'Our man didn't. Too busy reading, apparently.'

'Too busy seducing little girls, from the sound of it,' said Loveless, bringing the car to an abrupt halt. 'Say what you like about me, but I like my women over twenty-one. This is Park Parade, I fancy. Big green in front and row of rather dull houses behind. What number are we looking for?'

'Seven.' The two of them got out, and stood for a minute, getting their bearings. From the green, came a sharp smell of newly-mown grass. They walked a few paces along the terrace of houses which overlooked it. 'Here we are,' said Loveless, touching his friend on the arm. 'Number Seven. I suppose we'd better get this over with...'

'Wait. You'd better see this, first.' Rowlands took the envelope containing the note to Diana Havelock from his breast-pocket. 'Are you wearing gloves, by any chance?' he asked. 'I am, as a matter of fact,' was the reply. 'Rather smart, pigskin ones—for driving, you know.'

'Good. Keep them on while you take a look at this. I don't want the evidence contaminated any further than it already is.'

Loveless read the note. When he had done so, he gave a low whistle. 'You're not planning to confront our man with this, are you?'

'That's precisely what I'm going to do. I want you to watch his face very closely when he reads it...'

'Perhaps he's a poker-player,' said Loveless.

'Perhaps. But do it, will you?'

A short, tiled path brought them to the front door. Rowlands pressed the enamel bell-push, producing a jangling sound within the house. After a brief interval, footsteps could be heard approaching. The door opened and someone—the maid, evidently—looked out. 'Yes?'

'I'd like to to speak to Professor Harding,' said Rowlands. 'Master's out,' said the girl. 'Then perhaps your mistress would spare me a few minutes?'

'Well...' She sounded dubious—and also very young, thought Rowlands. A local girl, newly inducted into service. 'I don't know as she's at home to visitors.'

'Perhaps you could find out?'

'I'll enquire,' was the reply. 'What name shall I say?'

Before Rowlands could supply this, a querulous voice called from within: 'Who is it, Millie? I've told you you're not to stand gossiping... Oh!' Because at that moment the speaker—Harding's wife, Rowlands assumed—came out into the hall, catching sight of her two visitors as she did so. 'Mrs Harding?' said Rowlands. 'I'm sorry to disturb you. I was hoping to speak to your husband—but I gather he's out.'

'That's right. He's usually at the Cavendish, when he's not teaching. Or the University Library... All right, Millie,' she added to the maid, who still stood there. 'I'll deal with this. These girls!' said Mrs Harding, when the servant had taken herself off. 'They don't have the faintest idea... What did you say your name was?'

'Rowlands. And this is Mr Loveless.'

'I'll tell my husband you called,' she said. 'As a matter of fact,' said Rowlands. 'You might be able to help me.'

'Oh?'

'Yes. I understand that you and Professor Harding got back from a visit to the Lake District recently? Can you tell me what day it was?'

'I...' ('If you've ever seen a rabbit mesmerised by a stoat,' said Loveless afterwards, 'then that describes the expression on her face.') 'I don't recall exactly. Three or four days ago. Sunday, I think it was...'

'Are you sure it wasn't Saturday?' said Rowlands.

'Perfectly sure. May I ask what concern it is of yours, Mr... er...?'

'Just interested,' said Rowlands. 'Only a friend *swore* he saw Professor Harding in Cambridge on Saturday. Matter of fact, we had a small bet on it. I've just won five shillings, I fancy.'

'I do not approve of betting,' said Mrs Harding coldly, as she went to shut the door in their faces. 'Yes,' said Rowlands. 'It's insidious, isn't it? Once you start, it's hard to know when to stop. Like lying.'

'Her face when you said *that*,' Loveless remarked, as they sat over their—very agreeable—pints in the back bar of the Pickerel, 'was like a study for one of the Hon. John Collier's execrable Problem Pictures. "A Guilty Thing Surprised" or "Caught Out" might do for a title…'

'Yes, she seemed very uncomfortable when I asked her which day they returned from their holiday,' said Rowlands. 'Which suggests that Harding might very well have been in Cambridge on Saturday night, and that he could have killed young Sedgwick.'

'I must say,' chuckled Loveless. 'I'm rather glad you didn't ask her about that note. There was an awful moment when I was afraid you were going to.'

'That would have been cruel,' said the other. 'I'm sure the poor woman has suffered enough on account of her husband's philandering, without having her nose rubbed in it… Even so,' he added, taking a meditative draught of his beer, 'I wish there was some way of establishing that Harding wrote that note, before I hand it over to the police.'

'There is,' said Loveless, with the air of someone pulling a rabbit out of a hat. 'He wrote that note, without a shadow of a doubt. Here's the proof.' He took something from inside his jacket, and put it in Rowlands's hand. 'A letter? But… Where did you get this?'

'Took it from the Hardings' hall-table just now, when you were chatting to the maid. Poor little lass, I wouldn't be in *her* shoes for the world, with a sour-faced mistress like that…'

'You *stole* it?'

'Yes. What of it? The writing on the envelope's the same as in your note. There's your proof!' cried Loveless. 'I should have thought,' he added, sounding faintly aggrieved, 'that a vote of thanks was in order.'

'What—for committing a criminal offence? You do realise that's what you've just done?'

'Well, if it helps to trap a murderer…'

'Keep your voice down,' said Rowlands, because his sharper ears had registered the appearance of the landlord from the other bar. 'Everything all right, gentlemen?' he said. 'Yes, thanks,' replied Rowlands. 'Very nice pint, this.'

'We do our best, sir.' Having ascertained that all was as it should be behind the bar of the Snug, the man absented himself once more. 'I'll remind you,' said Rowlands in a low voice,' that his best friend's a policeman.'

'Oh, come off it, old man...'

'As soon as we've finished these, we're going to find a pillar-box and post that letter. Who's it addressed to, by the way?'

'The Gas Board,' said Loveless sulkily. 'All the more reason why we shouldn't hold on to it a moment longer.' Rowlands tapped his friend on the arm with the purloined letter. 'It probably contains a cheque. We don't want the Hardings having their gas supply cut off. And I *am* grateful, he added. 'You've convinced me that I'm on the right track, at last.'

17

It was not quite two o'clock when they left the pub. Loveless said he had to get back to St Gertrude's for the afternoon's sitting. 'Mustn't keep the divine Athena waiting, you know…' He offered to take Rowlands back with him, but the latter wanted to lose no more time before presenting the evidence he'd gathered to the police. 'It's a pity I can't show them that letter to the Gas Board, as corroboration that the author of the note was Harding,' he said (the letter having been safely posted in the box outside the newsagent's in Magdalene Street). 'But I expect they'll find other specimens of his handwriting when they search the house.'

'You're pretty set on catching this fellow, aren't you?' said his friend, as they took their leave of one another. 'I was the one who found two of his victims, don't forget,' said Rowlands. 'I owe it to them to do what I can to bring their killer to justice.'

Loveless said he would drive Rowlands back to the police station, but the latter refused. 'It would mean going back though the town. And you're already almost halfway to St Gertrude's.' Besides, he added, he felt like a walk. What he didn't say was that he intended to go the long way round along the Backs—a route that would take him past the new University Library. Hadn't Mrs Harding said that her husband might be found there, if he wasn't at the Cavendish? Rowlands thought it was worth a try. He'd no intention of speaking to Harding—just of ascertaining where he was to be found, for the next few hours. It would be the job of the police to arrest the man; but it couldn't hurt, he thought, to track him to his lair.

And so when Loveless, having delivered himself of the humorous injunction that his friend was to stay clear of the river, had roared away up Castle Hill in his motorcar, Rowlands set off at a brisk pace along the road that would lead him past the backs of the colleges. It was a fine, Autumn day, and the sun felt warm on his back. A pleasant smell of newly fallen leaves, from the trees that lined the path on which he soon found himself, mingled with the smell of smoke from a bonfire—no doubt composed of the same leaves; the college groundsmen being assiduous at keeping their lawns tidy, he supposed. He'd be passing some of Cambridge's most famous views, he recalled, from that long-ago, first visit. The backs of St John's and Trinity—with its Wren Library—were just across the way, beyond the little brook beside which he was walking. Trinity Hall, Clare College and King's, with its fifteenth century Chapel, lay further on; Queens' College beyond that.

He wished—not for the first time, since his arrival in Cambridge almost a week ago— that Edith was here with him. She was so good at describing things; one felt one could almost see them… But (he reminded himself) the beauties of smooth green lawns, pale stone and Gothic spires were not his concern. What mattered was to catch a murderer. In the past few days, while he'd been recovering from the attempt on his life, he'd been reflecting on the nature of the man who'd tried to kill him.

The picture that was emerging was of a formidable adversary—a man who, in the beginning, at least, had always been one step ahead of him. The way Diana Havelock's murder had been made to look like an accident had been a clever trick—and one the murderer had almost got away with. If it hadn't been for the doubt raised in Rowlands's mind by that odd detail of the green satin shoe—a doubt confirmed by what poor Julian Sedgwick had said—the girl's death would have been passed over, as it was meant to be. Then there was the matter of Thomas Findlay's death—again, made to look like an accident. Had it not been for the timing of this, and for the fact that young Sedgwick's death (another faked accident) had followed so soon after, that, too, would have passed unnoticed.

'You're very clever,' said Rowlands softly, addressing the man he was convinced had carried out all three crimes, as well as the attack on himself. 'Yes, you're clever—but maybe not as clever as you think.'

Footsteps—those of young person in a hurry—were approaching along the path. 'I say,' said Rowlands with a smile. 'I don't suppose you could direct me to the University Library, could you?'

'Why, it's just over there,' said the youth. 'I'm going there myself. I'll take you, if you like.'

'That would be very kind,' said Rowlands, feeling—as he always did when he had to ask for directions—as if he were eighty years old. Which was unreasonable, he told himself, as he and his companion crossed the road and walked along the lane that led to the library. It wasn't only the blind who got lost. 'Are you studying here?'he asked his new friend. 'Third Year Physics. And *don't* they make us sweat!' groaned the lad. 'You're a physicist, are you? Then you must be one of Professor Harding's students...'

'Bristow's my supervisor. Wave Theory. That's his field. I don't imagine,' added the young man with magnificent condescension, 'that means a lot to you?'

'Oh, it's starting to make sense,' said Rowlands. 'Thank you, Mr... er...'

'Kemp. William Kemp.'

'Like the Shakespearian actor,' murmured Rowlands. But if the boy caught the allusion, he seemed not to understand it. 'Here we are,' he said. 'Can't miss it, really, can you, with that dirty great tower? Well, cheerio.' They had reached the bottom of a flight of steps. Young Kemp ran up them, whistling under his breath. At the top of this was a revolving door—Rowlands waited until a couple of people had emerged from it, before trusting himself to the mechanism. He found himself in a large entrance hall. The echo of footsteps running up the stairs to one side of this indicated that Mr Kemp had already passed through the turnstile and entered the library.

Rowlands waited his turn at the central island, behind a young woman who was arguing with the librarian over the return of some books. 'No, no, no!' she was saying. 'I've *told* you I'll return the last two books by parcel post. I'm going back to Oxford tomorrow, so I won't be able to return them in person...'

'I'm afraid those titles are already a week overdue,' said the librarian patiently. 'We'll need them returned at once, so that they can be stamped with a new date.'

'But I've already explained,' replied the women, with barely concealed exasperation. 'I'm still working on my paper, so I'll need them for another month at least...' Her voice was familiar, thought Rowlands. But he couldn't put a name to her. Just then, one of the other library staff came over to where he was standing at the great circular desk. 'May I help you?'

'I hope so. I was wondering if Dr Harding had come into the library today?'

'Dr Harding? I'm not sure. I'll just check to see when he last returned or borrowed any books.'

She did so. 'It looks as if he *was* here, this morning,' she said. 'But I'm not sure if he's still in the library, or not.' She raised her voice above its near-whisper. 'Miss Pinkerton, have we seen Dr Harding today?'

'I saw him this morning,' was the reply. 'He usually lunches in the Tea Room, when he's working here.'

'Thank you,' said Rowlands. 'No, I won't leave a message, thanks,' he added, when Miss Pinkerton's colleague suggested this. He turned to go, and at that moment was aware that someone had come up to him. It was the woman who'd been at the desk in front of him. 'What is it you want with Robert Harding?' she hissed—and then he knew her at once. 'Why do you ask, Dr Bostock?' he said. He felt her clutch his arm; then to his dismay, she burst into tears. 'The man's a s-scoundrel,' she sobbed. 'I d-don't care who hears me s-say it. That he should be allowed to continue t-teaching at this university is a s-scandal...'

With some difficulty, Rowlands disengaged himself from her grasp. He took a clean handkerchief from his breast-pocket and gave it to her. 'Blow your nose,' he said. 'I think,' he added to the astonished librarians, 'that a cup of tea might be a good idea. I'm not a member of the library, but might it be in order for me to accompany Dr Bostock to the Tea Room?'

Having made their way along what seemed to Rowlands an admirably symmetrical system of corridors and staircases, they reached the Tea Room, which he was relieved to find wasn't crowded—with only a couple of elderly dons mumbling to one another in a corner, and a quartet of French exchange students discussing the evening's arrangements in another. Over a cup of refreshingly hot, strong tea, he listened as Evadne Bostock poured out her heart. 'I know you probably think I'm mad,' she began without preamble. 'Everybody thinks that. It's what *he* said to me,' she added with a shudder. '"Don't think anyone will believe your preposterous stories"—his very words—"You're lucky they haven't already locked you up..." That's what he told me. Lovely, wasn't it, from the man who'd sworn he was in love with me, only a few weeks before...' Dr Bostock's voice trembled. 'Sorry,' she said. 'I'll be all right in a minute.'

'You're referring to Dr Harding, I presume?'

'Yes. That swine,' she said. 'Of course, I was a fool to let it happen... but I was so lonely. After Oxford, this place was horribly cold and unfriendly... and he was so charming—at first.' From which Rowlands gathered that Dr Bostock had been another of Harding's conquests. He needed to be sure, however. 'He seduced you,' he said gently. 'That sounds so frightfully Victorian, doesn't it?' she replied. 'But I suppose that *is* what happened.'

How determined these young women were not to be deemed old-fashioned, thought Rowlands. 'Victorian'—that was the expression Diana Havelock had used in her journal, too. 'As I said, I was a fool,' said Evadne Bostock. Talking about the affair seemed to have calmed her. Rowlands risked another question: 'What happened after that?'

'He said we should stop. It might damage my career, if we were found out, he said. He meant *his* career, of course,' she said bitterly. 'When was this?' asked Rowlands. Dr Bostock thought for a moment. 'Towards the middle of the Easter Term, I think. He'd already started seeing that girl.'

'Diana Havelock, you mean?'

'I never meant any harm to come to her,' she burst out. 'I just wanted to expose her for what she was...'

'You wrote those letters.'

'Yes.' Her voice had shrunk to a whisper. 'I didn't mean to hurt her,' she said. 'I must have been mad. That's what he said, and he was right...'

'I don't think you're mad,' said Rowlands. 'Just unhappy.'

'I killed her,' said the girl. 'I drove her to it.'

'Nonsense,' he replied. 'Writing those letters wasn't a very nice thing to do, but it had no bearing whatsoever on Miss Havelock's death. She was murdered, Dr Bostock. Someone knocked her down, and then gave her a lethal dose of morphine.'

Evadne Bostock drew in her breath sharply. 'Do you think *he* did it?'

'That's what I'm trying to find out.'

'He was looking at her all through dinner that night,' said the girl miserably. 'Trying to catch her eye. She wouldn't look at him. Kept tossing her head in the affected way she had... Women like her,' said Dr Bostock with sudden venom, 'make me *sick*! Using their looks to attract a man, and then pushing him away...'

'Perhaps,' said Rowlands, 'she wasn't very proud of herself for getting involved with a married man?'

She laughed. 'Well, that's one in the eye for *me*!'

'I didn't mean...'

'No, you were right to say it. It was a pretty shabby thing to do. And yet,' she added, sounding very young all of a sudden. 'I couldn't help it. He was so *very* charming, in the beginning. Until *she* came along, with her red hair, and that painted face of hers...'

'She was his research student,' Rowlands pointed out. 'She could hardly help being in his company some of the time. As her tutor—supervisor, I mean—he had no business taking advantage of her...' Or of you, he thought, but did not say. The thrust must have gone home, for she said in a subdued voice: 'So you think Robert... Professor Harding... killed her?'

'That's for the police to decide. I'm just trying to get a picture of events in the order in which they occurred.' A thought struck him. 'Maybe you can help me, Dr Bostock? On that night—the night of the end of term dance—you left the dining hall with the Mistress and the other female dons, to go to the Senior Common Room, didn't you? The men followed later. Could you tell me at what time—to the best of your recollection—they arrived, and in what order?'

'I...' She had been holding her teacup; now she set it down

in its saucer with a clatter, as if it had suddenly become too hot to handle. 'I didn't go straight to the S.C.R.,' she said. 'Oh.' He guessed, from her embarrassment, that she'd been paying a visit to the Usual Offices. Perhaps she was more of a Victorian than she liked to admit. 'Never mind. It was just a thought...'

'I waited outside in the corridor. I... I wanted to speak to him... to Robert.'

'And did you?'

'No. I... I waited a few minutes—there's a notice-board outside the door to the dining hall, so I looked at that for a minute or two...' He could picture it. Her air of studied unconcern, as she waited for her former lover; her pathetic pretence of interest in the minutes of the Chess Club meeting, or the latest victory of the St Gertrude's Hockey Team. 'Then the door opened, and I thought it must be him. But it was only the Chaplain...'

'Go on,' said Rowlands, sensing there was more to come. 'I... I waited another minute or so, because I could hear voices... the door wasn't quite closed... so I knew they must still be inside. I was just about to give up, when the door opened again.'

'Was it Professor Harding this time?' Rowlands was conscious that he was holding his breath. 'No,' she said. Then she told him who it was.

Chief Inspector Douglas was busy, Rowlands was informed by the desk sergeant, when the former arrived, some twenty minutes later, at the Police Station. Nor could Inspector Brown spare a moment to see him. 'He's interviewing a suspect,' said the sergeant grandly. 'Both of 'em are, as it happens. My orders are that they're not to be disturbed. Was it something important?' he added, perhaps seeing Rowlands's exasperated expression. 'Very important. It concerns the murder case they've been looking into.'

'Does it now, sir?' The sergeant's tone of voice seemed to Rowlands a shade too jocular. 'Well, you just leave it with me, and I'll make sure to pass on whatever it is to the Chief Inspector. Reckon he'll be busy for a while yet. They've only just brought him in...'

'But surely, this is more important...' Rowlands started to

protest; then enlightenment dawned. 'It's a suspect for the murder case that they're interviewing, isn't it?' he said. 'Can you at least tell me who it is?'

''Fraid not, sir. All that's confidential,' was the reply. 'Now, if you'd like to wait…'

'It can't wait,' said Rowlands. 'I suppose I'll just have to leave a message.'

'That's right, sir,' said the policeman blandly. 'I've pencil and paper if you need 'em.'

'A typewriter would be of more use to me. My handwriting's a bit all over the place, these days.' Having secured the use of a typewriter in a conveniently empty office—'It's a bit irregular, sir, but seeing as how you're a friend of the Chief Inspector's…'—Rowlands typed as succinct an account of his findings as he could. There wasn't time to go into all the ins and outs of it, he thought, as he signed the letter, and handed it to the sergeant. 'Could you make sure the Chief Inspector gets that as soon as possible?' he said. 'It really is a matter of life and death.'

'I'll do my best, sir,' said the policeman—with which Rowlands had to be content. Emerging from the heavy oak doors of the building onto bustling St Andrew's Street, he berated himself for a fool: 'To miss what was in front of my nose, all this time! I've been blind as a bat,' he told himself. '*Preening* myself on having identified the right man, when all along…' It didn't bear thinking about. The fact that he'd believed himself to have been more than a match for his adversary was the final humiliation. 'He hoodwinked me, just as he hoodwinked everybody else,' thought Rowlands. 'What a fool—what an unutterable fool—I've been.'

It was five minutes' walk from the Police Station to Free School Lane—he knew the way now, and anger quickened his pace. As he strode along, he reviewed the events of the case—events which had begun on a beautiful evening in mid-June, and which had taken until this moment to comprehend. Yes, he thought, it all made sense: the killing of Diana Havelock; the subsequent murders of Thomas Findlay and Julian Sedgwick. He'd been right about the fact that they were connected: the two men had died because they both knew something the murderer wanted to conceal.

In Findlay's case, it was the identity of the man who'd gone to Miss Havelock's room on the night of the end of term dance, having left the dining hall a few minutes after Dr Maltravers, and a little before the two other men who'd been sitting at table with him. Findlay must have seen him—as Dr Bostock had seen him, not knowing that this was crucial information. Perhaps, thought Rowlands, he—the man in question—had been spotted by Findlay climbing the stairs that led to Miss Havelock's room; or perhaps he'd been seen coming out of the room itself—or dodging into one of the rooms beside it when he heard somebody coming? Honoria Fairclough had heard the sound of a door closing further along the corridor—although she hadn't realised at the time what it meant. Certainly Findlay must have realised the significance of what *he'd* seen, soon after Miss Havelock's body had been discovered. He'd attempted to blackmail the killer—with fatal consequences for himself.

As for Julian Sedgwick—he'd also discovered something: a motive for Diana's death. But that motive wasn't the one Rowlands thought he'd identified—an adulterer's fear of discovery—but something much more insidious. As he turned in at the gate of the Cavendish Laboratory, Rowlands felt the weight of the girl's journal in the pocket of his lightweight tweed jacket. It was all there, for anyone who was able to understand it, he thought. A motive for murder, trumping even that of illicit passion.

There was no one about in the courtyard, and he found the heavy glass doors of the Mond Laboratory unlocked; he pushed them open. With any building with which he was unfamiliar, it was a matter of getting his bearings. In the centre of what (from Gillian Mainwaring's description) he knew was a circular atrium, he stood and listened. Sounds, as ever, would tell him what he needed to know: was the place empty, or inhabited? Did the sound echo, suggesting a large, vaulted space, and hard surfaces—or was it muffled by low ceilings and soft furnishings? Here, there was only a dead silence, suggesting that efficient sound-proofing had been introduced into this uncompromisingly modern building. A space designed for scientists, which shut out all the distractions of the outside world.

Ahead of him lay a corridor; to his left, a staircase, which conformed to the cylindrical shape of the 'Crocodile's' atrium. On an instinct—or was it that he'd heard some faint sound from above?—he chose the stairs. Now, it was he who was the source of the sound: his footsteps echoing on the concrete steps as he followed their spiral upwards. Here was another circular space, and another corridor—presumably running parallel to the one on the floor below—leading off from it. He followed this, his fingers skimming its smooth tiled and plastered walls, along which doors were set at intervals.

He tried the handle of one of these at random: it was locked. Which was no more than he'd expected to find; from all he had gathered, during his brief foray into the main building, much of the work conducted within these walls was of a confidential nature. You didn't want just anybody wandering in. Yet he persisted, trying handle after handle, with the same result, until he came to the end of the corridor, and the last door of all. This time, the door opened to his touch. He went in. 'Well, well,' said a voice. 'Here you are at last, Mr Rowlands. I have been expecting you for some time.'

'It took me a while to work out that it was you.'

'That is because you allowed yourself to be guided by false premises,' said the other, with some amusement. 'A common error.'

'I knew it had to be someone who was at the end of term dinner,' said Rowlands. 'I eliminated all but two...'

'Three, surely?' was the reply. 'You surely have not forgotten our mutual friend, the estimable Dr Giles?'

'He didn't do it,' said Rowlands impatiently. 'He's not the murdering type. Besides which, he was away from Cambridge on the Saturday Julian Sedgwick was killed... when you killed him, I mean.' The other man laughed. It was a dry, un-amiable laugh, more like a cough or a clearing of phlegm from the throat. 'I killed him, certainly,' he said. 'But I think you will find that your friend Dr Giles is at present in custody for the crime. He lied to the police about his whereabouts on Saturday night. I know, because I happened to see him entering the door to his staircase—looking very furtive, I might add—when I was myself crossing

Old Court… for what purpose you may imagine,' he added slyly.

'That doesn't mean anything,' said Rowlands, although his heart sank a little at the news. Why had Giles lied? It didn't make sense… 'On its own, it is, as you say, of little significance,' agreed the other. 'One could put it down to mere forgetfulness. We elderly dons can be forgetful, you know…' His voice was suddenly that of the harmless old buffer Rowlands had taken him to be. Again, he laughed, and Rowlands realised that even this—the man's air of senile helplessness—had been a lie, designed to confuse the unwary.

'However,' went on the hateful voice—now shorn of its quavering notes—'the police, stupid as they are, will have found other evidence by now. Evidence which, added to his foolish lie, is more than enough to hang him. The handkerchief, with which I was obliged to anaesthetise young Sedgwick, will have been found in Dr Giles's room. Hidden behind a volume of Webster's plays. A nice touch, I thought. *The Duchess of Malfi* was always a favourite of mine. "Cover her face. Mine eyes dazzle. She died young."' The terrible words, declaimed in that dry, precise voice, raised the hairs on the back of Rowlands's neck. 'A perfect murder, don't you agree?'

'Which one are we talking about?' said Rowlands. What was taking Douglas and his men so long? He'd left as precise an outline of what he'd discovered as he was able—the name of the man they were seeking, and an account of his various crimes—for the Chief Inspector to find. He'd even said where he was going. If the police didn't get here soon, they'd miss the confession he was in the process of extracting from the murderer. 'You have a number of murders to your credit.'

'Indeed. But the first one was the really flawless crime. It worked like a dream, you know. I had intended to intercept her—the Havelock girl—as she made her way across to the marquee where that infernal dance was being held. The college grounds are large and dark, and there would have been ample opportunity for me to carry out my plan without being seen. She would not have been found until morning.' Bristow chuckled. 'You see, I had thought it all through! We scientists like to consider every contingency. But as it turned out, chance took a hand. I saw her enter the building, after exchanging some words with you—I wonder what *that* was all about! She was quite unmistakable, in that garish green frock. I followed her into the building and up the stairs to her room. Since she was not expecting me, I had the element of surprise on my side. Without wishing to employ a *cliché*, "she never knew what hit her."'

He sighed. 'Despite what you might think, Mr Rowlands, I am not a cruel man. She didn't suffer. Once she was, as it were, *supine*, the dose was swiftly administered, and strong enough to stop her heart almost immediately.'

'You stole her research, and passed it off as your own,' said Rowlands, disregarding this shameless self-exculpation. 'Oh, come now, Mr Rowlands! That shows how little you understand the academic community. Research does not "belong" to any one individual—least of all in the scientific world. It is shared, for the benefit of many.'

'Then why did you kill Diana Havelock?'

'She was greedy for fame,' was the reply. The bantering tone was gone, now. 'She insisted that the research on which I had allowed her to assist me, and on which I have now published not one, but two papers, should be submitted as her own. The idea that she—a mere chit of a girl—should claim credit for so important a piece of work was simply preposterous.'

'Why?' said Rowlands. 'Because she was young—or because she was a woman?'

'Women should never have been allowed into the University, in my view,' said the other. 'At best, they are fit only for the more humdrum work—the routine checking of results and the preparation of experiments—at worst, they are a snare and a delusion. Look at poor old Harding!' he chuckled reminiscently. 'Quite ridiculous, his philandering. Yes, if it hadn't been for the fact that he was absent from Cambridge when I was dealing with the Sedgwick boy, he would have made an ideal suspect for that and for the earlier business. *You* certainly favoured him, did you not?'

'What makes you think that?' said Rowlands. 'Why, because I myself put the idea in your head during our interesting little chat on the train from London,' said Bristow. 'I saw your face when I mentioned Harding's name in connection with the girl. Then it was a simple matter to provoke Harding himself into losing his temper during that fortuitous conversation in Hall about murder… Again, I watched you when Harding was speaking. Oh, you suspected him all right!'

'Perhaps I did,' said Rowlands. Throughout their several exchanges, he had remained by the door, conscious of the advantage that his adversary had over him—which was not only that of sight, but of familiarity with his surroundings. Now the other man seemed to become aware of this. 'You are a cautious fellow, are you not?' he said, with the condescension of an adept towards an ungifted pupil. 'You have been standing there all this while, as if you might take to your heels at the slightest provocation. But I assure you, I am unarmed and there is no river nearby. You have nothing to fear from me.'

'Unlike Thomas Findlay,' said Rowlands. 'I suppose he saw you coming out of Miss Havelock's room?'

'In point of fact, I was already descending the staircase at the end of the corridor when he saw me,' said the murderer. 'Being a resourceful young man, he put two and two together, and thought he could turn it to his own pecuniary advantage. In that, he underestimated me—as you have done all along, Mr Rowlands. Confess it: you never suspected me until just now—and then only because you could no longer go on suspecting Harding. Such a pity he was away on the night I visited young Sedgwick, otherwise *he* would be the one now sitting in a police cell.'

'As it happens, I've reason to believe he was in Cambridge last Saturday night,' said Rowlands. 'Indeed? I wonder who told you that?' said the other. 'If I had known… But no matter. As you are aware, I have an impregnable "alibi"—is that the word?—for Saturday night. Two hundred members of the Royal Society will confirm it…'

'Oh, I've no doubt that an examination of the train timetables for Saturday will show that you had ample time to give your talk, return to Cambridge, and—having killed Julian Sedgwick—return to London, in order to reappear in Cambridge next morning,' said Rowlands. 'I expect you concocted some story about wanting to retire to your hotel room early, in order to give yourself time to do this. You'd found my note to Sedgwick in his pigeonhole when you arrived at the college, and so you knew you had to act fast. You let yourself into his room with the set of keys you'd taken from the hook in the Porters' Lodge. When the boy was dead, you locked the door behind you, and returned the key to the lodge on your way out.'

'What an imagination you have, Mr Rowlands!'

'I admit that—for a time—I swallowed the tale you were at such pains to construct, Professor Bristow. But there were a few things that didn't quite fit...'

'Really? Pray enlighten me.'

'Oh, it'll all come out at the trial,' said Rowlands. 'It was just that I couldn't fit it into a pattern until recently. Diana Havelock's journal changed all that.'

18

FOR THE FIRST TIME since he'd walked in the door there was silence. Then: 'What are you talking about?' said the cold, dry voice. 'A journal?'

'That's right. We found it amongst her papers. I'm sure that a more thorough search will turn up the detailed research she was engaged in when you killed her. But the journal makes it clear that she knew her work had been plagiarised. It's what Julian Sedgwick discovered too, wasn't it? I think she confided in him about her fears that someone at the laboratory had stolen her work, and that—because he was jealous of Harding—he assumed that was whom she'd meant. Then after she died, he started asking questions at the Cavendish, and found that Miss Havelock had started working on a new project only a few weeks before. It was on Wave Theory—with which Dr Harding was not involved. But you were. It was *you* that Sedgwick was trying to warn me about. He confronted you with the fact that you'd appropriated Miss Havelock's research without her permission, and you killed him.'

'He made wild accusations,' said Bristow. 'He threatened to expose me...' The voice was cold with fury. 'I couldn't allow that.'

'No,' said Rowlands. 'It would have meant admitting the truth.'

'And what was that?'

'The truth that you weren't good enough as a scientist,' he said. 'That you'd fallen behind. Overtaken by someone younger, and cleverer. A woman, at that.'

'No, no. It wasn't like that.' But there was a note of uncertainty, now. 'What can you—a mere layman—know about such things? I tell you, my research—and it *was* mine, whatever you might say—will be of inestimable value, in the world we are building, my brothers-in-science and I. A world in which the strong and able will flourish, and the weak and useless will be eliminated. The weapons we shall build—weapons which this research of mine will make possible, Mr Rowlands—will be the most powerful the world has ever known. It is they that will guarantee our security now and for future generations. There! That is the *real* truth of the matter. My work, and the work of my associates in Germany and Russia, is of far greater importance than the lives of a few insignificant people.'

'You're insane,' said Rowlands. It struck him that, after all, Douglas and his myrmidons might not arrive in time. 'Not insane,' said the other. 'Just clear-sighted. Which you, unfortunately, are not.' Before Rowlands could react, he found the other man beside him, so close that he could feel the latter's breath against his cheek. 'Don't move,' said Bristow. 'Or it will be the death of you. I have a syringe in my hand—you can feel its point against your neck, can you not? It contains a dose of morphine large enough to fell an ox. I am quite prepared to use it, as must be clear to you by now. So you see, any sudden movements would be unwise.'

When Rowlands had indicated, by the merest flicker of his eyelids, that he understood, the point of the needle was withdrawn. Bristow was still close beside him, however; he could smell the sour breath, and the faint stench of chemicals that clung to his skin. 'The police know I'm here,' said Rowlands, his lips barely moving. 'If you kill me, they'll know it was you who did it.'

'Ah, but there you have underestimated me again,' said the scientist. 'I have another fate in store for you. Come, you will precede me out of the door and along the corridor to the stairs. And do not think you can attract attention by shouting—these rooms are all empty, at present. The young people for whom you seem to have such a high regard are all still away on their holidays. Only the truly dedicated remain. Move,' he added sharply. 'Or it will be the worse for you.'

Conscious that this was no idle threat, Rowlands began walking slowly, with a shuffling step, along the deserted corridor. He'd make a break for it when they reached the stairs, he thought. But before he could do so, he felt his arm firmly grasped. 'We will go down together,' said Bristow. 'I promise you, one false step will be your last.' They reached the bottom of the spiral stairs, and then the glass-and-steel doors to the building. 'Push them open,' hissed Rowlands' companion in his ear. With the syringe grazing his cheek, Rowlands did as he was told. Together, in a nightmare parody of fellowship, he and Bristow crossed the courtyard to the main building.

'Why are you doing this?' he said, as, repeating in reverse the manoeuvre by which they had exited the Mond Laboratory, he pushed open the oak doors that led into the Old Cavendish building. 'Why not kill me, and have done with it?'

'Come, come, Mr Rowlands! You are not a stupid man—far less stupid than those policemen in whom you have such touching faith… We will climb the stairs to the second floor, if you please. I know you are familiar with the layout of this building from your previous visit here.'

'It was *you*, talking to Harding outside the laboratory, then?'

'Of course it was I! I saw you and your young companion, as Harding and I came up the stairs. Your blindness does not make you invisible, Mr Rowlands. I followed you when you left the building. I knew it was my chance to get rid of you. I had planned an accident of some kind—the traffic along Trumpington Street is so very heavy, these days—but it suited my purpose admirably when I saw you turn down towards the river… Yes,' said Bristow. 'Keep going upstairs, please. It could not have been more fortuitous that you decided on that particular public house for your lunchtime drink. It was there, as you know, that I had arranged to meet the foolish Mr Findlay. *He* I incapacitated by slipping a sedative into his beer—otherwise I could not have effected his disposal. There was no time to achieve the same result in your case, and so I was obliged to resort to more violent means of rendering you unconscious. Fortunately I carry a heavy steel torch in the pocket of my waterproof. That—and the fact that you are blind—made it relatively easy to approach you. The noise of the waters covered the sound of my footsteps, too…'

'And yet I am still here,' said Rowlands. Francis Bristow

laughed. A chilling sound. 'You say that with such admirable bravado, Mr Rowlands! I find, as I go on, that the business of disposing of my enemies is more enjoyable than I had anticipated. With the Havelock girl I was forced to be quick. The Sedgwick boy, too. Only with Findlay—the credulous fool!—was there some pleasurable anticipation. But not as much as I am feeling at this moment. Have you ever seen a cat playing with a mouse, Mr Rowlands? Its sensations and mine are not so very different, I fancy...'

'I see,' said Rowlands, as step by step, they continued their slow ascent of the creaking stairs. 'That's really rather funny, you know—given that it was a cat who first alerted me to the fact that you killed Diana Havelock. You were coughing and wheezing that night in the Senior Common Room, weren't you? You pretended you had a cold, but of course it was an allergic reaction to the cat you found in Miss Havelock's room, when you entered it in order to kill her. I didn't realise at the time what it meant—your sneezing fit—but it all makes sense, now...'

'I detest cats,' said Bristow, 'Nasty, creeping little beasts. But none of this proves anything.'

'Unlike Miss Havelock's research papers,' said Rowlands. 'Which, with the assertions about plagiarism she makes in her journal, will be proof enough of your motive for murder.'

'Who knows about that—apart from you?' was the reply. 'And you won't be around much longer. Enough of this. We have arrived. Open that door, if you please.' But before Rowlands could obey this command, the door itself swung open. Someone looked out. 'Oh!' said a voice. It was Gillian Mainwaring. 'Professor Bristow. I didn't expect... Hallo, Mr Rowlands! What are you doing here?'

'Run,' said Rowlands. 'Get away as fast as you can!' But the girl just stood there. In a flash, Bristow had pushed them both inside the room, and slammed the door. 'I wonder, Miss Mainwaring—it *is* Miss Mainwaring, isn't it?—what exactly *you* were doing in the Radium Room?' he said. 'I...' She sounded flustered. 'I was just carrying out a bit of research.'

'Were you indeed? These young women!' said the professor, assuming once more a fussy, donnish manner. 'Always meddling in what does not concern them. You are aware of course,' he went on, addressing the girl. 'That access to the Radium Room is strictly limited to Fellows and fourth-year students?'

'Yes, I...'

'Nevertheless, you disregarded this instruction,' said Bristow sharply. 'Well, you may live to regret it.'

'I'm sorry. I...'

'Miss Mainwaring,' said Rowlands. 'You must get away from here. This man is dangerous—don't you understand?' It was too late. As he spoke, Rowlands felt the grip on his arm relax; a moment later, it was the girl whom Bristow had in his clutches. 'I'm afraid he's right, Miss Mainwaring,' said the latter. 'As I have explained to your friend Mr Rowlands here, this syringe—the one I am holding against your rather pretty neck—contains a lethal dose of morphine...' Gillian Mainwaring gave a gasp. 'So I'd advise you to keep very still. Now then. Are you playing attention, my dear?'

'Yes,' she whispered. 'Good,' was the reply. 'Now I want you to go to the cupboard and take out the jar containing the solution of radium—a discovery sometimes attributed to a woman, although it is far more likely that it was her husband, Dr Curie, who did the crucial research. That's right. Now remove the lid—it's a good thing you're wearing rubber gloves—and pour out a little into that petri-dish.'

'But...'

'Do as I tell you. There's no need to look so frightened. It isn't you who will suffer the effects of exposure to the substance, over the next hour or so. That will be Mr Rowlands's fate. It won't be a pleasant end, I'm afraid,' added Bristow. 'Nausea and violent headache, followed by vomiting and, er, other disagreeable symptoms—ending in catatonia and death. Yes, it's a pity that, driven by no more than idle curiosity, our inquisitive friend Rowlands will allow himself to become locked—accidentally of course—in what will shortly become a lethal chamber.'

'You monster,' said Gillian Mainwaring, with some of her old spirit. 'You won't get away with this.'

'Ah, but that's where you're wrong, my dear. As I was explaining to your blind friend here, the strong and decisive will always triumph over the weak and vacillating. Come, we are wasting time. You know how to drive, I take it?'

She seemed momentarily taken aback. 'Yes. My brother taught me last summer...'

'Excellent. You are to act as my chauffeur—or should that be "chauffeuse"?' He chuckled at his own poor joke. 'Since I cannot both drive and hold a syringe full of morphine to your throat.'

'Where are we going?' she said dully. 'Didn't I say? Why, to your Alma Mater, of course. St Gertrude's College. Where I intend to recover my property...'

'If you're referring to Diana Havelock's research papers?' said Rowlands, 'you won't find them.'

'Oh, but I will,' said Bristow. 'When we reach the college—"that infidel place", as a wiser man than I once called it—I will merely enquire of the Mistress where the papers are to be found. I will explain to her that as part of a piece of—alas, unfinished—research by the late Miss Havelock, they properly belong to the Cavendish Laboratory.'

'I'll tell her that's a lie,' said Miss Mainwaring; then drew in her breath sharply, as her gaoler tightened his hold upon her. 'What makes you think you will be there to tell her anything?' he said. 'Open the door, if you know what's good for you.' She did so, and he pushed her outside, following her out. 'Goodbye, Mr Rowlands. I have enjoyed our skirmishes more than you will ever know. Alas, like all good things, these must come to an end.' The resonant sound of the door falling to, and of the key turning in the lock, was like the closing of a tomb.

As the sound of their retreating footsteps died away, Rowlands flung himself against the door. But it was made of solid oak—no chance of escape *that* way. Next, he tried the window, which was sealed tight shut, he discovered. He could try breaking it, if he could find a suitable missile. First, however he'd do what he could to protect himself from the noxious vapours which must even now be contaminating the air within the room. In front of the window was a porcelain sink, with a cold-water tap. He pulled out his handkerchief (fortunately, he always carried a spare) and soaked it, before tying the wet cloth over his mouth and nose—a rudimentary gas-mask.

Then he turned with a feeling of dread towards the bench on which, a few moments before, Miss Mainwaring had placed the petri-dish with its deadly contents. He took off his jacket and—having first removed Diana Havelock's journal from the pocket, flung it over the place where he guessed the dish to be. Now for the window. On the bench next to the sink, he found and rejected a number of objects: a rack of test-tubes, a pile of clean petri-dishes… No use. Then his fingers closed on a heavier item—a glass bell-jar, with a round glass knob by which it could be lifted. It would have to do.

Forcing himself to slow down, so that he could calculate the effort needed more precisely, he picked up the heavy object and, having weighed it in his hand a moment, threw it with some force against the lower pane of the tall sash-window. There came a splintering crash. Glass flew everywhere—he turned his face away just in time. Clean, blessed air rushed in. Rowlands gulped it down in lungfuls. 'Help!' he shouted, when he had gained strength from this. 'For God's sake, help!'

He couldn't afterwards have said how many minutes passed before he heard footsteps outside the door, and the handle being tried—'It's locked!' he shouted—and the footsteps going away again and then returning, followed by the sound of the key in the lock. It had seemed an eternity. His only thought when the door opened at last was to fling himself through it—anything, to get out of this poisonous chamber. In his headlong flight, he crashed into a solid body. 'Steady on, old man!' said a voice. It was Percy Loveless. 'You nearly knocked me for six.'

'Shut the door,' croaked Rowlands. Only when it was done did he breathe again. 'I thought you were the police,' he gasped, still reeling from the horror of the past few moments. 'Sorry to disappoint you,' said Loveless. 'And after I tracked you down so cleverly, too! When I didn't find you at the police station, I remembered Harding's wife had said something about the Cavendish. I guessed you wouldn't be able to resist doing some more sleuthing…' Suddenly he dropped his facetious tone. 'I say, Rowlands, are you all right? You look like death warmed up.' At this, his friend was seized with a spasm of laughter that turned into a coughing fit. 'I very nearly was,' he said, when he could speak again.

It wasn't until they were seated in the roadster and heading, with as much speed as Loveless could muster, along the Huntingdon Road, that Rowlands finished putting his friend in the picture as to what had happened to him—and even then, his account was interrupted by frequent extortions to Loveless to 'get a move on, do!'—to which the latter was inclined to take exception. 'I'm going as fast as I can,' he said. 'We've been touching 50mph since we left the city centre. I don't imagine you want to add a few cyclists to your already impressive tally of corpses?'

'It's just that we don't have much time. If we could only catch up with them…'

'It depends what his car's like. Any idea what make?'

'None. But they only left a few minutes before you arrived—ten, at the most.'

'It's taken us another ten minutes to get this far. That's a twenty minute head-start. But I'll see what I can do.' With which he put his foot down, and the car shot forward at a speed which left Rowlands with the feeling that his stomach had been left behind him. He hoped this rising sensation of nausea was due to Loveless's driving, and not exposure to radium. God knows what that had done to him. It was probably best not to think about it.

They turned into the drive of St Gertrude's College at last. 'Let me out here, will you?' said Rowlands, as they reached the entrance to the Porters' Lodge. He dashed inside. 'Have you seen Professor Bristow and Miss Mainwaring?' he asked the Porter. It was Wainwright, this time. 'They must have arrived a few minutes ago…'

'Sorry, sir. Nobody's come in this door in the past half-hour,' said Wainwright. 'But I reckon that's Professor Bristow's car outside all right—the Morris.'

That was all Rowlands needed to know. 'They're here,' he said, as Loveless—having parked the Brough—joined him under the arch of the main gateway. 'The Porter hasn't seen them, so they must have gone in by the other door.' He pushed it open. 'Come on.' In the entrance hall at the foot of the Tower staircase,

Rowlands almost fell over someone who was kneeling on the floor, and was only prevented from doing so by Loveless's hand on his elbow. ''Ere! Watch where you're going!' said an indignant voice, which turned out to belong to one of the 'Gyps'. 'I'm doing my best to clear up this mess, without gentlemen falling on top of me…'

'I'm so sorry—I didn't see you,' said Rowlands. 'I don't suppose,' he added, 'that you've seen an elderly gentleman—Professor Bristow—with one of the St Gertrude's girls? Miss Mainwaring, I mean…'

'I don't know about any professors,' said the woman, getting to her feet with a groan, and a creaking of knees. 'And I haven't seen Miss Mainwaring. But *some* young lady's gone and dropped face-powder all over my stairs, which was only swept this morning.'

'It could be her,' said Rowlands to his friend. 'Come on. It's the best lead we've got…' Without further ado, he began racing up the flight of stairs two at a time, with Loveless, protesting a little under his breath, following at a more sedate pace. 'Hurry!' cried Rowlands, as he reached the first floor landing. 'All right, all right,' grumbled the other. 'Can you still see the trail of face-powder?'

'Yes. It continues up the stairs, as far as I can make out.'

'Then let's follow it.' His heart beating faster, Rowlands took the next flight at a run. 'I think I know where he's taken her,' he said. Because they had by now reached the top of the last flight of stairs, leading to the corridor Maud Rickards had referred to as 'Top Boots'. To one side of this was a door. 'The powder runs out just here,' said Loveless. 'She must have made it last as long as she could, plucky little thing,' said Rowlands.

He opened the door. 'In here,' he said. 'There's one more flight of stairs to climb. I hope you've a head for heights,' he added, setting his foot on the bottom step. Unlike the broad carpeted stairs up which they had come, this was part of a narrow stone spiral. 'Positively mediaeval,' murmured Loveless. 'One would think…'

'Quiet! We don't want to give him any more warning than we have to.' Up and up they went, each turn of the spiral bringing them closer to the top of the tower. What they would find when they got there, Rowlands wouldn't permit himself to consider. At last, the sensation of cool air on his face told him they were within sight of the top. He held back a moment. 'Can you see them?' he whispered to Loveless, who had come up behind him, and now stood getting his breath. 'Let me have look.' He craned his neck over Rowlands's shoulder. 'Can't see anyone—they must be out of my line of sight.'

'Unless I've made a mistake,' muttered Rowlands. 'But I felt sure…'

'If you come near me again,' said a voice from close at hand, 'I'll scream my head off.' It was Gillian Mainwaring. 'I said, keep away from me!' The laugh which greeted these brave words chilled Rowlands's blood. 'My dear young lady, you'd be better off saving your breath. We must be seventy feet in the air. Who on earth do you think will hear you, from up here?'

'I will.' Rowlands stepped out onto the roof of the tower. 'And I,' said Loveless, following suit.

There was a stifled exclamation from Bristow; then he recovered himself. 'Well, well, Mr Rowlands… so you haven't died—or at least, not *yet*. You've brought your friend, too, I see. But I still have the advantage, you know…'

'Look out!' shouted Loveless, but his warning came too late. A stifled scream from the girl told Rowlands that Bristow had her once more in his clutches. 'Come any closer and I'll finish her off,' he panted. 'Let her go, Bristow,' said Rowlands. 'What good is she to you now? Let her go, and throw down that abominable weapon, and the police may take a more lenient view…'

Again, Bristow laughed: a mad sound. 'Do you take me for a fool?' he said. 'What difference will the life of one silly girl make to the police, when I've already killed three people?'

'All the difference in the world,' said Rowlands. 'If you won't throw away the syringe, then at least take me as your hostage, instead of Miss Mainwaring. 'You've tried to kill me twice before—why not make it third time lucky? He took a step towards where he judged that Bristow and the girl were standing, on the far side of the tower's flat roof. There would be a surrounding wall, he guessed—perhaps crenellated, in Gothic fashion. 'Get back!' screamed Bristow. 'Or it'll be the end for her.'

Gillian Mainwaring began to sob quietly. For a long moment, all four of them—Bristow and his captive and the two would-be rescuers—stood frozen in a terrible *impasse*.

Then Bristow spoke—his voice a dead monotone. 'Stop that snivelling. No one's going to hurt you.' In the same moment, he shoved the girl violently away, so that she would have fallen, if Loveless had not caught her. 'He's trying to get away!' shouted the artist; but there was of course no escape route apart from the staircase in front of which he and Rowlands were standing. A moment later, the girl gave a cry. 'No!' Because by then it had become apparent what kind of escape the murderer intended to effect. He had taken advantage of the brief hiatus brought about by his release of Miss Mainwaring to climb up on the low surrounding wall. Now he stood there, balancing on the narrow ledge, as if in some game of 'I Capture the Castle'.

'Get down, man!' yelled Loveless. 'Do you want to kill yourself?' But Rowlands, who had guessed the truth of the matter, said: 'Can't you get the girl away from here? She oughtn't to see this...'

But it was already too late. As he started to move towards where he guessed Bristow was standing, the other cried out—it was hard to make out what he said, because the wind blew the words away. Afterwards, Rowlands thought it was something about the Kingdoms of the World. All such reflections were driven out of his head by what happened the next minute, however. 'Good God!' cried Loveless, in a voice of horror. Then there was nothing but silence. 'He did it,' muttered the artist, still holding the weeping girl in his arms. 'He stuck the thing in his neck and pushed the plunger home. I watched him do it.'

'He'd have been dead before he hit the ground,' said Rowlands. A great weariness overcame him. It was over, then. He realised that he felt nothing. He drew a deep breath of the cool, pine-scented air. Around the tower, a flock of crows was already wheeling.

BEGINNING OF TERM

19

After much discussion, it had been decided by the Fellows that the Mistress's portrait, as commissioned by the Trustees of St Gertrude's College, and executed by Mr Percy Loveless R.A., would hang in the Fellows' Common Room, not in Hall, with those of previous incumbents. 'Because,' said the portrait's subject, in a tone that indicated that this was the end of the matter, 'one wouldn't want to be always catching sight of oneself over the dinner table.' Present at the unveiling of the portrait on the first Saturday of the Michaelmas Term were senior members of the College and their guests, as well as the artist himself—and those he had, by special request, invited. One of these was Frederick Rowlands, and it was he who now stood, with his wife Edith, contemplating—as far as he was able—the reason why they were all assembled.

'I think he's really caught her,' Edith was saying in a low voice, as they stood in front of the portrait. This had been hung on the far wall of the F.C.R., so that one saw it from the full length of the room—a distance of thirty feet—as one came in the door. 'Her air of dignity... but also something else. It's her expression, I think. If one didn't know better, one would say she looks rather shy. But one can't be shy and be the head of a women's college...'

'Oh, I don't know,' said Rowlands. 'People are more than just their public selves.'

'Perhaps that's it,' she said. 'One gets a sense of the private woman behind the public role. Although he's captured that, too. She's wearing a rather splendid velvet robe. Scarlet. It sets off her dark hair beautifully. It might almost be an academic gown—but it isn't, of course. Her hand's resting on a pile of books...'

'Very appropriate,' he said.

'One of them's open… I can't quite make out the title.'

'That'll be her study of Aristotle, I expect. Ah, here's Loveless now,' he said, as the latter's resonant tones were heard. 'We can ask him.'

'Hello, old man—glad you could make it,' said his friend. 'And Mrs Rowlands, too. This *is* a pleasure. When are you going to let me paint your wife, Rowlands?' he went on, having kissed that lady's hand. 'Ask her,' was the reply. 'We've been admiring your latest work. What's that book she's resting her hand upon? I thought it must be one of hers…'

'Uncanny,' said Loveless to Edith. 'You'd almost think the blighter could see… Yes, it's some learned tome on that Greek fellow.'

'Aristotle.'

'That's the chap. How are you, Mrs Rowlands? I hope that husband of yours hasn't been getting into any more trouble since I last saw him?'

'No more than usual,' said Edith. And it was true that since his brush with death at the Cavendish Laboratory a month before, Rowlands had been leading a blameless existence. Catching the eight-fifteen to work every morning. Digging the garden for an hour or two when he got home from work. A Sunday walk along the river with Edith and the girls. It was all he'd ever wanted—a quiet life—and yet somehow he couldn't seem to help getting mixed up in things that were very far from quiet. 'Good,' said Loveless. 'So you approve of my painting?'

'Very much,' said Edith. 'I was just saying to Fred that you've caught her expression exactly.'

'Ah, that's the hardest thing to get right. People think it's the eyes that convey expression, but really it's the mouth. The hands are important, too. But here she is,' said Loveless. 'My distinguished subject. I hope *you're* pleased with your image, Mistress?'

'As long as the Trustees are satisfied, I'm content,' said Miss Phillips drily. 'How nice to see you, Mr and Mrs Rowlands. I hope you're enjoying your stay in Cambridge?'

'Very much,' said Edith. 'Of course,' Beryl Phillips went on, 'you see us in rather less clement weather than on your first visit. Although I sometimes feel that the Michaelmas Term is the *best* time to see Cambridge. We are a working community, you know, and this is the beginning of a new year...'

'Time for a fresh start,' said Rowlands.

'Indeed,' was the reply. A few further exchanges of no particular consequence followed, before the Mistress excused herself, saying that she had other guests to speak to. 'Magnificent creature,' murmured Loveless. Then he, too, was called away by social obligations. Both he and Beryl Phillips were, to a greater or lesser degree, 'on show' that evening, Rowlands thought. It was their public personae one was dealing with: the famous artist and the distinguished academic. Their private selves had been put away. The man who'd stood with Rowlands at the top of that fatal tower, a month before, and whose hands had been shaking so much as he poured them both a whisky in Rowlands's room afterwards that he'd spilled half of it on the floor, was the one who now dispensed his particular brand of charm around the Fellows' Common Room—and yet you'd hardly have known they were the same man. The stately Head of College who now moved among her guests was the woman who, on hearing Rowlands's account of all that had taken place in the weeks leading up to Francis Bristow's suicide, had said, in tones which betrayed her shock and pain, 'How will we ever recover from this, Mr Rowlands?'

Well, a month had gone by and both she and the College had recovered—or at least started to recover, Rowlands thought. That process, like his own, would take a long time. The poison Bristow had introduced into the body of the University would need to be expelled, if it were not to do lasting damage to that institution. In him, the hubris which was all too often a component of the scientific mind had combined with an even more pernicious arrogance. Believing himself above ordinary morality, he had sought to harness his gifts to the service of an evil system. The irony was, thought Rowlands, that if he hadn't tried to pass off Diana Havelock's research as his own, he might never have been found out.

His thoughts focused once more the conversation he'd

had a few days after Bristow's death, when he'd returned to Cambridge for the inquest. It struck him, as he got off the train and began the long walk into town, that this was becoming something of a habit. Who would have thought that this tranquil university town could have harboured so much spite and bitterness? Since he had time to kill, he varied his usual route by turning down Lensfield Road, in front of the Catholic church, and into Trumpington Street. Past the Fitzwilliam, past Peterhouse and Pembroke, and so to the junction with Botolph Lane—that led, he knew, to the Cavendish. Since his incarceration in the Radium Room, he'd had no inclination to revisit the place, even to see how Gillian Mainwaring was faring. She, from what Miss Rickards had told him, had recovered pretty well from her ordeal, and was now hard at work on her dissertation for Part II of the Tripos. But then the young were resilient, he thought.

As he crossed the little lane, and passed in front of St Botolph's church, he heard a shout: 'Hi, there! Mr Rowlands! A moment, if you please…' It was Robert Harding. 'Good afternoon,' said Rowlands, as the man caught up with him. 'I understand,' said the latter, very much on his dignity, 'that you wanted to speak to me. My wife said…'

'It doesn't matter now.'

'Oh, but it does,' say Harding, drawing level with Rowlands, as the two of them passed the gates of Corpus Christi. 'I won't have my wife bullied, do you hear?'

'You lied about the day you returned to Cambridge from the Lake District, Professor Harding. Your wife merely confirmed the fact.'

'Agnes never said a word about that,' blustered the physics don. 'She didn't have to,' replied Rowlands. 'I don't think,' he added, 'that Mrs Harding enjoys lying.'

'Of course she doesn't!' snapped the other; then, perhaps realising that this was a kind of admission, added, in a cooler tone: 'What does it matter, anyway—whether we came back a day earlier or later?' They'd reached King's Parade, and the turning for the Market Square. 'I think you know why,' said Rowlands. 'I'm going down here, so…'

'If you're on your way to the inquest, so am I,' said Harding. 'It doesn't start for half an hour yet.'

'I know. I'm going to have a drink in the Eagle first.'

'I'll join you. I want to know,' said Robert Harding, 'exactly what that pathetic female told you...'

'If you're referring to Evadne Bostock, it was she who put you in the clear,' said Rowlands, as they reached the Eagle's gateway. 'I hardly think,' said Harding, 'that telling you I was in Cambridge on that Saturday night—meeting her, as she'll have explained, no doubt—was putting me in the clear. It could have landed me in a *very* awkward situation—not least with my wife.' To say nothing of the police, thought Rowlands. 'Yes, Dr Bostock did tell me about that meeting,' he said. 'I gather she felt remorse for what she saw as her part in Miss Havelock's death, and intended to go to the police about it. She merely wanted to warn you of her intention...'

'She threatened me, all right,' said Harding bitterly. 'Said all that business with her... and with Diana... was bound to come out. I had the devil's own job to persuade her to hold her tongue. Told her she'd be seen as vindictive—which she was, of course...'

'And yet it was she who established your alibi for the night of Diana Havelock's murder,' said Rowlands coldly. 'I think you might be grateful to her for that.'

'Wait,' said Harding. The self-righteous note was gone, now. 'You surely can't think that I...' He lowered his voice as a noisy group of undergraduates pushed past them into the pub. 'I loved her—Diana. I'd never have hurt her—never!'

'Is that why you broke it off with her?'

'I didn't... I say, do let's go in and sit down, like civilised beings,' said Harding. No more was said until after they'd entered the venerable building, where successive generations of the warring tribes of Town and Gown had drowned their differences in pints of strong ale. 'What'll you have?'

'Half a bitter,' said Rowlands. It seemed all wrong to ask the man he'd come close to getting hanged for murder to buy him a pint. Besides, he wanted to keep his head clear. When they were seated, with their drinks, in a quiet alcove towards the back of the pub, Harding went on, in an undertone: 'It was Diana who broke it off with me. I… I begged her to reconsider, but she was angry. She wouldn't listen to me.'

'And so you arranged to meet her in the rose garden that night?'

'Yes. I hoped to make her see reason.'

'But you didn't turn up.'

'I… I had second thoughts. She'd been avoiding my eye all evening. I realised it would be hopeless to try and win her round…'

'Yet she went to the rose garden after all,' said Rowlands. 'She waited for you. When she realised you weren't coming, she became quite distressed.' He wasn't sure exactly why he wanted to make Harding suffer. Perhaps he felt the handsome don had got off rather too lightly. Something of this seemed to strike the other, for he said in tones of affronted dignity: 'I thought I was *sparing* her, by letting her go. I cared for her, you see. She and I… I don't suppose I can make you understand… but we were everything to one another…'

'You're a married man,' said Rowlands. His beer tasted sour. Perhaps it was the end of a barrel. 'You had no right to get involved with a young girl—someone who had her whole life ahead of her.'

'Oh, I don't suppose *you've* ever looked at another woman, Mr Rowlands,' sneered Harding. 'I can tell you're the virtuous type…'

'Was the reason she broke it off because you wouldn't do anything to help her? said Rowlands, choosing not to answer the implied question. 'I mean,' he added, 'to stop Professor Bristow passing off her work on Wave Theory as his own. Wasn't that why she was angry?' Harding took a sip of his drink. 'Diana was very young,' he said. 'She didn't understand how things work in the world of scientific research. It's quite usual for scientists working in a particular field to collaborate. She was only a PhD student, after all.' He gave an indulgent laugh. 'A very bright girl—make no mistake—but in a fairly lowly position, as regards the Cavendish hierarchy…'

'Who are all men,' said Rowlands. 'Indeed,' was the reply.

'But women can hardly expect…' Harding broke off. 'This is all beside the point,' he said. 'The fact of the matter is, when I tried to explain the way things were to Diana, she flew off the handle. Accused me of betraying her! Which was ridiculous of course,' he added, with a complacency Rowlands was starting to see as characteristic of the man. 'Without my support, she'd never have got the Studentship. As I tried to explain to her, if she'd only taken the long view, she'd have gained the recognition she deserved—might even have been appointed to a Junior Fellowship, in due course. But she wouldn't see reason, I'm afraid.'

'She was your research assistant,' said Rowlands. 'Didn't it bother you that Bristow was stealing her work?' Harding sighed. 'I can see that you don't really understand,' he said. 'One paper more or less…'

'A paper Professor Bristow delivered to considerable acclaim at the Royal Society,' said Rowlands. 'I hardly think that's a negligible misdemeanour.'

'It's all rather beside the point now, isn't it?' said Harding. 'As I tried to explain to that young hothead, Sedgwick…'

'I guessed it must have been from you that he learned the truth.'

'Yes. He came roaring after me, accusing me of all kinds of perfidy,' said the physicist. 'I'd seduced his lady love—I assure you, she was perfectly willing—and purloined her research. I set him straight on *that* score, I can tell you!'

'I'm sure you did,' said Rowlands. 'You put him onto Bristow, who'd already killed twice, to protect his reputation.'

'I didn't know that then.'

'No. But didn't it strike you as suspicious afterwards, when the boy was found dead?'

'Not at all,' was the cool reply. 'I thought he was the suicidal type, if you want to know. Ranting on about the girl, and how I'd taken her away from him. I'm afraid it didn't surprise me in the least when I heard what he'd done…'

'Except that he didn't kill himself, did he? He was murdered—by your colleague, Professor Bristow,' said Rowlands. 'Don't you feel the least bit of guilt about that?'

'None at all. I'm sorry about the boy, of course—but Bristow was mad, it stands to reason. I should have thought *you*, of all people, would agree with that.'

'There seem to have been others who were prepared to overlook his madness,' said Rowlands quietly. Harding laughed. 'You're referring to my colleagues in Germany, I take it? And I *do* regard them as my colleagues, just as poor Francis Bristow did. We scientists are an international community, you know. Our work transcends politics.' Or is harnessed to serve its ends, thought Rowlands. Until that moment, he'd never really believed that scientists could have a different way of looking at moral questions from that of ordinary folk. For such men—and they were almost all men—everything else was subordinate to the ruthless pursuit of knowledge, and its no less ruthless application. The lives of a few 'insignificant people', as Bristow had put it, were nothing compared to this.

Leaving Edith talking to Maud Rickards, he strolled outside into the little courtyard, where he lit a cigarette. Through the open French doors of the room behind, voices drifted out into the cool October evening. 'I think you'll find that theory's been discredited…' That was Miss Hall, in conversation with a fellow historian, presumably. 'I simply can't wait to get back to Delphi,' said another voice—was it Miss Sissons or Miss Crane? He'd never quite managed to tell the difference between them. 'Harold and I,' said Miss Merriweather, to whom the remark had been addressed, 'have been thinking of Greece for our honeymoon.' The voices murmured on, in civilised accord, or disputation. 'Of course, what Coleridge really *means* and what he *says* are two different things…' Dr Maltravers. And then kind little Miss Glossop, always so anxious to please. 'Oh, I'm sure you must be right, Chaplain! It's just that in my own paper on Coleridge, I did make the point that…'

Yes, he thought, they would recover—singly and collectively. Too much was at stake—the future of St Gertrude's College, of women's education; perhaps of Europe itself—for them not to do so.

Someone had followed him outside. 'Mr Rowlands, is it not?'

'Good evening, Miss Kruger. Nice party, isn't it?'

'Oh, yes. It is, as you say, a nice party. I heard what you did,' she went on, with what he recognised as a characteristic directness. 'You saved that girl. Oh, I know you English do not like to boast of such things—it is not "cricket"... is that not the expression? But I wanted to say that I have heard about this, and that I thank you for it.'

'Mr Loveless did as much as I did.'

'I am sorry, but I think that is not so,' said Miss Kruger. 'It was you who found out who killed Diana. You who brought that man to justice. Although I should have liked to see him hang for what he did,' she added, the quietness of her tone making the words more chilling. 'She was my friend,' said Ilse Kruger, meaning the dead girl, Rowlands guessed. 'I'm sorry,' he said. 'There is nothing to be sorry for,' she said. 'We were both—how do you say this? Misfits. I think that is the word. *She* because she was so exceptional a student—even in this place of exceptional students—and I...' She gave a choked little laugh. 'I seem not to fit in anywhere.'

On Sunday morning after Chapel, Rowlands and his wife, accompanied by Maud Rickards, went for a walk along the Backs. It was a beautiful Autumn day at the beginning of a new term, and the atmosphere in the university town was one of hope and expectation. It was, as Rowlands had said to Miss Phillips, a time for fresh starts. As they got off the bus at the bottom of Castle Hill, a flock of 'Gertie' girls on bicycles came careering past, whooping with excitement. 'Silly young things!' said Miss Rickards affectionately. 'Anyone would think they *wanted* to break their necks...' She was once more acting as the Rowlandses' guide to the beauties of the city—a role she appeared to relish. The three of them turned down Bridge Street. Having stuck their heads into Magdalene's Great Court, to admire the display of bronze and gold chrysanthemums against the Tudor brick—'Such rich colours Fred!' exclaimed his wife. 'Like a Turkey carpet'—they crossed Magdalene Bridge, pausing only to laugh at the antics of a group of Magdalene men—who, having taken the College punt out, seemed unable to avoid steering it into the riverbank.

'I expect this is my last day of freedom,' said the Bursar, with a resigned air, as they continued their walk into town. 'Full Term starts on Tuesday, with another crop of freshers to settle in—and all that that implies. Lost luggage, mix-ups over rooms, girls wandering the corridors like lost souls...'

'Go on with you! You enjoy every minute of it,' said Edith. The Bursar gave a sniff. 'I suppose *somebody* has to keep our little flock of geese together, so that they can be turned into swans in due course,' she said. Rowlands was reminded of the last time he'd heard that proverbial phrase—or a version of it—on his first afternoon at St Gertrude's. It seemed a hundred years ago. 'More Geese than Swans now live; more Fools than Wise,' he murmured. It was as true now as it had been when the words were written. 'What's that?' said Miss Rickards. 'Oh, nothing,' he said.

Outside St Jude's College, Rowlands parted company with his wife and her friend, having arranged to meet up with them at the Mill, for a cold lunch. He was also going to seek out the man who'd rescued him from drowning—whose name he had at last managed to obtain from the boatyard, where his saviour worked, it transpired—so that he could stand him the best pint of beer money could buy. First, however, there was someone he had to visit. Crossing the Tudor court of the men's college, he reflected on all that had taken place in the three months since he had first set foot there. He remembered thinking it a haven of peace in a darkening world; now he knew it, too, had contained darkness.

Professor Giles was expecting him; even so, Rowlands thought that the older man seemed flustered at his appearance. 'Come in, come in,' he said, with a heartiness that struck the other man as feigned. 'What can I get you?'

'Nothing for me, thanks,' said Rowlands. 'I'll smoke, if I may?'

'Yes, yes, by all means do.' Giles seemed unable to settle, nervously rubbing his hands together as he stood there, in the middle of his little sitting-room. 'I feel I owe you an apology,' he said, as if this was something he'd been wanting to say for a long time. 'I can't think why,' said Rowlands. Although it wasn't hard to guess what it was Giles meant. 'If I'd been straight with you in the first place…'

'That's water under the bridge.'

'I just couldn't risk bringing her name into it, you see…'

'There's really no need to explain.' Rowlands was starting to regret having agreed to this meeting. Because, as he'd discovered during the conversation he'd had with Chief Inspector Douglas, in the aftermath of Francis Bristow's death, the man the police had arrested on suspicion of murder, and whom Douglas and his colleague had been interrogating while Rowlands was confronting Bristow in the Mond Laboratory, had indeed been Austin Giles. If it hadn't been for that, Bristow might have been arrested before he'd had time to attempt another murder. He'd have been saved for the hangman, too—although, unlike Miss Kruger, Rowlands couldn't help feeling glad that circumstances had prevented this.

Yes, Giles had lied to Rowlands and to the police about the date he'd returned to Cambridge. He'd been in his college rooms the night of Julian Sedgwick's murder—but he hadn't been alone. The married woman with whom he'd been conducting a discreet affair was none other than the estimable Mrs Clark—his 'bedder', as it happened. 'If her husband found out, it'd be terrible for her,' said Giles. 'The man's a brute. It was to protect her—Emily—I lied.'

The planting of the incriminating handkerchief in his colleague's room by Bristow had seemed to make the case against Professor Giles watertight, the Chief Inspector had explained, somewhat sheepishly, when he and Rowlands had met to discuss the affair after the inquest. 'He was always a suspect, you know. He was with the other two in the dining hall at St Gertrude's that night. None of them had alibis.'

'Yes, but only one of them left the dining hall early,' Rowlands had pointed out. 'I only discovered who it was when I talked to Evadne Bostock.'

'We don't always get things right first time,' said the Chief Inspector. 'Although we'd realised by the time we got your note that Giles wasn't our man. We got to the Cavendish only a few minutes after you and that artist friend of yours had left. Just as well he was on hand to get you out of there…'

'Just as well,' agreed Rowlands.

'No, I'd never have forgiven myself if anything had happened to you,' Giles was saying. It struck Rowlands that it was rather late in the day for such regrets, but he said nothing of this. 'Fortunately, it all ended well,' he said. 'And so there's nothing to forgive.'

'So no hard feelings, then?'

'No hard feelings.'

After this, they talked of more general things. The worsening political situation in Germany. College news. Professor Harding, it transpired, had been offered a post at Imperial College. 'Running a department, I rather think,' said Giles. 'I've an idea Cambridge was always too small for him.'

Leaving the college by its back gate—which was the most direct route onto the Backs, Giles told him—Rowlands found himself surrounded by a group of young people heading in the same direction, apparently. One of them was Angela Thompson—he recognised her crisp tones at once. 'I say, come on! You are a slowcoach, Miles! I thought Jude's men were supposed to be athletic...'

'Some of us have other virtues,' said Miles Rowntree. 'I can't think what... Oh, hello!' she said, on recognising Rowlands. 'How nice to see you again. Are you in Cambridge for long?'

'Not long,' he said. 'My wife and I return to London tomorrow.'

'What a pity—otherwise you could both have come to supper, couldn't they, Miles?'

'Rather,' said Rowntree. 'How *are* you, sir?' Was there a shade of nervousness in the enquiry—a suggestion that the boy was recalling the last time they'd met, and under what circumstances? Perhaps, thought Rowlands—but then again, perhaps not. 'I'm very well, thanks,' he said. 'We wouldn't expect you to hike all the way out to Gertie's,' went on the ebullient Miss Thompson. 'Would we, Miles?'

'Not a bit of it,' muttered the young man. 'No, we'd have it in Miles's rooms, wouldn't we, my sweet? Miles orders a very nice dinner,' confided Miss Thompson to their prospective guest. 'Such a pity you can't join us.'

'It is,' agreed Rowlands. 'Some other time, perhaps?'

'Why not?' was the bright reply. 'Well, lovely to see you again, Mr Rowlands. We're walking to Grantchester,' she added, as if it were the other side of the moon. 'Come on, Miles. Brenda darling, if you don't get a move on, the Green Man will have called Last Orders…'

When the little party had moved off, Rowlands lit a cigarette, and strolled on at his own more leisurely pace. Such a beautiful day, so late in the year, deserved to be savoured, he thought. The fact that the girl, after the first nervous start of recognition, had made no allusion to what had brought them together, nor to the grim *finale* of the affair, was not, he thought, unduly surprising. She was young—and it was in the nature of the young to look forward, rather than back. A new term beckoned, with all its potential for triumph and disaster. The young women of St Gertrude's and Newnham—and the young men of Trinity, Magdalene, Christ's, King's, Peterhouse, Emmanuel, Queens', St John's, Jesus, and all the rest of their peers—would be racing to lectures on bicycles, and filling the quiet streets with their laughter and chatter. All that had happened in the closing week of the Easter Term could be consigned to oblivion.

He walked on, his feet crunching lightly on the gravel walk that ran beside the river. On Trinity lawn, a groundsman was sweeping up the leaves. As Rowlands passed the great iron gate that led, along a double avenue of limes and cherry trees, to the back entrance of the college, he heard the clock in Great Court striking twelve.

Lightning Source UK Ltd.
Milton Keynes UK
UKHW04f0747220918
329314UK00001B/32/P

9 780992 746773